A STEEP AND SAVAGE PATH

JJA Harwood is an author, editor and podcaster. She has published two YA fantasy novels: the *Sunday Times* bestselling *The Shadow in the Glass* and *The Thorns Remain*. You can also find her on the silly and sweary D&D podcast *Lads on Tour*.

Also by JJA Harwood

The Shadow in the Glass
The Thorns Remain

A STEEP AND SAVAGE PATH

JJA HARWOOD

Magpie

Magpie Books
An imprint of HarperCollins*Publishers* Ltd
1 London Bridge Street
London SE1 9GF

www.harpercollins.co.uk

HarperCollins*Publishers*
Macken House,
39/40 Mayor Street Upper,
Dublin 1
D01 C9W8
Ireland

First published by HarperCollins*Publishers* Ltd 2025
This paperback edition 2026

1

Copyright © JJA Harwood 2025

Internal illustrations copyright © Charlotte Day/Central Illustration Agency 2025

JJA Harwood asserts the moral right to
be identified as the author of this work.

A catalogue record for this book is available from the British Library.

ISBN: 978-0-00-851800-4

This novel is entirely a work of fiction.
The names, characters and incidents portrayed in it are
the work of the author's imagination. Any resemblance to
actual persons, living or dead, events or localities is
entirely coincidental.

Set in Sabon Lt Std by Palimpsest Book Production Ltd,
Falkirk, Stirlingshire

Printed and bound in the UK using
100% renewable electricity by CPI Group (UK) Ltd

All rights reserved. No part of this publication may be
reproduced, stored in a retrieval system, or transmitted,
in any form or by any means, electronic, mechanical,
photocopying, recording or otherwise, without the prior
written permission of the publishers.

Without limiting the exclusive rights of any author, contributor or the publisher of
this publication, any unauthorized use of this publication to train generative artificial
intelligence (AI) technologies is expressly prohibited. HarperCollins also exercise their
rights under Article 4(3) of the Digital Single Market Directive 2019/790 and
expressly reserve this publication from the text and data mining exception.

For Mum, Dad and Lucy, who I would walk into Hell for
(even if it means taking the bins out)

PART ONE

The wedding went better than everyone expected; not a single drop of blood was spilled. It was a clear, cold morning, the breath of the mourners turning to mist, sunlight peeking over the slopes of the Carpathians. Irina's wedding clothes fitted her well, even though the embroidery was a little plainer than she would've liked and her linen shirt smelled of the musty chest it had been kept in. There was still snow on the ground, but one of the villagers, a girl around her age, had found snowdrops lurking at the foot of a vast pine tree and braided them into Irina's dark hair. Her bridal crown itched but that was to be expected; with so few flowers to be found it was mostly pine, and the needles were digging into her scalp. They'd even found a beaded bridal choker that was the right size. It was not exactly what she had hoped for, but she supposed it would have to do. Her own village was miles away, and with the pass to Bukovina snowed over for the best part of a week, there was no hope of sending for her own things until it had cleared. Not that she would try and get a message home; the last thing she wanted was for her parents to find out where she really was. She shivered at the graveside with her hands clasped and her head bowed, trying to look as if she were listening to the priest and not observing the crowd.

Black headscarves; black felt and fur hats. The tips of noses and ears red in the cold. Blue shadows under every eye. Long, deep lines on every cheek. Hollow faces made hollower in the icicle-shaped shadow of the sharp church spire. Some of them would not look at her at all, their gaze sliding past to the pale-faced priest. Some of them could not look anywhere else, the hope in their eyes almost unbearable. Most of them kept glancing at the forest at their backs, pressing in on every side, the shadowy line of the trees curling around the village like fingers about to close around an ankle. It was still dark, between the trees. The sunlight hadn't reached them yet. Irina supposed that was the point of having the wedding so early in the morning; a half-hearted attempt to pretend the groom was participating. The thought felt like stepping onto a thin sheet of ice, but she supposed someone had to let him know that he was getting married.

Not that the groom was in any position to complain. He was dead.

Father Simeon was nearing the end of his sermon. Ordinarily, there would be songs, dancing, laughter, feasting. But the crowd was silent. Hands and feet were too heavy for dancing, and no one had laughed in the village since the first attack. In the dead of winter, and with their harvest stores slowly dwindling, none of them would have turned down a feast – but that was tainted, too. No one liked to think of hunger, at the edge of the forest.

Irina shivered. Her wedding clothes were linen, made out of what could be spared. Embroidered red flowers ran down the length of her sleeves in long, thin lines, and whenever she saw them she could not help but think of claw marks, scratched into her flesh. Her overskirt, wrapped around her waist and secured with a wide belt, was red too, and covered in geometric patterns in black, white and green. At least that was a little warmer, but she wished they hadn't put her in so much red. It felt like tempting fate. Suddenly nervous, she risked a glance at the forest. Nothing

A Steep and Savage Path

– well, nothing she could see. If only the priest would hurry up, then she could go inside and start preparing. It wouldn't be safe to pack until she was truly alone – something that, working as a servant in the house of a wealthy farmer, she had sorely missed. Irina had no complaints about anyone under Mihai's roof, but there always seemed to be someone under it when she had things she needed to do in private.

Father Simeon reached across and lifted the bridal crown off her head. The crowd murmured. Anticipation lurched through Irina; she tried not to let it show as the priest passed the bridal crown over the grave beside her. This was it.

Carefully, the priest placed the crown back on her head. He blessed her, blessed the crowd, and said nothing more about the empty grave before him. She tried not to look at it, and failed, her eyes dragged back to the dark earth – no wooden cross but then again, there was no one buried there yet. If they'd been able to find the groom's body, he wouldn't be causing so much trouble. Father Simeon took a deep breath and closed his eyes, tilting his face to the rising sun. Irina could have sworn she saw the glimmer of a tear clinging to his lashes. It was only then that she started to feel guilty. These people had been through enough. If her plan didn't work, she would condemn them to much more suffering.

The crowd of mourners that made up her wedding party was already starting to trickle towards the little house at the edge of the woods. Half of them remained waiting with her, watching her. She still wasn't sure of all their names. She knew them by the names of the ones they'd lost: Anton's daughters, still hollow-eyed after their father's passing; Eugen's greying wife, widowed too soon; Marta's child, plummeting into adulthood with the speed of a mountaineer tumbling from a peak. They watched her with tears in their eyes, and the only way she could hold her head high was to pretend she did not see.

Father Simeon cleared his throat. 'Irina? Are you ready?'

She nodded, and joined the procession. Picking her way past the line of freshly dug graves, drawing ever closer to the hem of the forest, Irina set her jaw and tried not to think of all the things that could go wrong. She was not chasing a fairy tale, she told herself. She was not sending herself on a fool's errand, tearing after the first thing that looked as if it could stand a chance of helping Catalina. She was going to get her sister back.

At the edge of the forest, the procession slowed. Father Simeon beckoned her forward. The crowd parted, swelling up behind her and to the sides, cutting off her escape routes; some of them were even resting their hands on the hilts of their knives. If it hadn't been for the blades, she probably could've pushed her way through the crowd. Short and stocky, Irina was strong after years of taking food up to shepherds on the mountainside, lifting great packs of wool onto the back of her father's wagon, and barrelling through flocks of sheep to rescue the chicks getting under their feet. If she wanted to, she could be out of the village before the sun was high in the sky. Not that she was going to try and escape, Irina thought. She was exactly where she needed to be.

Irina stood at a rough-hewn wooden gate – barred from the outside, of course – that was set into a hastily erected fence. She knew exactly what she would find beyond it, because she had seen the villagers working on it: the small, single-storey house they said had once belonged to the groom. When she'd first come to the village it looked as though it was one gust of wind away from keeling over. Now, it had been repaired, the holes in the steep roof patched, the shutters freshly painted, the dirt steps up to the front door levelled off. The woodstore had been filled, the well in the courtyard had been mended. Still, the windows looked like empty eyes, the fence posts a row of jagged teeth.

A Steep and Savage Path

'You will want for nothing,' Father Simeon said, as the bar was lifted aside and she laid a cautious hand on the gate. 'Everything you need has been provided – food, firewood, blankets. I shall set good strong men to patrol the forest to see that you come to no harm. In the day, of course.'

Irina thought of the empty grave she had stood beside. 'Of course,' she said.

'It is only one night. You'll be safe,' the priest said, and Irina could not tell if he was trying to convince her or himself. 'We put a good bar by the door, and the gate is strong. And I shall be holding a vigil for you, in the church. You'll be perfectly safe.'

Irina kept her eyes on the patched wooden walls of the little house, trying not to glance back at the thick, high walls of the church.

'Will you need anything else, before the sun sets?'

'Warm clothes and good shoes,' Irina said immediately, 'and my pack. Having my own things will be a comfort,' she added, hoping her excuse was convincing.

The priest looked around at the crowd. 'Are her things in there?'

There was a general murmur of assent.

'And the clothes and the shoes? They're all . . .'

Another murmur.

Father Simeon clapped his hands together, looking slightly manic. 'Well,' he said, 'if that's everything you need, then perhaps it's time to . . .'

'Yes,' said Irina. 'It is.'

She pushed open the gate. Tension slid out of the priest's shoulders. The crowd ebbed back from the fence with a sigh. Nerves and excitement and fear tangled through Irina's thoughts like briars. Soon, she thought. Catalina wouldn't have to wait much longer.

'Thank you,' the priest whispered.

The words lodged themselves between Irina's ribs and twisted.

'There is garlic,' he continued, leaning close to the wooden gate. 'I could not leave you with nothing. I have prayed night and day that the wedding will be enough to let him rest, but . . . you know not to open the door to him, if he asks to be let in?'

There was desperate guilt in the priest's voice. Irina did not move. If she turned to look at him, all her secrets would come spilling out of her, like a pot of salt that had been turned over.

'I will be careful, Father,' she said.

'I asked if anyone could keep watch over you, but they could not be spared,' he whispered, in a rush. 'I am sorry. But with four of us already dead, we must think of our own families. I will give you all the protection I can, with my prayers.'

Irina frowned. There were five fresh graves in the churchyard. One was empty, dug for the ceremony she had just taken part in. Three more were for the remains of Anton, Eugen and Marta. But as she stood looking into the yard of the little house, she realized she did not know who was buried in the last grave.

'Father,' she began, trying to keep her voice light, 'I only know about Anton, Eugen and Marta. Who else have we lost?'

'Do not speak of such things,' Father Simeon hissed. 'Do not even think of them! Not when you have such a task ahead of you. Please, child. You must keep your mind clear and pure. Think only of the Lord, and do not entertain any doubts. He will use them, if you do.' The priest let out a long, juddering sigh. When he spoke again, his voice sounded as if it would splinter. 'I hate that we must ask this of you. But we shall all be thinking of you and praying for your safe deliverance.'

Irina tried to keep the relief from showing. Even though fear curled its tendrils around her thoughts, there was no denying that if the villagers had set someone to guard the little house at the edge of the woods, the rest of her plan would become much more difficult. If they found out what she was planning, they would never forgive her. If it failed, it would be hard to forgive herself. Still, she had to try; it would never work if they interfered.

She squared her shoulders. She took a deep breath. Gathering her secret plans close to her chest, she arranged her features into what she hoped was a suitably innocent expression. Then, she looked at him.

Guilt and grief were scrawled across Father Simeon's face. His beard was scraggly and unkempt, shadows pooled underneath his eyes. When she had first come to the village he had been a sturdy, sun-weathered man, short and stocky and strong. Now, he seemed to have withered, shrinking in on himself with each scream in the night, each splash of blood on the snow, each dark square of fresh-turned earth in the graveyard. She had the power to stop this. But that wasn't her plan – not until she'd got what she wanted.

Irina took the priest's hands in hers. 'Don't worry, Father,' she said, her voice gentle. 'I have faith.'

Tears sparkled in the priest's eyes. 'Bless you,' he murmured.

Irina let go of his hands. Then she turned and went into the house to prepare to meet her husband.

On the whole, Irina thought, the villagers had done a decent job. She wouldn't have guessed that the house had been abandoned until now. The door creaked a little, and there was a slight smell of damp from where the roof had been leaking. But there were no cobwebs tangling in the corners, no dust furring up the walls. The house smelled cold and clean, as if it had been recently aired.

It was only one room, with whitewashed walls and a dirt floor. Dark wooden beams ran across the ceiling. A narrow bed was pushed up against one corner, curtained off from the rest of the room by a frame hung with heavy, embroidered blankets in black, red and yellow. There was a wooden table in the centre of the room, with two roughly hewn wooden chairs. The second one was already starting to unnerve her; she dragged it over to a wooden chest set against the far wall. A stone oven large enough to sleep on was built into the opposite corner of the house, with a shelf above it for pots and pans. Bunches of dried herbs were suspended from the ceiling, and several rings of garlic. The simple canvas pack she had arrived with was sitting in the centre of the wooden table as if it were a vase of flowers. It was the plainest little house she had ever seen, and she could not help but wonder how much of the monster they'd had to scrub out of the place before she'd seen inside. She noticed a dent in the wall, hastily covered over; a series of hooks with nothing hanging from them; a man's forgotten hat, lodged in the rafters. Had it been his? She shivered. She didn't want to know.

Flinging her bridal crown on the table next to the pack, she lit the oven. It would warm the house through, and she would have a long, cold day ahead of her. She opened her pack to see how much room she had for food, and swore. Her own clothes were missing – those had been made from good, strong wool, warm enough to travel in and sturdy enough to endure the harvest. Snow lay thick on the ground; if she left the house in the wedding clothes she'd borrowed, she would freeze. The message was clear: she wasn't to go anywhere.

She set the thoughts of her missing clothes aside; food and a stake were more important, and there, the villagers had been generous. As well as a pail of water, and pork fat for cooking, she'd been left dried sausages, jars of pink and green pickles and a sack of cornmeal; she wrapped the preserves in cloth as best she could and placed them inside a cooking pot. She mixed up a cornmeal dough, then dug out three water-flasks from her pack and filled each one from the well. By then, the oven was hot, and she fried up a pile of crispy jumări while her cornbread baked, the smell of pork fat and paprika making her stomach rumble. She grabbed a small pouch of salt, pulled dried herbs from the ceiling and sharpened some of her kindling into stakes. When her food was prepared and cooled, she wrapped it up in cloth and placed it carefully into her pack, making sure that nothing would break if it was jostled around. Then, with shaking hands, she fished out her most prized possession from the secret pocket sewn into the lining of her pack. It was a necklace of wooden beads, some of them slightly chewed, worn smooth from years of fiddling.

Catalina's necklace.

Irina slipped the necklace over her bridal choker, clutching it tightly, and tried not to think of how idiotic her plan was. But there was no getting around it. The smart thing to do would have been to accept that the sister she had known – the cheerful, lively seven-year-old with a penchant for tall tales – was no longer the sister she had. It wasn't as if anything unusual had happened to her; people hit their heads all the time, and it was only natural that some of them would never quite recover. The tree Catalina had fallen from back in the summer had been tall, and she had landed badly. Her family would never be able to afford a doctor, but they'd done what they could, taking care to support her neck and head when they'd brought her inside. She'd been lucky to have survived at all, even if she had not left her bed – had not even lifted her own hand – since the accident. If Irina were a sensible-minded young woman, she would accept the fact that, now, all her sister could do was lie in bed, her eyes empty, and swallow the food and water their frightened parents brought to her lips. Catalina was lucky to be alive after the accident, but she was not lucky enough to be herself. Irina ought to be grateful that she had not passed. That was what her mother had told her.

But Irina was not grateful. Nor was she sensible. And so, instead of thanking God that there was a pulse in Catalina's wrist and no life in her eyes, Irina had gone looking for answers.

In the village where Irina grew up, there had been a witch. She lived at the edge of the forest, in a small wooden house ringed by a fence, much like the one Irina found herself in now. She had spent most of Irina's childhood treating toothache and soothing fevers, and after so many years watching her mix up poultices and brew teas it was almost a surprise to learn that she could see the future in the palm of someone's hand. After Catalina had woken up empty-eyed, and her family had spent weeks spooning water into her slack mouth, Irina had sought out the witch, knocking on the door of the little hut in the middle of the night.

'Please,' she had whispered, handing over a sack of cornmeal, 'tell me what's wrong with her.'

The witch examined the cornmeal, letting out a grunt of satisfaction. Like every other woman in the village, she wore a headscarf; hers was black and patterned with red and green flowers. Her face was deeply lined, though she was not old, and there was always dirt lodged underneath her fingernails. But her eyes were quick and clever and – faced with a long silence that she was desperate to fill – Irina was reminded that here was a woman who knew exactly when to speak up and when to fade into the background, sliding beneath the notice of the village priest.

'She hit her head, then slept for days. She's awake now, but she isn't . . . herself. It's been weeks,' Irina continued.

'I know,' said the witch, setting the sack aside. 'Your mother asked me to look at her when she woke up. I warn you, Irina, she did not like my answer. Neither will you.'

'Tell me.'

The witch sighed. 'Her soul is not in her body.'

That night, hearing the words from the witch's lips had felt like being thrown into cold water. Even the memory made Irina shiver.

'Your sister was badly injured,' said the witch. 'Her body came back from death. Her soul did not. She is alive, but she is not living.'

Suddenly, Irina had felt aware of every shadow, every creak. Hair prickled on the back of her neck. 'Is she human?' she whispered.

'Of course she is,' the witch snapped. 'She's just empty.'

'But . . . but how . . .'

The witch motioned Irina inside. Her house was small and plain, with only a table and chairs and one narrow bed for furniture. The oven was lit and everything was scrupulously clean. She pulled out a chair and Irina sat down. 'Think of it like a chicken coop,' the witch said, sitting across from her. 'It is only a chicken coop when it contains a chicken. Otherwise it is only an empty structure, without the thing that gives it purpose. It is the same with your sister. Her body has recovered, but her soul – the thing that makes her *her* – has fled.'

'Fled where?' Irina asked.

The witch shrugged. 'Into the land of the dead, I imagine.'

'The land of the . . . that's not what they say in church.'

The witch's face smoothed over into a careful expression. 'Of course it is not,' she said calmly, 'that is why I told you I only imagined it. It is what they said long before the churches were built – in ancient times, when Rome still ruled. Of course,' she said, assessing every inch of Irina's face, 'you and I know that such teachings are false.'

Irina had heard similar stories before: ones where men met Death on lonely roads in the shape of an old woman. They'd never been mentioned in church, but the priest had never stopped the storytellers, either. She glanced over her shoulder. The door was still closed. 'I won't tell anyone, I promise. Please, just tell me what you know.'

'I do not pay attention to heresies, you understand,' the witch said, casting a look at her shuttered windows, 'but I can tell you that they used to believe that the land of the dead was where people went before they learned the truth about Heaven and Hell. And that there are stories of living people visiting it.'

Hope sparked into life. 'So it's a real place? Does that mean Catalina's soul could be brought back? Would she be herself again?'

The witch leaned forward, lowering her voice. All her pretence vanished. 'That is a very dangerous idea, Irina,' the witch said. 'You would do better not to think of it.'

'But could it be done?'

The witch sighed, pinching the bridge of her nose. 'In theory, yes. In practice?' She made a dismissive noise. 'Your parents have two daughters. Losing one to an accident is bad enough; losing the other to sheer stupidity would be more than they could bear.'

Irina leaned forward, jabbing a finger into the table. 'Could it be *done*? Could I get into the land of the dead and bring back Catalina's soul?'

The witch shushed her, glancing at the door and windows again. 'Keep your voice down! But . . . perhaps. The way doesn't open for the living. You'd need a guide. Something that could walk between the worlds of the living and the dead.'

'Like what?' Irina breathed.

The witch shot her a sharp look. 'Like a mistake waiting to happen. You have heard the stories of the dead that walk, Irina. Even when they are compelled to return to those they loved in life, they bring nothing but suffering.'

A Steep and Savage Path

'But those are just stories, aren't they?'

'If stories is all they are, do not waste your time in seeking them out. Go home to your family, tend to your sister, and put this madness out of your mind.'

After a full day of cooking, packing, and sharpening stakes, Irina was ready to go, her pack bulging on the kitchen table. She opened the window and a cold breeze stung her fingers. A copper-gold sunset burned across the sky, the edges of the clouds glowing like embers. The jagged shadows of the forest spilled across the floor, long and sharp as knives. Irina lit a candle and drew her chair closer to the oven, and covered her legs with the warmest blanket, settling her bridal crown back onto her head. That, more than anything, would mark her out as a bride; it would make it clear to her husband exactly who she was, and what he owed to her. A sharpened stake was pressed against her thigh, hidden underneath the brightly coloured blanket. That would make it even clearer.

Irina gripped the stake in one hand, her eyes on the open window. She wouldn't have long to wait. He would be hungry.

The attacks always followed the same pattern. The sun went down. Wrapped in darkness, he would come home to the village, dragging himself out of whichever lonely forest grave he had been hiding in. That was why he was here. If they'd given him a proper funeral, he never would've started walking, but no one seemed to know when or where he'd died – or if they did, they weren't telling her. They'd searched the woods for days and never found where he'd been buried; without knowing where he slept during the day, they had no hope of killing him. He started with the little house, prowling through his former home though it had stood empty for months. Then, he would move into the village proper, scratching at shutters until someone swung them open.

One extended arm was all it took. Freezing fingers latching around a wrist. A flash of teeth. And then, the screaming. The lucky ones escaped him with a few fingers missing. People had learned fast, after those first few swipes. But in November, Marta had become convinced she'd heard one of her children trapped outside, and had insisted on searching the yard with a candle. December winds had torn off one of the shutters on Anton's windows, and he'd gone out to fix it in the dark. And in January, Eugen had lost track of time visiting his father, and thought that his old Austrian imperial sword would be enough to keep him safe in the forest. All of them had been dragged into the dark. They'd been deposited outside the church the next morning, their throats torn open and without a drop of blood in sight. Even though only four people were dead, the rumours had travelled fast, reaching Irina's village a few weeks after the first attack. And Irina knew she had found her guide.

She'd packed a bag and told a lie: that she was going to Timișoara, to look for work as a servant. She'd worked there before; her parents, focused on Catalina, suspected nothing. Within weeks she was working in Mihai's household, listening to the scratches at the window every night. The footsteps, shuffling through the snow with a rhythm that did not seem fully human. Terrified bleating and stamping of hooves came from every pen as he prowled past the livestock. She could track his every move by listening to the screaming and kicking of horses that had scented something dead on the air. He did not kill often – from what she'd gathered, it was perhaps one person a month – but his presence hung over the village like a shroud. Shivering in her bed, listening to him stalk through the village, her plan no longer seemed quite so brilliant. How was she even supposed to talk to him, if no one was safe enough to leave their homes after dark? Would he listen to her at all, or would he simply lunge right for her throat? Should she leave him an offering, or a note?

But in the end, the villagers had solved that problem for her. One Sunday in church, Father Simeon had talked about the dead man. In a trembling voice, he had told what he had heard of the dead – that they returned after a bad death, that they were compelled to return to the people and places they had known and loved, that fulfilling a wish could sometimes lay them to rest. The vampire that was plaguing them had died unmarried, and no one that he had loved was left alive. That was when the priest had proposed a wedding of the dead. It was a ritual that Irina was familiar with: if someone died unmarried, a living person would be married to the dead person during their funeral. It was only ever a formality, but it would give the dead person's soul some peace, and stop them from coming back. They'd never found the dead man's body and never had a funeral, and he had already risen – but still, the priest was desperate. If anyone would agree to be married to the dead man, Father Simeon had pleaded, that might be enough to stop him. All the unmarried women had been unable to meet his eyes, apart from Irina. The priest seized on it. *Think of the souls you could save*, he had urged, but Irina had only thought of one.

She huddled into the blanket, watching the shadows fade with the light. Her heart was pounding. Could he hear it? Would the sound of her pulse call to him across the forest, like a soldier marching to the beat of a drum? Perhaps he wouldn't need it; they said the dead always came back to their homes in life. Perhaps simply being in his house, sitting in his chair, cooking food on his stove and sleeping in his bed, would be enough to drag him out of the grave and up to her door. Perhaps some part of him knew that, now, he had a wife, and he would haul himself up from the earth to find her no matter where she was. Irina's hand tightened on the stake. The sun was setting. She was about to find out.

Shadows bled into darkness. The wind lifted a lock of Irina's hair; the pine fronds of her bridal crown stirred in the breeze. Beyond the open window, there was silence. The last doors in the village had closed long before the sun had set. All she could hear was the faint shift of embers cooling in the fire, and the rustling of leaves in the wind.

No. Not the wind. Irina sat up a little straighter. What she'd first taken for pine needles rustling in the breeze was something different: the slow *ssshhhhh-sssssshhhhhh* of something pushing past the branches, stalking through the leaves. She knew that gait. She'd heard it on the other side of the wall, almost every night since she'd arrived in the village.

It was him. Her husband.

Irina shifted in her chair, placing her weight on the balls of her feet so she could spring up at a moment's notice. Her pulse fluttered in her neck. Her hand went to her throat. It was so vulnerable. So easily torn out – the choker she wore would not keep him from hurting her. She took her hand away, taking a deep, steadying breath. She *had* to seem vulnerable, or he would not come.

Outside, all she could see was darkness and the press of trees, pine needles glinting blue in the gloom. Something moved. Irina sat up straight, peering into the night. The wind rustled through the trees; was that all she had seen? Or had he been looking back at her, clawed hands curling over the edge of the window frame, his dripping teeth bared? Something glinted in the dark. Her mouth went dry. Was it an eye? A gleaming, pointed tooth? Or the blade of a knife? She was a woman alone on the edge of the forest, the inside of her empty house lit up against the night like a jewel waiting to be snatched. The dead were not the only things to worry about, and Father Simeon would have called back the men patrolling the forest by now. It wasn't that there would be no one to hear her scream; after a few months in the village, Irina knew exactly how far a scream would carry. It was that no matter who was out there, no one would be coming to help her, with a dead man prowling through the woods. She was completely alone. Irina swore. She'd been so focused on finding a guide to the land of the dead that she'd forgotten about the living.

Footsteps, crunching across the forest floor. She could hear the snap and crush of every broken twig, they were so close. She turned her head, trying to follow the sound. Faltering, uneven steps. The fading of owls' cries as they fled the thing dragging itself towards the house. A pause. Had he seen her, or scented her, or however it was he found his prey? Then, a sudden *bang*. Irina flinched, almost dropping the stake. Something fell into the snow. Her hands began to shake. This was a bad idea, she *knew* it was a bad idea and yet here she was, listening to a dead man creeping around outside her house. She peered out of the open window, her heart in her throat. Father Simeon had said the unmarried dead might be appeased with a living wife, but that was supposed to stop them from coming back at all and here he was, picking his way through the snow. The wedding was supposed to be enough, but could the ritual have worked, with no body in that grave? Or had the villagers left her here, waiting to see if the dead man would do something that would leave him content to crawl back into his grave with no more taste for blood?

The footsteps stopped. Irina listened, staring into the dark square of the open window. Distant wings, as something took off into the night. Her own heartbeat, fast as a chittering bird.

And, when she had been staring at the open window, the long, slow creak of the door being pushed open behind her.

He was here.

Cold air rushed in. The candle flickered. Irina froze, unable to turn and look at him, all her plans swept away on a tide of fear. What was she doing? She had allowed herself to be married to a dead man – a *dead man*, who had ripped and slashed his way through the village until everyone living there had agreed that throwing him a living girl might be the only way to make him stop. What had she been thinking? She shifted, ready to run, and the beads bumped against her breastbone. The warm touch of smooth wood brought her back to herself. She had been thinking of Catalina.

Irina took another deep breath and tamped down her fears. Floorboards creaked behind her. He was already inside – how? Too late, she realized: he didn't need an invitation; it was his house. She tightened her grip on the stake.

'I've been waiting for you, husband,' she said.

The footsteps stopped. An ember shifted in the silence, and Irina flinched. Then came the voice, from somewhere over her shoulder.

'Husband,' the voice repeated.

She flinched. There was a rasp to that voice, as though it was some time since it had been used. Part of her had expected his words to be spat out from behind fangs as long as her fingers. But he sounded disconcertingly human. Irina sat frozen in her chair, torn between the urge to gawp at the monster that had been stalking the village for months, and the urge to keep staring straight ahead, pretending that the man standing behind her had not crawled out of a grave to get here. Her hand on the stake was slippery with sweat. There'd be no going back once she turned around and faced him. But there was already no going back. She had married him. He was here. She'd put herself in this mess for a reason. It was time to see what she could make of it.

She licked her lips. 'Are you going to skulk about in the darkness all night?' she asked, forcing every ounce of bravado she had into her voice. 'Or are you going to introduce yourself to your wife?'

'Wife,' the voice rasped, almost thoughtful.

What was he thinking? She tightened her grip on the stake. Would he want her to actually *be* his wife? Or was he only thinking of her as a meal? Was he even thinking at all? He'd only repeated what she'd said. Some guide he would make, if those were the only words he could say. Had she trapped herself in here for nothing? 'Yes, that's what I said,' she said, gathering all the scraps of her courage. 'Now come here. I want to talk to you.'

There was a moment's silence. Then, footsteps. Panic flashed through Irina like lightning. And, at last, she saw her husband.

He moved with the slow, rolling gait of something waiting to spring. Shoulders hunched forward, head raised, his eyes never left her face. If it hadn't been for the way he moved, she would never have guessed he wasn't human. If he stood up straight, he would have looked like any other boy in the village – not much older than her, dark hair and dark eyes, wearing a plain linen shirt and trousers. It was unnerving, to think that when he was alive, he could have been so much like her. But there, the similarities ended. Rangy and drawn, hunger was written in every line of his body. His skin was pale but for his hands and feet, which were pitch-black, purple-tinted darkness crawling up his arms and legs. His clothes were torn, caked in dirt. Dried blood was smeared across his chin, the collar of his shirt stained rusty brown. He stalked towards her, arms hanging loose in front of him, as if he was about to drop onto all fours and bound across the floor. Looking at him, she had the unnerving sense that, despite his nearly human appearance, some last tether to life had long since snapped. She couldn't see his teeth. Irina wasn't sure what she was going to do when she did. Probably try and kill him, she thought, and felt a little better.

Her husband came to a halt just in front of her chair. He leaned forward, placing a hand on each of the arms of her chair. She could smell the rich forest earth clinging to his clothes, and the cold bite of snow. He was staring at her, his dark eyes roving over every inch of her face. Irina held his gaze and tried not to look at the blackness crawling up past his wrists. She'd seen it before, but only on dead men who weren't leaning over her.

'You do not give me orders, *wife*,' he growled, each word dripping with derision. His eyes drifted down to her throat. His lips parted and now she saw his teeth – pointed. Glistening. Her breath caught. Not now. It was too soon. She couldn't let him bite her; not before she'd even mentioned her plan.

Irina's hand shot up, pressing the point of the stake into his chest. She tried not to let it shake. 'Yes, I do,' she said.

He stilled. His eyes were boring into hers, black as the night sky. Irina set her jaw. She wasn't going to look at his teeth. The teeth that had torn out the throats of three people she knew – was that Anton's blood, dried on the collar of his shirt? Or Eugen's? Had they told themselves not to stare at the monster's teeth, as she was doing? Had they held a stake in their hands, just as she did?

'Are you going to be reasonable about this,' Irina asked, shifting her weight onto the balls of her feet, 'or do I have to find myself another husband?'

'Reasonable,' he laughed. 'Do you reason with your dinner? You will not survive the night. Why should I—'

Irina tackled him.

A Steep and Savage Path

Throwing herself out of the chair, she lunged forward, putting the weight of her whole body behind the stake. Even as she moved, she knew it was a mistake. The vampire rolled to one side, the point of the stake scratching across his chest, and Irina slammed into the floor, the words *stupid plan stupid plan STUPID PLAN* rattling around her head. She scrambled up, clutching the stake.

The vampire was nowhere to be seen.

Irina's heart was pounding. She drew herself up, summoning every scrap of bravado, eyes roving around the room. 'Are you hiding from me?' She turned in a slow circle, taking in the bare table, the fallen chair, the front door hanging open. She paused, staring into the night. Running was so tempting – unless that was what he was hoping she'd do. Could he have left? No. That would be too easy. He could be on the bed, behind the blankets hanging from the bed-frame. Or in the chest. Or in the pantry. He could be anywhere, she realized, the thought settling on her like a frost. This was his house. There could be a thousand hiding places here that she would never know – loose floorboards, trick panels in the furniture, gaps in the rafters. He could be watching her, right now, and she'd have no idea until she let her guard down and it was too late.

She had to draw him out. 'I know you're here.'

Nothing. Not even a creaking floorboard. Fear trickled through Irina's thoughts. What was he waiting for?

She stalked around the table. The open door swinging behind her, cold air tickling the back of her neck. She hated turning her back on it. She was only presenting a target.

'I married you for a reason,' she said, her eyes scanning from corner to empty corner. 'Don't you want to know what that is?'

The bed-hangings were drifting gently in the breeze. Irina tightened her grip on the stake. She could see the gap in the blankets, the thin line of darkness where the cloth had been parted. There. She'd found him.

'I only want to talk to—'

A faint, almost delicate scratching, over her head. Dust drifted down from the ceiling. Irina threw herself under the table as the vampire dropped to the floor, snarling. The stake flew out of her hand, rolling across the floor. He scrabbled after her, teeth bared. A swipe of his blackening hand caught her across the ankle. Cloth tore. She kicked at his fingers. The heel of her boot smacked into his chin and he swore, clutching his face. Irina scrambled out the other side of the table and snatched up the fallen chair. He scrambled after her. But just as he ducked out from underneath the table, lunging for her legs, Irina brought the chair around in a wide arc and hit him with it. He was knocked off balance, sprawling sideways. Irina darted forward and shoved the back of the chair underneath his chin, pinning him to the floor by the neck.

Holding the chair by the legs, Irina pushed down, panting. The vampire struggled, hissing like an angry cat. It was unnerving; he looked far too human to be moving like an animal in a trap. He was not choking – if anything, Irina thought, she was more out of breath than he was – but having the combined weight of a well-made chair and a strong young woman bearing down on his throat was certainly not an experience he was enjoying.

Irina was bleeding; that swipe across the legs had broken the skin. Her shoulder hurt from throwing herself to the floor, her legs were shaking, she was dripping with sweat, and if she thought too hard about the fact that she had started a fight with a dead man she was going to start screaming and never stop. But this was what she had come here for. It was, unbelievably, all going according to plan. Apart from the fact that the stake was halfway across the room and she'd have to put the chair down to pick it up, but she wasn't going to think about that.

'Can you please just listen to me?' she panted.

The vampire struggled. The chair bucked in Irina's hands. It almost flew out of her grip but she snatched it back just in time, holding it in place. He glared up at her, clawed hands slackening against the scratched wood. All the bones in his hands stood out sharp against the skin, and she wondered if one person a month was enough for him to feed on.

'Fine,' he spat. 'Talk.'

'I have a proposition for you,' she said.

'Apparently,' he said, shooting a disdainful look at her bridal crown, 'I'm a married man.'

'Not *that* kind of—'

The chair jolted. One of the legs flew out of her hand. He squirmed, shoving at the wood pinning him down. Irina grabbed the other chair leg and bore down, hard. He went still, his black eyes calculating, and too late she realized his tactic. She took a deep breath. He was trying to get a rise out of her, hoping that she would loosen her grip.

'That's not what I want from you,' she said.

He rolled his eyes. 'You want me to leave the poor, innocent villagers alone, I've no doubt. The thing is, I haven't been able to find any.'

She shook her head. 'That's not why I married you.'

'Wait.' He stopped, considered her. 'You married me for a reason? You weren't just left here? Is this . . . is this *your* idea?'

Irina hesitated. Fear and embarrassment had settled on her plan like dust. It already seemed foolhardy in her own head. Saying it aloud would be all it took for her enthusiasm to flake away into pieces. But the thought of saying nothing when she'd married herself to a dead man and tried to kill him pricked at her pride. She'd come this far. Surely she wasn't going to falter at the beginning of the road.

'I want you to take me to the land of the dead,' she said. 'Can you do it?'

He blinked at her. All the resentment vanished from his face. 'Sorry, what?'

'Well? Can you?'

The vampire's face turned thoughtful. His black eyes swept her up and down. Unsettled, Irina wracked her brains, trying to remember if any of the stories she'd heard of the walking dead had said they'd been able to read thoughts.

'Who *are* you?' he asked.

'Excuse me?'

'You're not from the village. You're a stranger to me – but you clearly know who I am, because you sought me out. You married me for a reason, apparently, despite the fact that I'm dead. But you didn't marry me to throw yourself on my mercy for the sake of *them*,' he said, his lip curling as he nodded in the direction of the village. 'You want to get into the land of the dead instead. So who are you? Why do you want to do something so stupid? And how did you settle on the most idiotic plan to get what you want?'

Irina's temper flared. 'It isn't stupid!'

The chair lurched in her hands. She wasn't ready. It slipped through her fingers. The vampire hissed in triumph and Irina sprinted across the room, lunging for the stake. Fingers brushed against the end of her braid. Irina dived for the stake, wedged against the chest of blankets, and snatched it up. A growl came from somewhere by her ear. She slammed into the floor with a grunt, rolled over, and saw the vampire crouching over her, his face inches from hers.

'Isn't it?'

She pressed the point of the stake against his heart. He froze. 'It isn't stupid,' she repeated.

'No. Stupid was letting go of the chair.'

Irina ground her teeth. Despite her fear, she was starting to get annoyed. 'Are you going to let me answer your question?'

'Fine. Why does a nice girl like you want to go to the land of the dead?' He grinned. 'I can always send you there the old-fashioned way.'

Irina hesitated. She didn't want to tell him about Catalina; the idea of him even knowing her sister's name sent a fresh spike of panic through her. But she'd have to tell him something. 'There's someone there I want to find.'

'Oh, I've heard this one. If it's your lover, you definitely shouldn't have married me.'

'Would you just—' She took a deep breath; she couldn't afford to lose her temper with him all but pinning her to the floor. 'Look, all I want from you is for you to take me into the land of the dead, help me recover a soul, and take me back to the land of the living. I can't get in by myself. I need a guide. That's you.'

Thoughtfully, he ran a purple-black thumb across his teeth. Irina tried not to think of rotting fruit. 'Why should it be me?'

'Because if you don't, I'll kill you, and find someone else to take me.'

The vampire snorted. He glanced down at her. 'I can see that's going well.'

Irina ground her teeth. The vampire grinned. She pushed the stake into his chest a little harder, and his smile curdled.

'I do actually have something I can offer you, you know,' she said.

'Aside from your scintillating company, darling wife?'

She glared at him.

He rolled his eyes. 'Fine. What would you offer me?'

Now came the part she had been dreading. Irina shifted, adjusting her grip on the stake. 'Well,' she said, avoiding his eyes, 'aren't you hungry?'

Silence.

Then, '*Always.*'

Irina shuddered. 'I'm not saying you can kill me,' she blurted, 'I'm going back to my family when this is done. But . . . you could have some of my blood. In small amounts. Whenever you wanted – as long as I'm well enough to keep going on the journey, of course. You'll get much more blood if you keep me alive than if you drain me in one go. You don't get to eat very often, do you?'

The vampire made a thoughtful noise. 'And what happens after we return to the land of the living, when you have the soul you came for?'

'I go home. I never see you again.'

'Abandoning your husband so soon? Heartless.'

Irina ignored him. She was already wishing she'd picked a less irritating vampire. 'I promised the villagers I would marry you. That's it. They're the ones who thought that'd be enough to kill you. Give me enough time to get away from the village and you can do what you like. You'd be stronger if you were eating regularly in the land of the dead.'

His face twisted. 'They sent you to do their dirty work. How very like them.' He paused, the disdain melting into a pensive expression that she had never expected to see on a face covered in old blood. Irina met his gaze, keeping her grip on the stake. 'Leaving them to die isn't enough,' he said, 'but you can give me something better. Invite me in.'

'Invite you where?'

'Into their houses, idiot.'

'But what will you do?'

A Steep and Savage Path

'Kill them, of course. Did you not notice the teeth?'

Guilt seeped into Irina's thoughts like a bad smell. She remembered all those frightened faces by the graveside, and the tears in Father Simeon's eyes. Leaving the vampire alive – for want of a better word – to keep ransacking the village would be unforgivable, let alone helping him do it. She needed a guide. But when her journey was over, she wouldn't need him any more. There'd be no need to uphold her end of the bargain.

'Well?'

'It's not my village,' she said. She hesitated, then pushed a little further. 'It's like you said. They sent me to do their dirty work. Why should I have any loyalty to them?'

He smiled slowly. Irina shivered. 'Fools. They should have chosen more wisely when they were picking me a wife.'

'Are you going to take my deal or not?'

The vampire considered her for a moment. 'You really don't care if I stay here and kill them when our bargain is done?'

Irina shrugged. 'Not particularly,' she said, trying to sound nonchalant.

'Then, yes. I accept. Or should I say "I do"?'

'Maybe you could try not saying anything,' Irina muttered.

The vampire rolled his eyes. 'You were the one who married me. This is *your* plan. There are other ways to get a dead man's attention than marrying him, you know.'

He stood up in one fluid motion. Irina scrambled to her feet a lot less gracefully, careful to take two big steps back. She still hadn't let go of the stake.

She cleared her throat. 'So should we leave now, or . . .'

'On one condition. Get rid of that,' he said, pointing at the stake.

Irina tightened her grip on the stake. 'How do I know you won't kill me if I do?'

'How do I know you won't kill me if you don't?'

Irina scowled. That was a good point, but it didn't mean she couldn't be annoyed about it. 'So you'll have your teeth and your claws, and I'll have – what? The chair?'

'Could it fit in your pack?' he asked, his face completely blank. Irina ground her teeth. 'Take a knife, then,' he continued. 'Just not something deliberately made to kill me, please.'

'Fine. Is that it?'

He waited. After a long, long moment, Irina put the stake on top of the chest. The soft *click* as she set it down echoed all around the little house. Her hand still hovered over the stake. The vampire watched it, and she was surprised to see some of the tension ebb out of his shoulders when she pulled her hand away.

'Thank you. Now, we seal the deal.'

She held out her hand.

'Not like that,' he said, taking a step towards her. 'I am *hungry*.'

Irina snatched her hand back, heart beating very fast. Her eyes flashed to the stake. 'You won't take too much?' she asked, hating the uncertainty in her voice.

He shook his head. 'You will have to trust me if you want this to work,' he said. 'Start now.'

Irina hesitated. Her eyes were drawn to the dried blood caked around his mouth, staining his shirt. How long had it been there? Whose was it? When he'd bitten those people, had they tried to reason with him? Had they stood in the light of a dying fire and tried to trap him in a bargain, only for him to tear their throats out?

Her hand found the necklace. She thought of Catalina, pointing to a blackberry bush no higher than her knee and telling her confidently that there was a bear living inside it. Catalina, crouching in the dirt courtyard of their home, watching a snail and asking Irina how long she thought it would take for the creature to slither across to the other side. Catalina sitting beside her mother's chair, head nodding as she stared into the fire and tried not to fall asleep. Catalina on her father's shoulders, giggling. Catalina as Irina had last seen her – propped up on pillows, staring straight ahead and seeing nothing, alive in the cruellest sense of the word.

With shaking hands, she pulled her braid over one shoulder and unfastened her choker. She lifted Catalina's necklace over her head, careful not to meet the vampire's eyes. The thought of his dead hands brushing against the beads was like imagining her sister's face starting to rot. She didn't even want him to look at it. She wound the necklace around her hand, rubbing her thumb over one of the chewed beads; her sister would gnaw on anything if it stayed still long enough. Then, she curled her hands into fists, and said 'Do it.'

The vampire came closer. The scent of recently turned earth clung to his clothes, rich and strong. Close to, she could see how thin his linen shirt and trousers were; he'd clearly died in the summer. There was something that might've been a scar on his chin, but she couldn't make it out. It was covered in too much blood.

She looked away. The beads were digging into her palm. She stood like a bowstring, drawn tight enough to snap. The vampire placed a freezing hand on the side of her neck, gently tilting her head away from him, and she clenched her teeth, biting back a whimper. Eyes fixed on the ceiling, she tried not to feel her pulse fluttering in her throat, tried not to hear her own sharp, panicked breaths. This was all part of her plan. She had to make peace with it. She'd known exactly what this bargain would cost her – she was the one who had proposed it. Surely that had to mean she wouldn't be afraid.

He placed his other hand on her shoulder. Irina swallowed.

Now there was no way out. He could snap her neck if she tried to run. She heard him open his mouth, right next to her ear. Felt him draw closer. His grip tightened.

'Wait,' Irina whispered. 'What's your name?'

There was a pause. A noise that was something between a growl and the sound an ordinary man might make when he was interrupted at dinner. Then, 'Stefan,' so close she could feel the name on her skin.

'Irina,' she said.

He sank his teeth into her neck.

In a way, it was almost a relief. Pain throbbed along her throat, and she did not want to think about the strange pulling sensation of having her blood drawn from her veins, but at least she wasn't standing there, waiting, dreading the scrape of teeth across her skin. It wasn't exactly pleasant, but it didn't hurt too much.

He pulled away, sooner than she expected. A pulse of pain rippled through her when his teeth finally came loose. Irina stepped back at once, slapping a handkerchief onto her throbbing neck while he was still wiping his mouth.

'Satisfied?' she asked.

'No. But we have a deal. I will take you to the land of the dead. Sleep, and eat as much as you can.'

'But aren't we leaving now?'

He shook his head. 'Not until I search the woods. If I find anyone waiting for me there, I'll kill you. Besides, you'll need your strength.'

'Why?'

The vampire smiled, his mouth glistening red. 'I told you. I am always hungry.'

The moment he was gone, Irina bolted the door. She slammed the shutters closed. Dragging the high-backed chair in front of the window, she hauled the chest across the door and collapsed in a heap in front of the oven, waiting until she had stopped feeling like she wanted to throw up. She felt as if all the strength in her body had been boiled away, like bones in a bubbling stock pot. Trembling, she huddled into a blanket and snatched up the plate of jumări, shovelling crunchy, salty pork into her mouth by the handful.

So, she thought. *That was her husband.*

Even after meeting him, Irina still could not decide if he was what she had expected. Somehow he was both more and less human than she'd imagined. Part of her had been expecting a slavering, relentless corpse whose capacity for reason had long since rotted away. Part of her had been expecting a sinister older man, well dressed and with manners refined by centuries of practice. She hadn't expected a boy close to her own age, who seemed to treat his humanity like a coat he could slip on and off at will. Nor had she expected the hands, cold as winter and turning black almost to the elbow. Still, at least the teeth hadn't been a surprise.

But then again, almost everything else about him had been. The villagers had told her nothing about him, not even his name. All they'd said was that he was a monster. They could not kill him without disposing of his body, so until they found his grave, she was their last hope. Perhaps it was too painful for them to speak of. The dead only rose from their graves when they had died badly, and he couldn't have been more than eighteen when he died. She wasn't surprised they didn't want to talk about him.

Irina reached for another handful of pork and found the plate empty. She felt hollow, but also annoyed; she'd planned to take some of it on her journey. One of the few things she knew about the land of the dead was this: don't eat the food. Don't drink the water. All the stories agreed on it. She didn't know how long she would be there. She couldn't afford to eat an entire plate of salty pork every time she had a shock, even if it had made her feel better.

Licking the grease off her fingers, she shifted closer to the oven, and tried not to think about how little she had heard about the land of the dead. In church, the priests had always been firm: there was Heaven and there was Hell, and any rumours from villages close to the dark press of the forest were not to be given quarter. They were only rumours. But priests living in villages like hers – easily three days' travel from the nearest town – had to be practical men. The wise ones recognized that there was a lot of room for rumours between the sanctity of Heaven and the sins of Hell, and as long as it was not heresy, sometimes it was better to leave such things alone. Not far from where she'd grown up had been the ruins of an old fortress, all but crumbling on the hillside. As children, they would creep up there, and once or twice Irina had seen fragments of paintings on the old walls: a long face with wide eyes, a dog with three heads, an instrument that looked a little like a cobza except the strings were set between two curved handles instead of running along a neck. The witch had always said the paintings had told a story, but it had stopped being told long before her time.

Fragments of it lingered. Coins placed over the eyes of the dead; Irina had asked the priest in her own village why they did this, and he could not answer. Bowls of food and drink laid out around the house at every wake; the priest had not been able to tell her why they did that, either. Covering the mirrors, propping the door open, the stub of a candle placed in a corpse's darkening hand – but here Irina could ask no more questions, because the priest had all but thrown her out of the little wooden church, telling her to stop being impertinent. But the truth burned inside her chest like a flame. The priest had not wanted to answer her questions, because he knew he could not answer them without blasphemy. No coins over the eyes had ever been mentioned in all Irina's years in church. This was something else. She could see the shape of it, like the dim outline of a house shrouded in mist. There was something there. She knew it. It was something finely balanced against everything she'd been told in church; not undermining it, but intertwining with it. The same thing that made the witch work the name of the Virgin into her spells made the priest lay cold coins over the eyes of a dead man, and people did not want to turn away from the church any more than they wanted to shun the witch's cures when they fell sick. But whereas Irina had been taken to church every Sunday and learned about the Lord since she was a child, no one had ever wanted to tell her what the dead needed those coins for in the first place.

Bruises were already blooming across her skin. One of her shoulders was almost completely purple, and when she saw it, she instinctively looked for Catalina. A hollowness settled over her. She tried to tell herself it was just as well that Catalina wasn't here – you could never show that girl a bruise without her trying to poke it – but it didn't work.

She unpacked, made more food, and repacked, desperate to have something to do with her hands. She wished once again she could've changed out of her wedding clothes, but they were all she had; she would have to wear those into the land of the dead. If Stefan even held up his end of the bargain. If he even *could* – he was so young, how much would he know about the journey ahead of her? Eventually she gave up and started pacing, stalking around the room like a wolf circling the village. Irina peered at the hat in the rafters again and stood on a chair for a closer look: it was black, wide-brimmed, and looked too large for the boy she'd met last night. She set it back where she had found it, puzzled. Had Stefan had family here, before he'd died?

Surely if he had, they would've arranged a funeral for him – and there'd been nobody living here when she'd arrived. There was only one narrow bed, pushed up against the wall, and she knew for a fact that nobody had wanted to take anything out of a house of the dead. What if he came back for it?

He must have lived alone. Unusual, she thought, but not unheard of. That must've been why he returned from the dead. They always said that those who didn't get a proper burial would end up demanding one, dead or not. If he'd died alone, with nobody to organize a search for his body and conduct a proper funeral – and a wedding of the dead in the process – that could explain why he'd come back. But this wasn't a large village. Had no one thought to check on him? Surely they must have noticed when he stopped coming to church. The little house wasn't that isolated. Even if he hadn't had family, someone must have seen the animals going unfed and the chimney growing cold.

Irina shook her head. If she wanted to know more about Stefan's life, she could simply ask him. But that was not a good idea if she was going to kill him once she got back to the land of the living.

There was no getting around it, she thought, as she started getting ready for bed. He would have to die. He'd killed people. He would have killed her already if she hadn't offered him a deal. She couldn't walk away from the village and leave him standing, and she certainly couldn't invite him into their homes before she left. Every time she looked at her sister, she'd be reminded of what she'd done, and she didn't want to make Catalina carry that burden for her. If she'd been a better person, perhaps she would have felt guilty. He was her husband, after all, and something had clearly happened for him to have come back in the first place. But Irina wasn't sure what to make of having a husband at all. It had always seemed like a nice idea but rather distant, in the same way that it might be nice to visit Bucharest. The same had been true for kissing, before she'd tried it. The idea of kissing someone she actually liked was fine, but both times she'd tried it the whole experience had been decidedly underwhelming. Marriage would be no different. She'd have to actually like Stefan to give not staking him through the heart a second thought, and if tonight was anything to go by, that was extremely unlikely.

Irina had a minute's warning.

She'd been dozing, her neck still aching after the bite. Then, a long, low creak from outside. She scrambled out of bed, tumbling gracelessly through the hangings as the footsteps came closer. She shoved her feet into her shoes, looking frantically around for a weapon, as once again, Stefan pushed the door open.

Moonlight streamed in through the open doorway, but he cast no shadow at all. Though she couldn't quite see his face, silhouetted against a sky full of stars, she knew he was looking at her. Only one of his blackening hands was clear in the gloom, resting on the open door; the greyish light made it look like a dead thing, dredged up from the bottom of the river. Perhaps he had drowned. She didn't know.

He stalked towards her. Although her own blood was still slathered across his chin, she could see the hunger glittering in his eyes. Fear skittered through her. He crossed the room in two long strides, already reaching for her – and paused, his eyes fixed on her outfit.

'You're still in your wedding clothes,' he said.

Irina plucked at her sleeves, fighting the urge to back away. They suddenly felt a lot thinner. 'They didn't leave me anything else.'

He made a noise of contempt. 'Of *course* they didn't. Why would they waste money on you?'

'What do you mean by that?'

He ignored her. 'You can't go to the land of the dead in that. You look ridiculous.'

'I look like your wife,' she said, grabbing the bridal crown and jamming it onto her head. If her wedding clothes could knock Stefan's bloodlust off course, perhaps they'd be more useful than she'd thought. 'And if we're going to be talking about the way we look, you should wash your face. It's covered in blood.'

He rolled his eyes. 'Are you ready?'

She nodded, shouldering the pack. 'Do you need anything from here before we go?'

'My things were all burned,' he said, holding the door open for her.

'Burned?'

He ignored her. 'Follow me.'

Irina stepped out into the courtyard. Under the moonlight, it was bitterly cold. Freezing fog curled between the fence posts, tangling around the hem of her skirts and making the snow look deep enough to drown in. All the colour had been leached out of the little courtyard, like a vein emptied of blood.

She shut the door behind her and followed Stefan, who was heading towards the forest. Bleached of colour by the snow and the moonlight, she could only see him by the darkness of his hair and his bare hands and feet. He seemed to slip in and out of his humanity as it suited him; one moment walking over the snow with his strange, hunched gait, the next skittering over the wooden fence like a lizard. Irina had to climb over it, trying not to snag her skirts on any splinters. She hopped down from the fence with an enormous tearing sound, as Stefan was already at the treeline. She yanked her skirt free and hurried after him, her pack bumping against her shoulder.

Irina was used to the woods the same way she was used to

the stars: she was familiar with them, but only at a distance. As the backdrop to her time in the village, they were comforting. The delicate rustling of pine in the wind soothed her when she could not sleep; the steady *thunk* of axes at work and the smell of fresh-cut wood reminded her that a warm fire was never too far away. But she'd never been sent into the woods. Close to, she was dwarfed by the trees. Twisted roots bubbled out of the ground like reaching hands. Bats chittered overhead. She caught the flash of an owl's wing out of the corner of her eye. Everything was painted in shades of darkness, and in her red-and-white wedding clothes, she felt like a target.

Stefan's stained white clothes rippled in front of her like the sails of a wrecked ship. Dirt and blood were smeared across his back, and, as he ran, she could have sworn some of them were in the shape of handprints. Irina stumbled through the undergrowth, twigs cracking under her feet and leaves rasping against her clothes, but he didn't make a sound. Hunched over, he ducked under branches and sprang over roots with the loping, silent grace she'd always associated with wolves. Once or twice, she lost sight of him, and started when he appeared out of the darkness, much closer than she'd realized.

There was a narrow dirt path twisting through the forest, but soon Stefan veered away from it. Pushing back the undergrowth, he pressed through dark pines as Irina struggled to keep up. A tangle of trees closed around them. Irina could barely see more than a foot in front of her, and if it were not for Stefan's filthy shirt, she would have lost him completely. Then the ground sloped up under her feet and the trees began to thin. After a few minutes of climbing, they emerged from the woods, face to face with a wall of dark stone. Irina panted as she waded through the snow, her thighs burning from the effort of the climb. She leaned against the rock face, too tired to be embarrassed at her own lack of stamina. It helped when she wasn't looking at Stefan. There was no sign of exertion on his face at all. He hadn't even broken a sweat. With a jolt, Irina wondered if he was even capable of that.

He watched her catch her breath, an unreadable expression on his face. 'Are you ready?' he eventually asked.

'Is this it?'

'There are many ways in,' he said, walking along the base of the mountain, running a hand over the stone. 'This is one of them.'

He stopped. Irina saw a dark gap in the stone. It looked tiny. In fact, she thought, it looked like exactly the kind of place that a monster might take a girl with a very poorly thought-out plan so that he could safely murder her away from the village. He turned back to look at her, her own blood still smeared across his face, and as he gestured her towards the entrance Irina was unable to drag her eyes away from his bloodstained chin.

'You can't be serious,' she said.

'Did you expect a signpost? A city gate?' he scoffed. 'This is the land of the dead. It isn't going to be at the side of an ordinary road.'

Irina crept closer, tamping down her fear as she rummaged in her pack for a tinderbox and a candle. She struck a light and peered into the crack, keeping half an eye on Stefan. It was larger than she'd expected, fanning out into a wide cavern of dark stone. Not exactly the coffin she'd half-thought he'd dragged her to. It looked solid enough underfoot.

'How do you know all this?'

He gestured at himself, taking in his bloodstained clothes, blackened hand and pointed teeth in one disdainful sweep.

'I got that,' Irina snapped, trying and failing to swallow her irritation, 'but that doesn't explain how you knew it was here.'

A Steep and Savage Path

He made a frustrated sound from somewhere at the back of his throat. 'Am I going to have to explain everything to you? I am *dead*. This is where I am supposed to be. Of course I know where it is. It calls to me.'

Irina stared at the entrance of the cave. 'It does? I don't hear anything.'

'Again, *dead*. You know, if you keep stopping to question my every move, we aren't going to get very far. You have to trust me at some point.'

'I left the stake behind, didn't I?'

He looked shocked. 'You did?'

'Well, yes. That was what we agreed.' She looked at the mouth of the cave again. Under the moonlight, with snow thick on the ground, a chill seemed to roll out of the cave like smoke. She glanced back at Stefan. He was staring at her, looking completely thrown, one hand halfway to his chin as though he was about to wipe his face.

Irina turned back to the cave, squaring her shoulders. She could see nothing beyond the entrance, only darkness. She waited, listening for the call Stefan had mentioned, and heard nothing but a faint whistling. Her heart stopped – she could hear it too – but then the breeze caught the hem of her snow-soaked skirt. It was only the wind. Whatever was calling was not calling to her. With a deep breath, she slipped inside.

She was standing on a ledge in an enormous cavern, shadow swallowing the rock on all sides. Candlelight lapped against dark stone, glimmering grey, brown and black. Droplets of water froze on the rock at her back, along grooves of white, raised stone that reminded her of burrowing maggots. She shuffled closer to the darkness, holding the candle high, and saw two vast stalagmites in the flickering light beyond the ledge, shadows dancing across their pitted surfaces. When she cleared her throat, it echoed.

Stefan appeared at her shoulder. 'There.'

Irina flinched back, nearly dropping the candle. 'What?'

He smirked and pointed into the darkness.

She held the candle a little higher. 'It's just a cave, isn't it?'

He stared at her, shocked. 'You mean you – come on,' he said, turning away and walking along the ledge. 'We'll take a closer look.'

Irina followed him into the darkness. The ledge sloped downwards, snaking along the outermost wall of the cave. Loose rocks skittered across the floor with every step; Irina had to keep a hand on the wall so she would not lose her footing. Every rattle of the pebbles echoed across the cave. She tried not to think about how long they kept bouncing. How far she had to fall.

Soon, the ledge levelled out into the wider cave floor. Stefan headed towards the two stalagmites, stopping just in front of them. They were enormous – each one easily as wide as the hut she had been staying in – and several hundred feet apart.

He waved at them. 'How about now?'

Irina looked at the stalagmites. Close to, they were paler than the rest of the cave, made of a bone-white rock that fell in long, thin fronds. It looked a little like a frozen waterfall, but they seemed no more remarkable than the rock they were made of. She held the candle a little closer. Was there a carving she was supposed to have noticed? She couldn't find one. She looked around, but there was nothing else there – nothing but Stefan, gawping at her with an expression of disbelief on his face.

'You can't see it, can you?' he asked.

'See what?'

'See *this*,' he said, and walked between the stalagmites. He was visible for a few seconds, and then, while he was still standing in the circle of candlelight, he disappeared.

Irina's mouth fell open. No one had ever told her the dead could do that. Was it a trick? Was he going to appear behind her again, and plunge his teeth into her neck? She scrabbled for the knife at her belt. She couldn't let him catch her undefended. How had she ever thought he'd hold up his end of the bargain? She wasn't planning to hold up hers; why should she expect something better of him?

But then, he slid back out of the darkness, as if he was stepping through a parted curtain. She'd been staring right at the spot where he appeared, and she had no idea how he'd done it. He was frowning at her like she was a puzzle that needed to be solved, and in that moment, the truth dawned on her.

'There's something here, isn't there?' she whispered. Gazing up at the vast stalagmites, listening to the hiss of her words echo around the cave, she felt like a mouse that had crawled into a church: suddenly confronted with something far bigger than her and impossible to understand.

He nodded. 'It's the gate.' He rubbed his chin, still looking thoughtful; his fingers came away bloody.

'I thought you said there wasn't going to *be* a gate to the land of the dead,' Irina said, unable to keep the snideness out of her voice.

He ignored that. 'I don't understand,' he muttered. 'I can see it. Why can't you?'

Maybe it's only visible to the annoying, Irina thought. She bit back the words. As much as she wanted to give Stefan a piece of her mind, the sight of her own blood smeared across his chin was enough to make her think twice. 'Can't I walk through it anyway?'

'You could try.'

Irina walked forward. The stalagmites towered over her. She kept walking. Nothing changed. But perhaps it wasn't supposed to change. Perhaps if she kept going, she would—

'No, that's not working,' Stefan called. 'Come back before you hit something.'

She turned around and headed back, nerves mounting. What if she couldn't get into the land of the dead at all? She'd have no way of getting Catalina back and, she realized, she'd be trapped in a quiet, dark space with a vampire who wanted her blood. No one would even know she was here.

'This doesn't make sense,' he muttered, frowning. 'You should be able to see it. Why can't you see it?'

Irritation rippled through the fear. It wasn't her fault she couldn't see whatever she was supposed to see. 'Maybe it's only visible to the—'

'—to the dead,' he said, his eyes widening. Irina clamped her teeth shut on the word 'annoying' just in time. 'Of course. It all makes sense,' he breathed. 'How can you see a gate to death if you aren't touched by death? Of *course* you can't see it.'

Irina grabbed his wrist experimentally. Nothing happened, except that Stefan gave her a perturbed look. 'You said touched by death,' she snapped, letting go. 'You're dead, aren't you? It couldn't hurt to try.'

'I think it might need something a little stronger than that.'

For a moment, she didn't understand what he meant. Then she realized that his eyes had drifted down to her neck. Irina felt a prickle of unease. Being bitten was the only real leverage she had, but she couldn't say she enjoyed the experience. How could he want more blood already? Was his hunger that endless?

'I . . . I'm not . . .'

He smirked. 'This is the arrangement we made. *Wife*. Don't tell me you—'

'All right, all right,' she said, moving her hair aside with shaking hands. 'You've made your point.'

In two strides, he was in front of her, one hand already

reaching for her throat. She flinched. His mouth was open, his fangs bared. Irina fought the urge to slap his hand away as she took off the bridal choker and Catalina's necklace. His fingers curling around her neck, tilting her head back. A flutter of panic ran through her. His other hand on her shoulder, exposing the length of her neck. She felt like a piece of meat, waiting to be pulled apart.

He stopped. 'Wait,' he said. 'Turn around. You should see it.'

Irina turned around. Despite her fear, a small part of her was relieved that she could roll her eyes in peace, even though she could sense Stefan's eyes on the back of her neck. Now she was staring into the blackness beyond the two stalagmites, wondering what, exactly, she was supposed to see. Stefan's cold hand gripped her jaw and tilted her head to one side. She tried not to flinch at the touch of his freezing fingers.

'How will I know if this works?' she asked, clutching her necklaces in shaking hands. 'How close to death are you going to take me?'

She'd expected a sharper reply, but when he spoke, there was no edge to his words. 'Tell me when you see it. Then I'll stop.'

His teeth sank into her skin. Irina winced. She couldn't decide if it hurt more or less than last time, but the sensation of her blood being pulled from her veins was far more unsettling.

Something shifted in the darkness.

Irina went still, her heart pounding. She squinted. There, at the base of one of the stalagmites, was the faintest patch of light. It was spreading, coiling up the rock, growing brighter as each delicate frond reached higher up the stone. Across the cave there was another, spiralling up the other stalagmite like ribbons wrapped around a maypole. The light looked as delicate as spiderwebs, red and orange and gold bursting into life like clouds along the edges of a sunrise. As she watched, the blood pumping out of her, the two strands of light thickened, brightened, coiled towards each other, as though they were vines around a frame. She stared, transfixed, as a thousand tiny points of light burst into life over her head in rose-pink, copper, and scarlet, joining the two columns until she was staring at an enormous arch. In the sudden glow, the cave around her was transformed. Glittering veins of quartz sparkled in the walls. Lacy fronds of stalactites hung from the ceiling. All the colours of rock glowed around her: warm browns, rich greys, golden yellow and shining white, all of them woven together in a living tapestry. And beyond the lights, at last, was a glimpse of what she had been searching for. The land of the dead, shimmering behind a veil of stars. All she could see of it was a patch of darkness, hovering behind the lights, and a watery shine in the gloom.

'*Oh*,' she gasped.

She wanted to cry. She wanted to laugh. The land of the dead was real. She hadn't risked her life on a fairy tale. Her plan could work. Her sister's soul was waiting for her, on the other side of the darkness. Catalina had a chance. If Irina could find the land of the dead, then she could find her sister.

Stefan pulled away. Irina staggered forward and slapped a hand over her bleeding neck, suddenly dizzy. She couldn't look away from the gate, but out of the corner of her eye, she saw his bloodstained mouth curve into a smile. It was a little strange: he'd tried to kill her when they first met and had drunk her blood twice, but despite the fact that he showed no signs of liking her, he still wanted to show her something beautiful. It was an unexpected gift, and she found herself wanting to offer something in return.

She fished out a flask of water from her pack and held it out to him.

He looked perplexed. 'I don't drink . . . water.'

'No, for your face. You've got a little – well, quite a lot of blood, actually.'

'Oh.' Looking even more confused than he did before, he splashed some water on his face and handed the flask back to her. 'Are you ready?' he asked.

Irina nodded. She was full of hope and fear and wonder, and a sense of how little she knew, and was not sure if she could trust herself to speak. What could she say, in the face of the beauty that had been revealed to her?

Stefan patted her on the shoulder. She thought he was trying to comfort her, until he took his hand away and licked the blood off his fingers.

'Let's go,' he said.

Footsteps echoing around the cave, they walked into the arch of swirling lights. Irina kept her eyes focused on the patch of darkness in front of her. She didn't feel right. Perhaps it was just the blood loss, still oozing underneath her linen collar, but her limbs felt heavy, sluggish. With every step she became more aware of her own heartbeat, feeling it twitch under her skin like a creature desperate to escape the confines of its cage. Stefan was striding ahead as though nothing was wrong, but she felt as though she was wading through thick porridge. Irina ground her teeth. Of course it was easy for him. He was dead. This was a gate to the land of the dead; he was designed to pass through it. She was not.

She wasn't meant to be here. She wasn't meant to even know this place existed. It had taken a brush with death to even see the way in. The land of the dead was not going to make things easy for her. Well, Irina thought, forcing one foot in front of the other, that was fine. It could make things as difficult for her as it liked; it wouldn't make a difference. She would force her way in, she would find her sister's soul, and she would bring her back home, where she belonged.

The patch of darkness was barely six feet from her, and sweat was pouring off her from the effort of reaching it. If she turned around now, her load would lighten with every step. But she was close enough to see that the darkness was not true darkness. In the gloom she could see rich blues and purples, rippling and shimmering in the same way that water caught the light. There was a whole other world in those shadows, and it would not keep her out.

A cold hand closed around her elbow. Irina started. She'd almost forgotten that Stefan was there; she'd been straining so hard to take each step she hadn't even noticed him double back to stand beside her. He gave her a long, assessing look. It unnerved her. Was he trying to make her turn back? Was he going to bite her again?

He said nothing. He simply turned to face the portal and, hand still clutching her elbow, yanked her forwards, his grip a little stronger than before. Irina staggered, stomach roiling; he kept going, dragging her closer to the gate. Shaking with the effort, every muscle in her body aching, Irina hauled herself up to the darkness. With Stefan's cold fingers still locked around her arm like an anchor, she stepped through.

PART TWO

The first thing Irina noticed about the land of the dead was the darkness. After the glimmering lights of the gate, the blackness was startling. The moment she stepped through the portal, the pressure she had been straining against lifted, and she lurched forward. There was a wrench in her shoulder as something caught her mid-fall: Stefan, his blackening hand still locked around one of her arms.

She stood up straight, adjusting her bridal crown. 'Thank you.' The gate glimmered behind her but when she turned away from it, she could see no light spilling out into the dark. For a moment, she panicked – what if it had vanished altogether? – but when she turned back, it was still there.

'Wait,' Stefan said, his voice taut. 'What's happening to the gate?'

Irina stared at it. It looked exactly the same. 'What do you mean?'

Stefan's eyes were wide. 'It's fading! How will we get back?'

The gate burned as brightly as ever. 'No, it isn't,' Irina said, confused. 'It's right there.'

He frowned at her. 'What are you talking about? I can see it fading, the way is closing, it's . . .' He trailed off, his eyes flicking between her bloodstained shirt and the gate. '*Oh*,' he breathed, the panic fading a little. 'It works both ways.'

'What do you mean?'

'You had to be touched by death to get through to the land of the dead,' he said, still staring at the sparkling gate. 'It looks like I have to be touched by life to get back to the land of the living.'

Relief flooded through her. If he wanted to finish tormenting the villagers, he'd have to keep her alive long enough to get back to the gate. And, she realized, she wouldn't have to try and kill him at all – she could simply leave him behind, once they'd rescued Catalina's soul. He wouldn't be able to follow her. She turned, looking around, and caught Stefan looking at her, a calculating expression on his face. He smoothed it away at once, but Irina was still uneasy.

It took her eyes a little while to adjust to the gloom. She could still see the afterimages of the lights in the gate, like fireworks in the night. When they had faded, she saw that they were standing in a cave that looked similar to the one they had left behind. There was stone under her boots and over her head, though it was hard to see much more than twisting, towering rock in the semi-darkness. An undulating indigo light from somewhere off in the distance was casting strange shadows on the ceiling. Irina shrank into herself a little at the sight of it; it made her think that something was swooping over her head.

'Well, here we are,' said Stefan, gesturing into the darkness. He peered up at the shadows on the ceiling. 'What is *that*?'

Pain throbbed in Irina's shoulder. She reached up to massage away the sore spot, her hand pushing aside the linen collar of her shirt with ease. It took her a moment to realize what this meant.

Her pack was gone.

Irina spun around. Her things were nowhere to be seen. Panic lurched through her. 'Have you seen my pack?'

A Steep and Savage Path

'Hmm?' asked Stefan. He was still staring at the roof of the cave. 'Oh, that. No. What do you think that blue light is?'

'Oh, no.' Irina dropped to her knees and started scrabbling around on the floor. Her hands were shaking. 'Oh, *no*.'

Still with thoughtful eyes on the ceiling, he waved a vague hand in the direction of the gate. 'You must have dropped—' He stopped, and started to laugh.

'What's so funny?'

'Don't you see?' he said, turning to face her.

She glared at him. 'No, I don't. All my food and water was in that pack, Stefan, so I don't really see what the joke is.'

He gave her an insufferable smile. 'You can't take it with you. Isn't that what they always say?'

Fuming, Irina got to her feet. 'Hilarious,' she muttered. 'You know I'm not supposed to eat or drink anything down here? I'll starve without that pack.'

'Imagine being driven mad by hunger,' he said, his voice completely flat. 'Truly, no one knows how you have suffered.'

Irina started patting down her pockets. 'I don't know why you're so calm,' she snapped. 'If I starve, so do you. How much blood is there in the land of the dead, do you think?'

He frowned. Irina felt a little glimmer of smugness; he clearly knew she had a point, and hated it. 'Then we'll leave.'

'We're not going anywhere without—'

'Fine. Then *I'll* leave, and you'll stay here and die.'

Irina stared at him. 'You can't.'

He leaned forward, grinning. 'Watch me.'

'No, you *can't*. Can you even see the gate any more?'

Stefan straightened up, glancing from side to side, clearly trying to check for an exit without giving her the satisfaction of seeing him do it. He ground his teeth. 'How do you *know* you aren't supposed to eat or drink anything here, anyway?'

53

'Weren't you about to leave?' she asked in her sweetest voice. He bared his teeth, red and glistening. The urge to needle him vanished. 'Stories,' she said, a little too quickly. 'That's how I know.'

'You're really going to put your faith in stories?' he jeered. 'Did you plan this journey on superstitions and sayings? How many other old wives' tales do you believe in?'

She raised her eyebrows at him. 'What, like "you can't take it with you"? Or the wedding of the dead? Or how vampires are made in the first place?'

Cold fingers seized her by the wrist. His hand had moved so fast she hadn't even seen it. He pulled her forward, yanking her off balance, and leaned down to whisper in her ear.

'Do you want to find out?'

All she could see was his teeth. She tried to pull away. 'Don't touch me!'

'Then don't push me.'

Irina tore her hand away and backed off a few paces. Her wrist stung; his grip had been hard to break. Stefan watched her go with the steady gaze of a cat tracking a mouse. Irina turned away and patted her pockets, unable to look at his empty eyes a moment longer.

To her surprise, she found something. Her clothes and shoes were still intact, although stained and torn, and she was still wearing Catalina's necklace. The stub of the candle she'd lit in the cave was still there, but no tinderbox, and she'd turned up a handful of pfennigs she hadn't spent yet in her pockets. She stared at them, unsure why these had been left to her when her food and water had not. But then she remembered the conversation she'd had with the priest, and all the wakes she'd attended where coins and candles had been pressed into the corpse's hands. Evidently there were some things you *could* take with you.

Too late, she realized what she was missing. Her knife. The one thing she had that would give her a fighting chance against a monster who could tear her throat out in a heartbeat. She froze, dread sweeping through her in a flood. She couldn't let him know. If he realized that she had nothing to defend herself with, he could drain her blood and stride back into the land of the living, leaving her for dead.

'Well,' she said, slipping her things back into her pockets with shaking fingers, 'we'd better get moving. I don't want to starve. The sooner we find Catalina, the better.'

'Who's Catalina?'

It felt strange, hearing her sister's name in a dead man's mouth. Irina's hand flew to Catalina's necklace, as though keeping it hidden would let her sister stay safe. Doubt curled around her thoughts like shadowy fingers. Stefan could not harm her sister in the land of the dead – here, she was only a soul, and had no blood to interest him. But when they returned to the land of the living, what was to stop him from finding them again, and lifting the shutters on Catalina's window?

Irina's jaw tightened. She'd kill him first. She strode off in the direction of the shimmering blue lights. Stefan followed, catching up to her on silent feet.

'Do you actually know where you're going, or did you just walk off so you could avoid answering my question?'

Irina kept walking. 'If I knew where I was going, I wouldn't need a guide,' she retorted.

'Oh, I *see*,' said Stefan, 'it's not just your plan that's foolhardy and poorly thought out. That's just you, as a person. Tell me, darling wife, what is the point of engaging a guide unless you are going to let them lead the way?'

Irina stopped dead in her tracks. Despite her fear, the urge to stamp her feet was *so* tempting. Stefan stopped too, smirking, then started heading off in the same direction, towards the blue lights.

'Oh, come *on*,' Irina groaned. The second she found Catalina, she was going to find the nearest pointy object and shove it straight through his chest. She'd sharpen the candle if she had to.

The blue lights were growing brighter. Shadows of stalactites swelled and snapped back into shape with every shifting wave of indigo. The rock around them gleamed smooth and black as tar. Irina was half-tempted to try and slide her feet across it, to see if it felt like she was ice-skating. But then she noticed the shapes in the distance. Not shapes – figures. Looking around, striding forward, or standing perfectly still as if they were staring; the darkness ahead was full of them. She only noticed them when the lights moved, and a tendril of brilliant blue sent their shadows careening across the floor.

She seized Stefan's arm. 'What are those?' she whispered.

'The dead,' he replied.

Fear oozed through her thoughts like icy water. 'Are we safe?'

Stefan kept his eyes fixed on the figures. 'I don't know.'

They crept forward. No one seemed to have spotted them. Whatever the dead were doing, it didn't involve Stefan and Irina at all. Whether they had fallen to their knees or were heading towards the lights, the dead were not paying any attention to the two of them. Undulating light showed Irina glimpses of them, and with each flash of a face – a beard, a pockmarked, drawn cheek, dull, lank hair – she realized that when they were moving, they too were heading towards the blue light. They seemed far more human than Stefan did; they hesitated, looked around for someone to walk alongside them, or held their heads in their hands and wept, whereas Stefan loped through the darkness, perpetually about to pounce.

Irina ignored them and kept walking, following Stefan and trying not to stare. She did not want to see them – she would feel much, *much* saner if she never knew what the dead truly looked like – but all the same, she could not help feeling curious.

Blue light bathed them, as strong as moonlight. They were not far from the source now – it was growing brighter with every step – and Irina realized it must be coming from somewhere below. High, arched shadows swept up the planes of Stefan's face, pooling around his eye sockets. In the blue light, the blood on his collar looked black. Lights danced along the ceiling, indigo and navy and purple and azure, shifting and sparkling, and Irina realized, at last, what she was looking at.

The light was coming from a river.

Not just any river. As she hurried to catch up with Stefan – he was taller than her, and had a longer stride – she caught a glimpse of it. Carving through the dark rock were all the shades of blue she had ever seen. Swathes of lapis and sapphire, sparkling as it flowed. Bright splashes of cornflower and duck-egg blue, speckled across the darker shades like stars. The richness of navy, almost purple and black. The colours moved like water, swirling and streaming together in the same direction, but she had no idea if it really was water that she was looking at. It was more like staring into the depths of the Milky Way.

'What is it?' she breathed.

'The first crossing-place,' said Stefan, his voice low. 'When we cross it, we're truly in the land of the dead.'

She frowned. 'Aren't we there now?'

He shrugged. 'Partially. It is like coming into a courtyard; you are inside the walls, but not the house.'

Irina bit her lip, thoughtful. 'If this is more of a border between life and death, should we search it before crossing the river?'

'If you want to search it, then we can search it,' he said. 'But if the soul you are trying to bring back has truly died, then it will be on the other side of the river. Do you know where Catalina is?'

Irina bristled once more when he said her sister's name. She should never have uttered it; the less he knew about her sister, the safer Catalina would be. She reached up for the wooden necklace, needing the familiar feel of it in her hand.

It moved.

Irina yelped. Stefan whirled around. 'What is it?' he hissed.

Irina pulled the necklace over her head, staring at it. The beads that Catalina had chewed and played with hung limp in her hand, until suddenly, they didn't. Irina held the necklace perfectly still, but it started swaying under her fingers, rocking back and forth in the direction of the river. She had a sudden image of holding a lizard by its tail, and nearly dropped the necklace.

'Are you moving that?' Stefan asked.

'No,' she whispered. 'No, I promise I'm not. This is how we find her, isn't it?'

Stefan stared at the necklace, mesmerized. 'Is that something of hers? Of Catalina's?'

Irina nodded. 'Have you seen anything like this before?'

'No, never. Why is it doing that?'

Irina did not answer. She did not know any more than Stefan did. Glancing around surreptitiously, she looked to see if anyone else was using something to guide their way, but the dead were empty-handed. But, she reasoned, perhaps it wasn't that unusual that the necklace was behaving strangely. Both she and Catalina were alive, even if Catalina's soul was no longer in her body, and neither of them was meant to be here. She adjusted her grip on the necklace, holding it between finger and thumb. It jiggled a little as she moved, but the moment her hand was still it started pointing to the river again.

He straightened up, sighing. 'I suppose we cross the river, then.'

Irina slipped the necklace back over her head and started walking again, squeezing the beads tightly. They had stopped moving but were warm in her hands. Tears pricked at the corners of her eyes. She *would* find her sister.

As they approached the banks, more dark figures slipped out of the shadows. Fear rippled through her. Each one of them was dead. Close to, they looked ordinary enough. Old men huddled into sheepskin coats. Old women with floral headscarves tied under their wrinkled chins. A few soldiers in Austrian imperial uniforms. A young mother, clutching her newborn baby. One or two lost-looking children. They cast shadows and seemed solid enough, and even in the dark she could see they did not have the waxy, greying look she'd seen on corpses. If she'd passed them in the street, she wouldn't have given them a second glance. But the soldiers had slashed-open jackets, dark with blood. The mother's white shift was completely black from the waist down. Irina looked up at the ceiling to avoid noticing what was wrong with the children, feeling oddly guilty when she could not meet their eyes.

They were all congregating around the banks of the river. Up ahead was a dark mass of the dead, milling around and chatting in the strange, blue light. Every so often, the crowd would shift, and Irina would catch a glimpse of a long, dark shape setting out on the river. It was a lotca – a long, thin boat that sat low in the water, cutting smoothly through the stream of blue light to get to the opposite bank.

'So . . . do we borrow a boat?'

Stefan shook his head. 'There's only one crossing at a time. I'm not sure, but I think we'll need to pay the ferryman to reach the other side. Do you still have those coins?'

'Of course I've still got the coins,' Irina hissed, eyeing the mass of the dead. So far, no one appeared to have noticed them, next to the glowing river. 'What do you mean, you're not sure?'

'Well, it's not as if I've been here before.'

'You – you're supposed to be a *guide*!'

'You didn't specify that I should already know my way around. That wasn't what you asked for.'

'Yes, it was!'

'No,' Stefan replied, a smug twist to his smile, 'you asked me to take you to the land of the dead, help you recover that soul, and then take you back home. You didn't say anything about me knowing the way.'

Irina went scarlet. She *hadn't* checked if he had visited the land of the dead before – but really, what else had he thought she meant? And now here she was, surrounded by the dead and with a pedantic, self-satisfied vampire smirking at her. Doubt ran a cold finger along her spine. She'd always known her plan was poorly thought out, but what else had she overlooked in her desperation?

She took a deep, deep breath. This was no time to lose her head. First things first: get past the dead. 'You could have told me you hadn't actually been here earlier,' she said, every word loaded with anger. 'Why did you have to wait until the dead showed up?'

'Oh, don't act so shocked. They were always going to be here.'

'You didn't think that maybe it might be better if you admitted that you didn't know what you were doing *before* we were surrounded by walking corpses? What if they attack us?'

'Then I'll tear them into pieces,' he said matter-of-factly. 'I don't know why you're so surprised. What exactly were you expecting to find in the land of the dead, Irina?' he asked, dropping his voice to a whisper. 'Were you expecting it to be full of flowers in copper, silver and gold? This is Death. Surely you didn't think it would be empty.'

'That isn't the point!' she retorted. 'The only kinds of dead people *I* heard about that are walking around were those who wanted to harm the living, and I *am* living, so excuse me if I'm a little bit—'

'What makes you think they want to harm you?' he cut in, baffled. 'They haven't even looked at you!'

She put her hands on her hips and glared at him. 'Well, so far the only dead man I know is *you*, and you tried to kill me when we first met!'

'You knew what you were signing up for,' he scoffed. 'You all but invited me in – to my own house, by the way. You made yourself at home quickly, I noticed.'

'To have a conversation with you, not to – and what does it matter that I settled in? You weren't even living there when—'

'It's *my* house! Of course it—'

'Trouble in paradise?'

Irina squeaked. Stefan started. An old man in a sheepskin jacket had sidled up to them under cover of the argument, and neither of them had noticed. He had a broad, tanned face covered in a mass of lines, and barely came up to Irina's shoulder. He was giving Stefan a commiserating smile, and it would have been an expression that encouraged a lot more confidence if the tip of his nose had not been frozen off. It was cool in the cave, but not cold, and it took Irina a moment to realize exactly what she was looking at. This was how the old man had died.

'Perhaps I could . . .'

Stefan cut across him. 'No,' he snarled. 'Leave us alone.'

The old man held up placating hands. The tips of his fingers were gone too. 'Young man, I only meant to offer some advice.'

'Whatever you're offering, I don't want it,' Stefan said, with a step forward. 'Leave us *alone*.'

Irina laid a hand on Stefan's arm and propelled him out of the old man's reach. 'I'm sorry,' she said, giving the stranger an apologetic smile, 'as you can see, my husband and I were having a disagreement. He's a little hot-headed. I hope we weren't disturbing you.'

The old man gave her a worried look. Irina tried very, very hard not to stare into his blackened, empty nostrils. 'Clearly. If a son-in-law of mine lost his temper like that, I should be worried for my daughter. But you can't have been married long if you're still . . .'

'Still what?'

He gestured to her bridal crown and wedding clothes. Irina looked down; her shirt was stained with a considerable amount of blood, right around the collar. With the beaded choker hiding Stefan's bite marks, it looked as though someone had tried to slit her throat.

'No,' she said weakly. 'We . . . we had some trouble at the ceremony.'

The old man made a sympathetic noise from somewhere at the back of his throat. 'You poor children,' he said, taking Irina's hand, 'I suppose in those circumstances—'

A shadow passed across his face. All the joviality drained out of his eyes, and suddenly, he looked utterly stricken.

'Ileane,' he murmured. 'Who will take care of her? She's so young.'

He was crushing Irina's fingers. Fear raced through her. The tighter he held on, the darker his hands became, swelling and blackening and turning colder and colder. His face was changing too. The warmth was leaving his tanned skin, his greying cheeks cracking and blistering, ice crystals sprouting from his eyelashes and lips. Irina tried to tug her hand away but he held on tighter, his shortened fingers almost frozen around her hand. Pain pulsed through her fingers. She winced, but he didn't appear to notice. There was a desperate fear in his face.

'Please,' he said, 'you have to tell her I—'

Stefan grabbed the old man's hand and wrenched it away with a *crack*. Irina staggered backwards, heart pounding. Her hand was ice-cold where the old man had touched it, and her wrist was throbbing from the force of Stefan's blow.

'Go,' Stefan said.

The old man's shoulders were heaving. He backed away, clutching his hand. His fingers sat at odd angles. 'She . . . I don't . . .'

Stefan shifted his stance, moving in front of her. '*Go*,' he repeated, and the old man fled into the crowd.

Irina cradled her hand against her chest. Flexing her fingers in case they froze solid, she stared after the old man, feeling sick. 'What happened?' she whispered.

'I don't know,' Stefan muttered. 'He seemed fine until you touched him.'

'I didn't touch him; he touched *me*,' Irina muttered. 'I didn't do anything.'

Stefan was peering at her hand, a thoughtful expression on his face. 'Can I see?'

Irina held out her hand. He examined it, his blackened fingertips turning her hand palm-up and peering at the whorls and creases on her skin. It seemed perfectly ordinary to Irina. Her hand looked as it always did: a little square but firm, with nails she was trying not to bite. It didn't have frostbite, which was the important thing.

'I have an idea,' he said, 'but you'll need to test it first.'

'*I'll* need to test it?'

He nodded. 'If I'm right, I can't help you with it.'

'Fine,' she muttered, yanking her hand back. 'What's the test?'

'Go and pat that child on the head,' he said, nodding to a boy of around five years old a few steps behind them.

Suspicion flared up like a firework. 'Why?'

'Because I need to know if I'm right about something.'

'Is he going to get hurt?' Irina asked, alarmed.

Stefan gave her a withering look. 'That depends on how hard you pat him on the head, doesn't it?'

Irina chewed the inside of her cheek, wondering how much of a bad idea it would be if she pushed Stefan into the river and asked literally anybody else to help her find her sister. Perhaps that five-year-old would do, if he had a decent sense of direction. She took a deep breath and headed towards the boy Stefan had pointed out. A small child, he looked like he was made entirely of pointy elbows and knobbly knees. All his clothes were too big for him, the collar of his shirt gaping around his shoulders. He'd be tall, when he was – with a jolt, Irina realized that he wouldn't ever be fully grown. He was dead.

Plastering on a smile, she approached the little boy, hoping her fear and confusion weren't showing. He had a mop of untidy brown hair and a slightly bemused expression, and when he saw her, he seemed to wilt a little, as if he'd been hoping she would be someone familiar. 'Excuse me,' she said, putting a hand on the boy's shoulder, 'are you—'

She stopped. The moment her fingers had touched the boy's shoulder, thousands of tiny red, raised spots had blossomed across his skin. His face had turned grey, his lips blue-black. Eyes wide and filled with horror, he looked up at her, tears brimming in his eyes.

'Where's Mama?' he whimpered. 'Did she get better?'

A Steep and Savage Path

Irina yanked her hand away. Heart hammering, she staggered back. His tiny hands snatched at her skirt, pulling her towards him.

'I'm sorry,' she said, her throat suddenly tight. 'I didn't know – I'm sorry.'

The little boy ignored her. 'Where is she?' he wailed. 'Where *is* she?'

Stefan appeared out of nowhere. He pointed to the mother and baby, who were walking up to the banks of the river. 'There she is,' he said. 'If you hurry, you can catch her before she gets on the boat.'

The little boy let go of Irina's skirt and set off, calling 'Mama!' as he ran. Irina watched him go, trying not to recall his blue-black lips and the spots that had rippled across his skin. Measles, if she was any judge. The boy clearly hadn't been lucky enough to survive it.

'How did you know that was his mother?' she asked Stefan.

'I didn't.'

She rounded on him. 'What?'

He grabbed her by the elbow and pulled her close. 'Keep your voice down,' he whispered. 'I needed him out of the way. So do *you*.'

'What do you mean?'

Stefan steered her away from the riverbank and the slow stream of the dead heading for the boat. 'I have a theory. I don't know what else it could be, but . . . I think you make them remember what it means to be dead.'

Irina went cold. 'What?'

'Think about it,' he hissed. 'This is the land of the dead but most of the people here,' he waved a hand at the crowd around the crossing-point, 'don't seem all that dead. You've seen corpses, haven't you? Corpses don't look anything like these people.

They might be wounded but they're all walking, talking – nobody's screaming, or praying, or crying. They clearly know that they're dead, but I don't think they feel it. They don't understand what it means. They're almost normal. Almost alive. But life – *real* life – isn't what's keeping them upright. That doesn't have a place down here. And then, along you come, and you *are* the real thing. Whatever is propelling them forward doesn't even compare to what's pumping through your veins. And when you touch them, they know that. That's why they started looking dead, why they started asking about their families. It's like you make them remember what they are, and what they left behind.'

Puzzled, Irina opened her mouth to argue. Surely it wouldn't be that bad if she reminded the dead of the loved ones they'd left behind. She couldn't imagine wanting to forget Catalina, or their parents. But then, the full weight of Stefan's words started to sink in. The dead would remember those they'd left behind, true. They would remember their mothers' screams, their children pressing their hands, their fathers' mouths set into lines tight enough to hold back the tears. All the love they had known would come rushing back – and all the grief, and the fear, and the pain. It would be like a wound that only started bleeding when the sword was pulled free, and Irina's hand was on the hilt. What would they do to her when they realized she'd been the one to hurt them like that? And, Irina thought, that was saying nothing of the physical effects of death. The old man had clearly frozen to death; the little boy had succumbed to measles. What had that been like? Had the old man been lost in a snowstorm, squinting into a blizzard as he tried to wade through drifts as high as his chest? Who had been waiting for him to come home? Had he felt the moment when his body slipped from life into death, or had all the feeling been frozen out of him by then? And as for the little boy – Irina squeezed her eyes shut, desperate to shield herself from her own imagination. It didn't work. She could picture a weeping mother, a pale-faced father. Had it hurt, when the boy died? She prayed it hadn't – prayed the fever hadn't burned, prayed the rash hadn't felt like knives, prayed he hadn't panicked when his breathing started to falter. But even if it hadn't hurt, she realized, that didn't matter. At her touch, the boy had still remembered his family's grief, had still felt the weight of his own mortality slipping away, had still had his loneliness thrown into sharp relief.

She'd done that.

Irina pressed a hand over her mouth. For a split second, she felt a flash of panic at her own touch. What would she remember, in the land of the dead? But there was nothing – nothing but her own guilt.

She looked up at Stefan, horrified. 'And you wanted to test that on a child?'

His face hardened. 'Better a child than a soldier.'

'*What?*'

He took a step forward, his jaw set. 'You heard me,' he growled. 'I did what I did, and I won't apologize for it. I had a theory, and I needed to test it in a way that we wouldn't both end up hurt. Do you think everyone here had an easy death, Irina? Do you think shedding a few tears is all they will do, when you remind them of what they've lost? A child running for his mother is much better than a soldier reaching for his sword. Now you know what you can do, before anyone has tried to hurt you.'

'But . . . but you just used him and sent him off into the dark! How do you know he won't tell someone what happened? You can't just – and you used *me*, too! Why didn't you tell me that was what you were going to do?'

'Then you wouldn't have let me do it.'

Fury bubbled through Irina's veins. 'It's cruel. It's cruel, and you know it is.'

'Yes,' he snapped. 'It *is* cruel. But so am I. You asked me to see you safely through the land of the dead and I will do this, because I gave you my word. But I did not claw my way back from death by being a kind and gentle person, Irina. I hurt people. I kill people. You knew that when you sought me out. Do not expect me to pretend otherwise, just to spare your feelings.'

Irina's hands were curled into fists, fingernails digging into her palms. She couldn't think of anything to say. She could only glare at him, boiling in her own anger, jaw clenched so tightly she felt like it could crack in two.

Stefan was right. He was a vampire. She had known he was a monster when she set out to make this bargain. She'd seen exactly what he'd done to the villagers. He'd filled four graves in the churchyard. But when he'd stepped through the door, disconcertingly human and reaching for sarcasm in the same way as any other boy her age, she'd caught a glimpse of what he used to be. Human.

But he wasn't human any more.

Irina drew herself up to her full height. She put her shoulders back and looked him dead in the eye, gathering her purpose about her like a cloak. This would only make things easier when she stabbed him in the back.

'You're right,' she said, her voice cold. 'I forgot what you were, for a moment.'

He went still, all the little human imperfections draining out of his movements. Irina thought of wolves, preparing to pounce.

'Good,' he said, his voice clipped. 'Then let's go. We have a boat to catch.'

* * *

Now that she knew what she was capable of, Irina walked differently. She took small steps, keeping her elbows tucked in, her hands clasped in front of her chest. As they approached the banks of the river, her nerves grew. There were so many people, and they were all so close. Whether they were peering curiously at the blue river or looking around for a familiar face, for now, the dead seemed perfectly normal, but her slightest touch could send their worst memories rocketing through them, and all the rage and grief and terror of dying would be pointed straight at her. Bump against the mother and baby, and she could make them remember bleeding out in childbed. Brush too close to the group of soldiers slapping each other on the back, and they would remember sabres sliding into their guts, or the moment a musket ball burst through their chests. If one of the children playing around the banks ran into her, they would—

Irina shook her head, clenching her hands tighter. She wasn't going to think about what the children would remember, because she didn't know. Guessing would only torture her. She would be better off keeping her limbs tucked in close and her wits about her.

It had taken them half an hour to pick their way down to the banks. She wove her way through the crowd, steering the widest possible path around the dead. Stefan had kept close behind her, moving silently as mist. Irina was grateful for the quiet. She had no idea what she would say to him, or if she should say anything at all. It was never a good idea to make conversation with a monster; it only let you forget about their teeth.

The sparkling, shifting expanse of blue streamed alongside her, splashing indigo, teal, and royal blue light up the left side of her body. They stood in a long queue behind a couple of soldiers. As they talked they would throw out an arm, laughing, and Irina would flinch. Only a few dozen feet from the head of the queue was a dark platform set into the water, with a small group of people standing on the other side. Every so often, the long, thin boat would glide across the light and pull up at the dock, propelled by a dark figure Irina only saw in snatches. Sometimes they would shake their head at a passenger, and refuse to move until they got off the boat and waited on the other side of the platform. When a handful of the dead climbed into the boat, it would set off for the opposite shore. Irina couldn't see what was on the other side. The river was wide, and glowing too brightly.

They were almost at the front of the queue now, though it was moving slowly. Irina took a deep, calming breath; not long now until she was away from the press of people. The soldiers in front of her were waving to their friends in the boat – Irina took a step back – before the blue light of the river hid them completely. Neither of them seemed to mind the dark circles of blood on their uniforms. Nor did their comrades, who, ignoring the sticky mass that covered the fronts of their shirts, were waving enthusiastically as the boat lurched beneath their feet.

'What do you think is on the other side?' one said to the other.

His friend shoved him in the arm. 'A riverbank, idiot.'

The first soldier put on a high-pitched, sing-song voice. '*A riverbank, idiot.* Use your imagination, Andrei. It's glowing blue! There's got to be something good on the other side.'

'Wine. Women. A field of horses that can ride swifter than the wind. I don't know, Doru! We'll find out when we cross.'

The first soldier – Doru – looked around, curious, and caught sight of Irina. He smacked his friend in the stomach – right in the middle of the puddle of blood, in fact, but Andrei did not seem to notice. 'Keep your voice down about the women,' he hissed. 'There's a girl behind us.'

Andrei looked over his shoulder, the least successful casual expression Irina had ever seen on his face. He was perhaps a year or two younger than her, no more than seventeen. The moment he caught sight of her, he flushed. He turned back to his friend, there was a flurry of whispers and nudging, and then both of them rounded on her with enormous smiles. Dread pooled in the pit of her stomach. Just what she needed when she'd learned she couldn't touch people: a couple of teenage boys desperate to flirt.

'Hello!' said Andrei, adjusting his uniform and puffing out his chest. 'I'm Andrei, this is Doru. What's your name?'

'Irina,' she said, putting her hands behind her back. Behind her, Stefan went still.

'Settle a bet for us, Irina,' Andrei said, as Doru's face slowly started turning red. 'What do you think is on the other side of the river?'

Irina stared across the glowing blue water. Despite her trepidation, she was curious. 'Aside from another dock, you mean? I don't know. I suppose some kind of judge?'

'A judge?' Doru asked, looking faintly nervous.

Irina shrugged. 'Maybe? They always say there's a Heaven and a Hell, don't they? Someone has to decide who goes where.'

Doru tugged on Andrei's sleeve. 'Andrei,' he hissed, 'Andrei, are we going to get—'

But Andrei wasn't listening. He was nudging Doru in the ribs and grinning at her. 'See, Doru? Smart *and* pretty. Girls like that don't come along every day.'

Irina shifted, trying not to make it obvious that she was leaning away from them. Talk like this had always seemed nice in theory, but in practice it made her feel uncomfortable when it came from a stranger. She didn't even know them. But she knew that grin. Any second now, Andrei was going to try and touch her, and blood would come splattering out of the rip in his shirt and his eyes would fill with fear and pain and he'd be looking right at her as he remembered the blade plunging into his guts.

He was still grinning. 'We can't be in Hell, when we're face to face with an angel. That settles it, Doru. We've gone to Heaven. Tell me, Irina—' he started reaching for her, one arm ready to slide around her shoulders, '—where is your husband, exactly?'

Something blurred past her; Stefan, barging past and grabbing Andrei by the lapels. 'Leave,' he snarled.

'Get off! What are you—'

'Hey!'

'Don't—'

A crowd had gathered, all of them staring. Irina could sense them at her back. Panic fluttered through her. Stefan was holding Andrei by the front of his jacket while Doru tugged at his hands, trying to loosen his grip. A middle-aged man behind them was frowning, while two old women started to whisper. If Irina didn't do something soon, someone was going to push past her to get to the fight.

She crept closer, careful to stay well out of Andrei and Doru's flailing, and laid a gentle hand on Stefan's shoulder. He let go, rounding on her with a snarl. Irina flinched, snatching her hand away. Stefan's face flickered.

'It's all right,' she said, keeping her voice carefully calm. 'It's just me.'

Silence spilled out around them like ink. Stefan's eyes darted around the faces in the crowd. Then he slung an arm around her shoulder – so fast that Irina wasn't sure if he was going to grab her by the throat – and pulled her to his side. He glared around the crowd, daring them to come closer. His purple-black hand was stark against the sleeve of her red-and-white shirt. Every eye was trained on them, and Irina wished she was invisible.

'This is Stefan,' she said into the silence. 'We're married.'

'Really?' Andrei began, but Doru cut him off.

'We didn't know. So sorry to have troubled you,' he said, grabbing Andrei by the arm and forcibly turning him away.

'What are you doing?' Andrei hissed. 'We need to do something! Did you see how he grabbed her?'

'Yes, I *did* see, and that's exactly why we shouldn't get involved. He's . . . wrong.'

Stefan's arm stiffened around Irina's shoulders.

Andrei rounded on Doru, whispering frantically. 'We can't leave her!'

'You'll make things worse. Trust me.'

Doru and Andrei's argument receded into a flurry of whispers. Stefan leaned forward to whisper in her ear. 'Do you really think we will be judged?' he murmured in her ear.

'What was that?' she hissed. 'Everyone was staring at us! What were you thinking?'

'I had to do something, he was going to grab you! Well?'

She pinched the bridge of her nose. 'I don't know if there's going to be a judge. I'm guessing,' she snapped.

'Because that could be a problem.'

Irina was on the verge of asking why when the boat slid back into view. The soldiers it had been carrying were nowhere to be seen. There was only one figure onboard now: a tall, dark figure propelling the boat forward with a long staff, half-hidden in the shining water. Underlit by gleaming shades of blue, it was difficult to see them clearly. They were swathed in a dark robe that rippled as they moved, like the water swirling beneath them.

The boat bumped against the dock. The soldiers fell quiet, eyeing Stefan and Irina as they stepped back. What were they planning? Irina tried to ignore them, pulling out two pfennigs and handing them to Stefan. She didn't know if the ferryman was dead, but she didn't want to risk accidentally touching their hand and watching them wither before she'd made it across the river.

She glanced at the small group of passengers on the other side of the platform. They seemed to have little in common: old, young, men, women, children; bloodied, bruised, cheeks livid with consumption or spattered with pox marks. They were digging through their clothes, scrabbling around the edges of the platform on their knees, wandering along the riverbank and staring at the rock beneath their feet. The realization dawned on her. They had no fare, and so the ferryman had turned them away.

A little girl stood at the edge of the group. She looked to be about seven – the same age as Catalina – and she was crying. Her face and neck were swollen with mumps and her feet were bare. Before she knew what she was doing, Irina's hand was closing around another pfennig.

Stefan's fingers locked around her wrist. 'What are you doing?' he muttered.

'We can't leave her here. I've got the money, why shouldn't I pay her fare?'

'But why? We don't need her.'

Irina glared at him. 'She needs us! And it's none of your business what I do with my money, thank you.' She held out another handful of coins; there was enough to spare, even accounting for their passage back. 'Go and give them to her, if you're so worried.'

Shock flashed across his face. 'But . . . but this is – don't you need this?'

Irina shooed him towards the rejected passengers. 'Not as much as she does. Go on.'

Still looking perturbed, Stefan shoved the fistful of coins into the child's hands. Her eyes went wide. The rest of the group crowded around her as she started handing them out. The moment Stefan left her side, Andrei stepped forward.

'Excuse me,' he said, 'are you all right?'

'I—'

Instantly, Stefan was between them. 'She's fine.'

Andrei glared at him. 'I wasn't asking you.'

Irina laid a hand on Stefan's arm, sure that her smile looked false. 'I'm well, thank you.' She glanced at the ferryman. It was impossible to see their face under the hood of their cloak, but it was clear they were watching her. The darkness under the cowl was pointed straight at her, and a too-long hand was wrapped around the pole like a snake, one many-jointed finger tapping against the wood.

Andrei was still looking at her. 'You don't have to go with him,' he said.

'She doesn't have to go with *you*, either!' Stefan snarled.

The ferryman planted a foot on the dock, clutching their pole with both hands. The hood moved as they looked between Stefan and Andrei. Irina felt a flutter of panic. Any second now, they would take a swipe with their pole and end the fight. If Stefan got knocked into the water, there'd be no one to stand between her and the dead.

'This is ridiculous,' she snapped, gathering up all her irritation and forcing it into her words. 'I decide where I go, thank you, and I have decided that I am getting into that boat. Stefan?'

She climbed onto the dock, arms folded, and waited. Stefan scrambled after her, blocking Andrei before he could reach out and shoving the coins into the ferryman's hand. For a moment, no one moved. Stefan and Irina stared into the darkness of the cowl – what *was* under that hood? Irina wondered – and silence spilled around them. Then, the ferryman stepped aside and Stefan helped Irina into the boat, shepherding her towards the prow. Irina's shoulders sagged. She felt so much better not staring into the ferryman's empty hood.

The boat was simple, with wooden seats worn smooth by years of use – perhaps centuries, Irina thought with a shiver. She found a seat at the front, well away from the ferryman and the two soldiers, who had climbed in after them. The moment she sat down, Stefan was behind her, snatching her in his arms and pinning her against him. His grip was as tight as a winding-sheet.

Irina stiffened. 'What are you doing?' she muttered.

'Making sure they don't get any ideas,' he replied, glaring over at Andrei and Doru. 'What happens if they try and grab you, out on the water?'

There was a certain logic to that, Irina had to admit. She didn't want either of them remembering their battlefield deaths in a small, confined space where she had no way of escaping but jumping into the water – and that was saying nothing of the ferryman. She wasn't even sure if they were human, let alone dead; there was something almost avian about the way that they moved, and their hands seemed to have too many bones. But Stefan's arms were cold and his face was pressed into the crook of her neck. She was sure that any minute, she was going to feel the prick of teeth. She shivered. Undead soldiers and a ferryman who never showed their face suddenly seemed a lot more appealing.

'Everyone's going to think you're jealous,' she said, 'and you had better not bite me. Not in the boat.'

'I wasn't going to,' he said, a little sulkily. 'Not in the boat.'

Behind them, something slipped into the water. The boat leapt forward; Irina clutched the sides, heart pounding. The ferryman had started propelling them across the river – there was nothing to worry about – but she hadn't expected them to start so soon.

'Let's use that,' he mused.

'The boat?' Irina asked, before she could stop herself.

'Of course not the boat!' Stefan hissed. 'The whole "jealous husband" thing. It's the easiest way to make sure the dead don't touch you.'

Irina thought for a moment. She could see the merits of the plan, but she'd be lying if she said she felt any enthusiasm for it. It was one thing to explain away her bridal crown, but another to pretend that she and Stefan were actually in love. Marriage had only ever been something she'd pictured with some vaguely perfect template of a man she'd put together in her own imagination. The thought of pantomiming it with a stranger who wanted to eat her was hardly what she'd been dreaming of. She didn't even know him; how was she supposed to fake something like that? She stared across the glowing blue water, lost for a moment in bursts of cornflower-blue light.

'Couldn't we say you were my manservant, instead?'

'I'm not being your manservant,' he said at once. 'Don't you think it's a good plan?'

'I think it would be a good plan if you actually acted like my husband,' Irina sniffed.

'I'll just scare anyone who comes too close to you. That's all we'll need.'

'It is *not*,' she muttered.

He went still. 'What do you mean?'

Indigo shadows pooled around their feet. Irina's red-and-white clothes were a shifting mass of blue, almost ghostly in the light from the river. She could barely hear the ferryman's pole carving through the water. She wondered if their voices would carry, and how much she should say with at least two creatures probably capable of killing her within earshot.

'Look at it like this,' she muttered, throwing caution to the wind. 'I look like I've been murdered in my wedding clothes. We should be the newest of newlyweds. If you want people to think you're my husband, fine, but you'll have to behave in a way that would make people believe that someone would actually want to marry you.'

'So will *you*,' he hissed.

She ignored him. 'All you've done since we got here is pick fights, threaten me, and use me to test a strange, cruel theory without telling me – and that's not even mentioning the fact that you tried to kill me when we first met. If you're acting jealous and possessive as well, that's not going to make people want to leave us alone. If anything, it'll make them want to help me get away. That's what they're already doing. Didn't you hear what those soldiers said?'

There was a loaded silence from somewhere behind her shoulder. Irina swallowed back her nerves. She tried to focus on the droplets of sparkling blue spraying against the dark wood of the boat, and not the monster at her back.

Then, he spoke. His voice was full of something she could not place. 'What makes you think they will be so eager to intervene on your behalf?'

She shrugged. 'It's what people do.'

'It's what *you* do. You didn't need to give away those coins – why would you do that?'

'Well, you can't take it with you,' she said, with a smirk.

The other side of the river was coming into view now. Like the bank they had left behind, there was a long, dark platform set into the shore. Glowing blue water underneath the dock cast the striped shadows of planks onto the ceiling. Beyond that, there was a dark mass of people walking away, but the river was too bright for Irina to see what they were heading towards.

'What exactly are you asking me to do?' Stefan asked, his voice wary.

'I don't want you to kiss me,' Irina said immediately. 'Nothing like that. But if we want people to believe that we're newlyweds, we're going to need to act like newlyweds. You know. Cuddly. Sentimental. No grabbing at me. Be jealous, if you want, but if you're obviously enamoured, at least then people won't think I'm in danger.'

'Would you like a pet name?' Stefan asked, his voice loaded with sarcasm.

Water slopped over the sides of the boat as they drew near the platform, sloshing close to Irina's shoes. It left a sparkling blue puddle in the bottom of the boat. She reached out, curious. Would it feel like water at all, when she touched it?

Stefan caught her hand and pulled it back. 'If you wanted a proper husband,' he said, 'you shouldn't have married me.'

'Oh, I know I'm just a meal to you,' Irina replied, resisting the urge to elbow him in the stomach, 'but that's no excuse. This might not be a real marriage, but that doesn't mean you get to treat me poorly.'

'I wasn't – fine,' he muttered, as the ferryman turned the boat alongside the dock. 'I can play whatever part you wish, but it will only be a part. Do not forget that.'

The ferryman planted one foot on the platform and held out a hand to the soldiers, helping them off the boat. Irina saw a flash of claws under their cloak. 'You've made that quite clear,' she said. 'Don't worry. I know exactly what I signed up for.'

'Excellent.'

Stefan stood up and climbed onto the dock. Irina got to her

feet, wobbling slightly, and before she knew it he had lifted her out of the boat and onto the jetty. He set her down gently, beaming through gritted teeth.

'Better?' he whispered, tucking her arm through his as they walked towards the shore.

Irina gave him a smile as fixed as his own. 'It'd be more convincing if you washed more of the blood off your clothes,' she replied.

'You are completely mad if you think I'm getting any of that water on me,' he said, patting her hand with a little too much force.

'Why?' she hissed, her smile slipping in the force of her curiosity. 'What's wrong with the water here? I know we can't drink it, but we could touch it, couldn't we?'

He shot her a wry look. 'Can't you just accept that your husband knows best?'

Irina smothered her anger and plastered the toothiest smile she could muster on her face. 'I really wish I'd brought that stake with me,' she said, fighting to keep her tone light.

Stefan chucked her under the chin. He was still giving her the least sincere smile she had ever seen, but there was real amusement in his eyes. 'You probably should've brought the chair. You might've had more luck with that.'

So far, Irina thought, as she trudged away from the glowing blue water, one riverbank looked much like the other. There was the same dark stone under her feet, the same stalactites clustered on the ceiling. There was even the same stream of people heading into the dark, although they had managed to lose Andrei and Doru amidst the groups of people waiting by the riverbank. Blue light shone on a sea of retreating backs: linen-shirted, fur-coated, wool-clad. Irina saw patterned headscarves, felt caps, the cockaded hat of an army officer. No bridal crowns, she noticed, although there were a few trailing shrouds. Not for the first time, she clutched at her skirts with a sweaty hand. After the scene on the far riverbank, she would have preferred to slip through the underworld unnoticed, but living or not, people always remembered a bride.

Slowly, the blue light faded to an indigo darkness. For a moment, she stumbled on outcroppings of rock, stubbing her toes. Stefan seized her arm, keeping her upright with a grip of iron.

'Watch where you're going,' he whispered.

'How?' Irina asked, waving her hand into the expanse of black. 'I can't see a thing.'

There was a pause. 'Can't you?'

She sighed. 'Not this again.'

But then, she saw it. Up ahead: the faintest glimmer of colour, glittering over the heads of the crowd. After the blues of the river, it looked startlingly yellow. She squinted into the distance. More light. More shadows. More dead faces, clustering closer to her than she had thought.

'It looks busy,' she said, standing on tiptoe for a better view. 'What do you think is up there?'

Stefan kept a firm hold on her arm. His grip felt like a jailer's. 'That judge you were talking about. I'm sure of it.'

The light was growing stronger now. The cave had changed. It was no longer a cave at all. At some point in the shadows, the stalactites had receded into the ceiling, and what Irina had taken for glittering sparks of quartz in the rock were moving. Bright pinpricks of light swarmed over their heads like fireflies. At this distance, she could not tell if they were stars or sparkling creatures swooping over her head. Under her feet was a wide dirt road, the same colour as spilled wine. It had been pressed flat and worn smooth by thousands – millions – of feet, she realized, and if she pushed forward she could glide as if she were on ice. She could not see the edges of it, there were so many people on either side, but she was sure she heard the rustling of leaves beyond.

The pace of the crowd was slowing now, shuffling forward as if they were trailing behind a coffin. Irina peered over their heads. In the distance, the sparkling lights clustered together, spinning and spiralling around each other. There were flashes of colour, a burst of darkness, and then the pattern of moving lights started up again.

'Give me a boost,' Irina whispered. 'There's something up there.'

'Everyone will see you,' Stefan muttered.

'Do you want to find out what it is when we're too close to get away from it? Just lift me up so I can see.'

He looked irritated, but bent down, put his arms around her waist and hoisted her up. Wobbling slightly, but with her head and shoulders well above the crowd, Irina stared into the lights.

At first, she was not sure what she was looking at. At the front of the crowd, bright lights in every colour she had ever seen were zipping across the path. They shuttered back and forth faster than she could track, leaving trails of colour behind them. She blinked, and several lines of coloured lights hung in the air. She blinked again, and several more hung beneath them. She blinked again – and the picture became clear. The lights were weaving a shimmering tapestry across the path, flying back and forth like the shuttle on a loom.

Irina craned her neck, pushing down on Stefan's head to try and lift herself a little higher. He grunted; she ignored him. She was too busy staring at the picture. The lights had woven an image of an unknown woman in a bridal crown, wild roses framing her anguished face. A figure stood in front of the lights, watching.

'Are you finished?' Stefan said, sounding a little strained.

Irina let go of his head. He put her down, looking extremely annoyed. 'It's a tapestry!' she said, as soon as her feet touched the floor. 'That's what the lights are making! There's a woman, a bride, and she's crying—' She broke off, as another flash of light broke over the crowd. 'Are they weaving something new? Stefan, lift me up again so I can—'

'No.'

Irina stood on tiptoe, craning to see over the crowd. The top row of lights was just visible; it was now a heavy grey, like snow clouds pressing close. 'Oh, come on! Please?'

A woman standing nearby tutted loudly. Stefan's fists clenched automatically, but then she said, 'Your husband said no, child. You must learn to listen to him.'

An expression of absolute glee spread across Stefan's face. He turned to Irina, grinning, and mouthed 'your husband said no,' while Irina was still floundering for a response.

'And you,' said the woman, rounding on Stefan, 'you are only encouraging such behaviour. It is not proper for a married woman to behave so, even if she is young.'

Irina tried to look contrite as she trod on Stefan's foot; his hands were still curled into fists. He took the hint and put an arm around her. 'Oh, I know she is wayward. Flighty. Foolhardy. Unrefined—'

Discreetly, Irina kicked him in the ankle.

'—but I just can't say no to my little wife,' Stefan finished, flashing the sickliest smile Irina had ever seen in her direction. 'Even though she is—'

'Oh, stop it, my love,' said Irina, before he could get started. 'You're making me blush.'

The woman sniffed. The sound went right through Irina. The woman was middle-aged with tanned skin and a long, lined face, and though Irina had never met her before she had the uncanny feeling that this woman had been disapproving of her all her life. She had a black headscarf embroidered with flowers tied neatly under her chin and a matching shawl around her shoulders. Every item of her clothing was meticulously clean and neat, the stitches on her embroidery almost indiscernible, they were so small. Under her judgemental gaze, Irina simultaneously wanted to stand up straight and slouch even further down out of sheer spite.

Still, she tried to be polite. 'I'm sorry,' she said, attempting a smile, 'I was only curious about what was up ahead.'

The woman sniffed again. 'That much is clear.'

'I don't suppose you—'

'I wouldn't care to speculate,' said the woman, tucking her hands into her sleeves. 'Those are people's lives in the tapestry. It is not my business – and it certainly is not yours.'

Curiosity burst into bloom. Irina stared at the lights, only catching flashes of colour as they zipped across the path. 'People's lives? But why are we being shown this, if we aren't supposed to see? What is it for?'

A man standing in front of them turned around eagerly. He was plump, perhaps fifty, with warm, brown skin and a pair of tiny round spectacles balanced on the end of his nose. Dressed in a green silk coat and britches and with a waterfall of white lace at his throat, he was easily the wealthiest person Irina had ever seen.

'Now *that* is an intriguing question,' he said, as if he'd known Irina all her life. 'Doctor Emil Nicolescu.' He held out a hand.

Stefan lunged for it – Irina flinched – and shook the doctor's hand before he could get close enough to touch her. 'Stefan.

This is Irina. We're—' his throat worked, as if he was trying to dredge something up from right at the back of his mouth, '—married.'

'Then congratulations are in order,' the doctor said, glancing at Irina's bridal crown. 'Or perhaps not, if you – er – didn't have time to change, before . . . arriving.'

Irina ignored this. 'What's an intriguing question, Doctor?' she asked.

He looked relieved. 'Well, my dear, the classics are my discipline, and on my way down here I couldn't help but notice several intriguing similarities between this place and my field of study. Do you know much about the *Aeneid*?'

'What's that?'

'My *dear*!' Doctor Emil exclaimed, clasping his hands together. 'You have no idea how lucky you are. To experience the *Aeneid* for the first time – goodness, I hope I can do it justice! Settle in, settle in – although I should ask, are you familiar with the *Iliad*? The Trojan War?'

'Um . . .'

'God in Heaven! Not at all? Achilles? Hector? No?'

Stefan shifted Irina backwards. Doctor Emil waved his hands a lot when he spoke, but she was still annoyed. Stefan was leaning forward, eager, all but shoving her out of the conversation completely. 'Doctor, perhaps you could tell us a little more about your theory first?'

'Yes! Yes, an excellent idea.' He clapped Stefan on the shoulder; Stefan's frozen smile cracked a little. 'Smart lad. Well,' said the doctor, 'in the *Aeneid*, there's a passage where our hero, Aeneas, must journey into the underworld. He is taken across a river by a mysterious ferryman and witnesses the workings of Hades – including the judgement, where the dead are sent to one of three places: the fields of Asphodel, Elysium, and

Tartarus. Information about these places is rather limited, but we do know that the fields of Asphodel were for ordinary mortals, Elysium was for true heroes, and Tartarus was for the wicked.'

Irina's mind was racing. She thought of the boatman and their too-long hands, the glowing river, the coins she had given to the dead – the same coins, she realized, that were used to cover the eyes of corpses at every funeral she had ever been to. She clutched at Stefan's arm, her eyes wide – and saw a look of sudden fear on his face.

'So if that's all true,' Irina said slowly, 'now that we're across the river, will we be judged?'

'I believe so,' Doctor Emil said, his eyes shining. 'Now, if you saw an image of a woman at the head of the crowd, that posits an interesting question. Why? Surely it must be a part of this judgement – after all, there must be something upon which we are judged, no? At the head of this queue we will be separated into sinners, saints, and souls left between, and shuffle along to whichever part of the underworld fits us best. What do you say to that?'

Clarity settled on Irina. It made sense. She had been to church all her life, and she had never heard about a river, or a ferryman, or a rather public kind of judgement. But the doctor evidently had. According to him, this was all to be expected, even if it was in no story Irina had ever heard. She thought back to all the funerals she'd attended, the coins and the candles and the cakes set aside for the corpse. Those were not Christian things, and yet they still did them. Evidently, there was more reason to do them than she had first thought.

'Who's going to judge us?' Stefan asked, his voice quiet.

'I've no idea,' said Doctor Emil, sounding much happier than Irina would've done in his position. 'If I recall correctly, the ancients believed it would be three kings, but that business with the lights suggests something different. How exciting!'

'So does this *Aeneid* tell us what the underworld will be like?' she asked. 'Do you know what we can expect?'

'I'm afraid it's not so straightforward,' Doctor Emil replied. 'There are a number of sources that discuss the Greco-Roman underworld, you see, and all have slightly different interpretations – oh, it will be *such* a treat to discover which is correct! Although,' he mused, looking thoughtful, 'the vast majority of them mention the five rivers, and of course we have already seen one of those, so it stands to reason that—'

'The five rivers?'

'Yes! You must know the Styx, everyone does – the river of unbreakable oaths, which we crossed thanks to the ferryman. But there's also the Acheron, the river of sorrow; Cocytus, the river of wailing; Lethe, the river of forgetfulness; and – how appropriate,' the doctor said, chuckling, 'right after I mention the Lethe, I forget if the last river is Phlegethon or Pyriphlegethon! You'll know that when you see it, of course. It's the river of fire.'

Dark red light washed over the crowd. A sudden shout. Irina whirled around, staring, but could see nothing but the topmost slice of an image hanging in the air, red as an ember. Silence was rippling out from the front of the queue.

'What was that?'

'Nothing to worry about, I'm sure,' said Doctor Emil, desperate cheer underlying every word. 'I suppose not everyone is going to the Elysian Fields – or Heaven, as the case may be.'

Stefan leaned forward. 'We need to talk,' he muttered in her ear. 'Get us out of here.'

'This is all so fascinating,' she said. 'I'd love to know if your theory is true. If you'd be willing to keep our place in the queue,

Doctor, perhaps my husband and I could take a closer look at this judgement and let you know what we find?'

Doctor Emil looked delighted. 'Oh, how wonderful! Be sure to take in as many details as you can, my dear, and tell me everything!'

Stefan put an arm around Irina's shoulder and pushed sideways through the crowd, moving aside anxious-looking children, frail grandmothers, priests, rabbis, miners, farmers, sailors. After what seemed like an age, they reached the edge of the path.

At first, Irina could see nothing but blackness. But looking away from the tapestry of lights, she saw the shapes of tree trunks – row after row of twisted yews. Each one was charcoal-grey, the leaves bone-white, the berries black as pitch. Stefan led her into the trees, and the moment the path was out of sight, he yanked his arm away, as if Irina's shoulders were a burning brand.

'What is it?' she whispered.

'The judgement,' Stefan said.

Irina bit her lip. 'I was wondering about that.'

Stefan looked over his shoulder. Irina could see nothing but trees behind him, fading into the distance like smudges of ash blurring together. 'If we stand before those lights, they'll see everything we've done. They'll reveal to everyone that you are living, and that I am . . . not.'

'It won't be a problem for you, surely,' said Irina. 'You're meant to be here.'

'That's not the point!' he hissed. 'We need to find another way in.'

Irina looked around the forest. Only those trees near the edges of the path were clearly defined. The further away from the wine-dark road they got, the fuzzier their edges became. She had the uncomfortable thought that if she walked into the haze, the edges of her own body might start to blur too. '*Is* there another way in?'

His face twisted. 'There has to be. There *has* to be! I won't – I'm not – look,' he said, leaning forward, his eyes darting all around the colourless forest. 'I don't care what you have to do, just find another way through that gate!'

Irina considered him. The muscles in his jaw were working as he clenched and unclenched his teeth.

'Why do *you* not want to go through the gate?' she asked, her eyes narrowed. 'I'm the one who should be worried. What don't you want everyone to see?'

'I'm not worried!'

'Stefan.'

Resting a blackened hand on the tree behind her, he leaned close. 'It's you I'm thinking of, Irina,' he said, every word ringing hollow. 'What if . . . what if you get turned back at the gate, and everyone sees your secret, and you can't ever find this Catalina? What will you do then?'

The words sent panic slicing through her, but she could see the insincerity in his eyes. He wasn't thinking of her as anything more than a meal; hadn't he told her so himself? No, she realized, thinking of the look on Stefan's face when the doctor had talked about judgement. This was not concern; this was a distraction.

'It's *only* me you're thinking of, is it?' she asked, folding her arms.

He hesitated. Restless energy propelled all his movements, and there was a frantic look in his eye she did not like. He was either going to tear out her throat, or tell her everything.

He looked over his shoulder again. 'I know where that tapestry will send me, Irina. Tartarus. Hell. The bad place.' He leaned forward, trying for a smile. 'I know I've done terrible things,' he said. 'I know I should be punished. But . . . Irina, you have to help me get through without being judged. You need me. Anyone else here would remember their own death the moment they touched you – who else is going to keep them away? You must see that no one else can . . .'

His voice trailed off. He looked almost feverish, with desperation lighting up his eyes. She'd seen that look on people's faces before: in bad winters, when brimstone preachers came to town and put righteous fear into the congregation. At times like that, certain people learned to fade gently from view – Jewish merchants, the Roma passing through, or the witch living on the edges of the forest. It was safer for them to be out of the reach of zealots, but Irina always felt sorry to see them go.

'Of course I'll help,' she said. 'Let's see if we can get round the edges.'

Stefan blinked at her. 'You will?'

Irina glared at him. 'I said I would, didn't I? We made a deal. Besides, I need to get past the barrier, too.'

Suspicion stole across his face. 'Just like that?' he asked. 'You aren't going to . . .'

'Going to what?'

He shrugged. 'I don't know. Shout, or throw things, or call me names.'

Mystified, Irina had to remember to keep her voice quiet. 'Why would I do that?'

Stefan opened his mouth. No words came out. He ran a hand through his hair, looking utterly lost.

'Stefan, we made a bargain. We have to work together. How would behaving like that help us find a way through?'

The unmoored expression on his face was unsettling. It was like looking at someone who'd heard the creak of a falling tree in the forest and knew they had no time to move. Irina stepped aside, unnerved. No creature that could tear her throat out had any business looking so adrift.

'Come on,' she said, turning towards the lights, 'let's get a closer look at the barrier.'

She set off between the trees, keeping the path on her left. After a moment Stefan followed her. Light blazed across the trees in every colour as the scenes were woven, sending pillars of shadow across the forest floor. Every so often, the multi-coloured lights would stop, and the blaze of a single colour would wash over the trees: mostly blue-grey, but sometimes blinding white, and sometimes wine-dark red. The forest was oddly quiet. No twigs snapped under her feet, no leaves rustled in the wind, no branches creaked over their heads. All she could hear was the noise of the crowd on the path. Chatting, singing, laughing, crying. The occasional scream and, sometimes, pleading. An 'ooooohhh' from further back as the lights zipped across the path, as if they were watching a shooting star. Closer to the front, complaining – evidently waiting was just as boring when you were dead as it was when you were alive – and an endless round of commentary from those who could see the tapestry of lights. People tutted at abandoned children, gasped at battlefield bravery, asked each other why he had married the innkeeper's awful daughter when that lovely neighbour was *right there*. Irina cringed. The fact that everyone here was watching each other's lives play out was bad enough. They didn't have to make it worse by commenting on it. She caught her foot on a tree root and stumbled, nearly pitching over. When *she* died, was this crowd of people going to watch her life like a play and comment on it too? The thought made her feel sick.

Something rustled in the smudge-grey mass of trees to her right. Stefan caught up to her. 'Don't trip,' he whispered. 'We need to keep quiet, this close to the barrier.'

'I *know* that,' she muttered. 'Can you see anything?'

He put a finger to his lips and crept a little closer to the crowd. Stealing up to a large, twisted tree, he sheltered behind it, peering at the mass of people.

'You were the one who started talking,' Irina complained under her breath, and followed him.

They were nearly at the tapestry now. Next to it, Irina felt like an ant. It towered over the heads of the crowd, showing the life of the woman standing before it in brilliant, blinding lights. There was no sign of the judges Doctor Emil had mentioned, but then again, Irina reasoned, she did not know who was weaving the tapestry. If she had been in the queue, only a few dozen people would have been in front of her, and every single one of them was craning their necks to see the tapestry. The faces of several smiling children were being painted in shimmering lights, and at the foot of the tapestry, a woman in a long, white headscarf was staring up at them, her hands pressed over her mouth and her eyes full of tears. Guilt prickled at the back of Irina's neck. It felt like a sin, watching this woman weep over her children from between the colourless trees.

The image of the children faded. The woman reached out with a trembling hand. Then, suddenly, a sheet of white light blazed across the path, slicing across the forest. Irina flinched, pressing herself closer against the tree. The woman walked into the light, and when it had faded, she was gone.

The person behind her – a lost-looking child – stepped up to the front of the queue and the tapestry started weaving again. In the woods, Stefan darted forward to the place where the light had splashed across the ground, crouching down for a closer look. Irina followed, peering over his shoulder. It looked like ordinary earth to her, as deep and dark as the tramped-down path they had slipped away from.

'What do you think?' she whispered.

Almost absent-mindedly, Stefan reached up and pulled a snowdrop from Irina's braid. She'd forgotten it was even there; the wedding seemed so long ago. He threw it across the ground where the light had been. Nothing happened. He made a thoughtful noise, then stuck his hand over it as well. Still nothing.

'What are you doing?' she asked.

'There's no gate here,' Stefan explained. 'It's not a fixed point on the path through the woods. I think we could keep walking through the trees for miles and never get into the underworld proper. The real gate is the light.'

'Are you sure?'

'Not even a little bit,' said Stefan, straightening up and brushing the soil off his hands, 'but I think it makes sense. That woman just walked into the light and disappeared. You clearly have to stop and go through something, or the queue would just be constantly moving. And according to that doctor, there's three different places you could end up and we've seen three different kinds of light. It's as good a theory as any.'

A wash of blue-grey light blazed across the path. Irina started forwards, the necklace at her throat rattling. Stefan grabbed her arm and hauled her back.

'What are you doing?' he hissed. 'I thought you were going to get me through the gate!'

'I was! You said to go through the light!'

The light disappeared. So, too, had the child at the head of the queue. Stefan dragged her back, seething. 'You can't go charging off! We have to work out which light goes where first!'

Irina yanked her arm out of Stefan's grip. 'Well, it obviously wasn't going to the bad place,' she snapped. 'That was a child.

What sins could they have committed? Nothing that merited eternal punishment, I'll bet.'

Stefan opened his mouth, and then closed it again. He looked even more annoyed, and Irina felt a thrill of triumph. She was right, and he hated it.

'It doesn't really matter where we end up as long as it's not Tartarus. Or Hell. Whichever one that is,' she muttered, shuffling a little closer to him as the trees rustled somewhere off to her right. 'Catalina won't be there, so there's no point in looking, and you don't want to go there either. So all we need to do is work out which one of the lights means a bad judgement has been made, and not go through that one.'

'And how are we going to do that?'

Irina pointed at the tapestry. Stefan's mouth twisted. With the lives of the dead playing out before them, it would be easy to spot a true sinner.

'Fine,' he muttered. 'But we're not going until we know which is the gate to Hell.'

Wrapped in velvety smugness, Irina pressed closer to the tree and peered up at the tapestry of lights. An old man was standing before it now, and far over his head streams of colour flashed backwards and forward like comets. A vast stone kitchen was shining in front of him, filled with sweating cooks, white-capped servants, and children turning a roasted goat on a spit in the fireplace. The scene dissolved into blinding blue-grey light. Irina shielded her eyes, and when she took her hand away, the old man was gone.

Stefan sidled up to the tree beside her. 'How do you know she won't have gone to Hell, anyway?'

'Of course she hasn't,' Irina snapped. 'She's a child. She hasn't had time to do anything that would send her to Hell. Maybe she's a little annoying, and she certainly isn't a saint, but there's no way she's there.'

Stefan looked away. 'Some people are rotten all the way through, right from the beginning,' he said, his voice quiet.

'Not seven-year-olds! Who told you that?'

He didn't answer.

The queue kept moving. Catalina's necklace pointed straight in front of them, until light cut across the path. Then, it writhed, juddering and twitching in all directions like a snake thrashing in a trap. Catalina had clearly passed through the gate, but Irina had no idea which light she had gone through; something about the gates' appearance seemed to send the necklace into a frenzy, and she could not read its movements.

A young woman in a dirty apron watched herself scrubbing a wooden floor; she disappeared into the blue. An impossibly hairy man in a hermit's robe stared at a vast image of himself pottering around an empty cave; he stepped into a pale gold light brighter than the sun. Another child, too young to do anything but chew on their own fingers and look around, lost; blue light engulfed them. A monk watched himself doodling in the margins of an illuminated manuscript; he stepped into the blue. A girl of ten watched her shining hands lift a baby bird back into its nest; pale gold light reached out to meet her, warm as a mother's hand. And, at last, a man in a soldier's uniform, who watched himself slice neck after sleeping neck as the crowd grew quiet. Light like red wine spilled across the path. The man bolted, running for the trees. Someone stuck out their foot. He fell. He screamed. In a burst of light, he was gone.

Silence spilled over them. Beside her, Stefan's hands were curled into white-knuckled fists. She stole a glance at his face. All she could see there was fear. A strange kind of guilt pricked at her. Monsters shouldn't be afraid – at least, not in front of their prey.

She shook the feeling away and went back to watching the lights. Another child was standing in front of them, sucking their thumb and pulling on their earlobe as they stared up at their own receding back, chasing a chicken on sturdy little legs. Irina tore her eyes away from the lights and nudged Stefan. He flinched.

'Let's go on this one,' she whispered. 'Get ready.'

'But how do you know if it'll be—'

She gave him an unimpressed look. 'Stefan, that child can't be more than four years old. What could they possibly have done that would send them to Hell?'

He didn't answer. He just glared, and ground his feet into the dirt, ready to run. Irina did the same, shuffling away from the tree so the roots wouldn't trip her. Off to her right, something rustled.

'Ready?' Stefan asked, as the child stared up at an image of themselves on their sickbed.

She nodded.

Silver-blue light blazed across the path. Stefan sprang forwards. Irina bolted after him, running into the light. It blazed all around her, searing hot. Something sizzled under her boots. Still, she kept running. A bright, swirling mass of blue and grey pressed in on every side, so close and so vivid that there was nothing else to see, not even the flash of her own arms and legs as she ran. Something was burning. It wasn't her shoes, or her hair, or anything she could see and touch. It was something she could feel right between her ribs, like a brand sizzling in her heart.

She faltered. It hurt so much. White-hot agony had carved out a hollow at the centre of her chest, and it was all she could feel. She should turn back. She still had time. She still had coin. If she walked through the trees, she could find her way back to the ferryman, and pay for passage back to the land of the living.

Without Catalina.

Irina gritted her teeth. A scream strangled itself somewhere in her throat. She forced herself to keep moving forward. Her hand scrabbled at Catalina's wooden beads, knocking against her breastbone as they thrashed around her neck. She wouldn't let her go. She couldn't. Pain scorching through her, razing everything it touched, she pushed herself forward – and the light vanished.

Irina fell to her knees into grey-green grass. The pain had gone. She felt like it had taken half her bones with it. There was no strength in her. All she could do was tremble around the hollow space where the pain had been and try not to retch, ignoring the necklace still rattling against her chest.

Her vision was distorted, blotches of colour dancing in her eyes after the brightness of the light. They seemed to be in an enormous field, full of grasses that were tall enough to hide in. She could just about make out a pair of blackened feet coming into view, peeking out of dirty linen trousers. Moments later, Stefan was crouching down, peering into her face. He didn't look like someone who felt like an invisible red-hot poker had just been jammed into their soul. He was calm, collected, and a little bemused. Although she felt as if something had scraped her raw, Irina still had the wherewithal to be annoyed with him.

'Wait,' she rasped. Breathing deeply, she tried to focus on something – anything to distract her from her roiling stomach. But she could see nothing but the grasses, long and slender and coming up past Stefan's waist. Even the sky was featureless: a shade of grey that reminded Irina of dirty paper. There were no clouds, no birds, no treetops – nothing to break up the empty expanse.

'We can't. We need to keep moving,' he said, hauling her upright.

Nausea rose at the back of her throat. Irina clapped a hand over her mouth. Her limbs felt like ice about to thaw.

'Come on,' he growled, slinging an arm around her shoulders. 'We don't know if anyone saw us.'

Irina threw up. Stefan jumped back, nearly dropping her. He swore. Then, he bent down, grabbed her around the thighs and threw her over his shoulder. Winded, for a few moments all Irina could do was wheeze.

'What are you—'

'We need to get away from the barrier before someone else comes through,' he snapped. 'We can't stay here. I'll find us a place to wait. Don't throw up down my back.'

Irina took slow, deep breaths, and tried to blink her vision back. 'I'll try.'

Stefan set off. 'I had better get to eat after this,' he muttered.

It took Irina a long time to feel like herself again. She felt scooped out, hollow. At some point, when she was trying not to throw up, Stefan had deposited her onto a rustling floor. Irina closed her eyes and held out her left wrist. To her surprise, he hesitated.

'Let's wait. You aren't well.'

She nodded, and closed her eyes. When she felt steadier, she held out her wrist again, trying not to flinch as his cold hands rolled up her sleeve and his teeth sank into the flesh of her arm. Nausea rose as the blood was pulled out of her; she tried to think of soothing breezes and cool waters as her stomach roiled. Not, she realized, that she had seen much of either in the land of the dead. The water had been more than water, and though the trees had been rustling back at the barrier she'd felt no wind in her hair. So far, the underworld had been cool and still.

Eventually, when Stefan had stopped eating, she sat up and straightened her bridal crown, her bitten wrist twingeing as she pushed herself upright.

They were still in the vast plain, with no sign of the caves they had left behind. It stretched for miles either side, rolling gently away into the distance no matter which way she looked. Sitting down, she was almost completely hidden by the tall, grey-green grass, each blade perfectly still. She felt like a dormouse, safe in its nest, listening for the approach of a cat. There was no sun in the pale grey sky. No shadow on the ground, except her own. No tree to shelter under, no mountains clustering at the horizon. Without them, there was nothing to mark how much time had passed before she felt well again; she felt oddly unmoored, without the length of a shadow or a shade of light to anchor her. There was only the grass, and the sky, and a vague feeling that something was missing. She tried not to feel small. At least the glowing river had been something to navigate by. Here, there seemed to be nothing.

Stefan was sitting close by, eyeing her still-bleeding wrist as she cradled it. He was licking the blood off his fingers and wiping his chin. Irina was reminded of a cat trying to clean itself.

'Where are we?' she asked.

He shrugged. 'It's been like this since we went through the gate.'

Irina sat up straighter, peering over the top of the grass. 'Where *is* the gate?'

'Don't tell me you've forgotten something.'

She was about to spit out an irritated reply when a thought occurred to her. 'You don't know, do you?'

'I think it's that way?' he said, pointing somewhere off to the left. 'I'm not sure, though. I walked for a while, but I haven't seen it since we passed through. Or any other people, for that matter.'

Irina swallowed, her mouth suddenly dry. If the gate was only an entryway, it would not matter if she found Catalina's soul. She'd never be able to bring her back. She raised a hand to the necklace; away from the gate, it was still.

Stefan cleared his throat. 'What happened back there?'

'What do you mean?'

He stared at her as if she'd just asked him what her own name was. 'You collapsed, you threw up. When we were going through the gate, I heard you trying not to scream. What was wrong with you?'

Irina's temper flared. 'What do you mean, "what was wrong"? Going through the gate was what was wrong! Didn't you feel it?'

'Feel what?'

She stopped. 'Wait,' she said, 'you mean it didn't hurt?'

'No. It was just running and a lot of bright light.'

Irina ground her teeth. 'You mean you didn't get any of the weird chest pain, or the burning, or anything like that?'

He shook his head.

A horrible thought occurred to her. 'Turn around,' she said, 'and close your eyes.'

'Why?'

'Can't you just do it?'

His eyes narrowed. 'What are you planning?'

She glared at him. 'I am *planning* to see if that weird chest burning feeling I had earlier actually burned something off,

Stefan, and I would really appreciate it if you gave me some privacy while I—'

'All right, all right!' he said, turning around and screwing his eyes shut. 'I was only asking because you tried to kill me, remember.'

'That was *once*,' Irina snapped, peering down the neck of her shirt. Everything looked fine, and she let out a sigh of relief. 'And besides, you tried to kill me first. I only wanted to have a civil discussion.'

There was a moment of silence. A little of the tension eased out of Irina's shoulders; looking at Stefan was so much easier when she couldn't see the blood staining his collar. After a moment's stillness, he started plucking at the blades of grass, running them between his fingers like a ribbon. Watching him play with something was surprising; she hadn't thought a vampire could still want that. Something brushed against Irina's left wrist; a green shoot was peeking through the blades of grass, curling gently towards her. She moved her hand carefully away. She had never been much of a gardener, but it seemed a bad idea to bleed on the plants.

'Are you done?'

Irina debated seeing how long she could make him sit there for. She relented; Catalina needed her, and the sooner they found her the sooner Irina could take her home. Besides, after the first few minutes, making Stefan wait would stop being funny; he'd only lose his temper. 'You can turn around now.'

He stood up, looking anywhere but at her. 'Shall we go, then?'

'I suppose we should,' she said, hauling herself to her feet and fumbling around for a handkerchief. She still felt a little light-headed and her stomach was growling, but she doubted she was going to vomit again, so that was something. Careful not to touch the beads with her bloody hand, she took off

Catalina's necklace and held it between finger and thumb. For a moment, it was still. Panic lurched through her. Were they in the right place? But then it began to sway back and forth, pointing across the vast grass sea, and hope burst into bloom.

'Have those beads been chewed?' Stefan asked.

The green shoot had grown taller, brushing against her bleeding hand. She shook it away, and shoved the necklace back over her head. 'Yes. Not by me,' she added, as she set off in the direction the necklace had indicated. 'She was teething.'

Alarm flashed across his face. 'She's not your daughter, is she?' he asked, falling into step beside her. 'She can't be. Not if she's seven years old.'

Irina hesitated, fingers curling around a handkerchief. She had no idea what it would mean for Catalina if Stefan thought she was her own daughter. Would he be kinder to her when they found her? Would it make any difference at all?

'Sister,' she muttered.

'Why didn't you tell me?' he asked, as they waded through the grass.

Irina hesitated. How frank could she afford to be? If she told him the truth – that she was prepared to risk her own life by trusting him, but not Catalina's – would he listen? Or was letting him know how much she valued her sister only handing him another way to hurt her? She stumbled. A drop of blood flew from her throbbing wrist, disappearing into the green. She shook out the handkerchief and tried to bind it up one-handed, avoiding his eyes.

'Aren't you going to answer me?'

She tied off the knot with her teeth, glad of a few moments to collect herself. What she wanted to say had to be phrased carefully.

'All right,' she said, as another green shoot brushed against the back of her hand. 'I did not tell you about Catalina because Catalina does not concern you.'

He frowned at her, confused. 'But we're going to—'

Irina held up a hand. 'You made a bargain with *me*. It's my blood you want. Nobody else comes into it. Ever.'

Silence settled on them like snow. The confusion had bled out of Stefan's expression. Now, he just looked empty.

'I suppose that's sensible,' he said, his voice heavy.

The slightest prickle of guilt wormed its way into Irina's thoughts. 'You told me you were cruel,' she said quietly.

His face closed over. He kept walking. After a moment, Irina followed him, unsure what she wanted to say – if she wanted to say anything at all. Everything she'd said was true. Stefan was a dead man who killed the living to stay upright. He'd told her so himself. But now, as she watched his shoulders slump, she wondered what a life like that might do to a boy who remembered enough of his humanity to be concerned by the possibility that she might have had children too young.

She shook the feeling away, hurrying to keep up. And behind her, where drops of her blood had fallen into the long grass, red peonies bloomed.

Irina was not sure exactly how long they trudged through the grasses, not speaking. With no sun in the sky, it was hard to keep track of the time. No shadows lengthened underneath their feet. Nothing moved across the sky. Nothing moved at all, but for them. When Irina looked behind her, all she saw was the trail they'd cut through the grass, and a few distant spots of red. The long grass hissed as they waded through it, and the sound echoed around the plain so strongly that it seemed to be coming both from their own path and from much further away. The only way of knowing that time had passed was her growing hunger. Her stomach was growling like an angry cat, and that was saying nothing of her thirst. She didn't think her mouth had ever been so dry.

Stefan had not said a word to her. He had not even turned to look at her. They had simply kept walking in the direction the necklace had indicated, in total silence. His head was bowed, his shoulders slumped. Did she feel guilty? She could not decide if she was looking at a man so dejected and broken he could not bring himself to look at her, or a sulking teenage boy. Either way, she didn't feel bad about it. He'd told her he was cruel. Why would he expect her to act as if she hadn't heard him? Catalina was seven years old. What kind of sister would Irina be, if she didn't try and shield Catalina from a creature that had confessed to murder and refused to apologize for it?

She took off the necklace and held it up again, just to make sure. A memory stirred: Catalina, chubby-cheeked and only just crawling, gnawing on the beads with her first tooth. How many times had she prised this necklace out of her sister's tiny hands?

Irina ignored the wistful pang and focused on the necklace. Holding it between finger and thumb, she let it hang loose until the beads started to move. It swung back and forth, rocking in her hands – and pointed straight back the way they had come.

'Stefan!' she called. 'I think we've gone too far.'

He trudged back through the grass, still not looking at her. Irina turned to look in the direction the necklace was pointing, and saw nothing but the path they had carved through the foliage, and a distant dip in the grass further up the plain. She set off, still holding the necklace like a talisman. After a few steps, it stopped pointing, hanging limp in her hand.

Irina swore. She shook the necklace, starting to panic. Had she broken it? She backed away, shuffling along the path she'd taken – and the necklace sprang back into life, leading her back in the direction she'd just been going.

'What's wrong?' Stefan asked.

Irina gave the necklace another shake. 'I don't know. It stopped working for a second.'

She kept walking, and after a few steps, the necklace fell still. Irina faltered. 'Oh, for—'

'Wait,' said Stefan, 'keep going.'

She did. Rustling through the grass, the sound echoed all around her. She made it five paces before the necklace sprang back up again, pointing in the opposite direction. At last, she realized. The necklace hadn't stopped working. It was simply pointing down.

Had they found her?

Excitement and fear surged through her. Irina shoved the necklace back over her head and dropped to her knees, flinging huge handfuls of grass aside. There was nothing there – nothing but more grass, tamped down so tightly it formed a hard mat beneath their feet. Irina's thoughts stuttered over the discovery. Was something underneath it? There had to be earth down there somewhere, at least. Surely all those plants were growing from something.

'Are you sure she's down there?' Stefan asked, hunkering down beside her.

'She has to be,' Irina said, pulling up a handful of long grass and throwing it aside. No soil clung to its long, white roots. 'Where else could she be?'

'It's just that if she was buried, there'd be signs of a grave here.'

'She isn't buried!' Irina snapped, hauling up another handful of grass with a ripping, rustling noise. 'She isn't even dead!'

He stared at her. 'Then what are you doing here?'

'That's not your business.'

'It *is* my business!' he insisted. 'Is this a trick? How do I know the villagers haven't paid you to leave me stuck here? Where did you get all that money from, earlier?'

'Would you just—'

He grabbed her by the shoulder. Fear glimmered in his eyes. 'Tell me the truth!'

Irina shook him off, glaring. The rustling grew louder. 'If I was helping the villagers to kill you, I would've done it in the land of the living. But Catalina's soul is here. Her body isn't. She isn't *dead*, Stefan. She's fine—' Irina crouched down and ripped up another handful of grass, flinging it over her shoulder. 'She's just stuck here—' another handful went sailing into the grass, '—and I'm going to bring her home.'

'You could have told me,' he muttered, straightening up. Irina kept digging. Her hands were bleeding now, covered in dozens of tiny cuts from the long blades of grass. But there, underneath the mat of closely knotted grass, she could see a spot of black. Hope caught her by the throat and squeezed. She'd found something.

She lunged for it. Tearing handfuls of grey-green grass away, the dark spot grew wider. But as she threw the grass aside, green shoots were wriggling towards her, blood-red buds already starting to sprout, squirming towards her bleeding hands like maggots.

Somewhere over her head, Stefan swore. 'Irina, something's – what are you doing?'

'Help me!'

He fell to his knees. Red peonies burst into bloom all around them. Stefan ignored them, tearing at the little spot of blackness with a ferocity that made Irina remember all those torn-out throats. Scarlet petals and grey-green grass flew through the air.

The hole in the ground grew wider. Irina stuck her hand into it, calling 'Catalina?'

No soil, no tangling roots – not even a surface brushing up against her fingertips. All she could feel was the wriggling, writhing plants. Dry and cool, it was as if a tangle of discarded snakeskins were pushing against every cut on her skin, blind heads pushing for a way in. Bright peonies were bursting into life all around the hole, squirming up towards her. They were closing around her wrist, stalks winding around her arm, crawling up towards her shoulder . . .

Stefan tore the flowers away in one swipe. There was a ripping sound and Irina felt something tear – not in her physical self, but in some gossamer-thin thread the world was tied together with. She yanked her hand free, and the sides of the hole crumbled inwards, one long, wriggling shoot still squirming into the cut on her wrist. The hole was now wider than her thigh, and there was something glimmering in the darkness on the other side.

She tore the shoot away. Blood spattered across the ground. More flowers slithered towards her hand. Irina snatched it away, kicking the hole until it widened. Stefan's hand slashed through the air, sending crimson petals scattering. Behind them, the long grass rustled.

Stefan glanced over his shoulder, then into the hole. He snatched another handful of peonies away from Irina's arm. 'What are you doing?'

'We're going in!' she yelled, cradling her bleeding hands to her chest.

He swore. 'Fine.'

Irina threw herself into the hole, screwing her eyes shut. Something snagged in her hair – Stefan's hand, or a burst of wayward flowers, she could not say. Either way, she was falling, tumbling into the blackness in a flurry of skirts and red petals, one hand clamped on her bridal crown. Behind her, she heard Stefan swearing frantically, lost in the rush of wind.

She hit the floor with a *thump* and a roll, pain blossoming on her left side. Moments later, Stefan crashed down beside her, groaning. For a moment, Irina lay on the ground, panting. She reached up to touch the necklace with a throbbing hand. It was still there, and she sagged into the earth, relieved.

Then, a small voice said, 'What's that lady doing on the floor? Did she fall down?'

Irina opened her eyes and scrambled upright, cramming the bridal crown back onto her head. She appeared to have fallen into a village on a summer's day, with no sign of the fields of grass or the darkness of the cave. Two children were staring at her: a chubby little girl of about four years old and an older girl, who could not have been more than nine. Both of them were neatly dressed in clean white shirts and black woollen vests, carefully embroidered in red and yellow, and wide, striped skirts. They had identical flowered headscarves tied under their chins, and they were holding hands. At the sight of the younger girl clinging to the older one's fingers, anguish twisted its knife. Where was Catalina?

She looked around as Stefan got to his feet. There was no sign of the hole in the ceiling, because there was no ceiling over their heads. Instead, there was a vast expanse of blue, brighter than a summer sky. Something like a heat haze hung in the sky, no wider than a foot across. When she squinted at it, her head began to ache. The ground was rich, brown mud, but it had not clung to her clothes. Dotted around them were several small houses with high thatched roofs and brightly coloured shutters, no door taller than her shoulder, no window higher than her hip. Each home had a byre, housing the fluffiest animals Irina had ever seen: goats, sheep, donkeys, cows, horses, chickens, ducks. Then she saw their eyes, and her stomach turned over. They were enormous, almost taking up half of the animals' heads. Further back stood a ring of conical haystacks, surrounding the little village in a perfect circle. Several of them looked like they had been jumped in.

Something brushed against her hand; another red peony, winding its way towards the blood dripping from her fingers. Stefan ripped it from the earth, looking wary. Irina ignored him and focused on the children. 'Hello,' she said. 'I'm looking for my sister. Have you seen her?'

But the girls did not answer her question. They had seen her bridal crown, and gasped. 'Are you getting married?' said the older one.

Stefan dropped the peony and massaged his shoulder, and the girls turned identical stares on him. He was filthy and surrounded by bits of smashed peonies, and his blackened hands and feet looked almost profane in this soft, brightly coloured part of the underworld. The younger of the two girls shrank back. 'I don't think you should get married,' she said.

'Elena!' the older girl snapped. 'Don't be rude to the lady!'

Elena tried to shuffle behind her. She looked like she was about to cry. 'I don't like him, Anca,' she mumbled. 'He's all mucky, and his hands are scary.'

Stefan opened his mouth to say something. Irina threw out an arm before he could get started. 'He is all mucky,' she agreed, 'but we can clean him up. Do you know where my sister is?'

A little hand tugged on the back of Irina's skirt. Panic engulfed her. Irina looked over her shoulder. A boy of about five was holding onto the cloth. The child was going to relive his own death, and she hadn't even realized he had got that close. She was going to watch his tiny, rotting face staring up at her, fear flooding his clouded eyes, his mouth slack with horror, blood pouring down his –

'Can I have some of your flowers?' he said.

He was still blonde, blue-eyed, and rosy-cheeked; a far cry from the shrunken, decaying face she'd been expecting to see. But, she realized, he just had a handful of her skirt. He hadn't actually touched her.

'Yes,' she croaked, keeping her hands out of his reach, 'take as many as you like.'

He scrambled off, scooping up handfuls of flowers and running off to a byre containing a fluffy white donkey as more children came out of the houses. The animal stared straight ahead, chewing peacefully, as the little boy stuck flowers in its mane. Its jaw moved in exactly the same way with every bite; down, around, and back up again, although she couldn't see what it was eating.

'Anyway,' she said, shuffling a little closer to Stefan, 'my sister . . .'

A clod of mud sailed through the air. It hit Stefan in the side of the head. He whirled around, snarling, and Irina tried not to snigger. Two boys disappeared into another of the tiny houses, shrieking with laughter.

'Stop that!' Anca yelled, stamping her feet. 'That's not nice!'

A tiny face appeared at the window, sticking its tongue out. Elena pointed at it, yelling, 'He's making faces! He's not allowed to make faces!'

Another little girl appeared at Irina's elbow. She looked about seven years old and was dressed in a man's embroidered shirt, trailing on the ground as she walked. Her eyes massive, she stared up at Irina. 'Can I come to the wedding?' she asked. 'Please?'

A boy swaddled in heavy furs and a conical hat toddled up

behind her. 'Will there be cake?' he asked. 'I'll come if there's cake.'

Irina backed away, holding her hands out of reach. There were easily a dozen children now. Anxiety bubbled in the pit of her stomach. She couldn't do it. She couldn't make them relive their last moments.

A child of eighteen months toddled out of a house on unsteady legs, babbling and pointing at her. A ten-year-old boy followed him outside, shouting 'Sergiu! You have to be the bear – oh.'

Another clod of mud soared through the air. This time, Stefan caught it, and a group of small boys cheered. Startled, he dropped it, and when it slopped onto his shoulder they collapsed into a heap of giggles.

The haze in the sky seemed to be pulsing. Irina stared at it, the headache building behind her eyes. Not pulsing – juddering, she realized, as though something was hitting it from the other side. Then, something smacked into her. A sheep that looked like a walking pom-pom had barged into the back of her legs. She staggered forward; a girl of about six was holding one of the sheep's ears and steering it towards her. 'This is Mioară,' she said, 'you can pet her if I can be in your wedding.'

Stefan's hand closed around Irina's elbow. Children surrounded them on every side. His eyes darted from tiny face to tiny face. 'Do we run?'

'They're children,' Irina muttered.

'Dead children,' he retorted. 'What happens if they think it's a game, and chase you down?'

Panic twisted like a knife. They seemed like perfectly normal children now. But all it would take would be one of them demanding a hug or trying to hold her hand, and they would start to rot before her eyes. She'd catapult them back to the worst moments of their lives, while two dozen of them surrounded her. She had to distract them. Then she could find out if they'd seen Catalina.

Irina clapped her hands together. 'We're playing a game!' she yelled. 'Last one to sit on the floor loses!'

The children shrieked and threw themselves onto the ground, giggling. Soon, Irina and Stefan were the only ones standing. They exchanged a look.

'You have to sit on the floor!' Anca called. 'That's the rules!'

Stefan shrugged. Irina gathered up her skirts, moving them out of the way so she could sit, and the children exploded into laughter. When she looked up, it was to see Stefan sitting on the ground next to her, smirking. 'You lose,' he mouthed.

Irina resisted the urge to make a rude gesture. Instead, she put a hand to her forehead, and said, 'Oh no! You beat me!' in an unconvincing voice. The children laughed; Stefan mouthed a swear word at her.

'Everyone stay sitting down,' Irina said, ignoring Stefan. 'I've got another game we can play.'

'What's the game?' the girl with the sheep asked, her arms locked around one of its legs. It was chewing in the exact same way as the donkey – down, around, and up – with an identically placid expression on its face. Irina tried not to stare at its enormous eyes.

'It's a finding game,' she said. 'I'm looking for my little sister, Catalina. I think she might be here. She's about seven years old, with blonde hair and a chipped front tooth. She likes telling stories. Anyone who can help me find her gets a prize.'

The little boy who'd asked for her flowers put his hand up. 'I know her!' he said, excitedly. Irina's heart lurched. 'She told me if we could find some blackberries we can turn my donkey purple.' His voice trailed off, sounding lost. 'She . . . she made me think about . . .'

'You can't get purple donkeys,' Anca interrupted.

'You *can*,' the boy retorted, suddenly bright again, 'Catalina said you can *make* them purple if you get a big pot of blackberries and mash them all up. Then you can put them on the donkey and their fur goes purple, so ha!'

'That doesn't count—'

Irina held up a hand. Her heart was beating so fast, it felt like it was going to burst out of her. 'So Catalina was here? Where is she now?'

'They took her away,' Elena said.

Fear curled around Irina like a fist. 'Who took her? Where?'

Elena had her fingers in her mouth. 'Away,' she mumbled.

'They said she wasn't supposed to be here,' Anca said. 'She made people sad.'

At once, Irina remembered how, at her touch, measles had blossomed across the dead boy's skin. She hated that she could do that to people, but at least she was old enough to understand what was happening. Catalina would be horrified. 'Did . . . did she change people?'

Anca shook her head. 'They just got sad. And quiet. She was nice, but . . . she put funny thoughts in your head. The guardians said she wasn't supposed to do that. So they came to put her somewhere she couldn't get us.'

'Funny thoughts?' Irina asked, fighting to keep her voice gentle. 'What kind of funny thoughts?'

The children fell silent. Anca had a faraway look on her face. 'I can't remember,' she said. 'It's gone a bit fuzzy, since the guardians visited. I think I thought about a bed? And . . . and a face?'

Irina opened her mouth to ask another question. Stefan

coughed, too loudly, and she took the hint. Anca had a lost expression; Irina did not want to push any further.

'These guardians, the ones that took her. Did they give you a name?'

Anca looked thoughtful. 'I don't think they have names,' she mused. 'They're just the guardians. They come and check on us. Sometimes they bring cake. Sometimes the cake turns up on its own. Oh, sometimes, when people's families get here, they take them to meet them, so they can all be together.' She tilted her head. 'Why didn't they take her to you, if she's your sister?'

Irina opened her mouth, but Stefan cut across her. 'We are married,' he said, sounding almost bored. 'That means she's part of my family now.'

The girl with the sheep started welling up. 'But I wanted to be in the wedding!'

'So, the guardians,' Irina said quickly, 'what are they like? Where did they go?'

Anca pointed over Irina's shoulder. 'They went that way. They went through the door. Can you have another wedding, so we can join in?'

The children made enthusiastic noises. Someone was yelling about cake at the back of the group. Stefan looked revolted, but that seemed to be because a toddler was trying to climb into his lap. Only Irina seemed to have noticed that the haze in the sky was juddering. She could not look at it for more than a few seconds – her head hurt trying to focus on it – but something about the movement made dread trickle down her spine.

'I'll ask the guardians if you can have another wedding,' said Anca. 'They look after us, so they'll look after you, too. They bring us everything we ask for, so they'll give you everything you need. Even your sister! Then you won't have to go looking for her. They'll have told her to stop making people sad now, so she can come back.'

The toddler was attempting to crawl over Stefan's knees. Irina tried to catch his eye but he was distracted; now the baby was trying to touch his face. 'Please stop that,' Stefan muttered. The other children were ignoring him completely, their eyes fixed on Irina.

'If you stay, you can tell us stories,' Anca said, 'and pet the animals, and we can braid your hair, and—'

'Can I make the bridal crown? Yours is just twigs.'

'*I'm* doing it, *I've* got the flowers!'

'Give them here!'

'Please do not climb on me. Whose child is this?'

'—and you can tuck us in when we want to sleep, and you can stop the boys from fighting and throwing things—'

'She can't stop me, I'm really good at throwing—'

'Please, someone come and get this child. It is sticky.'

'—and there'll always be someone here to look after us, and play with us, and you won't ever have to leave,' Anca finished, beaming up at Irina. 'It'll be so much nicer if you stay.'

Dozens of imploring eyes were fixed on her. Guilt crawled across her thoughts like a spider. They were children. It would be cruel to leave them alone, even if they did have these guardians bringing them food and checking up on them. But she couldn't leave Catalina. The guardians had taken her, and Irina had no idea if she would be safe with them. It didn't sound like she would be, if she had been 'put somewhere' away from the other children. Regardless of if Catalina was safe, Irina had to leave, and quickly. Even if the sky had not been juddering, she thought, trying not to look at the animals with enormous eyes and unsettlingly gentle expressions, there was something off about this place. Animals weren't supposed to look like that.

Donkeys kicked. Chickens squawked right when you were about to fall asleep. Sheep, particularly the fluffy ones, were completely brown at the back end. She'd never once met any animal that was so clean, so soft, and so content to let a child drag it around by the ears.

The truth didn't dawn on her. It slammed into her, as if she'd been headbutted in the stomach. They weren't animals at all. They were toys. Whatever had put them together had made them everything they thought a child would like – soft, placid, cute, and in a vaguely familiar shape. But why? Why not give the children real toys, instead of these unnerving facsimiles of farm animals with no farm to house them? What else were the animals for?

The sky shuddered. Irina saw the haze move out of the corner of her eye, and winced as pain flared in her head. For a second, all the animals were perfectly still. Then they all resumed their strange, circular chewing. Irina shivered.

'You can come and stay with Elena and me,' Anca was saying, 'there's lots of room in our house. And you can stay up as late as you like – everybody can, but you have to tell us all stories before we go to sleep. Otherwise we won't—'

'That's very kind of you,' Irina interrupted, 'but I have to find my sister first.'

Anca frowned. 'No, you don't. The guardians will find her for you. Stay here with us.'

Elena's eyes were full of tears. 'Are you going away?' she asked, her voice wavering.

'No!' Anca snapped. 'She isn't going anywhere! We need a big girl to stay and look after us. She can't go!'

Unease prickled at the edges of Irina's thoughts. Every motionless animal turned its head, their overlarge eyes fixed on her.

She plastered on a smile. 'All right,' she said, 'I can stay.'

The children cheered. Stefan looked up, alarmed.

'Do you promise?' Elena asked, her little face lighting up. 'You'll really stay and be our mama?'

Guilt slammed into her like a musket ball. 'Yes,' she said, 'I promise.'

Elena threw her arms around Irina's legs, hugging them tightly. Panic struck Irina like lightning – she was going to watch this child rot – but when Elena pulled away, her face was smiling and serene. She too had only touched Irina's skirt, not her skin. 'Thank you,' Elena said. 'The bigger boys aren't nice, sometimes. But they'll have to listen to you if you're Mama.'

Disgusted with herself, Irina fought to keep her smile in place. 'I promise I'll make them listen,' she said, 'but I had better talk to the guardians first if I'm going to be Mama. Can you tell me how to find the door, so I can wait for them?'

Beaming, Anca pointed over Irina's shoulder. 'It's through the ring of haystacks,' she said, 'you'll know the ones when you get close. You can see the other place, if you turn around three times first – only if you turn right, though. But you shouldn't look. It's not as nice as here, in the other place.'

'I'll be very careful,' Irina said. 'And while I'm waiting, we can play another game – a hiding game. I'll go and wait by the door and close my eyes. You can all hide, and then I'll come back and find you when the guardians get here.'

The children cheered and sprang to their feet. Irina threw up her hands, staggering back from them. She couldn't let them get close.

'Wait! Wait until I'm by the door before you hide,' she called. 'Otherwise I'll find you all, quick as blinking. And . . .' she laid a finger on her cheek, trying to look thoughtful and not like she was barely repressing the urge to run. 'And I think I'll need help looking for you. I bet you're all really good hiders. Stefan, maybe you could . . .'

He took the hint, getting up at once and all but flinging the toddler at his brother. 'Of course.'

Irina kept backing away. The animals were still staring at her. Not one of them had moved since they'd turned their heads. They hadn't even blinked. 'Everyone sit back down!' she said, shuffling away from the children with her smile still fixed in place. 'If you move before I get to the haystacks, I'll know where you're hiding.'

They sat back down, giggling. Some of them were already glancing at the houses, the byres, the pile of perfect mud. One or two of the older children were looking straight at her. She had no idea if they'd realized what she was planning to do.

She turned her back. There was a flurry of feet, and a burst of hushed squealing. Irina flinched.

Stefan caught up to her and muttered, 'What was that?'

'There's something in the sky,' Irina whispered. 'I said what I had to. Are any of them following us?'

He started to turn his head. Someone shrieked, 'You can't *look*!'

'They're hiding,' he whispered. He fell back and started walking directly behind her. A little of the tension ebbed away from Irina. At least this way, a child wouldn't barrel into her legs: Stefan would be the one on the receiving end instead, when the child ran into him. 'We're leaving, aren't we?'

She nodded. 'I can't stay. And those animals . . . something's not right.'

'They're watching you. Keep smiling. I don't think they want the children upset.'

'They're not coming after us, are they?' she whispered. They were out of the little village now, past the last diminutive house. The ring of haystacks was not far, separated from the village by a border of the softest, greenest grass Irina had ever seen.

A Steep and Savage Path

There was a pause. Then, 'No,' Stefan whispered, and Irina's shoulders sagged. 'But those flowers are growing again. You need to be more careful.'

'Why?'

He pointed to her bitten wrist. 'It's your blood,' he muttered. 'I couldn't see clearly, in all that grass, but here . . .'

Irina yanked her hand away. A drop of blood from Stefan's bite hit the earth; a shoot started squirming up to meet her, the red peony already blossoming. 'If anything, *you* need to be more careful. This wouldn't happen if you weren't a messy eater.'

'It's your blood.'

'It's *your* dinner!'

They were nearly at the haystacks now, and there was no doorway in sight. But when she checked the necklace, it pointed her towards the haystacks. Emerald-green grass was soft and pliant under Irina's boots. It was warm, although she felt no sun on the back of her neck, and she could smell pastry baking in an oven, although she had seen no smoke curling from the chimneys. Her stomach rumbled. For a moment, she hesitated. It was cruel to lie to those children and slip away like a traitor under cover of a game. It was a move she had used often with Catalina, when looking after her younger sister had become too much of a chore for a teenage girl. Guilt slid between her ribs like a knife. Sooner or later, the children would start to look for her. They needed her. They'd wonder where she'd gone, and they'd never find out. But she could not stay. Not when Catalina was not here.

Irina squared her shoulders. It was time to go.

Even though there was not a literal door, Anca had been right. Drawing close to the ring of haystacks, it was immediately clear which ones were set aside for children to jump in, and which ones made up a doorway to another part of the land of the dead. All but two of the haystacks looked soft and inviting, despite the fact that the enormous piles of straw towered far above their heads. A thick layer of straw ran around the base of those haystacks, there to cushion a fall, and when she put out a hand, Irina found the straw as soft as a pile of tangled ribbons. But two of them stood taller than the others, looming over Stefan and Irina like statues. With every step, Irina's sense of unease mounted. Walking towards them was a little like hearing the forest go quiet before spotting the thing that had scared the smaller creatures away.

Between them, there was nothing but empty sky and empty fields: an undisturbed expanse of rippling blue and gold. But if she squinted, Irina could see a slight shift in the air between the haystacks, as though she was staring into the same kind of heat haze she'd seen hanging in the sky. From over her shoulder, she heard giggling, slamming doors, and many pairs of feet, sprinting for a place to hide. She waited until the noise had died down, staring into the flicker in the air. The last thing she wanted was for any of the children to come running up to her, accusing her of cheating.

When the last door slammed, Irina took a deep breath. She glanced over her shoulder – there were no children in sight, but every animal was staring at her, and the patch of sky over the village seemed to be pulsing as though something was scrabbling at it.

Beside her, Stefan swore softly. He was staring up at the sky. 'What is that?'

Irina ignored him. She spun clockwise on the spot, three times. Staggering to a halt, she gasped.

Through the haystacks, she saw another place entirely. It was as if a strip of cloth had been torn away, leaving a wide stripe of the other world suddenly in plain sight. On either side of the haystacks, the sky was still blue, the fields still full of golden wheat. But between them was a slice of dark forest, filled with the twisted shapes of skeletal trees. It was painted in every shade of darkness, lit by strange bursts of green and pink light that clustered around the roots. A place of tangled shadow and muted colours, it seemed a far cry from the soft, brightly coloured world they had fallen into. Fear slid underneath Irina's skin. This was the underworld she had been expecting: dark, secretive, foreboding. Was it wise to leave the safety of this little village and venture through the woods?

It was not. That much she was sure of. But then again, she told herself, neither was she.

Squaring up to the panel of darkness, Irina set her jaw. A dull buzzing started up in the back of her head, getting louder the closer she drew. She reached out a hand and her fingertips started to prickle, a lesser version of the pain she'd felt forcing her way through the vast gate of light. Dredging up a shred of hope, she tried to tell herself that it wouldn't hurt as much – clearly, this smaller door was not the same as the glowing light she'd pushed through. She checked Catalina's necklace again; it was not rattling against her breastbone like it was trying to escape, as it had done at the gate, but steadily pointing her forward. Perhaps she'd be all right.

Stefan stood beside her. His eyes darted between her fingertips and the world she was reaching for, then back over her shoulder, at the distant village. He scooped up a handful of peony petals and threw them into the dark, gloomy space between the haystacks, and watched them flutter to the ground.

'Interesting,' he muttered, and stuck his hand through the gap. Nothing happened. 'Interesting,' he repeated.

Taken aback, Irina stared at his outstretched hand. 'Didn't that hurt?' she asked.

'We need to get out of here,' he said, looking back at the

village. 'That patch of sky looks like someone's hammering on the other side of it.' He slipped through the haystacks and into the gloomy forest on the other side, jerking his head towards the distant trees. 'Come on.'

Irina took a slow step towards the door. Already it felt like she was walking through a storm cloud, a myriad of sharp, prickling pains blossoming across her body. A whimper lodged in her throat. She clamped her mouth shut at once. What if the children heard, and came running?

Stefan sighed. He thrust a blackening hand towards her, his greying skin looking even more unnatural in the bright light of the village. 'Irina, if there is something in the sky—'

'I know,' she snapped. She gave Catalina's necklace a quick squeeze and closed her eyes. She wanted to pray, but in that moment, she had no idea who she would be praying to.

Stefan let out an impatient snort. Cold fingers latched around her wrist. Her eyes flew open as he dragged her into the darkness.

Pain burst across her body like fireworks. It felt as if her whole body was suddenly malleable as dough, and she was being squeezed and twisted into a new shape, bones grinding together underneath her skin. Irina clapped a hand over her mouth, holding back something between a sob and a scream. Stefan's hand felt like a manacle on her wrist. Agony rippled through her. Her own fingernails cut into her cheek, as she fought not to make a sound. And then, suddenly, she was through. The pain disappeared. Staggering forward, she crashed into Stefan, who dropped her wrist as if it had scalded him.

Irina fell to her knees, shaking. She'd had worse, she told herself – she'd had worse that very same day. Going through that little door hadn't been as bad as going through the glowing gate. She could handle it. If she could stay here a moment, taking slow, deep breaths in this cool, dark place, she could handle it. If she didn't have to stand up too fast, if she could have a cold cup of water, if she could stay perfectly still and not move a wrung-out muscle, she would be fine.

Stefan was looking at the gate thoughtfully. 'Wait there. I want to try something.'

Irina waved a hand; it felt oddly boneless, after the pain had vanished. Stefan spun around three times, anticlockwise. There was a feeling of pressure being released and the forest grew a little darker. When Irina looked over her shoulder, the door behind her had been closed.

'We shouldn't stay right by the door,' Stefan said. 'We need to move.'

Irina nodded. She eased herself back onto her haunches. After the brightness of the village, the dark was a sudden shock. Once again, there was no sun in the sky, but this part of the underworld was much darker. Lit by small points of coloured light, she could just about make out the suggestion of a path, tall trees, and the shape of Stefan standing in front of her.

He crouched down, peering at her. He was looking at her like she was a puzzle to be solved. With his bloodstained clothes and blackening hands and feet, his head slightly tilted, he looked like some kind of carnivorous bird, perched on a branch and looking for his moment to swoop.

'It's the barriers,' he breathed, after a long moment. 'Of course.'

Irina would have liked to ask him to elaborate, even if Stefan was clearly going to use the opportunity to make himself look clever, but she was too busy taking slow, deep breaths and trying not to throw up. She waved a hand at him instead; it hurt so much it felt like the motion might make it fall off.

'I think that might be what the necklace is pointing you towards – the gates and the doors your sister went through. I think they're different. But it's not as easy for you. You can't pass through them without it costing you something,' he said, getting to his feet. 'But of course you can't. You're living. You aren't meant to be here, so every barrier we come across is going to be designed to keep you out. If you want to get past them, you're going to have to fight your way through.'

Irina's stomach was beginning to settle. She didn't feel anywhere near as hungry as she had done back in the village, but that was probably for the best. Eating anything when she felt like her body had been squeezed through a piping bag was likely not a good idea. She held out her hands, just to check that they were the same shape as she remembered. They were, and she sagged in relief.

'What does it feel like?' Stefan asked.

Irina started flexing her fingers. It was not that they felt stiff, more that they felt loosely attached. 'Horrible,' she muttered.

'Then why do you do it? You don't have to.'

Irina glared at him. 'She's my sister.'

He shrugged. 'And?'

'And I'm not going to leave her!' Irina snapped. 'She's seven years old, her soul and her body have been split apart, God knows what kind of trouble she's in with those guardians, and she's *my sister*. What kind of coward do you think I am, that I'd give up just because it hurts?'

He folded his arms. 'But that's not the only reason you're doing this, surely.'

Irina hauled herself upright. It took longer than she would have liked; her legs were unsteady. 'Of course it is! She is a *child*. She's part of my family and I love her, and I will do whatever it takes to get her back home safe. That's all the reason I need! Do you understand me?'

His blackened hands twitched, clutching his elbows tight. In the half-light, they looked like spiders crouching on his arms.

'Oh, I understand you,' he muttered. 'I understand you much better than you think. I thought I was supposed to be the cruel one, *wife*, but the way you handled those children? Making them feel safe, lying to their faces, and leaving the moment their backs were turned? They'll be looking for you. How long do you think they're going to sit there, hiding, waiting for you to come and find them?'

Guilt churned through her. He was right. She shouldn't have lingered. The right thing to do would've been to get the directions she needed and leave as soon as she could. But she'd panicked, and before she knew it she'd been promising to stay and speaking to them the way she spoke to Catalina. A new regret spread its tendrils through her thoughts. Had Catalina ever felt abandoned in the same way that Irina had left those children behind?

'Who else are you going to lie to? What else are you going to do to find your sister?'

'Whatever it takes.'

Stefan took a step forward. He was no longer clutching his own arms as though he was afraid he would break apart. His fists were clenched, and there was something vicious and desperate in his eyes.

'Admit it. It was cruel. You made them trust you, and then you left them. You promised them you would stay, you told them you would be their family, and you left them. You *left them*. It's easier to leave, isn't it, rather than look what you did in the eye? You're just like everyone in the village. You took the coward's way out and ignored what was happening, because it was easier. You're selfish, you're thoughtless, you *left them*!'

He was spitting the words with such venom that it took her

a moment to realize what, exactly, he had just said. The village had been full of children – children who, if she so much as patted them on the head, would find the full weight of their own mortality crashing into them as they withered into corpses. And that was saying nothing of the animals that had turned their heads towards her in one smooth motion, or the strange guardians that the children kept talking about, or the mother-shaped shoes the children had seemed to want her to step into. Leaving the village was the right thing to do, even if she hadn't handled it perfectly. Stefan had admitted they couldn't stay. So why was he so angry?

He wasn't talking about that village at all. He was talking about his own village, in the land of the living.

A sense of calm drifted through her, like falling snow. She held herself like a general, head up and shoulders back. Stefan faltered. For a moment, the hard lines of his face slipped.

'I told you,' she said, her voice quiet, 'that I would do whatever it takes. I meant it. I know it was cruel to leave them like that. But, *husband*, I have not killed people. I have not dragged people from their beds and drained them of blood. I have not spent months hounding an entire community every single night, making them dread the moment the sun goes down. I have lied. I've made promises I had no intention of keeping. I'm sure I'll do so again. But there's no blood on my hands.'

His jaw clenched. Shadows drenched his hands well past the elbow, the blackening skin lost in the darkness. With his monstrous hands and feet hidden by the gloom, and his bloodstained mouth made into a smear of darkness, he looked more like a boy than Irina had ever seen him. But she was not fooled. There was a line of graves in the churchyard which showed what he was capable of, and she could not forget it.

She took a step forward, close enough to reach out and slap

him right across the face. 'I know exactly what I've done, and I can look it in the eye,' she continued. 'Can you?'

Stefan said nothing. His mouth was set into a thin line. The muscles in his arms flickered; he was clenching and unclenching his fists under the cover of darkness. Eyes fixed on her, his expression was a mask. Irina almost pitied him. It must take so much effort, she thought, to keep up all that cruelty.

She was the first to look away. Her hand strayed to Catalina's necklace, and the moment her fingers touched the wood, Stefan was forgotten. She took off the necklace, held it carefully between finger and thumb and watched it swing into life, pointing her down a dark and winding path. She set off, barging past Stefan, who was still motionless, still silent. Ignoring him, she kept walking, and after a long moment, he followed her.

All Irina could think about was her hunger.

She and Stefan had been walking the gloomy path for what felt like hours, still not speaking to each other. The twisting trail wound through the trees, and their every footstep sounded as loud as cracking bone in the silence. Cool, dark and quiet, the narrow track would have felt peaceful if she'd been able to see where it led, but all she had to go on was the movement of Catalina's necklace. Tall, dark pines crowded either side of the path, lit from below by clusters of mushrooms glowing pink and green. They clung to the trunks and glimmered between the roots, throwing long, deep shadows over every ridge in the bark. Irina had been walking past them for enough time to make her mouth go dry and her legs ache, and all she could think about was what they would taste like. Fried up in butter until they started to go brown – or perhaps maroon or forest green, she wasn't sure – and sprinkled with thyme. Stewed to richness in a sour soup. Cooked up with garlic and dusted with dill, laid on a generous bed of *mămăligă*. Irina didn't know if the mushrooms were poisonous. She'd never eaten anything that glowed before, but it seemed unlikely that the mushrooms could harm her. What was the point in having poisonous plants in the land of the dead? Everyone here had already died.

Stefan padded along behind her. He had said nothing since their argument, but she could feel his resentment radiating off him, like a cold wind tugging at her hair. Irina did not care. Her anger was still smouldering, and her hunger was fanning the flames. Worse, she was sure that he was feeling exactly the same way, and she hated that they had even that in common.

Nothing he'd said had been a lie, she acknowledged, as she forced herself to walk past a clutch of glowing green mushrooms shaped exactly like chanterelles. She was still deciding exactly how ashamed she was after lying to the children to get away from them. They'd all cheered and grinned when she'd said she would stay, and the memory of their delighted faces was already weighing on her. But it had been her best option. And while lying to the children may have been unkind, it paled in comparison to the blood dripping from Stefan's hands.

He might not have told a lie, she thought, but he'd said those things to hurt her. Why? Was that just who he was? Was her undead husband someone who, at his core, could not wade through the mire of his own guilt unless he dragged someone else along with him? Or was there something else at play?

Irina's stomach growled. The image of a pot of bubbling golden *mămăligă* rose in her mind's eye, and her mouth began to water. She forced herself to keep walking, to not think about the silky taste of cornmeal. Over her shoulder, Stefan let out a dismissive snort. Irina's temper flared, like a candle in a gust of wind. One of the first things he'd told her was that he was always hungry. Why did he care that she was hungry too? Irina glared at a large clutch of glowing pink mushrooms, trying desperately not to think about the smell of paprika in a bubbling stew. There was something wrong with that boy.

But what?

Talking about Catalina had started the fight. Well, she admitted to herself, blushing, truthfully *she* had started the fight. Stefan had simply been asking her why she was bothering to retrieve her sister – but that was a ridiculous question, Irina thought, her temper flaring again. Of *course* she was going into the land of the dead to get back her sister's soul. She wasn't going to leave Catalina on her own, surrounded by the dead. She was family.

Surely Stefan must understand that. He'd been living, once. Surely he remembered having family of his own. Surely he hadn't forgotten them. How long had he been dead? No one had told her. Irina had been living in the village for a few months when she'd been asked if she'd be willing to be married to a dead man. It had taken a week's journey to reach the village, and perhaps a few more before that for the rumours to spread to her own village. He couldn't have been dead for all that long. Long enough for his house to have fallen into disrepair, but it was a hard winter following a restless, storm-laden autumn, and such things could happen quickly in poor weather. A year at most, she guessed – perhaps less, if he'd only killed four people. Certainly not long enough for the memory of what it meant to have a family to have faded – but she couldn't think of any other reason why he'd lost his temper like that. It didn't make sense for him to become so cruel so quickly.

The path crunched under Irina's feet. Quickly, she checked the necklace: still straight ahead. She held her scratched hands close to her chest, like a penitent sinner, in case another drop of blood fell to the ground and sprouted a flower that wanted to wind itself around her ankles. It was perfectly still in the forest, and silent but for the sound of rustling leaves and their own footsteps. Her shadow was the only thing that moved, splashed across the path like a pool of blood.

But, she supposed, as she picked her way down the path, perhaps he didn't have a family. His house had been standing empty. Perhaps it had just been him, sitting alone in that little house on the edge of the woods. But that didn't sound right. She'd found a man's hat in the rafters which clearly hadn't belonged to Stefan, and he'd told her that when he died, all his things had been burned. Someone must have done the burning. She tried to recall what had been said of Stefan's family, back in the village. Nothing came to mind. No one had talked about the empty house on the edge of the forest. No one had mentioned Stefan's name, not even during the wedding.

Unease slid through her thoughts. No one in that village had ever talked about Stefan as he had been in life. It was as if they'd all detached the monster that stalked their village from the person he had once been: it was impossible to see the man under the shadow of the monster. They must have known him – they'd known enough about him to be certain that he had died unmarried, otherwise they would not have tried marrying her to him. But they hadn't buried him, she remembered, because the grave she'd stood next to was empty. Did they even know where he'd died? He'd lived with them. Died with them. Killed them. So why was no one speaking his name? How could a boy of no more than nineteen die with no one to mourn his passing?

Irina shivered. Stefan's footsteps were quiet, but suddenly they seemed to be all she could hear. Did he know that no one spoke about him, after he died? Did he care? She wasn't sure. It seemed like a bad idea to ask him, after their argument. After all, he could still kill her.

It was getting darker. The trees were starting to thin out, and with fewer glowing mushrooms clinging to the bark, the faint light was starting to fade. Irina could barely see the edges of the path ahead of her. She swallowed, suddenly nervous.

'Can you see in the dark?' she whispered.

Stefan's voice was rippling with venom. 'Oh, are we speaking now?'

Irina ground her teeth. How she had even started to feel bad for him when he was this petty, she had no idea. She walked to the base of a tree, one solitary glowing mushroom clinging to the bark. Carefully, she prised it away from the roots, watching to see if the pink light flickered.

'You are *not* going to try and eat that,' Stefan said, horrified.

'Of course not!' Irina snapped. She tugged a little harder and the mushroom came away, glowing pink in the palm of her hand.

'Then what are you—'

'I thought we weren't speaking.'

All she could see of Stefan was a vague shape in the darkness, but she could feel him glowering at her. She picked her way back into the centre of the path, holding the mushroom like a lantern, and kept walking. It did not help. After a while she realized that all it was doing was illuminating the palm of her hand. She threw it a few steps ahead of her; it shot through the darkness like a shooting star and landed with a small puff of glowing spores.

'Don't step on it,' she whispered, 'we'll need a marker if we turn back.'

'I thought we weren't—'

'Shut up.'

'Oh, for – hold on. I've got an idea.' Ripping a handful of glowing mushrooms off the nearest tree, Stefan dropped them on the ground and trod on them, crushing them into a glowing paste. Luminescent spores clung to the soles of his feet, turning them pink and green, and although Irina could not see his expression clearly, she knew in her bones that he was pulling a smug face at her.

'Now we can see where we've been,' he said, 'in case we lose the marker.'

'That's actually very clever,' Irina muttered grudgingly.

The glee in his voice was palpable. 'So sorry, I didn't hear you.'

'I *said* that's very clever.'

'That's odd, because I thought that we weren't speaking—'

'God*damn*it!'

Irina stomped around the glowing mushroom and kept going into the dark. Stefan followed. After a few more steps, the last of the mushrooms clinging to the trees faded from view. There was only blackness now. Irina had both her arms held out in front of her, the necklace clutched in one hand. If she felt it move, she changed direction, hissing to Stefan to follow her. He placed one cold hand on the back of her neck, and she tried not to think about how easy it would be for him to snap it. They always said the dead were strong, and now that he was feeding regularly, Stefan was getting stronger. But instead, he shifted his hand onto her shoulder, and a strange guilt stole through her. Of course he wouldn't kill her; she was his meal, and his only way out. The villagers might not have been safe from him, but she was.

Eventually, the darkness began to ease to a gentle gloom, and the necklace began to tremble. Irina's legs were aching from the walk, but up ahead she could see a glimmer of familiar white-gold light. The forest that had surrounded them had disappeared. So had the path. In the half-light, Irina could make out the heads of flowers beneath her feet – not the blood-red peonies that had sprung from the earth, lunging at her like venomous snakes, but wild orchids, irises, vetch. All of them tangled together in a soft, purple carpet, smelling sweeter with every step. She took a deep breath and closed her eyes, breathing in the scent, and that was when the buzzing started. Right at the back of her head, it was faint enough to ignore, but the sensation was enough to make her feel queasy with anticipation.

There was another gate ahead.

She held up the necklace and peered at it closely. For a second it was still, pointing straight ahead, then it started twitching and thrashing. She kept walking. The buzzing got louder and, now she drew a little closer, she could see that it was not one light in the darkness but a vast sheet of the palest gold drawn across the flowers like a curtain, much like the coloured light she had seen at the tapestry. The flowers shone like amethyst, but now the sound of the gate was ringing in her ears, the delicate, floral smell was making Irina feel sick.

She stopped. 'I'm going to need a minute.'

Stefan scowled at her. 'I thought you'd do *anything* for your family,' he spat.

'It just—' She ground her teeth, trying to swallow back the rising pain and nausea. 'It just doesn't feel good.'

He stopped. Something like guilt flickered across his face. 'Even from this distance?'

Irina nodded. She held up the necklace again. It lurched in her hands, twisting and pointing first left, then right, left again, up, down, right, down, as if she was trying to hold a snake by the tail. She grabbed it with both hands and it finally went still, pointing straight ahead once again, but dread was already seeping through her. The necklace looked like it was trying to get away. Did that mean Catalina was near, and it was trying to get to her? Or did it mean that there was something far more dangerous here, that threatened the only thing she had that would help her find her sister? And which way was she supposed to go – straight ahead, where it pointed more steadily, or towards the sheet of light, which made it writhe in her fingers like a living thing?

'What was that?' Stefan asked.

She held up the thrashing necklace. For a split second it went still, pointing parallel to the sheet of light, then it started squirming again, pointing in all directions the moment she shifted her weight a little closer to the light.

Stefan peered at the necklace, alarmed. 'Is it meant to do that?'

Irina shrugged. 'It did this at the gate, after we crossed the blue river, but not at the door. Sometimes it seems to point down the path,' she said, indicating a distant forest on the other side of the clearing, 'so I don't know if we should go that way or go and see what that is,' she said, gesturing at the sheet of light.

'It's your sister,' Stefan said, his voice just a little sour. 'You decide.'

Irina hesitated. When it was still enough to read the direction it was pointing, the necklace seemed to be leading her to the forest on the other side. But the presence of the light was unnerving her. Why was it here, and why was it making her makeshift compass act like this? Did it mean that Catalina was on the other side of the glowing gate? Or, like a compass exposed to a magnet, was the presence of the gate throwing off the only thing she had to navigate by?

'I suppose we should check while we're here,' she mused, 'who even knows if we'll find this place again?'

Stefan snorted. Irina ignored him and set off towards the gate. With every step that took her closer, the buzzing got louder. Her stomach roiled. Pain started to burn in the back of her head, smouldering like a pot that had boiled dry. By the time she was close enough to reach out and touch the wall of light, her whole body was throbbing with pain and the necklace felt like it was going to choke her. Raising her arm felt like dredging something up from the bottom of a river.

'Shall we?' she asked, through gritted teeth.

There was no answer.

Stefan's jaw was clenched. His eyes were fixed on the sheet of light, wide and frantic. His blackened hands were contorted, twitching. He looked like a branch, bent back to the point of snapping.

'Stefan?'

He nodded. He still didn't look away, but he raised a hand. Irina did the same, sticking her fingers into the pale gold light. She bit back a scream. It felt like she'd dunked them in boiling water.

There was a hiss. A smell of burning flesh. A strangled yell. Irina yanked her hand out of the light and whirled around. Stefan was staggering backwards, clutching his hand. The faintest shadow of a handprint was sizzling on the surface of the gate.

'What . . .'

Stefan was hunched over, cradling his hand to his chest. His shoulders were shaking, and Irina couldn't tell if he was trembling or crying. She couldn't see his face.

Irina's hand hovered over his shoulder. 'Stefan?'

'I can't.'

'You can't . . .'

'The gate,' he groaned, waving his uninjured hand at the wall of light. 'I can't.'

'Come on,' she said, patting him on the back. At the touch of her hand, he flinched. 'Let's move back a bit.'

She steered him away from the gate. She checked the necklace again; the further away from the gate they got, the less it writhed. With every step, she felt lighter, and the pain in her head dimmed to a low whine. She was not the only one. The further they went, the straighter Stefan stood, the easier he walked. Soon he was looking over his shoulder, glaring at the gate as though it had personally offended him.

'It doesn't make any sense,' he muttered. '*You* struggle with the gates because you're alive, but I'm dead. I shouldn't have any problems. Why can't I get through?'

Irina flopped down onto the flowers. Close to, she realized that there were no stalks and leaves beneath; only layers and layers of petals, each one perfect. Now that the pain had faded, she was bone-tired, and starting to feel a little faint. 'Do you think it goes back to the land of the living?' she asked. 'Maybe that's why it was keeping you out.'

He sat down beside her, still cradling his hand and glowering at the light they'd left behind. 'We've seen that gate – well *you* have, I can't see it unless I drink your blood. Besides, then you could've got through. It has to go to somewhere in the under-world, but—'

He stopped. All the anger and wounded pride fled his face so fast that, for a moment, Irina thought it had been slapped right out of him. She panicked. She hadn't done anything. She hadn't said anything. What had happened?

'Stefan?' she asked. 'Are you all right?'

He didn't answer. His mouth was slightly open, but she had no idea if he was about to speak or scream or sob. Staring at the gate, white-gold light reflected in his stricken eyes, he looked like he'd watched something die. Irina followed his gaze, wondering if he had seen something, and then she understood.

The white-gold light was familiar because she had seen it before: at the tapestry of lives, woven in front of the crowd of dead waiting for admittance into the underworld. It was not a door to another pocket of the afterlife that they could open and close; it had been one of the three colours blazing between the lives woven over their heads, and must lead to another part of the land of the dead entirely. The wine-dark light had led sinners to Hell, or Tartarus, whichever it was. The blue-grey light, that she'd seen most often, had led them here. And the pale gold, she realized, had flashed up after showing the lives of the hermit, of the kind-hearted girl who had lifted a sparrow back into its nest, of the mother and her smiling children. Pure lives. Pure people.

She was looking at the gates of Heaven – or the Elysian Fields, whatever Doctor Emil had said it was called. The eternal reward. The home of saints and martyrs and the lucky, worthy few. The thing that every priest had promised her might be possible if she remembered her prayers, honoured her mother and father, and lived her life as a good woman should.

And it would not let Stefan in.

He had been judged, and found wanting. Sins clung to him like vines crawling up a tree. She supposed she shouldn't be surprised, but then again, neither should he. He'd killed people. Of course his soul – if he had one – was not spotless. Had he really thought that, despite everything he'd done, he still had a chance at paradise? But watching him staring at a place of eternal joy and realizing that he was barred from it felt like stumbling across a house fire when it was already blazing. There was nothing she could offer but pity. Whatever he had done had clearly not been bad enough that the only door he could pass through led to Hell – he had passed through the blue light, after all. But whatever kept him from Hell was not enough to lead him into Heaven. He wasn't good enough. The thought dropped into Irina's mind like a leaden weight.

Was she?

She glanced down at the necklace. It pointed into the forest, but as she watched, it swung back around, shaking and squirming when she held it out in the direction of the gate. The only clear path it pointed her down led her right past that sheet of light. She could look. She could force herself through the burning gate and check the Elysian Fields without someone to keep the dead from touching her. But she did not know that Catalina was even there, and besides, that would mean leaving Stefan slumped outside the walls, staring at a gate to a better world that he could never pass through. He'd spent a lot of time insisting that she was cruel. She didn't want to prove him right.

'Let me see your hand,' she said.

He flinched. 'I . . . I . . .'

Gently, she reached for him. He shrank back, cradling his hand to his chest.

'I just want to see if you're hurt,' she said.

His voice splintered when he spoke. 'Why?'

She turned her hand palm up, and said nothing. Stefan watched her for a long moment, his eyes darting from her hand to her face. Irina kept perfectly still. She had the feeling that if she moved at all, he would think she was trying to slap him.

Eventually, he gave her his burned hand.

Truthfully, Irina had no idea exactly how bad it was. She had never treated a burn before. His hand had already been turning black well past the wrist, fading to the greyish-purple of a bruise halfway up his forearms. Away, at last, from the half-light of the forest, she could see the colour carried itself along his veins, like wisps of smoke in the wind. Apart from the colour, it looked and felt much like a normal hand, if a little cold. Scars made ridges across his knuckles. Two of his fingers were a little crooked. The lines on his palm deepened as he tried to curl his hand into a fist, then stopped. Irina had never learned how to read palms – her mother had said that was best left to witches – but she caught herself wondering which one was Stefan's lifeline, and how short it would be.

Then, at last, she noticed something she was actually looking for. The skin had broken in several places: his fingertips, the heel of his hand, and the top of the palm. Ridges of blackened skin peeled away in tiny rings, revealing flesh that oozed like rotten fruit. Irina fought to keep the disgust from showing on her face. At least it didn't smell.

'Let's look for some water,' she said, glancing around the field of flowers. 'There has to be some, somewhere.' Cold curiosity seeped through her thoughts like melting snow. 'Can . . . do you heal? I'm sorry, I don't know how this works.'

When he spoke, his voice was shaky, small. 'Not the way you do.' He glanced at his hand and looked away, quickly. His throat worked. 'It won't heal on its own. I need to eat.'

Relief dawned like a sunrise. She could fix it. Irina took off Catalina's necklace and unfastened the beaded choker, winding both carefully around one hand. 'Go on, then.'

He didn't move. He was watching her smooth her dark braid over one shoulder, looking utterly lost. His body was twisted towards the gate at his back, hesitant.

'Aren't you hungry?' Irina prompted.

'How can you . . .' He stopped, ran his uninjured hand through his hair. 'That's what got me in this mess,' he hissed, waving his burned hand at her. 'How can you ask me that, now? I'm not good enough. I'm a sinner. I—'

'I don't think that's true,' Irina said.

Shock flashed across his face. 'What?'

She shrugged. 'Think about it,' she said. 'There's a Hell, here. Or a Tartarus. I really should've asked that doctor to explain the difference – anyway. *That's* where the sinners go. Not here. If you were truly evil, you wouldn't have been able to get into this place at all.'

'You . . . you don't think I'm . . .'

'I think you've done bad things,' she said. 'You said so yourself. I'm not sure if that makes you a bad person. Maybe that place,' she said, nodding to the sheet of light that split the field in two, 'is just for people who were really perfect. You know. Saints.' She gave him a small smile. 'They probably don't get to have any fun at all.'

Stefan's eyes were wide. For the first time, she realized that they were not black, but very dark brown, the colour of a rich tisane. They were fixed on her, filled with an expression she could not place. Shock, anger, hope or pain, she had no idea how to read him. But as soon as she had seen it, he folded the expression away, schooling his features into something even less open. Irina was filled with a sudden sense of unease. She had seen something she shouldn't, and she had no idea what it was.

'I suppose they don't,' he said.

Irina cleared her throat. 'So, should I put my jewellery back on, or . . .'

'Oh! No. Not yet.'

She turned her head aside as he drew closer. It felt strange to look him in the eye, as he was opening his mouth and showing those pointed teeth. It would be stranger still to meet his gaze after she'd glimpsed his turmoil. It wasn't hers to see.

Cold fingers touched her shoulder. She flinched. 'Sorry,' she muttered. 'Cold hands.'

He gave her an apologetic smile. 'I can't do anything about that, I'm afraid. But I don't have to bite you.'

'You *do*. You need both your hands. Just do it. I'll be fine.'

Teeth sank into her neck. Irina clamped her mouth shut at once, strangling the whimper at the back of her throat. His teeth were sharp. When the pain faded, the tug of blood being drawn from her veins grew. With her head tilted to one side, and something tugging at her throat, she felt like her neck was in a noose. When he was done, she straightened up, and the motion sent a wave of dizziness right through her. She clapped a hand over her bleeding neck, trying to blink her vision back to some semblance of order. Stefan, however, was staring at his hand. He held it up, and Irina saw the skin of his palm knit itself back together. It moved like worms wriggling through the soil, and Irina's stomach heaved.

'I think I need to lie down.'

'Wait until it stops bleeding,' he said. 'You don't want any more of those flowers.'

She nodded. It made her feel sick. Still keeping her hand clapped over the wound, she brought her bandaged wrist to her mouth and worried at the knot with her teeth until the handkerchief came loose, then pressed the cloth to her neck. It helped. Without the slick feel of blood underneath her fingers, it was a lot easier to ignore the rising tide of nausea.

Irina waited. Her limbs were heavy, her eyelids drooping. She felt utterly empty. When had she last slept? She wasn't sure. In the land of the living, she'd waited up for Stefan. In the land of the dead, she had no idea how much time had passed. Had she spent days forcing herself through all those gates, or merely hours? Either way, it was catching up to her. All she wanted was sleep.

'I'm going to lie down,' she mumbled. 'If something happens, fix it.'

'Fix it? You can't just—'

But she was already asleep.

Irina ached all over when she woke up, and in her opinion, that was profoundly unfair. She had slept, hadn't she? It ought to have made a difference. But her stomach was still rumbling, her arms and legs were sore and her neck was throbbing. Perhaps a few more moments of keeping her eyes blissfully closed would help. She stretched, straightening her arms – and felt something tug on her left wrist. Her eyes flew open. Her arm was completely overgrown with vines, the purple flowers around it stained red. Fear flooded through her. She tried to sit up. Pressure cut across her throat; they'd grown around her neck, too. They were not squirming for the open wounds, as they had done in the great grass fields. Instead the vines had gently and firmly grown over the scraps of bloody cloth at her wrists and neck, holding her in place.

'Stefan?' she whispered.

Swearing, from somewhere over her shoulder. Then, an explosion of rustling as he lunged towards her. When his face finally came into view, it was lit with panic.

'I'm so sorry,' he said, scrabbling at the roots closest to her neck, 'I was looking at the forest, I thought you wouldn't want me to watch you sleep . . .'

He tore away a handful of vines. Irina sat up at once, yanking at the vines around her wrist with her free hand. The moment she was free, she sprang to her feet. Everything spun. Stefan jumped up beside her, steering her away from the vines. They moved like earthworms in turned-over soil.

'I'm sorry. You're not hurt?'

Her heart was hammering and the world was still lurching slightly, but the vines had not actually hurt her. Her makeshift bandages were still in place. Irina staggered backwards. She'd left an impression in the flowers, a depression curled up on its side in the position that she slept in. But under the imprint of her head and at the tip of the shadow of her arm, all the flowers had turned red.

'Let's get out of here.' Her mouth was so dry it came out like a wheeze. She cleared her throat. 'Sorry,' she rasped, 'thirsty.'

He looked alarmed. 'Were they choking you?'

'Let's just go.'

He stared at the dark shape of the forest encircling the field. Irina could not take her eyes off the impression she'd left in the grass. The red flowers blooming in the shadowy shapes of her own neck and wrist made her think of a winding-sheet wrapped around a corpse, with everything bleeding through. A wave of dizziness washed over her. She blinked it away, desperate for a sip of water. 'Shall we carry on down the path?'

'I'm not sure what else we'd do,' he said, placing a steadying hand on her elbow. He led her a few steps away, glancing back at the still-stirring vines. 'I . . . I really am sorry. I thought I heard something in the woods, so I wasn't paying attention, and I didn't want to stare at you while you were sleeping, and . . .'

He trailed off. Twisted half-away from her, shoulders high, he seemed already braced for a blow. His eyes were fixed on his now-unburnt hand.

'What did you hear?' she asked.

'Rustling, I think? But it sounded like it was coming from

further away, not from those vines.' He still wouldn't look at her. 'We can stay here a little longer if you want to get your breath back.'

'No,' Irina said, her hand flying to her throat. The necklace was still there. When she checked it, it pointed to the forest across the field, but as she turned to look over her shoulder at the glowing sheet of light, it writhed in all directions, thrashing and spinning. 'We should get away from that gate. I don't think the necklace works around it.'

'All right,' he said, setting off for the forest. 'We should try and find some people, as well.'

'Is that a good idea?' she asked, following him.

'All we know about this place is that Doctor Emil told us it has five rivers,' he said, as they approached the dark edge of the woods. Not that it truly looked like woods next to the blinding light of the gate; Irina knew that the trees were hidden in the shadows, but all she could see was a smear of darkness across the path. 'We've already crossed one of them, obviously, but we've got no idea where we are in relation to it now, or those guardians, or your sister.'

'We've got the necklace.'

'And we're just running around, following wherever it points us,' Stefan continued. 'If it's even pointing us in the right direction. We should try and find someone who knows more about how this place is put together. Like that doctor. He liked you, he'll explain things.'

'How much do you think he knows, though?' Irina asked, scanning the darkness. 'I don't think I've ever heard a story which maps out the land of the dead. Is that even possible?'

'I'm not sure,' Stefan said. 'How would you begin to map a place like this? That village full of children seemed to span for miles until we found the door leading us here, and there's no sign of the village in this forest now. I think it's more like ripping up a bunch of maps and stitching the pieces together. The only way we'll make sense of it is if we ask someone.'

Irina could see the sense in that. There was no real direction to their journey, except the one the necklace pointed out. If they had some idea of what lay ahead, they could plan for it. But after watching measles blossoming across a dead child's skin, and frostbite withering a dead man's face, she had no desire to seek anyone out but Catalina.

'If we're going to find people,' she said, hurrying to keep up, 'then I'm going to need some gloves.'

She expected him to argue. He was, she had noticed, very good at that. Instead he nodded, and kept walking towards the pool of shadows that concealed the trees. 'Then we'll find you some.'

Now, they stood at the edge of the darkness. The slightest rustle sent a jolt of nerves through her; she kept looking around, convinced she'd see vines snaking towards her ankles. Irina squinted, and saw nothing. Her stomach rumbled.

'You're sure you don't want to retrace our steps?' he asked, as she strode into the darkness of the woods. 'The only people we've seen on this side of the gate are those children.'

'I don't want to double back on ourselves. Besides, do you really want to go back the way we came?' she asked, putting her hands out in front of her like a sleepwalker. 'With all those creepy animals? I know you want to find people to help us, but those children can't answer our questions. We need real adults.'

They were deep enough into the darkness that she could no longer see even the vague outline of her hands in front of her face. Stefan's cold fingers gripped her shoulder; she nearly yelped, it was so unexpected. 'And you're going to find these real adults by charging off into the woods, are you?'

Irina shrugged. 'We don't have a map. How else are we going to do it?'

There was a moment of silence. Then, he swore. Irina grinned. She always loved knowing she was right.

They stumbled forwards, unseeing. Their footsteps rang through the darkness. Slowly, the sound began to soften, the echoes swallowed as the ground grew softer and the trees closed in.

'You're really sure about not going back there?' he asked, his voice quiet. 'I'll wait, if you want to check the Elysian Fields for your sister.'

'I don't think she's there,' Irina said. 'The necklace is pointing us away from the gate now – and it wasn't really pointing us towards the gate anyway, it was just shaking. I'm not sure if I want us to try and get into somewhere that isn't actually going to help us find her.'

'*Us?*' he muttered.

She ignored him and kept walking. Stefan fell into step beside her, finally taking his icy hand off her shoulder.

'It . . . it hurt, just to get close to the gate,' he said. 'Touching it was . . .' He cleared his throat. 'Is that what it's like for you, when you cross over?'

Irina nodded. Too late, she realized that he probably couldn't see her. 'Did it start with a headache that got worse as you came nearer? And then your whole body started aching and it felt like you might throw up?'

There was a pause. 'Something like that,' he muttered. 'That's really all you felt?'

Irina let out a hollow laugh. There was a faint glimmer of green ahead; another luminescent mushroom, growing from a tree. Relief flooded through her; she'd missed the light. 'Oh, no. That's just the start of it. When I went through the blue gate, I felt like I was being set on fire.'

'And you still wanted to go through that other one?'

'I didn't want to. I had to.'

'But—'

Irina cut him off. 'Let's not have this conversation again. I know you don't think I should go after her, but I'm going to, so you may as well get used to it.'

'But it hurts you.'

She shrugged. 'She's family. Anyone else would do the same if they were in my position.'

He fell silent. They passed a smattering of glowing green mushrooms clinging to the base of a tree. Further ahead was another cluster, and another. Pinpricks of green and pink light were strewn through the darkness, as if someone had thrown them through the trees in the same way that Irina threw corn to the chickens.

She picked her way along the path, her eyes slowly adjusting. After so long in darkness, the gentle spots of glowing pink and green were almost blinding. The mushrooms were beautiful in a way she had not appreciated, stomping moodily down a similar path hours before. They sat in frills along the roots of trees, or rose against the trunks like enormous fans. Dappled pink and green light was cast across their faces from below. Pass one group, and Stefan would look sickly and pale; pass another, and the light would give him an unnatural blush. The ridges of their footprints from earlier stood out sharp against the path, casting deep shadows ahead. Stefan seemed to want to say something to her. He kept glancing at her, half-opening his mouth. But then he always looked away.

Eventually, Irina got bored. 'Why mushrooms?' she asked.

'I'm sorry?'

She waved a hand at the trees around them. The glowing mushrooms had multiplied as they walked, climbing up the trees until the tallest ones sprouted well above their heads. A fine layer of glowing spores dusted the edges of the path. 'Don't you wonder why there's so many of them?'

Stefan peered at the nearest tree. 'I suppose they might do something. It could just be that we're in a cave, though.'

'We're in a forest, Stefan.'

'Yes, but the forest is *in* the cave. Don't tell me you've forgotten how we got in.'

'But this is clearly a forest.'

'We're in a cave! Just because—'

Irina pointed to a tree. The rest of his sentence was lost in a groan of frustration.

'I don't know if this place works like that,' Irina mused. 'We know there's three different areas, and those rivers, but . . .' she sighed. 'It's like you were saying earlier, about ripping up maps and stitching them together. They don't seem to fit together like places in the real world, you know? We dug a hole and ended up falling from the sky. It's not put together in the way that normal places are.'

'So what you're saying is that we *could* still be in the cave.'

Irina opened her mouth to argue, then saw that he was grinning. She pulled a face at him instead.

'It is strange, though,' he murmured, his grin fading as his face turned thoughtful. 'There's so many different places, all strung together. I was always taught it was just Heaven and Hell. But here there's so many different pockets.'

Irina shrugged. 'I was, too, but I think that part makes sense. Different people believe different things, but if they all end up in the same place . . .'

'Don't let Father Simeon hear you say that,' he said, smiling.

'Did you know him?'

The question had slipped out before she meant it to. The

moment she asked, Stefan's face closed off. All the ease was buttoned back into place, leaving his face carefully blank.

'Yes,' he said, his voice toneless. 'I knew everyone in the village.'

Taken aback, Irina blurted out the first thing that came into her head. 'They don't talk about you. Not . . . not about how you were, before.'

Stefan nodded slowly. He was staring straight ahead. The pink and green light cast strange shapes across his face. Whichever way the shadows fell, the blood around his mouth looked black. There was nothing in his expression that she could read.

'No,' he said, his every word measured. 'I suppose they would not.'

They walked for a long time. Glowing mushrooms overshadowed them, covering everything in a fine haze of luminescent spores. The closer they grew to the path, the more colours Irina saw, pinks and greens blending into peachy orange and soft lilac. Just as the light had grown almost blinding, it began to fade. The mushrooms shrank, the trees grew thinner. Only this time, instead of walking into darkness, they saw a yellow glow between the leaves, and heard a snatch of voices.

They stopped before the edge of the trees, listening, but could not make out the conversation. Irina adjusted her bridal crown, shook the glowing spores out of the folds of her clothes, and repositioned her choker so it covered the wounds on her neck. She started forwards, but Stefan held her back.

'Wait. They could be dangerous.'

'Everyone here could be dangerous if I touch them,' Irina replied. 'Besides, aren't we looking for people?'

Stefan looked annoyed but didn't argue. 'Just remember to stay out of their way.'

'I was *going* to,' she muttered. 'Give me your arm.'

'What? Why?'

'We're supposed to be newlyweds, aren't we?' she said, threading her arm through his. 'We'd better act like it.'

In the shadow of the trees, he pulled a face at her. Then it was smoothed away, and the two of them stepped out of the shadowy haze of the forest, arm in arm.

The first thing Irina noticed was the fire, right in the centre of the clearing. It was a small, neatly constructed thing, but something about the flames did not look right. Hanging from a tripod over the fire was an iron pot, swinging on its hook and bubbling. Irina's stomach growled. Surrounding the campfire were a couple of well-constructed shelters, each large enough for two men to sleep in. One was a cone of branches tied at the top with twine and covered with moss. The other was a lean-to of leaves and vines propped up with sturdy branches. A small group of men were sitting around the fire, laughing and passing a bottle between them. One of them was strumming a cobza, another was messing around with a set of pipes. Unfamiliar stars shone over their heads. Irina glanced up and, for a moment, she could have sworn she saw them suddenly settle into place.

The men looked up when they approached, smiling. The piper shoved his pipes away, looking a little embarrassed. One of them threw something into the iron pot; Irina caught a whiff of rosemary. Her mouth began to water.

'Good . . . evening?' Irina asked, glancing up at the sky. It was a rich, dark blue, and once again, the stars seemed to still when she looked at them. 'Or is it morning?'

One of the men shrugged. Around forty, with a thick, dark beard, he reminded Irina a little of her father. 'We're not sure. It's been like this for a while.'

Stefan craned his neck to look. 'No sun or moon, either. How long have you been here?' he asked, frowning.

The man shrugged. He didn't look particularly concerned. Nor did his companions. The cook turned his attention back to the pot; the cobza player and the piper shuffled a little closer together and began talking in low voices.

'You must have some idea—'

'What my husband means to say,' Irina said, cutting across Stefan before he could get started, 'is that it's nice to meet you, whatever time of day it is. I'm Irina; this is Stefan.'

The man chuckled. 'Radu,' he said. 'That's Teodor at the pot, Alexandru and Constantin are the musicians. You're lost, I take it.'

Irina stared at him. 'How did you know?'

'You have that look about you,' Radu said, pushing Alexandru with his foot until the younger man moved to make space for Irina and Stefan to sit by the fire. 'You're neither of you hunters, are you?'

Irina and Stefan exchanged glances. They sat. Stefan put an arm around Irina and pulled her into his side, looking warily around the circle. Radu snorted. Stefan ground his teeth.

'Thank you,' Irina said quickly. 'It's kind of you to make room for us. You're right, we aren't hunters. I take it you are?'

The men nodded. She could have guessed as much. They were dressed practically, the sleeves of their linen shirts rolled up, wide leather belts around their waists carrying every tool imaginable. Their shelters were clearly made of what they could find or carry, and blended into the grey-green palette of the dark forest. There were bows and arrows around the camp, nets, shovels, a stick on which to tie down deer and carry them back home. But the more she looked, the more Irina realized that there was no evidence of any animals. No skins. No antlers. No meat, except for whatever was bubbling in the pot.

'Is there much hunting to be had here?' she asked, curious.

'Ah,' said Radu, his eyes gleaming, 'so you haven't seen it.'

'Seen what?'

The musicians smiled at each other. 'The beast,' Radu said, leaning forward eagerly. 'It's enormous. I thought at first it might be a large wolf, but it's stranger than anything I've ever seen. Three heads, each one with teeth longer than the last, but covered in scales rather than fur. Its front paws are massive, as big as your torso, easily. But its back half doesn't have any limbs at all – just the tail of a snake. You'd be terrified if you saw it, but it can't have been in your part of the forest,' he said, nodding to the trees behind them. 'It cuts a swathe through everything it passes. You see that pile of firewood, just beside you?'

Irina nodded.

'That was once the tallest tree in the forest,' Radu said, 'but the beast slithered past, and with a brush of its tail . . .' He swiped his arm out to the side in a chopping motion, smacking into Teodor's arm. Stew splattered into the fire as Teodor dropped the spoon into the flames.

'Mind the stew!' he snapped.

The musicians exchanged a look and sniggered. Chastened, Radu cleared his throat. 'Sorry, Teodor.'

'It smells lovely,' Irina said.

Teodor smiled at her. 'Thank you, dear.' He turned to Radu and his smile sharpened. 'At least *someone* appreciates it.'

Radu tugged his beard. 'I do appreciate it! I just didn't realize your arm was there.'

'It sounds like you know the forest well,' Irina interrupted. 'Do you know the way through the woods? I'm looking for my little sister, I think she may have passed through here.'

A Steep and Savage Path

Radu was still pleading his case. 'I'm sorry, you *know* I wave my arms around when I talk – what was that? Oh. Oh, yes, we know our way around. I've not seen a little girl, though. Just as well, with that beast wandering about.'

'It's part of how we find each other,' said Teodor, his face softening as he looked at Radu. 'People tend to find each other here.'

'What do you mean?'

Teodor peered into the pot. He scooped out a piece of meat with a wooden spoon and poked it with the tip of a wickedly sharp knife that had been tied to his belt. 'Not done yet,' he muttered, dropping the meat back into the pot. Irina watched it disappear back into the stew, her mouth watering. She was half-tempted to lunge forward and yank it out of the stew with her bare hands, she was so hungry.

Teodor tapped his spoon on the side of the pot, flicking the sauce off. Irina jumped. 'How much of this place have you seen?' he asked.

'A little,' she replied, trying to keep her voice light. Did the dead usually travel through the underworld? She decided to err on the side of caution. 'I haven't travelled much.'

'But you've seen enough of this place to note how different it is,' said Teodor, pointing at her with his spoon. 'You saw the river and the cave before you landed in the woods, at least?'

She nodded.

'Those are the only two things everyone here sees,' said Teodor, reaching for a potato from a pile of vegetables that Irina was sure had not been beside him moments before. 'You go through the gate, the same as everyone else. But we all come out in different places, depending on what you want to find. For us, it was the forest. But if you keep going that way,' he said, pointing off into the trees, 'you'll reach a town the size of Brașov, and if you head that way,' he said, pointing over their heads, 'you'll come to three villages in a row. Every single one of them is filled with people who've never seen between these trees.'

Irina leaned forward. 'But why? Aren't they curious?'

Radu laughed. 'Most people aren't. Well, not curious enough to risk running into the beast, or whatever else might be lurking in the woods.'

'We prefer it that way,' said Teodor, grinning at her. 'It took me a long time to perfect my lurking.'

Stefan had gone still beside her, his hand clutching one of her shoulders like a vice. She ignored him. 'What else is beyond the forest? I heard there were some more rivers?'

Radu leaned back against a log that Irina could not remember seeing behind him, stretching his feet to the fire. 'I imagine there would be. There must be fishermen here, they would want a river or two. There's every sort of place for every sort of person,' he said. 'We only go so far, you understand. If we need anything from town, we can get it, but the real sport is in the forest. Everything we want is right here – unless we want to go to town, and then it is there. Why would we go further?'

'I don't understand.'

'You really haven't travelled, have you?' he said, amused. 'You'll realize how it works the more time you spend here. It isn't like how it was before. You'll find what you're looking for much more easily – or it will find you. You don't need to search for the things you want. If you decide you want to go somewhere, then you'll be there before you know it. You'll see. Your sister will turn up in no time.'

Teodor sliced off a coil of peel and split his potato into quarters, dropping the pieces into the pot. 'Just give her a map, Radu.'

With a sigh, Radu sat up. He leaned forward, brushing some

of the debris away from the forest floor, and sketched a rough map into the dirt with his fingers. Three small crosses sat close to a wiggly line. Some distance away, a larger cross. Beyond that, another wiggly line, but this one drawn with two fingers zig-zagging across to thicken it.

Radu flicked the dirt off his hands – 'Radu! Mind the pot!' – and pointed to the thin wiggly line. 'That's the edge of the forest,' he said. 'We're not far from it – if you move that rock a little to the left, that's us. These,' he said, pointing to the row of three small crosses, 'are the three villages. You'll find most things you need there. This larger cross is the town, and if you can't find what you need in the villages, you'll find it there.'

'Is there a market?' Irina asked.

'In a sense,' said Radu. 'You don't need money. Whatever you do, don't go here,' he said, pointing to the thick line.

'Why?'

'It's the Grey River,' he said, 'like the one before the gate. It can be crossed, but you should not try. Did you see what the Blue River could do?'

Irina shook her head.

'Its water forges unbreakable bonds,' Radu said. 'Swear an oath with that water – well, it's not really water, I suppose – and you won't be able to break your promise. The Grey River is similar. Its water isn't really water, either. It is sorrow.'

His words sparked something in Irina's memory. Hadn't Doctor Emil said something about a river of sadness? What would that even look like? 'I . . . what? How?'

Radu shrugged. 'I don't know *how*, I only know that you should not go there, no matter what anyone tells you about the dance.'

'What dance?'

Teodor groaned. 'You are hopeless,' he said, throwing a

potato at Radu. 'If you didn't want her to go, you shouldn't have told her.'

'What dance?' Irina asked. Radu clamped his mouth shut, looking panicked. Irina turned to Teodor instead. 'What dance?'

'Apparently there's a dance on the other side of the river,' said Teodor, glaring at Radu over the bubbling stew. 'People from the town go sometimes. But it isn't much to talk about, dear,' he said, turning back to Irina. 'I've not met anyone who's ever been – a few who've gone, of course, but none of them are back yet. It doesn't sound like much of an evening. It's called the Totentanz, though I can't imagine why.'

Irina froze. Teodor went on peeling potatoes and flinging them into the stew. Radu scuffed over the map, looking embarrassed. On the other side of the fire, Alexandru and Constantin started playing again, pausing to whisper to each other every so often. Irina's own heartbeat was so loud that she was sure it had an echo to it. She could feel her pulse twitching in her neck. Hands shaking, she pulled her plait in front of it, praying it could not be seen.

Irina had grown up knowing about the Totentanz. Everyone did. It was painted in frescoes in the village church, on the walls of the monasteries in Bucovina. Woodcuts were printed of it in cheap pamphlets; she'd used them for kindling once she'd read the news of the French king's downfall, the Ottoman janissaries rebelling against their sultan, or the Russian tsar deposing his father. A few times, a group of travelling players had acted it out for them in the village. The dance with death had woven through her childhood nightmares the moment she had seen the frescoes of all those skeletons taking the hands of priests, noblewomen, peasants and kings. There was no way that Teodor and the other hunters could not know what it was.

A Steep and Savage Path

Did they know that they were dead?

Irina wracked her brains. They had to know. Doctor Emil had spoken about the underworld with a kind of frank excitement that made the fact that he was dead seem like an intellectual exercise. The old man with frostbite had all but asked them how she and Stefan had died. She'd seen people on the riverbanks with clothes black with blood. Surely they remembered how it had got there. She and Stefan were both spattered with blood, too, and nobody had said a thing. If they didn't know they were dead, surely they would've said something. Irina certainly would've done, if she'd seen someone stumble into a forest clearing with bloodstains spilling down their front like wine.

But Teodor could not imagine why a dance in the land of the dead might be called the Totentanz. Radu knew that he was a hunter, but there were no carcasses in sight. None of them seemed to question why they did not need money at the market, or wonder why they had not seen the sun. And though everyone who had gone through the gate had seen their life flash before their eyes, still dressed in the clothes they had died in, now there were no more bloodstained people to be seen, and she'd heard no one speak about death since she passed through the gate.

Irina tried to nudge Stefan, but he was holding onto her so tightly that she couldn't get the elbow room. His face was completely blank, but his eyes were darting between the men around the campfire, fast as flies. Had he realized the same thing she had? Irina flicked his leg to get his attention, and he flinched. Clearly not, she thought.

'Your shelters are very good,' she said, casting around for a question that wasn't 'Do you know you are dead?' and settling on that. 'How long did they take you to put up?'

'Oh, that's all Radu's work,' said Teodor, smiling fondly at the other man across the fire. 'He's good with his hands.'

One of the musicians sniggered and Radu blushed. Stefan shifted beside her, still holding on tight. Ignoring all of this, Irina turned back to Radu. 'It must've been a lot of work. How long did it take you?'

'Oh, not that long,' he said, waving away the question. 'I've been doing it all my life. You get used to it.'

Curious, she pushed a little further. 'Days? Weeks?'

Radu frowned. He tugged on his beard, confusion deepening in every line on his face. 'I . . . I'm not sure.'

'Perhaps they were here when you arrived. How . . . how did you arrive?'

The confusion cleared. 'I crossed the Blue River and came through the gate, just as you did.'

Irina hesitated. Stefan was stock-still beside her. She could not tell if that meant he wanted her to keep pushing, or to drop the conversation entirely. Then she decided it didn't matter. She wanted to know.

'I actually meant . . . before that.'

The music stopped. The fire stopped crackling. The pot stopped bubbling. Silence strangled them all like a choking hand. Radu's frown changed. Worried lines appeared between his eyes. Shadows curled around the edges of the circle of firelight, the sharp lines of the shelters deepening, darkening, until they looked like something that could draw blood.

And then, like a distant whisper, Irina heard something, from deep in the woods.

Rustling.

The hunters jolted out of their reverie. Radu's head snapped around to the source of the noise, his eyes gleaming. 'There,' he said, 'in the woods.'

A Steep and Savage Path

Sound rushed in. Bubbling stew, crackling fire, and the clatter of men reaching for their weapons. Now that the flames were moving again, Irina realized what was wrong with them; they all moved in exactly the same way, swaying and snapping in unison like reflections caught between two mirrors.

Alexandru dropped the cobza and darted into one of the shelters. 'So close to camp!' he called, coming back with a coil of rope over his shoulder.

Teodor was scanning the trees. 'You'd better go. The sound came from there,' he said, pointing down the path that led to the forest of glowing mushrooms. 'Head in the opposite direction.'

'But what about you?' Irina asked.

'Bless you for asking! We'll be fine. Nothing bad has ever happened hunting here – oh, Irina, you've dropped your handkerchief,' said Teodor.

The bloody piece of handkerchief that had been tied around her wrist had come loose, fluttering to the forest floor. Red peonies were already beginning to bloom where the bloody cloth touched the soil, but slowly, lazily. Irina frowned, curious – was it only fresh blood which sent the flowers springing up, snatching at her arms and legs? – and saw Teodor's hand pick it up, and freeze.

Panic struck Irina like lightning. He looked the same: there was no blood blossoming on the front of his shirt, or flesh withering off his bones. But something in his face had changed. Eyes wide, mouth slack, he looked as if something had been torn from him in one vicious swipe.

'Radu,' he muttered, and the horror in his voice hit Irina like a crossbow bolt, 'are we . . .'

'Lovely to meet you all!' Stefan said again, snatching the handkerchief out of Teodor's fingers. Grabbing Irina by the hand, Stefan dragged her off into the trees, towards the three villages Radu had marked on his crude map. He marched through the woods, squeezing her fingers tight enough that she started to lose feeling in them.

'Stefan! Let go!'

He glanced over his shoulder. 'Not here,' he mouthed. 'Too close to the hunt.'

Ducking under branches and stumbling through bracken, they pushed their way through the trees. When the sounds of the camp had faded and there was no more orange light flickering through the trees, Stefan stopped, his jaw set. Irina leaned against a pine tree, rubbing a stitch in her side. Her stomach growled.

Stefan jabbed a finger back towards the clearing. 'What did you say to him?'

'Shouldn't we keep moving? What about that beast?'

He scoffed. 'That was all talk. Now, what did you say to him?'

'Teodor? I dropped my – wait,' she said, confusion catching up to her before her temper carried her away. 'You were right next to me. You heard what I said.'

'That doesn't matter,' he said, avoiding her eyes.

'Yes, it does,' Irina countered. 'Something wasn't right, back there. Didn't you notice?'

He looked away, rubbing the back of his neck.

'I thought you saw it too,' Irina pushed, watching him closely. The more she looked, the stiller his face became. 'You froze. Your fingers were digging into my shoulder – I'm going to have a bruise there, by the way. I know you realized something.'

'It's nothing. And anyway, we're talking about what *you* did back there.'

Irina folded her arms. 'No, we aren't. Not until you tell me what made you freeze up like that.'

Suddenly, he was close. Inches away, fists clenched, she could almost feel, rather than hear, the growl building in his chest. Her eyes were level with his glistening teeth. 'You do not give me orders.'

Irina put her hands on her hips. 'Or what?'

He faltered. 'Well . . . or I bite you.'

'You're doing that anyway,' she snapped. 'And you're doing it with my permission, which I can withdraw at any time. Don't forget that.'

'I don't need your permission,' he hissed, reaching for her throat.

She knocked his hand away. 'Yes, you do. You don't get to walk all over me just because of the bargain we made. Back out if you want, but if you do, I'll go back to the land of the living without you.'

It wasn't a smile on his face. He was baring his teeth. 'You make a lot of threats.'

'So do *you*.'

'I could snap your neck right—'

Irina waved it away. 'Yes, yes, you're very scary. But you've spent a lot of time telling me that you're cruel, Stefan, and not a lot of time acting that way. You think I didn't see you letting that baby climb all over your lap, or carrying me when I couldn't walk? You aren't cruel, and you aren't going to kill me. You can't get back without me. Are you cold? Yes. But that's not the same thing as being deliberately, maliciously cruel, and I think you know that. So stop pretending you're about to tear my skin off and tell me what you saw.'

He stopped. Lips slightly parted, face full of shock and confusion, he seemed to have no idea what to do with his hands. They were frozen in the act of reaching for her, blackened fingers suddenly soft in the wake of what she had said. Before, he'd held them curved like the talons of a bird of prey, but now all the menace had slid away, like water dripping from the tips of his fingers.

'You . . . you aren't scared of me?'

Irina rolled her eyes. 'Stop trying to dodge the question. I know what you're doing.'

Stefan shuffled back. He looked away, running a hand through his hair.

'They were—' He stopped, fussing with the collar of his shirt. 'Those men. They—' He stopped again, smoothing down his bloodstained linen with a blackening hand. 'They were . . . together, weren't they?'

Thrown, Irina struggled to understand what he meant. 'Well, yes,' she said. 'They were cooking dinner.'

'That's not what I—' He still wouldn't look at her, speaking instead to the forest floor. 'Together in couples, I mean.'

'Oh.' Swiftly, Irina ran through her memory of the conversation between Radu and Teodor. Now that she thought about it, it sounded a lot like her parents arguing. 'Yes, I think they probably were.'

Stefan looked up at once. Suddenly, all his attention was fixed on her. Irina could feel it blistering. 'You don't mind?'

'Why would I? It's not my business.'

'So it's not a problem for you?'

Confused, Irina tried for a reassuring smile. She had no idea why he was asking her this, but it was clearly important to him. 'No,' she said, 'it doesn't bother me. They aren't the first couples like that I've met, actually. I worked in a household in Timişoara for a while where the widow next door had an understanding with the landlady, and they were – it doesn't matter. They were happy, that was the important thing.'

Stefan's face was a mask, but she could see the strings that held it in place. A muscle in his throat was working, and his eyes were darting across her face.

'Timişoara,' he said, his voice quiet.

She considered him for a moment. 'You know, that's not what I thought you were going to say at all. I thought you'd realized the same thing I had.'

He cleared his throat. 'What was that?'

'That they didn't know they were dead.'

'*What?*'

Irina threw up her hands. 'Why are you so surprised? You were there! You heard everything I said – you dragged me out of the clearing!'

'I was thinking about something else,' Stefan snapped. 'It was only Teodor's face that let me know you'd put your foot in it.'

'I dropped my handkerchief by accident, Stefan! It's not like I asked him how long he'd been dead. I'm not an idiot. I know you think I'm bad at this, but I'm not about to tap a stranger on the shoulder and ask them how they died.'

'You wouldn't *need* to ask, if you tapped them on the shoulder,' he snapped. 'They'd show you, right when their face melted off.'

She jabbed a finger at him. 'That was uncalled for.'

'It's—' He caught himself, closing his mouth with the expression of a man who had resentfully realized that he was being an idiot. He changed tack. 'Why would you ask something like that, anyway? I thought they knew. That professor certainly did.'

'That was before we went through the gate,' Irina said. 'Things could be different on the other side.'

As quickly as she could, she explained what she'd put together – the Totentanz, the lack of questions over their bloodstained clothes, Radu's blank look when she'd asked him where he'd been before he crossed the Blue River, the quiet terror that had crept across Teodor's face when he'd touched her bloodstained handkerchief. The more she talked, the graver Stefan's expression became.

'I think you might be right,' he said, when she had finished.

Irina could not hold back the urge to bask in her lovely smug glow. So she didn't, and smirked at him. 'What was that?'

He gave her a withering look. 'There is a *small* chance that you might possibly be onto something this time, instead of blindly crashing into things and hoping for the best. Doctor Emil seemed to know exactly what was going on, and so did that woman we met before him. You'd think they'd know why it was called the Totentanz if they remembered where they were. We'll need to be careful. Well, you will.'

'So will you, if we can't even talk about the fact that everyone here is dead!'

'Yes, but I can keep a secret and you seem to have a five-second grace period before blurting out whatever thought comes into your head.'

The sentence *it must be easy to keep a secret when nobody wants to speak to you* was already curling around Irina's tongue. She clamped her mouth shut before it could escape. If she said it, he'd be *right*. 'Look, we've got to get away from that beast. Are we going to these villages or not?' she snapped.

'Beast,' Stefan muttered, pinching the bridge of his nose. 'Honestly. You want to go to the villages? Fine. We'll go to the villages.'

'*You* were the one who said we should find some people! Where else are we going to—' Irina cut herself off, massaging her temples. Stefan liked to start fights, she had realized. Whether he was covering something up, enjoyed the back and forth of an argument, or had simply spent so long away from the living that he'd forgotten how to have a civil conversation, she wasn't sure. All she knew was that she was annoyed. Why did the dead have to be so irritating?

'Great,' she said, after a deep, deep breath. 'Let's go to the villages.'

She set off, heading in the direction that Radu had pointed out – or at least, as close as she could remember. Stefan fell into step beside her. Vast pines loomed over their heads, roots tangling under their feet. Sinuous ivy curled up the trunks. The forest floor felt springy underneath Irina's boots, but when she looked down, there was no carpet of pine needles softening the earth. She thought back to what the hunters had said: *people tend to find each other here.* And from what Radu had said, it seemed that people found the places that suited them best, too. Had the hunters living off the forest found a place where the cold earth was soft as a feather bed? She hoped so. They'd been kind. They hadn't deserved to be needled with endless questions until their faces went blank. Perhaps it was better that they didn't remember that they were dead. It couldn't be an easy thing to carry with them. Better, by far, to lay the burden down.

'Timişoara,' said Stefan thoughtfully.

Irina jolted out of her reverie. 'What?'

He flinched. 'Nothing.'

She stole a glance at him out of the corner of her eye. He was carefully not looking her way, his eyes fixed on a point in the middle distance, his mouth set in a tight line. Irina snorted. She wasn't sure if he could truly say that he was good at keeping a secret when it was so obvious that he had one to begin with.

'There was something else,' she said, as they kept walking. 'Back in the clearing, when it all went quiet, I heard something.'

'What was it?'

Irina shrugged. 'Rustling, I think? It could've been the wind, but . . . have you noticed any actual weather since we've been down here?'

There were no pine needles, twigs or grass under their feet. Without them, their footsteps sounded oddly soft, like they were brushing over cloth. It was so unlike the crackle and crunch of a real forest that Irina felt unsteady on her feet. If she closed her eyes, she could almost believe that she was walking across a linen sheet, stretched tight, and any minute now it was going to buckle and tear underneath her.

'No,' Stefan said slowly. 'No sun. No rain. No snow. No fog. I . . . I thought I saw some wind earlier. Up in the grasses.'

Irina nodded. 'I saw it too.' She remembered the way the grasses shook. They hadn't bent and swayed in a wide arc as a breeze tumbled across the plain. Instead, a swathe of them had juddered and twitched in a long line that headed straight for them. And, she realized, they had stayed flattened after they had stopped moving. A path had been carved through the grasses – one that led straight to them.

Irina's mouth went dry. At once, the soft sound of their footsteps was as loud as the gunshot crack of sheets of thawing ice. Her skirts brushed against her legs as she walked: flimsy, useless. She had nothing to keep her safe – nothing but a candle and a handful of coins. Her hands itched for something to hold – a knife, a rope, even a big stick would be better than her defenceless, empty palms. Why were they looking for gloves, when they should be looking for armour?

Stefan's voice was slow and measured. 'I think we're being—'

'Please don't say it,' Irina whispered.

They moved as quietly as they could, their strangely muffled footsteps the only sound. Irina could not help but wonder how far the noise would carry. She hadn't heard any more rustling.

Perhaps keeping quiet had paid off, and whatever had been following them had lost interest. Perhaps it had just been an animal – the hunters' improbable beast – straying too close to the campsite. Perhaps it had only been the wind.

She fiddled with the sleeves of her shirt, fighting the urge to look over her shoulder. She checked the necklace discreetly; it hung limp in her hand for a heart-stopping second, then lurched into life, pointing straight ahead. With no sign of the frenzied thrashing it had exhibited when it was brought close to the gate, Irina was comforted.

There was no change in the trees. Tall pine after tall pine, encircled with identical fans of bracken, Irina saw the same patterns in the moss, the same roots bubbling up under her feet. Her temper flared. She stopped in the middle of the path, folded her arms, and tried to resist the urge to stamp her foot.

'We're *lost*,' she hissed. 'Where are those villages?'

'How are we lost?' Stefan whispered. 'We've been going in a straight line!'

Irina glared at him. 'The wrong straight line, clearly. Can you remember the way back to the camp?'

Stefan shook his head. 'You can't be serious. We've been following your necklace, we can't be lost. Besides, we can't go back to a place where you revealed your secret in front of everybody—'

'I didn't do anything of the kind!'

'—and head straight back towards whatever is coming after us,' Stefan continued, remorseless. 'We just have to figure out where we are on the map. They said the villages weren't far.'

Irina snorted. 'Maybe for them. Don't they say that the dead travel fast?'

She was expecting a retort. Stefan certainly seemed to be gearing up for one; his mouth was already opening, and he looked irritated. But then, he stopped. 'You know,' he said, the annoyance smoothing itself away, 'you might be onto something there.'

Taken aback, Irina stood up a little straighter. 'I am? I – yes. Of course I am.'

He ignored her. 'Things work differently here,' he said, studying the trees around him carefully. 'We've had to pass through doors to different parts of the underworld. Maybe the dead don't. Those hunters said that people tend to find each other here – maybe it's only because they're dead that they can find what they're looking for so easily. Their souls are drawn to whatever they loved in life, but the living still have to search for it. The dead – well, the *true* dead – don't have that hunger. They can rest.'

Irina thought about it. He had said the word 'maybe' too many times for her to completely trust in his theory, but she had to admit that the idea had a certain amount of sense. The afterlife meant different things to different people. Different churches made different promises; different people had different ideas of what was diabolical and what was divine. It made sense that the land of the dead held many things, to satisfy the many people in it.

'So does that mean you can find your way around that easily?' she asked. 'Seeing as you're . . .'

'Dead?' he drawled, shooting her a sideways glance.

Irina blushed. 'Well, I didn't want to be blunt about it, but yes.'

'I'm as lost as you are,' he said, his voice careful. 'I might not make the dead wither when I touch them, but I don't think I'm dead enough to get any of the benefits of this place.'

Irina bit back the words *that can be arranged*; she didn't want to start another fight. 'And how do you explain the children?' she asked. 'They clearly didn't have everything they wanted, otherwise . . . otherwise they wouldn't have asked us to stay.'

Stefan thought for a moment. 'The guardians,' he mused, 'the children said the guardians came when their families arrived, and took them to meet them. Maybe that was just a safe place for the children to wait before their families die.'

Irina flinched. She'd seen the bloodstained clothes of the dead and watched their deaths blossom across their faces, but still, the reminder of it was like a slap. They'd seemed so full of life.

'Look,' he said, staring around at the forest, 'why don't we try spinning around three times and seeing if a gate makes itself known? It worked back there. It might work now.'

'All right,' Irina said. 'I suppose we don't have anything to lose.'

She spun on the spot, three times, and staggered sideways; her empty stomach was making her feel light-headed. Stefan sniggered.

'You did that on purpose,' she muttered.

'Yes. It was funny.'

Irina made a face at him and pulled Catalina's necklace over her head. Holding it between her finger and thumb, she glared at it rather than look at Stefan. It reared up in her hand, pointing them in the direction they'd been heading.

'Well, maybe we aren't lost after all,' she said, putting it back on.

The glee drained out of Stefan's face. 'Unless we end up back at . . .' He trailed off, clearly remembering the blinding white light and the sizzle of his own flesh. Pity fluttered through Irina's thoughts. Annoying he might be, but he didn't deserve that reminder.

She gave him a gentle nudge. 'We won't know unless we keep

going. Besides, that's not what Radu said was on the other side of the forest.'

'He could've been lying.'

'Why would he do that?' Irina asked, setting off in the same direction. A little unsteady on her feet, she noticed. Her stomach growled. She'd feel so much better if she could eat something.

Stefan fell into step beside her. 'I don't know. People lie all the time.'

'Well, yes,' Irina said, rubbing at a stitch in her side, 'about whether they like your new shirt, or who left the door to the chicken coop open. But not to two young people asking how to get out of the forest. That's different.'

He said nothing. Irina shot him a sideways glance. His jaw was set, every line of his body tight enough to snap. He was very carefully not looking at her. Irina considered him, studying his thin linen clothes, his bare feet. His shirt was poorly made, fraying at the hem, and plain. There was a split in the seam of his trousers, so that one leg was surrounded by loose panels of flapping linen all the way up to the knee. No shoes, no belt, no waistcoat. Not even pockets. They were underthings, really.

'What are you looking at?' he asked, his voice wary.

She blushed. 'Nothing.'

They kept walking in silence. Thirst made Irina drowsy, her tongue dusty and heavy in her mouth, but she barely registered it. Stefan's secrets cast a shadow over her thoughts, and the creeping sense that they were deeper and darker than she had suspected was crawling up her spine like a spider.

How, exactly, had he died? And when? No one in the village had said anything; by the time she arrived, they'd been too afraid to even speak his name. He was a young, strong man, with no wounds or signs of sickness. She'd thought that he'd died in the summer, his clothes were so flimsy, but now she wasn't sure. Had those been all he had?

She bit her lip, starting to feel queasy. His clothes were not the only sign that something had not been right when he was alive. From what she had heard, the dead only came back when they had died badly, whether that was from vengeance or from not being properly laid to rest, so the fact that he was here at all was proof enough that something terrible had happened. But it was the silences that worried her the most. He dragged them after him like manacles attached to his ankles, and when she strayed too close to certain topics, it was as if she could hear them clanking. Family. The village. Trust. He was so quick to snap back, always ready with a retort. So why did he fall silent, when his tongue was so sharp? And when he wasn't silent, the things he let slip were even more worrying. He expected the worst of her, and was startled when she did not behave like a monster. He'd begged her not to let him be dragged away and punished for his sins, but he'd never once disputed them. For a moment, back at the tapestry of light, he'd even seemed half-convinced that a child could have committed sins bad enough to condemn them to an eternity of pain and torture. How had he come to expect these things?

What had happened to him?

The more she thought about it, the more uneasy she felt. Asking him outright would do no good, she was sure. She had the vague sense that it would be rude to ask someone how they died, especially when it was likely a painful memory. It would feel like asking them what they wore to bed; it wasn't anyone's business but theirs. Besides, if she so much as looked like she wanted to ask a personal question, Stefan would probably sew his own mouth shut rather than answer. But something was wrong, and it was gnawing at her.

There was a dull whine in her ears and a pressure building behind her eyes. Irina kneaded her forehead as she walked. This was the last thing she needed. If she could only have a decent meal and a glass of cold water. But every step made her feel sick with worry, and she was so tired that her limbs felt like they had been coated in lead.

Realization struck like a bolt of lightning.

'Stefan,' she said, quietly. 'I think we're near another door.'

He stopped at once. They were still in the forest. Pine trees towered over their heads, stretching out for miles in all directions. There was nothing she could see between the trunks but swathes of bracken, low-hanging branches and the endless roll of the forest floor. But the headache was there, buzzing at the back of her skull like a trapped fly.

'I don't see anything,' he murmured.

'Turn around three times. Maybe that'll—'

He rolled his eyes. 'I'm not falling for that.'

Irina took a tentative step forward. It jolted through her. 'Fine,' she said, through gritted teeth. She placed a hand on his shoulder. 'Stay still.'

'What are you—'

Irina ignored him and began to turn on the spot, propelling herself off Stefan's shoulder as bile bubbled up in the back of her throat. She staggered to a halt, one hand clapped over her mouth, and saw it.

There was no blinding light this time – evidently this door did not lead to a different domain in the underworld. A slice of the forest had been torn away between two tall pines. On either side, the browns and greens of the forest rolled off into the distance. But between them was a wide track under a clear blue sky, cutting through sloping green fields. A small clutch of white houses sat at the other end of the path, their high thatched roofs coming down to the top of the window frames. Irina couldn't see anyone else on the path. There was no smoke coming from the chimneys. There were no cows grazing in the fields, or chickens scratching in the dirt. She might as well have been stepping into a painting.

'All right. Fine.'

Stefan spun on the spot three times. When he stopped, he almost looked surprised to see the slice of road between the trees. He glanced at Irina, who was hunched over with her hands on her thighs, breathing hard.

'I thought you were making it up.'

Irina shook her head. She eased herself upright and checked the necklace. It pointed her down the path, as she had known it would. She groaned. 'I hate these things.'

Stefan strode towards the door. 'Come on,' he called over his shoulder. 'Let's get it over and done with.'

Irina shuffled after him. Her empty stomach was making everything worse. Every step made her feel queasier. Her brain felt like it was rattling loose inside her skull. The taste of blood burned in her mouth. By the time she was close enough to touch the door, pain was throbbing through her like a heartbeat and she was trying not to cry.

'What are you—' He stopped mid-sentence, his head half-cocked.

'What is it?'

But now, Irina could hear it too. A slow, stealthy sound, like a knife ripping through cloth – almost like rustling.

Fear jolted through her. She scrambled for the nearest tree, but the branches were too high to reach. The presence of the door throbbed at her back like an open wound. It didn't stop Stefan. He had scrambled up the trunk while she was still scrabbling for a hold. He peered down at her, eyes wide.

'What are you doing?' he hissed. 'Get up!'

The closest branch was a foot over her head. Irina jumped; her fingers barely brushed the bark. She landed with a *crash*. There was a moment of silence, the ripping noise gone. Then it started, louder than before, slicing towards her.

It had heard her.

Stefan dropped out of the tree. Without a word, he grabbed her around the thighs and hoisted her up. Irina snatched hold of the branch, hauling herself towards it. Stefan let go. Her legs swung in the air as she clung to the branch. Kicking frantically, her grip beginning to slip, Irina felt a hand on her shoulder. Stefan, already halfway up the tree, was hauling her onto the branch, one hand pressed flat against the trunk. He dragged her up into the higher branches, and soon they were both clinging to the trunk and staring at the forest floor, many feet below.

They waited. Irina's heart was hammering against her ribs. They were easily twenty feet in the air, perhaps thirty, and she tried not to think about how fast she'd be falling if she hit the ground. Pine branches obscured her view of the forest floor. The ripping noise was getting louder and louder, and part of her was tempted to peer around the branch she was standing on to see what was making it.

She did not have to.

The noise grew louder, as if the ground below them would be torn in two. It was not just one loud tear: hundreds of scratching, scraping things were dragging themselves along the ground, grinding against bark and crunching over roots. And, as it drew nearer, a horrible, deep snuffling, dry as dust. Irina clung to the tree, a sickening fear crawling up the back of her throat, and the creature below came into view.

She saw it in snatches, half-hidden by the many branches beneath her feet. A vast swathe of scales, the colour of dead things. Two enormous lupine paws. Three flat snouts wider than the tree she was standing in, all turning from side to side. A serpentine tail, severing branches when it flicked from side to side. Three ridged skulls; a glimmer of teeth.

Stefan's face was white. The thing beneath them wound itself between the trees, half-dragging itself along with its massive paws. Its slithering and scraping across the floor sounded like a blade sawing through wood. It stopped, raised its enormous heads. Sniffed. Irina froze. Had it scented them? They didn't stand a chance against a beast that size – not without weapons, or traps they could have set. She couldn't let that thing get them. She had to find a way to throw it off their scent.

Her eyes fell on the scrap of handkerchief around her wrist. The cut had stopped bleeding, but the handkerchief was stained red-brown. Keeping one hand on the trunk, Irina worried at the knot with her teeth until it came loose. Then she scrabbled in her pockets for the scrap of candle, stomach lurching when she had to take her hand off the tree. While the beast snuffled below, she tied the candle up in the handkerchief, making a little bloodstained parcel. Testing the weight of it in her hand, she caught Stefan's eye.

He looked at the parcel, then down at the ground, and panic flashed across his face. He shook his head, fast.

Irina nodded, trying for reassuring but only hitting manic. She peered through the branches and raised her arm, aiming for a gap between the trees.

Stefan reached out a frantic hand. 'What are you doing?' he mouthed.

Irina threw. The bloodstained handkerchief sailed out of sight. Her aim was true; instead of smacking into a branch, it flew between the trees in a wide arc. She did not hear it hit the ground the first time – the beast was snuffling too loudly for that. But then it stopped, its massive heads turned towards a sound she had not heard, and the tap, tap, tap of the little parcel bouncing and rolling across the forest floor sounded as loud as a hammer. The beast shot after it, bounding and slithering through the woods, spines along its back snagging on the trees. The trunk shook as it passed – Irina clung on – and, with a whip of a long, scaled tail, it was out of sight.

'Quick,' Stefan hissed, 'let's get through the door before it comes back.'

He scrambled back down the trunk while Irina picked her way from branch to branch. With each step, she felt worse and worse, the familiar headache throbbing in the back of her skull. By the time she dropped down from the lowest branch, she wanted to throw up.

Stefan darted through the door. 'Come on!'

Irina breathed deep. The sunlit road was all but smiling at her on the other side. A thousand tiny pains pricked across her skin. She had to go through – the creature could be back at any minute – but all she could think about was how much it was going to hurt when she forced herself through that door. She remembered the grind of bone on bone, the searing agony that flashed across every nerve. The memory of the pain was bad enough. Now, she was so close that it was as if she could sense the pain crouching at the ends of her fingertips, waiting to claw its way up her arm.

Stefan held out a hand. His dirty sleeve fell back to his elbow, revealing purple-black skin and a web of dark veins. 'We've got to go,' he said.

'I know,' Irina rasped. 'It's just . . .'

'Do you want me to pull you through again?'

She shook her head. Fingers trembling, she took his hand. It felt like ice. For a moment, she expected him to haul her through the door anyway, his dark eyes moving from her hand to her face and back again. But he didn't. He simply stood with her hand in his, while pain thrummed through all her thoughts.

'On three,' he said. 'One, two—'

Ripping. Crashing. Irina turned, and saw the beast heading straight for her. It dragged itself along the forest floor, forelegs bounding while the back half of its body slithered through the trees. It was enormous. Hundreds of yards away, its three slavering heads snapped off branches and splintered trunks. She could see its six yellow eyes, each ridge on each canine head, all the endless, endless teeth . . .

'Irina!'

She sputtered into life and threw herself into the door. Agony flared. It felt like running into a wall, only to discover there was a crack she could squeeze through; the impact was bad enough, but the rolling, pinching torture of forcing her body through a space that felt far too small for her was much worse. Muscles spasmed. Bones buckled. Her skin felt like it had been set alight – and then, suddenly, she was staggering through the door, still clutching Stefan's hand. The pain vanished so quickly it felt like it had been ripped away. Shaking all over, Irina half-wondered if it had taken a layer of skin with it.

She collapsed. Stefan fell after her; she still hadn't let go of his hand. She wasn't sure if she could – her fingers felt like they'd seized up. The two of them hit the dirt in a flurry of dust and dirty linen. Irina barely felt it. Something seemed to have been squeezed out of her, and she couldn't stop trembling.

Stefan swore under his breath and wriggled his fingers free. He got to his feet, brushing the dust of the road off his clothes and flexing his hand. 'How close was it?'

Irina opened her mouth to speak and retched. Stefan peered

into the slice of darkened forest they'd left behind, and swore again.

'Get back. If this doesn't work, keep going.'

He spun on the spot three times, anticlockwise. A flash of thigh-length teeth, a snarl – and then the slice of forest vanished, with no sign that it had ever been there. The two of them were standing on a path winding up a hillside in something like daylight, with the smoke of distant villages up on the hill. There was no sound of tearing. No snarling. But there were no sounds from the road, either, and the silence made Irina feel as if she was balanced on a precipice.

She was fighting the urge to vomit all over the road, but she hauled herself upright on shaking legs. She gestured vaguely at the distant village, not trusting herself to speak.

'You're not very convincing,' said Stefan. 'Sit down a little longer. The door's closed, we'll be fine.'

'What would you have done if that hadn't worked?' she rasped.

He shrugged. 'Died, I suppose.'

Irina opened her mouth, ready to respond, and something pulsed. It was as if the ground she had been standing on had suddenly been shunted forwards, and yet nothing seemed to have moved. She whirled around, nausea rising, and saw nothing – until something thudded into the place where the door had been, and rippled out across the path. Panic flooded through her. Could that thing break through?

Instantly, Stefan was beside her. 'Come on. I can carry you if you can't walk, but we have to go.'

'I can walk.'

He gave her a sceptical look. 'Fine. But if you throw up, I'm telling everyone that you're pregnant.'

'Don't do that,' Irina wheezed, rubbing her ribs.

'Well, don't throw up, then.'

The necklace was pointing them towards the village. Irina forced herself to move, hauling one foot in front of the other until the thrum of the door began to fade. She risked a glance over her shoulder. From this distance, she could no longer see where the door had been – until something slammed into the other side of it, and the world around her seemed to ripple.

The village seemed to sit on the horizon without getting any closer. Irina found she did not mind too much. Every step brought her back to herself, and further away from the monster in the hunters' forest. The rhythm of the walk settled her, and soon her steps were sure and her hands were steady. She didn't even feel all that hungry or thirsty any more; evidently her appetite had been drowned in the rising tide of nausea.

She could not say the same of Stefan. He was agitated, stopping and starting and glancing over his shoulder. There was nothing behind them – at least, nothing that she could see.

'It worked. You closed the door,' she said. 'That thing is impossible to miss.'

'It clearly got through the doors before. Can you hurry up? I want to get off the road.'

Irina glared at him. 'I would love to hurry up, Stefan. But I've only just stopped feeling like I want to vomit, so this is as fast as I can go.'

Stefan ran a hand through his hair. 'We're exposed. If that thing is still following us, we've got nowhere to hide.'

'I appreciate that, but—'

'Who's following you?'

Irina shrieked. Stefan swore. The pair of them whirled around. Behind them, much closer than he had any right to be, was a man driving a hay cart. He peered out from underneath a broad-brimmed straw hat, his weather-beaten face curious. The sleeves of his linen shirt were rolled back to the elbow, and his embroidered sheepskin vest hung open. There was nothing in the cart. More importantly, there was nothing *drawing* the cart. The man was holding reins that looped onto nothing, the shafts of the cart floating in mid-air. He didn't seem to have noticed. All his attention was focused on them, and as the man took note of Irina's bridal crown and Stefan's shabby clothes, a gleam came into his eye. Irina's heart sank. She knew that look. Here was a man who had scented gossip.

Stefan threw an arm around her, nearly punching her in the shoulder in his haste. 'No one's following us,' he said. 'We're fine, thank you.'

The man raised his eyebrows. 'Is that so?'

'Yes. Everything is—'

Irina let out a pantomime sigh. She laid a hand on Stefan's chest; there was the briefest flash of panic in his eyes. 'Darling,' she said, 'we can't keep it secret forever.'

Stefan's eyes flicked to the driver. He lowered his voice. 'What are you doing?'

'Uncle Anton is bound to notice sooner or later,' she said, her voice pitched just loud enough to carry.

The man in the cart leaned back, satisfied. 'So your families don't approve?'

'They'll come around,' Irina said. 'Once they've had some time to calm down. When they see how happy we are, it won't matter that we eloped.'

'Youths,' the man muttered. 'Well, if you're going into town, I can give you a lift.' He jerked his head towards the back of the cart. 'There's space enough for you in there.'

Irina exchanged a look with Stefan. She didn't want to get close to the driver, but if what Radu had said about the dead being able to find their way around easily was true, they'd travel much faster in the stranger's cart.

'We're actually looking for somewhere we could find some gloves for my wife,' Stefan said. 'And a map, if there is one. Could we find those, in town?'

The man frowned. 'Gloves? Winter's a way off yet. Why would she need gloves?'

Stefan gave Irina's shoulder a shake. 'To save her delicate hands,' he said, turning a syrupy smile on her. 'Only the best for my little cauliflower.'

Instantly, rigor mortis set into Irina's smile. *Cauliflower?* She stared at a point over Stefan's shoulder. She was already feeling like she was about ready to curl up into a ball under the force of her own embarrassment; if she looked either of them in the eye, she was sure she would desiccate into a thousand tiny pieces and blow away on the wind.

The man did not appear to notice. 'Gloves, certainly. A map, though . . . why would you need one of those? Can't you find where you're going?'

'Oh, yes,' Stefan lied. 'But we want to decide where to go first.'

'Fair enough. Up you get, then. And no mooning in the back of my cart, or you can find your own way into town.'

Stefan and Irina went round to the back of the cart, Stefan's arm all but sewn to Irina's shoulders. It was a wide, flat hay cart, open to the sky, with shallow sides and slats worn smooth from use. Open at the back, there was a ledge they could sit on and let their legs dangle over the road. Stefan lifted Irina onto the seat – it was little more than a plank, but surprisingly comfortable – and climbed up beside her. The man cracked his whip – *why*, Irina wondered, when there was no horse? – and they set off.

It was a beautiful day. Green fields sloped gently downwards, a pale blue sky soft and inviting over their heads. There was no sun, and no shadows on the ground, but it was warm enough that Irina unbuttoned her cuffs and rolled up her sleeves. If she had to guess, she would say it was late spring: after the first harvest of strawberries and spring greens, but before the harsh heat of summer began to beat down. Perfect for farmers, she realized, as the cart trundled past a conical haystack twelve feet tall and a plough propped against a fence. As they drew close to the cottages, far more quickly than she had anticipated, she began to pick out wooden byres and chicken coops, distant beehives, and pitchforks propped against whitewashed walls. Occasionally someone would come out onto the front step of their cottage to watch them go by: children with their fingers in their mouths, mothers with babies on their hips, old women who looked up without putting down their sewing. But there was nothing growing in the fields, and there were no animals that Irina could see in the pens. No one seemed to mind. Nobody looked hungry. Irina shivered. It was just normal enough that the rhythm of the cart lulled her into docility, and she could nod and smile at the villagers who came out to see who was passing. But then she would catch sight of an empty field, or remember there were no hoofbeats ringing out across the road, and icy tendrils of fear seeped into her head like fog.

It was only when the last house was receding into the distance that Irina leaned over and whispered in Stefan's ear, '*Cauliflower?*'

'I panicked!' he hissed.

'Clearly.'

He shot her an irritated look. 'Nicknames are normal. Couples do that sort of thing.'

'Yes, but *cauliflower*?'

'Look,' he whispered, 'you started making up all that stuff about us running away together, and I had no idea you were going to do that. I just had to go with it, so you can go with cauliflower.'

Irina glanced over her shoulder. The driver was watching the road, but she had no idea if he was listening. 'I had to say something,' she whispered. 'He was asking questions! What else were we supposed to do, tell him the truth? At least now we're moving – and we can see if that thing is coming up after us.'

Stefan folded his arms, scowling.

'I thought it was a good story, anyway,' Irina muttered. 'We may as well use it. If anyone asks, we can say my Uncle Anton didn't like you, and your father didn't like me, so we ran away together.'

His hands twitched, digging into the flesh of his elbows. 'No.'

'But—'

'I said no, Irina.' His knuckles showed pearl-grey, his hands were clenched so tightly. He was staring straight ahead, and suddenly Irina wondered if that was because he didn't want to look at her. She stole a glance at him out of the corner of her eye. A muscle was working in his jaw.

'All right, fine,' she murmured. 'We won't do that. But people are going to ask questions. We should decide what we're going to say.'

'People don't ask questions unless you make them,' Stefan snarled, his voice rough. 'Didn't you learn anything in the village? All we need to do is stay quiet. If they don't want to ask, they won't. They aren't going to be asking how we are and how long we've been married, Irina. They don't care.'

Irina snorted. 'You've been away from people too long. Do you have any idea how often I've been asked when I'm going to get married?'

'Well, now you *are* married, so they can stop asking,' Stefan retorted, his linen sleeves still scrunched underneath his fingers.

'I just think we should get our story—'

'Would you just leave it?' he snapped.

Smarting, Irina folded her arms and fell silent. If he wanted to get crotchety with her, fine. She would let him. In fact, the next time someone asked them something about their marriage she was going to make up something really embarrassing, and make him nod and smile and agree that it was all true. Maybe she'd tell people he wrote poetry, and get him to make some up on the spot.

She shot him a sideways glance. He was clutching his elbows, the knuckles of his purple-black hands still grey with tension. His jaw was clenched, his eyes fixed on the horizon, and his face was paler than she had ever seen it. Belatedly, she realized she shouldn't be surprised. She'd strayed too close to the edge of one of his secrets: family. Pity flicked at the edge of Irina's conscience. She probably shouldn't tease him. Not when something was so clearly wrong.

The last of the three villages was long gone. The houses had all been slightly different: the first village had houses with long, sloping roofs spilling over the edges of the window frames; the second had wooden verandas running alongside every door; the third was full of two-storey buildings with wooden staircases leading up to doors on the top floor. But though the buildings had varied, and the people had all been slightly differently dressed – some in heavy sheepskin jackets, some with trousers tied up to the knee in criss-crossing leather straps, some with long, white headscarves and some with short, brightly coloured ones – there was something eerily similar about each village. There were no animals, no plants. There were stacks of neatly chopped wood piled up in every woodstore, but no trees in sight. Sometimes, as the cart trundled past, Irina smelled cooking: the comforting, mellow bubble of mămăligă boiling in a pot, or the rich sizzle of frying onions. But she never saw anyone eating, nor anyone pulling corn off the stalk and taking it into the kitchen. Everything the villagers needed seemed to be provided for them, but she could not have said from where. She shook off the thought. All that really mattered was that, for now, there was no sign of the beast.

But now they were coming close to the town Radu had marked on his crude dirt map. The road had widened, the forest long out of sight. The cart rattled over cobblestones instead of trundling over earth, and Irina was sitting with her knees pulled close to her chest to stop her clothes being flecked with mud and travel dust. More vehicles were approaching: simple wooden carts like theirs, painted Roma wagons, and grand coaches with coats of arms glistening on the doors and velvet curtains at the windows. None of them were pulled by anything that Irina could see. The shafts of the carriages hung in mid-air, the drivers of the wagons held reins that looped over empty space. Irina tried not to look as if the sight did not make her want to crawl under something and hide. Was it that there was nothing pulling them at all, or was it that they were being pulled by something that she could not see?

Discreetly, she checked Catalina's necklace. For a heartbeat, it lay lifeless in her hand. Then, slowly – much slower than before, she realized with a jolt – it lifted itself up, pointing directly behind her. Clutching onto the rim of the cart, Irina twisted in her seat to look at the town.

It was enormous. A vast stone wall stretched around the city, ten feet high and made of thousands of rounded stones cemented into place. Four round towers were built into the walls, squat and notched with narrow windows. Ahead of the cart was a wide, low archway, which the press of people and vehicles were all slowly being funnelled through. Irina scrambled away from the ledge and back into the cart proper. If anyone were to bump into her now, she'd never be able to get away.

Stefan followed her. He lowered his voice. 'Is there going to be any trouble at the gate?' he muttered.

Irina stood up in the back of the cart, staggering slightly as it moved. She caught a glimpse of carts moving through the archway and onto a cobbled street before Stefan yanked her back down.

'We're supposed to be subtle about this!' he hissed.

'No, we're supposed to not look suspicious,' she shot back, 'and you're the one skulking about in the back of the cart.'

He scowled at her. 'There's not looking suspicious and then there's standing up head and shoulders above the rest of the crowd, Irina. Everyone's going to be staring at you.'

Irina looked around. No one was watching them. Most of the drivers were concentrating on steering their horseless carriages towards the archway, and most of the passengers were staring up at the walls of the city. 'Don't be ridiculous,' she said, 'no one's going to want to look at me. They're all concentrating on getting in. Besides, don't you want to know what I saw?'

He glared at her. Then, his voice loaded with resentment, he muttered, 'Yes.'

'I couldn't get a perfect look, but it doesn't look like there's anyone on the gate,' Irina said, ignoring Stefan's sulking. 'And the more I think about it, the more it makes sense. What would anyone be checking? It's not like we've seen anyone with papers here.'

'That's not what I meant,' said Stefan. 'If it's a gate – or a door, I suppose, if there's no light – are you going to be able to get through it without anyone noticing that you're – you know . . .'

Irina went cold. 'In terrible pain?'

'Yes, that.'

She looked around. They were surrounded by people. The nearest cart was almost two feet away on their left side, and on the right a small group of women in long, white headscarves were walking alongside them, chatting and carrying large baskets. If they hadn't been having a conversation of their own, they could have easily heard everything that Stefan and Irina had been saying. They were certainly close enough to notice if she started grimacing in agony.

'I think I can keep quiet,' she muttered, 'but I'm pretty sure I pull faces when I go through the door. Someone will see.'

'You *definitely* pull faces.' Stefan ran a hand through his hair, examining the cart. It was wide and shallow, the sides made of widely spaced wooden planks. 'You can't lie down, someone will see through the gaps.'

Irina glanced up at the city walls. The cart had slowed almost to a standstill, stuck behind a crowd of apprentices throwing things at each other and a long line of red-and-yellow Roma wagons trundling through. The door was less than a hundred yards away, and drawing ever closer. They wouldn't have long.

Stefan was staring at it, chewing on his bottom lip. 'How do you feel?'

'Nervous,' Irina replied. She concentrated. Her head was a little sore and her mouth was dry. The cart trundled over a bump in the cobblestones; sweat prickled across her palms. 'Very nervous.'

Apprentices shrieked up ahead, darting in front of the first wagon and ducking behind one of the front wheels. The driver swore, tugging on the reins, and the line ground to a halt. As the cart lurched forward, nausea swelled at the back of Irina's throat. What if she screamed, in front of all these people? They'd come running. They'd try and pull her out of the cart, and the second their hands found her skin, they would rot. They'd wither away, disease blossoming across their skin and wounds opening up on their foreheads while their last moments hurtled themselves back to the forefronts of their minds, and all that pain and suffering would be her fault. She wouldn't let them do it. She wasn't going to plunge someone back to the agonies of death because she couldn't keep her mouth shut.

The line of carts jolted back into life. The shadow of the archway loomed overhead. Irina grabbed Stefan's arm and squeezed.

'Don't let them see,' she whispered. 'If anyone notices . . .'

The next wagon moved forward. Towers loomed over their heads; Irina was sure someone behind the windows was watching. She dug her fingers into Stefan's forearm as their cart rumbled slowly forward. She had to stay calm. She couldn't panic. Panicking would only make it worse, so she had to stop it – stop feeling sick, stop wondering how far she'd get if she vaulted over the side of the cart and ran, stop staring up at those vast, vast walls and wondering how close she'd get before the pain hit and how hard she'd have to bite the inside of her cheek to keep from screaming and –

A blackening hand reached across and grabbed her by the shoulder. Irina jumped. She nearly shrieked, but then Stefan hauled her into a hug, so quick and hard that she nearly headbutted him in the chin. He didn't even flinch. Very carefully, he placed a hand on the back of her head, patting it awkwardly. With his arms around her, and her face buried in his shoulder, no one would see if her face twisted in pain.

'I'm sorry, I couldn't think of anything else . . .' he began.

Irina threw her arms around him and squeezed, grabbing fistfuls of the back of his shirt. She was shaking. It was going to hurt so much. She was already feeling queasy, her breath coming in short, sharp gasps. And it was only going to get worse. The cart was moving so slowly. She'd be dragged towards the pain by inches, like nails scraping across her skin. At least when she walked through the doors she could control it, but this . . .

'It's all right,' Stefan whispered. 'It'll be over before you know it.'

'Are we close?'

She felt him nodding, his chin knocking the top of her head. 'Oh, sorry. Forgot you couldn't . . . anyway. Yes, not long now.'

Irina wanted to throw up. She squeezed her handfuls of linen tighter. Something tore. 'What am I going to do if—'

'You won't.'

'You don't even know what I was going to say!'

The cart trundled over a few missing cobblestones; the jolting knocked Irina's head against Stefan's jaw. He grunted, but when he spoke, his voice was low and soothing. 'You're going to be fine. I've got you.'

'But what if—'

'I said, I've got you.' She felt him shift and twist to look up at the archway. 'Only one more cart ahead. Are you ready?'

Irina squeezed her eyes shut. Her whole body felt like thread pulled tight enough to snap. The cart started to move. Stefan's arms tightened around her shoulders. One of his hands was still resting on the back of her head, surprisingly gentle. Irina waited for the pain.

Nothing happened.

The cart moved forward. Around them, she could hear people chatting, laughing, the steady rumble of wheels over cobblestones.

There was a dimming and brightening of light. But there was no pain. Nerves crackled through her, and she was still feeling queasy, but nothing hurt.

She opened her eyes.

Peeking over Stefan's shoulder, she saw the archway, still close enough to touch. There was no haze in the air, no slice of the world torn away to reveal a completely different place – and, she realized belatedly, she had not had to spin around three times to make the door appear in the first place. The other side of the city walls – uneven, rounded stones held together with worn cement – was clearly visible.

Irina squinted. There was something written on some of the stones. Just before the cart moved away, she caught a glimpse of the closest one.

Sacred to the memory of
She gasped.

'It's all right,' Stefan whispered, 'it's all right, we're through, it'll be gone soon.'

'Not that,' Irina replied. 'It didn't hurt at all; I think these doors just lead into the city, not another part of the underworld. Stefan, that wall is made of gravestones.'

He froze. 'What do you mean? Aren't you in pain?'

Irina flushed. 'No. I . . . I think I was just expecting to be.'

'Oh. Well. Good.' He cleared his throat. Loosening his grip, his arms slid off her shoulders. 'What did you say about gravestones?'

'I saw one of the inscriptions, over the archway.'

He pulled away, peering back at the wall. 'That doesn't make sense. If people aren't meant to know they're dead, why build a wall out of gravestones?'

Irina shrugged. 'Don't ask me. Maybe those are one of the things you *can* take with you.'

A Steep and Savage Path

He snorted. There was a red mark on his cheek; the pine needles on her bridal crown had been digging into his face, and he hadn't said a word. As she turned to look back at the wall, his eyes strayed to her hair. 'Oh, sorry,' he said, reaching for the top of her braid, 'I think I squashed one of your flowers. Shall I . . .'

'They're still in there?' Irina asked, reaching for the back of her head. She could still feel the delicate petals threaded into her hair, but she couldn't work out how they were supposed to be placed without a mirror.

'Here. Let me.'

For a moment, Irina hesitated. Then she turned around and let him fix her hair. He was surprisingly gentle – but, she realized, she wasn't sure why she was surprised. Sometimes he could be clumsy, but he'd stopped trying to hurt her. Now, when he was carefully lifting the crumpled snowdrop out of her braid and threading it back into place, the soft pull was oddly soothing. She wondered how he could see what he was doing. Her hair was dark enough to blend with his purple-black hands.

He stopped. She could feel him hesitating, one hand resting on her plait as if he was about to test the weight of it. 'I think I fixed it,' he said, his voice quiet.

Irina's hand flew to her hair. It felt perfectly normal. The flower was where it should be, and her braid wasn't snarled up into a knot. She turned back around, and as she turned, she saw him pull his hands away from her, as though he'd been burned.

The city was a warren of narrow streets, walls as tall as pines looming over their heads. Stefan and Irina said goodbye to the driver and picked their way through the crowds, uneven cobbles under their feet. Irina held her hands close to her chest, out of harm's way, and Stefan had one of his arms clamped across her shoulders. If her heart had not started to race every time someone drew close, Irina would have been fascinated. The town was thriving. Wide, high-windowed houses with arched doors large enough for a hay cart to drive through surrounded them, their plaster faded to a soft, comfortable colour somewhere between peach and yellow. Wooden shutters hung at every window, carved and painted with flowers and animals. Red-tiled roofs gleamed in the light of a sun she could not see. And that was saying nothing of the inhabitants. She'd never seen so many people look so relaxed. Laughing women in colourful aprons strolled arm in arm. Three Jewish men in crocheted yarmulkes leaned against a butter-coloured wall, talking in serious voices. A gaggle of widows in black sat on a doorstep, gossiping. Men in sheepskin coats barged past soldiers in loosened uniforms; servants in stockings and breeches clung to the back of a gleaming coach; a cluster of young girls in embroidered vests shrieked and pushed each other as they walked, joking and complaining about boys. Irina had rolled down her sleeves and buttoned her cuffs at the wrist, but even though she walked with her hands well out of the way of the crowd, every new face made her mouth run dry. It was not that she had never seen so many people before. Her village was large. In the summer, they held dances. Sometimes pilgrims passed through on their way to the monastery, or imperial officials clutching sheets of paper for the census. And she had travelled a little: not just to Timişoara, but to Sibiu and Hunedoara. She was used to crowds. She was just not used to crowds that, at the touch of her hand, would wither into corpses.

They were all heading in the same direction: up the slope of a hill, to what she could only assume was a market. The smells of sizzling jumări, baking bread and sweet dumplings were drifting towards her. Irina's mouth began to water. A hundred different conversations floated down towards them, tangled with the sounds of cheap fiddles. Irina's hand drifted up towards the wooden necklace. Was it safe, to check it here? She wasn't sure. She didn't want to give people any more of a reason to look at her, when she was already walking around in her bridal crown.

'So we get the map and the gloves,' she said, her voice quiet, 'and then we leave.'

'And we don't touch anyone,' Stefan muttered.

Irina's temper flared. 'I wasn't going to touch anyone!'

He snorted. Irina resisted the urge to poke him in the side; she could get him right between his ribs, with his arm around her.

'We should probably ask around about those guardians, as well,' she said, 'or that monster. See what people know.'

Stefan glanced at her out of the corner of his eye, scepticism writ large across his face. 'Is that wise?'

'Probably not,' Irina admitted, 'but I want to know what to do if that thing comes back, and where the guardians could've taken Catalina.' Fear settled on her thoughts like falling snow. 'And if she's safe.'

He sighed. 'Fine. But don't go charging off. If you bump into anybody, they'll know about you.'

'You said that already,' she snapped.

'I was just trying to help.'

They turned a corner and fell silent. They had reached the market.

At first, Irina did not know what to make of it. Every other place in the land of the dead had seemed almost, but not quite, like the land of the living – never real enough to truly be mistaken for life, but close enough, as though she was looking at a perfect mask rather than a living human face. But the market was different. A thousand beautiful and unreal things lay before her – so impossible, and yet so tangible, it was as if that mask had winked at her. A hundred stalls were crammed into a vast cobbled square, larger than Irina had thought the city could hold. Some were simple wooden tables, some hung off the backs of carts, some were palatial tents of red, purple and gold. A thousand different scents hung in the air – paprika, raw wool, fennel, leather, woodsmoke, beeswax. Fires glimmered under bubbling pots. At least three troupes of musicians were playing somewhere among the stalls: Irina could not see them, but all the different melodies tangled together with the shouting of hawkers and the complaining of customers. Gold and silver winked at her from underneath crimson awnings. Rolls of silk glistened like jewels. A tray of papanași was practically ogling her, the perfect golden-brown balls of crispy dough dripping with sour cream and jam. Irina's mouth began to water. She shouldn't. She knew she wasn't supposed to eat the food here, and surprisingly, she wasn't actually that hungry, but surely one bite wouldn't hurt. Surely no one would miss a perfect mouthful of crispy dough, still sizzling, blueberry jam trickling down the sides . . .

Stefan leaned down to whisper in her ear. 'Gloves, and the map, remember?'

Irina didn't look away from the papanași. 'I know.'

Stefan made a sceptical noise. 'Stay close. If we get separated . . .'

'I *know*, Stefan,' Irina muttered, irritation finally snapping her out of her daydream. 'Let's get the gloves first. I keep thinking I'm going to bump into someone and make them wither away.'

She could have stayed among the stalls forever. Silks and brocades sat piled next to trays of eggs in every size and colour. Stews bubbled alongside piles of large pink shells. Skeins of thread were neatly lined up according to colour – in rainbow order, Irina noted with a certain amount of satisfaction. Icons of Byzantine saints. Jewellery, everything from simple beads to glittering crowns. Books, piled high, in more languages than Irina had ever known existed. The more stalls they passed, the stranger they became. Finely wrought plants of copper, silver and gold lay on a stall hung with emerald-green cloth. On a rough wooden table stood a pile of perfectly round stones on a large porcelain dish; each one was bleeding, and Stefan craned his neck to stare. Several masks hung from the side of a wagon; some with long, thin beaks, some that would only cover the eyes, some made to look like the faces of animals. As they passed by, one of them winked at her. But, Irina realized, everywhere she looked, there was one thing she was not seeing.

There was nothing living.

There was meat bubbling in the stews, eggs being inspected for cracks, piles of soft wool on the tables. But there were no animals. Likewise, there were no plants but those already sliced and sizzling on a griddle. Nothing growing, nothing changing. It was oddly unsettling, to be surrounded by so much food and to see none of the places where it came from. Irina was sure the only real flowers in the market were those in her hair – until she saw a stall piled high with red peonies. She froze. Were they going to come squirming and writhing towards her, like snakes slithering towards their prey? But the flowers lay lifeless. A woman with one leg stopped in front of the stall, leaning on her cane, and lifted one to her face. Irina's heart jolted, waiting for the rot to spread across the woman's fingers. But nothing happened. She simply stared into the blood-red petals, an utterly haunted look on her face. Guilt rocketed through Irina. What was the woman remembering?

Stefan had stopped in front of a stall piled high with clothes.

Several pairs of gloves were laid across the plain linen cloth, looking like supplicant hands. The stallholder – a young woman in a black-and-red striped apron and a dark flowered headscarf – beamed at them both, taking in Irina's bridal crown and Stefan's arm clamped around her shoulders.

'You can't have these,' Stefan was saying, gesturing to a pair of sheepskin mittens, 'you won't be able to use your hands. And it's far too warm.'

The stallholder held up a pair of black lace gloves. 'All the court ladies are wearing these,' she said, looking hopeful.

Irina shook her head. She may as well have used a fishing net instead, for all the good those gaps in the lace would do her. 'That's not practical for me. Have you got something simpler?'

'No, you need something nice,' Stefan said. He picked out a pair of fine kid gloves, dove-grey and buttoning at the wrist. Irina stared. She'd never owned anything as lavish as those gloves. The stallholder was staring too, her eyes fixed on Stefan's blackening hands. A frown was starting to pucker between her eyes. Irina bristled, unsure if the stallholder was worried that Stefan's hands would damage her merchandise or if she'd realized that something was wrong. Either way, Irina was on edge.

'We'll take them,' she said quickly. 'How much?'

The stallholder jolted out of her reverie. Her smile widened. 'What do you have to give?'

Irina reached for a sheepish, straightforward charm, and had no idea if she found it. 'I've just arrived,' she said, attempting an ingratiating smile, 'and I don't really know how this works. Could you explain it to me, please?'

'Well,' the woman said, 'I'll take secrets, if you have any of those. Your jewellery's not quite enough for these, I'm afraid. You could give me a kiss – one for each glove, of course,' she said, with a wink. 'That goes for both of you, by the way. What else? Er . . . no hair, I've no need for that. You could work for me, I suppose, although with that stitching it'll need to be for at least six months. And I am obliged to tell you that if you were to set fire to Filip's stall and burn it to the ground, that would not count as payment, but I might drop the gloves in the confusion, who knows. Does that help?'

Irina blinked at the stallholder. 'Um,' she said. 'How about . . . Stefan, could you grab one of the . . .' She gestured to her braid.

'Oh,' he said, delicately unhooking a snowdrop from Irina's plait. He handed it over. 'Here,' he said. 'You won't find another one of these in the whole market – apart from in her hair, of course.'

The stallholder's eyes widened. She held out both her hands. Stefan dropped the little flower into her palms and she stared at it, her movements as still and slow as if she were holding a baby bird. Irina tensed. Did the flower still count as a living thing? But the stallholder's face did not change; evidently, the little snowdrop was as dead as everything else in this place.

'Done.'

Stefan passed the gloves to Irina. She put them on quickly. They were soft and fitted her perfectly, although she was a little clumsy with the buttons. After watching her struggle for a few moments, Stefan helped her fasten them. His purple-black fingers made short work of the buttons, even though they were always so cold. She was surprised he could be so deft. Did his hands feel numb? Could he feel the cold at all?

'Thank you,' she said, flexing her gloved fingers.

He gave her a quick, soft smile. Then he ruined it, when a glint came into his eye and he said, 'Only the best for my little cauliflower.'

Irina's face set into the most angelic expression she could muster as she tried to kick him in the ankle. He stepped back just in time, smirking. Seething, Irina turned back to the stallholder, sure that her smile was splintering.

'I wonder if you'd be able to help us with something else,' she said. 'Not something we're looking to buy, but . . . I'm looking for my sister. I heard she was last seen with the guardians. Do you know where I can find them?'

'Oh, they'll find you,' said the stallholder, still staring at the flower. 'No need to go looking.'

Irritated, Irina tried to stop her smile becoming a wince. 'But how will I recognize them? There's so many people here.'

'You'll recognize them. Was there anything else?'

Irina opened her mouth, ready to argue, but Stefan put a hand on her shoulder. 'No, thank you,' he said, steering her away, 'you've been very helpful.'

He led Irina away from the clothes stall, past empty cages ringing with the sounds of twittering orioles, rows of gleaming knives, stacks of brightly coloured woven baskets, fried cheese and skewers of meat sizzling on iron griddles. Though she had her gloves, Irina still walked with her hands clutched to her chest. There were children barrelling through the stalls, older siblings chasing after them; stallholders reaching out from behind their tables to grab the shoulders of passers-by; couples strolling arm in arm; gaggles of young men who moved through the market shoving each other and puffing up their chests. Irina's whole body felt like a finely balanced instrument, one unlucky nudge away from breaking. She wouldn't feel safe until she was away from the crowd.

'Why didn't you let me talk to her?' she hissed. 'She might've known something.'

'She clearly didn't,' Stefan replied, as the two of them squeezed up against the side of a wagon to make way for a woman in a satin dress rolling past in a wicker bath chair. 'You were just going to draw attention to us.'

'No, I was going to find out more about the guardians!'

He sighed, pinching the bridge of his nose. 'Let's just see if we can find that map.'

There were three stalls selling things to read: one with stacks of brightly coloured novels and political tracts bound in leather, one with cheap pamphlets with thickly printed woodcut images, and one with stacks of thick, yellowing scrolls. None of them had any maps. The stallholders seemed confused when they asked for one.

'Can't you just get to where you want to go?' a spotty boy asked, when Irina unrolled scroll after scroll and found nothing but drawings of old plants.

'That's what we need the map for,' she snapped. 'Can you at least tell us about the rivers?'

The boy frowned. 'But you don't *need* a map,' he said. 'You just think about where you want to be, and then you're there. What do you mean, you can't find your way?'

Irina handed back the scroll in a huff, viridian leaves flashing past as she rolled up the parchment. 'We're new here,' she muttered.

'What my wife means to say,' said Stefan, cutting in with an attempt at a winning smile, 'is that we're still getting used to how things work, and perhaps if you had something like a map, that would help us work out where we want to be, and *then* we could . . .'

Stefan's words withered as he stared at the stallholder's confused face. The boy was frowning, one hand plucking at the skin on his top lip as he thought. 'But if you don't know where you want to go,' he said slowly, 'why would you want to go there? Don't you have everything you need right here?'

Irina was chewing the inside of her cheek, trying to keep a lid on her frustration. It didn't work. 'We are *trying* to find my sister, and if you would just tell us what you know, that would be appreciated.'

The stallholder's face cleared up instantly. 'Oh, that's easy. The guardians will bring her to you. There's a place for unclaimed children here, as well. Have you tried there?'

Irina groaned. Stefan's hand tightened on her shoulder; a muscle was twitching underneath his eye. 'Thank you,' he said through gritted teeth. 'You've been—'

He stopped. His grip loosened. Irina looked up; he was staring off into the crowd, shock scrawled across his face. Then, he left. He slipped between the crowds of people like a fish slithering through pondweed, leaving Irina and the stallholder staring after him.

'Stefan!' she yelled. 'Where are you going?'

He seized her by the wrist, dragging her after him.

He moved like water, twisting his body and rolling his shoulders to squeeze through the smallest gaps in the crowd. Irina staggered after him, barging into old men with heavy packs, servant women in matching white kerchiefs and aprons, and children holding half-eaten covrigi, mouths full of fried dough and lips frosted with salt. Each bump sent a flare of panic running through her. She craned her neck, looking for blood spilling from blue lips, for rashes spreading up grey necks, for bones poking through withering skin. But all she saw were annoyed faces staring after them. No blood. No disease. No wounds.

Stefan skidded to a halt near the far edge of the market. He ducked behind a green-and-yellow wagon, pulling Irina after him. His jaw set, he peered around the side, ignoring the bemused woman selling copper pans whose stall he was clearly hiding behind.

Irina yanked her wrist out of his grip. He was starting to squeeze. 'What are you doing?' she whispered.

Ignoring her, he stuck his head out a little more from behind the wagon. Seething, Irina did the same. There wasn't much to look at, in Irina's eyes. Some wooden benches were propped up against the stone wall of the market square, where a handful of people were sitting and eating their food away from the crowds. A cart loaded with discarded bits and pieces from the market: apple cores, bits of smashed glass, broken horn spoons. And a blonde boy, perhaps a year or two older than her, wearing a white linen shirt and trousers, a wide leather belt, and tall black boots. He was bending over, adjusting one of his boots, when he straightened up, turned around, and saw them.

'Stefan?'

Stefan swore. He darted back behind the wagon, trying to haul Irina after him again. She snatched her hand away before he could grab it. 'What are you—'

The boy rounded the wagon. Close to, it was easy to tell that he had been cared for. There was an intricate black-and-red border embroidered around the collar and cuffs of his linen shirt and an interlocking pattern of diamonds was tooled into the leather of his belt. He was short, strong, and clearly self-assured; he was sizing up Irina already, grey eyes darting between her and Stefan, his chin tilted up like he was about to start an argument.

Stefan grimaced. 'Hello, Danil.'

Danil was in the middle of giving Stefan the most thorough up-and-down look Irina had ever seen. Stefan rubbed at one of the bloodstains on his shirt; absolutely nothing happened. 'God, you look awful,' Danil said, when he was finished. 'What happened to your hands? And where are your shoes?'

'Maybe we should have this conversation somewhere a little more private,' Irina said. The stallholder was watching them with interest, not even trying to pretend she was not eavesdropping.

Danil shot Irina a disdainful look. 'Who's she?'

'No one you know,' Stefan muttered, rubbing the back of his neck. 'Come on. That alley looks quiet.'

'I've heard that one before,' Danil replied, with a smirk. Stefan ignored him, looking anywhere but at Irina. He pushed past them both and headed for a narrow street leading away from the market, between two tall buildings joined by a series of arches; it was dark, quiet, and away from the prying eyes of the crowd. Irina followed.

Danil glared over his shoulder at her. 'Why are *you* coming?'

'It was my idea,' Irina retorted.

Now it was her turn for an incredibly drawn-out once-over. Every inch of her felt like it was being weighed and priced, from the flowers in her hair to the pointed opinci peeking out from underneath her skirt. Danil's mouth twisted.

'Why is she in a—'

'Do you want to talk or not?' Stefan interrupted.

Scowling, Danil folded his arms. Stefan ducked underneath the first arch, clearly looking for a shadow to lurk in. When he couldn't find one, he backed up against the wall, turned to Danil, and said, 'You look well.'

Danil scoffed. 'Oh, is that the conversation we're going to have? You're not going to explain any of this,' he said, gesturing to Stefan's shabby clothes and purple-black hands and feet, 'or why you didn't show at the inn? Or who *she* is?'

'Something came up,' Stefan said. 'I couldn't get away.'

'Oh, *something came up*, did it? What could've possibly—'

'Someone,' Stefan cut in. 'I think you know who.'

Irina expected Danil to round on her. He did not. Instead, he looked frightened, glancing back into the market and along the silent length of the street. 'He's not here, is he? He didn't find out?'

Stefan shook his head. 'He didn't follow you, did he? After you left the village?'

'No, never,' Danil said.

'And you didn't go to see him, after I . . .'

Danil raised an eyebrow. 'Why would I want to see your father?'

Stefan's eyes snapped to Irina. As he met her gaze, his face suddenly seemed raw. Clarity dawned like a sunrise. Stefan was afraid of his father. Something had happened, something that the village had known about and ignored. That was why he hated talking about them all so much, why he expected her to treat him so badly, why his mood soured every time she mentioned family.

Danil had seen Stefan's panic. He turned to Irina, disdain dripping off his every word. 'I suppose this was his idea,' he said. 'Don't think I haven't noticed that bridal crown, by the way. It's a little rushed.' His eyes drifted pointedly to Irina's belly. 'Were you in a hurry?'

Irina blushed. 'I don't know what you mean.'

'Yes, you do.'

'Leave her out of this,' said Stefan, putting a hand on Danil's shoulder and dragging him around to face him. 'Listen, Danil, you're sure you haven't seen my father? Not . . . not on your way here?'

Irina's mouth fell open. Stefan couldn't ask Danil how he'd died. Whatever had killed him, it was safer for everyone not to know – just asking the question could send Danil spinning back into the memories of his own death. Not that she was feeling particularly concerned about Danil just now. He was smirking over his shoulder at her, like he was waiting for her to discover a secret he already knew.

'What's the matter?' he drawled. 'Are you afraid your bride will find out your dirty little secret?'

'All right,' Irina said, moving back towards the mouth of the alley, 'you two clearly have something you want to talk about in private. I'm going to wait over here.'

'Thank—'

'No, stay,' said Danil, grinning. 'Don't you want to know? I bet you're curious.'

She was, but Danil had taken a step after her and was close enough to snatch her hand. The gloves were still buttoned tightly at the wrists – she was safe there – but he was still far closer than she would like. 'Not really,' she said, backing away, 'Stefan's business is his own. I don't know what you're talking about, so I'll just wait here while you—'

'Then I'll tell you,' Danil said.

He snatched her wrist and pulled her towards him.

'Hey!' Stefan yelled. 'Don't touch her!'

Irina staggered forwards and slammed into Danil. Fear ricocheted through her. She glanced at his face, terrified: still human, still smirking. One hand still locked around her wrist, he leaned forward to whisper in her ear. She locked eyes with Stefan. His face was a mask of horror. And then dread billowed through Irina like smoke, as she felt the cold brush of Danil's bare hand against her cheek when he cupped his hand around her ear.

'Your husband and I,' he began, 'were—'

He stopped. His words were cut off in a strangled whisper. Tiny, shifting sounds crackled right next to her ear, like something desiccated crumbling into pieces. Drenched in horror, Irina was frozen, staring at Stefan. One of his blackening hands was clapped over his mouth, his eyes full of tears.

Something shifted against Irina's cheek, shrivelling away from her. Irina shrieked, staggered back, and saw Danil's face.

It was blue. It looked like it had collapsed, the cheeks were so sunken in. She could see the shape of his skull more than the shape of his face. His hollow eyes were glazed over, and for a moment, she wondered if she had killed him. But then she saw him staring at his hand. It, too, was bluish-grey, and so wrinkled around the fingertips that it looked like a poorly fitting glove. That, she realized, was what she had felt against her cheek: the skin of Danil's hand withering as she brought his death back to him.

'What did you do?'

His voice was like dead leaves, rustling against each other. The sound shocked Irina back to life. She yanked her hand out of his grip.

'Please,' he rasped, reaching for her, 'my mother. She can't – oh God. Who's going to—'

Stefan was still plastered against the wall, eyes wide and horrified. He was staring at the back of Danil's head, transfixed. Certainty dropped into Irina's head like a stone. She could not let him see Danil's face.

'Go!' she yelled.

Danil snatched at her sleeve with a shrunken, blue hand. 'You can't go,' he pleaded, 'you have to take a message to my mother. Please, she was the only one who survived the outbreak, she has to know I—'

Irina bolted.

Barging past Danil, she grabbed Stefan's arm and hauled him after her, staggering down the alleyway.

'We can't just leave him.'

'We have to!' she snapped. 'We can't fix him, Stefan!'

'Wait!' Danil screamed, in a voice like broken glass. 'Please!'

Stefan shuddered as Irina dragged him down the street. It was like running with an anchor scraping along the ground behind her, until his feet caught up with the rest of him and he finally started running with her.

Danil was howling behind them, pleading. She could hear him struggling to move on his wasted limbs, crashing into walls. And there were more voices, too – stallholders and shoppers coming to see what the fuss was about. Their screams echoed down the narrow street, bouncing off the arches over their heads. Irina ran faster. It sounded as if the alley was full of tormented, keening people, and she could not bear the thought of turning back to see what she would find. Had Danil's face stopped withering? Had the sight of him been enough to remind anyone who found him that they, too, were dead? How many people were in the mouth of the little street, the flesh sloughing off their bones, the horror of their own mortality looming over them like mountains they could not climb?

She didn't let go of Stefan's hand. She ran, tasting blood at the back of her throat, a stitch blossoming in her side. Stefan's fingers were locked around hers, squeezing so tight they felt like they were about to snap.

The end of the alley was in sight. They sprinted towards it. Shambling footsteps echoed after them. Stefan and Irina burst onto a wide cobbled street. The city wall loomed in the distance. It wasn't far. They could make it. If they ran, they could get through the gate and put the city behind them before Danil could stumble into the main street. Perhaps they could outrun him – they were young and strong – but as they pelted past a family of five and an outraged pair of grandmothers, one thought was pounding through Irina's head like the beat of a drum.

The dead travel fast the dead travel fast the dead travel FAST—

A cart with no horse pulling it turned out of a side street, blocking their path. Irina swore, skidding to a halt. Stefan's hand slipped out of her grip. He pushed forward, sprinting in front of the cart. She darted around the back, bursts of panic propelling her forward. She couldn't see him. There was a trail of outraged faces, but Stefan was nowhere in sight. Had she lost him?

From somewhere over her shoulder, there came a horrible, keening cry. Far too dry to be a living scream, it was cracked, splintered. Irina barrelled forward. Terror pounded in her chest, as Danil stumbled out into the street. He'd found her.

Another dry, cracked howl. She couldn't tell if there were words in it. Irina forced herself to keep running, not to look over her shoulder. She sprinted across the cobbles. Where the hell was Stefan?

'Irina!'

He was there, next to a rank of carts. His face was white. In the distance, the arch of a city gate was visible, at the bottom of a set of cobbled steps. They wouldn't reach it. Danil had already made it out of the alley. He'd catch them.

She crashed into Stefan, gasping for breath. 'He's close,' she gasped.

Stefan grabbed a cart. 'Get in.'

'Do you know how these things work? We don't know what's pulling them. Can we even use these?'

He swore. Then his eyes landed on the stairs.

'They don't know that,' he whispered. 'If we push one down the stairs, it'll look like it's moving on its own. We can hide up here while he goes after it.'

Irina darted around to the front of the nearest cart, untying the ropes that held it steady. Stefan hauled it into the middle of the street as soon as the knot was loose, teeth gritted. Then, they shoved it down the stairs, and threw themselves underneath the carts they'd left untouched.

Screams echoed along the street. Sweating and gasping for breath, Irina lay on her side underneath a hay cart, two massive wheels on either side. Cobblestone-shaped bruises were already throbbing underneath her clothes. Her bridal crown was lost; when it had slipped off her head, she could not say. Stefan was behind her, so still that if it had not been for one of his hands digging into the small of her back, she would not have known he was there. She couldn't even hear him breathing.

Then, she heard Danil.

The cry tore through her. Anguish, horror and rage tangled in a splintering scream. Irina flinched. She pressed her hands over her mouth. If she made a sound, even the slightest gasp, he would find them. But even though her hands were shaking and revulsion and fear crawled across her skin, she could not help but pity him.

Ragged footsteps echoed down the street. Danil's shining black boots came into view. They looked loose, gaping where the flesh of his calves had withered away. On unsteady feet, he lurched forward, and stopped.

Stefan shifted. Panic burst through Irina. Was he going to give them away? She glanced up at him. Stefan was staring at the slice of street visible from underneath the cart, his eyes fixed on Danil's boots. Guilt and fear were scrawled across his face. One hand was uncurling, reaching forward. As quietly as she could, she rolled over and took his hand. He didn't appear to notice.

The footsteps shuffled forward. The sound scratched at Irina like claws. Every instinct was screaming at her not to keep her back to the dead, to turn around, to see what was coming for her. But she ignored them. Stefan was craning his neck, trying to see out from underneath the cart. If Danil saw him . . .

Irina laid a hand on Stefan's cheek. He flinched. He wrenched his eyes away from Danil, and Irina wished he hadn't. Longing, curiosity, horror and shame burned in his face. He wanted to see Danil, and at the same time, dreaded it. Irina remembered the tickle of Danil's hand withering against her face, and knew she could not let Stefan look.

She shook her head. Held out her arms. Stefan buried his face in her neck. Irina held him, one hand tangled in his hair so he could not look up. Her pulse fluttered in her throat, but she ignored it. It was bad enough that she had to see what had become of Danil. For someone who had known him, and perhaps loved him, to see his face now would be torture.

From far below came the regular *thump, thump, thump* of the cart rolling down the steps. Another scream from Danil sliced into her. Stefan flinched at the sound, pulling her closer. And at last, the shambling footsteps picked up as Danil moved after the cart.

Irina listened to Danil clambering down the stairs, moving far below. Her heart was hammering. Irina loosened her grip and peeled away from Stefan, shuffling out from underneath the cart. The street was deserted.

Stefan followed her. He got to his feet, trembling. The expression on his face was something Irina hoped she'd never see again. Unable to look him in the eye, she took his shaking hand and led him away.

Getting out of the city was easy. After Danil had run screaming through the streets, people everywhere were scrambling for the arched gateways, pale and shaking. All Stefan and Irina had to do was blend into the crowd. Nerves rippled through Irina at the press of people around her. They were so close. She couldn't risk repeating what happened to Danil. This time, there'd be no getting away unseen, because they were surrounded on every side. They'd all see. They'd all know. Would they try and touch her too, when they saw what she could do? Would they try and pull her to safety, only to rot before her eyes, or would they turn on her and demand to know what she had done?

Stefan had clamped his arm around her. He wouldn't look at her. They didn't speak. But in the crowd of frightened people, no one noticed – she didn't even get any sideways looks for her uncovered hair, now that she'd lost her bridal crown. What was one more terrified couple, in a crowd of dozens?

Now, they were on the road again. After a few seconds of juddering, Catalina's necklace had led them trudging onwards. Much like the road that had taken them into the city, it was a wide and dusty dirt track, gently rolling over sloping green hills. Distant fields blazed gold and forest green in the light of the missing sun, and the air was filled with something a little like birdsong, although no birds were in sight. It should have been a beautiful day, with an easy road stretched out before them and a carpet of lush fields unrolling in the distance. But it did not feel beautiful. The last of the frightened people had left them behind long ago, and they were alone, but Irina could still hear their screams ringing in her head. Her hand kept drifting up to her cheek, to the place where Danil's dead flesh had touched it. She shivered. Wherever he was, she hoped Danil was all right, that whatever she'd done to him had not been permanent. He hadn't been kind, but he hadn't deserved that.

A new fear curled itself around Irina's thoughts like a snake. When she found Catalina's soul, what would happen? Would she wither away like Danil had? Irina shook the thought away, choked by panic. No. It wouldn't happen like that. It couldn't. Catalina wasn't even dead.

'So,' she said, desperate to have anything else on her mind, 'you two were . . . involved?'

Stefan flinched at the sound of her voice. He still wouldn't look at her. 'I don't want to talk about it.'

Guilty, Irina looked away. 'I'm sorry.'

'It isn't your fault.'

'Isn't it?'

Stefan let out a long sigh. 'You tried to stop him. *I'm* sorry, I should have realized. Things only ended when I . . . well,' he said, flexing a purple-black hand, his greying veins stark against his skin. 'He never liked hearing about any of the girls I'd been with, before. I should've guessed he might have got jealous.'

'Girls? And Danil?'

He gave her a small smile. 'I wasn't exactly a monk when I was alive.'

Irina couldn't decide whether to be thrown or impressed. Stefan couldn't have been much more than eighteen when he died, and yet he'd had time to get involved with at least three people, one of whom he would've had to keep secret from everyone. Where would he have found the time? Irina had kissed a couple of people, mostly just to see what it was like. It had been fine at best, and at worst, slobbery. She couldn't imagine putting in so much time and effort with either of the people she'd kissed just so she could keep doing it, especially when she'd had so little in common with them. She'd never felt any of the stirrings and flutterings that everyone said were supposed to happen, and she'd been quite disappointed. It had always sounded like something she'd enjoy. But perhaps she shouldn't have been surprised; in all honesty, Matei and Nicolai had been rather boring.

Stefan was watching her out of the corner of his eye, his hands plucking at his loose linen trousers. 'You . . . you never . . .?'

Irina shook her head. 'I never met anyone I liked enough.'

'What, not even kissing?'

'Oh, that. Honestly, it's been a bit of a let-down so far. Everyone makes it sound so much nicer than it actually is. I don't see what the fuss is about.'

He gave her another sidelong look. A smirk was twitching at the corner of his mouth, and she cut across him before he could say the joke out loud.

'Don't you dare say that I'm doing it wrong,' she snapped.

'I wasn't saying anything,' he said, that smirk still lingering on his face.

'It just doesn't work for me,' she said. 'I've tried it, twice, and it's just a lot of . . .' She found herself making a gesture like she was trying to put two halves of an eggshell back together and quickly stopped. Stefan sniggered; she elbowed him in the side.

He stumbled sideways. 'How are you so pointy?' he muttered, rubbing his ribs. 'I wasn't laughing at you. Well, maybe a bit,' he said, as she began to protest, 'but only because you were doing that thing with your hands. You looked like you were trying to catch a fly.'

'That's what it feels like,' she muttered, folding her arms.

He pulled a face. 'What, always?'

Matei had been very nervous, and kissing him had felt like he was trying to headbutt her with his mouth. Nicolai had been extremely enthusiastic about his tongue and she'd come away with a wet chin, which had been unpleasant. In truth, she wasn't sure why she'd bothered kissing them; it had seemed like something she ought to do because everyone else was talking about it. She barely knew them – it seemed impossible that she would want to spend time mooning over either of them. Irina had been hoping for the kind of kiss that was sung about: slow, soft and sweet. Part of her still hoped for it, although she didn't know where she would find it. Surely it had to feel like that with somebody, otherwise all those musicians wouldn't have got out their fiddles in the first place.

'Pretty much,' she said.

'Wait,' he said, frowning, 'are you telling me that this isn't something you like, and you're still being forced to—'

'It's not like that,' she interrupted, 'no one forced me. I just thought . . . look, everyone else was doing it and it sounded fun, but then I tried it and it wasn't. It wasn't bad, it was just a thing I did, like . . . like washing clothes.'

'Washing clothes?'

Irina felt herself go scarlet. 'Well, maybe not washing clothes, but you get the idea. But it's fine. Matei was back in Timișoara and Nicolai was only passing through. We didn't really know each other, so nobody's heart got broken. It was a bit disappointing, but that's it.'

Stefan stared out across the unmoving fields. 'Shame,' he said.

The road had grown steeper. Irina had been feeling the burn in her thighs for a long time. Anxiety fizzed inside her with every step. Catalina's necklace had pointed them along a winding track, the gently sloping fields slowly giving way to jagged rock. But when she pulled it out to check, it hung limp. Convinced they were lost, they had turned around and begun walking down the hill, and that was when it had started into life and pointed them back up the hill again. Breathing hard as she climbed, Irina could not stop herself from touching it. It was the only thing she had that could lead her to her sister. Would she be able to find her if it stopped working?

Before long, they were in the foothills of real mountains, sparse pines growing thinner and stragglier the higher they climbed. Irina did not like looking at the trees. There was something unsettling about them, some strange uniformity in their branches that made her certain they had not grown from the earth. She and Stefan kept to the narrow path, keeping the vast slabs of rock to their right, and a tumbling slope of grey to their left.

'Maybe we should stop for a minute,' Stefan said.

'Oh, are you hungry?'

He looked a little surprised. 'Well, yes, but I thought maybe you might want to rest for a while. It's been a long walk.'

Irina was breathless and sweaty and would have happily slept by the side of the path, but she shook her head. 'I can keep going.'

'Come on, sit down. Get your breath back. You could check the necklace again while we're waiting, if you want to stay busy?'

Her hand closed over the wooden beads. She was almost afraid to look at it, in case it didn't work. What would Stefan say if she held up the necklace in mid-air and it stayed resolutely still? What would she do?

'You should eat first,' she said. 'Find me a place to sit?'

Stefan went a little further up the path. The moment his back was turned, Irina yanked off Catalina's necklace and held it up. There were a few moments of heart-stopping stillness, and then it lurched into life, pointing them further up the mountain. Irina sagged with relief and followed Stefan, unsure why she had not wanted him to see her makeshift compass fail. What would it mean for their journey, if she no longer had anything that would guide her way?

Up ahead, Stefan had found a flat slab of rock on the side

of the road. Irina hurried over, cramming Catalina's necklace into her pocket and unclasping her choker before she sat down. Pulling her braid over one shoulder, she tilted her head so that he could get a better angle. 'Whenever you're ready.'

He was on her in seconds. Teeth sank deep into her neck. Irina hissed. It stung. Stefan did not appear to notice. He was holding her head and her shoulder like they were two ends of a pork rib. Hot blood dripped onto her collarbone as she tried to ignore the strange tugging sensation of life being pulled from her veins. Stefan released her, panting, his mouth slick and crimson.

'Next time,' said Irina, scrabbling for the remaining half of her handkerchief with trembling hands, 'you have got to be more gentle. I thought you were going to take out a chunk, it hurt so much.'

Stefan had wiped blood off Irina's collarbone with his fingers; he froze with them halfway to his mouth. 'It hurts? Why didn't you say something?'

Irina gave him a very old-fashioned look. 'Of course it hurts,' she said, slapping the handkerchief over the bite wound. 'You are eating me, more or less.'

'I'm not eating you,' he said, licking the blood off his hand. 'I'm not chewing or anything. Besides, you could have said something.'

'You don't chew soup, either, and that still counts as eating.'

'Depends what you put in the soup. And anyway, you drink soup, which is what I'm—' He cut himself off, eyes fixed on his bloodstained hands. A part of him seemed to wilt at the sight of her blood on his fingers. 'I'm sorry.'

'It's all right,' Irina said, setting off on the path again.

'Don't you want to rest?'

Irina considered it for a moment. She felt a little light-headed, but moving helped. 'Not particularly.'

Stefan was frowning, wiping the blood off his face with the back of his hand. 'Are you sure? You haven't eaten or had anything to drink. I'm still hungry. Aren't you?'

Irina thought for a moment. She didn't feel all that hungry or thirsty – she'd been able to walk for what felt like miles – but now that she had stopped to consider it, her mouth was starting to feel dry. Perhaps it was a little unusual, she thought, but this was the longest and strangest journey she had ever been on; it was just as well her body was getting used to travelling. It was a blessing, really; she could not eat or drink anything in the land of the dead, or she'd be trapped. 'I can manage. Are you coming or not?'

He fell into step beside her. The necklace pointed them up the mountainside, and soon Irina was sweating, the handkerchief at her neck soaked through. She longed for a cold breeze, or for the chill of snow glittering on a mountaintop. But those were things from the land of the living. In the land of the dead, there was no cold wind howling down the mountainside, no snow blocking the path in freezing drifts. There was no moss beneath her feet, either, nor lichen clinging to the rocks. No mountain flowers sheltering at the base of boulders, hidden from the worst of the wind. Once, she saw a shadow flicker across the path and looked up, searching for a cloud tumbling across the sky or a bird swooping overhead. But there was nothing. It reminded Irina of when her mother would cook; before she knew what she was going to make, there was an onion sizzling in the pan in melted butter. It sat there, glistening, for a long time before the rest of the dish took shape. The land of the dead felt similar, as if only the bones of the world were there and the rest had yet to be formed.

Eventually, the path came to an end. It flattened out onto a ledge of grey rock that looked as if half of it had been snapped off. The mountain loomed over them on their right, far too steep to climb; on their left, a sheer face of rock tumbled down into the valley below. At the edge of the platform was the end of a rope bridge, stretching over a vast gorge. Irina's stomach dropped. It looked sturdy enough – the bottom was made of three long strands of rope knotted together, each one as thick as her thigh, and two long ropes ran alongside it like handrails. Strong ropes joined the footrope to the two supports at regular intervals, so she supposed it did technically have sides, but somehow that didn't feel reassuring when she could see even from the ledge that the gaps between were wide enough for her to slip through and go plummeting down into the gorge. Irina's palms were sweating. She peered over the ledge, clutching one of the bridge posts for support, her mouth very dry. Far below, curling through the gorge like twisting smoke, was a silver river. It gleamed in every colour of grey she had ever seen: steel, pewter, slate, iron. A spray of water glittered like silver coins; another the colour of cracked black pepper. This was the Grey River that they had been warned not to cross: the river of sorrow.

Irina took out Catalina's necklace and held it up. It swung loose in her hand – *please work*, she thought, as it stayed motionless, *please, please work* – then pointed directly across the bridge. She groaned.

'Could we find a way around?' Stefan asked. He was peering over the ledge, too, not even trying to hide the trepidation in his voice.

Irina put the necklace back on and checked her clothes, making sure that everything was tightly fastened. 'Do you really want to go back to that city? Or risk running into the beast again?'

'No, but – you're going to do it no matter what I say, aren't you?' he said, as Irina took hold of the bridge posts, testing the ropes with one of her feet.

'I would have listened first,' she said. She kicked the footrope experimentally; it seemed solid enough. Not that she knew much about bridges, of course, but the fact that it was not immediately unravelling was a good sign.

Stefan winced. 'Please don't kick the knots.'

'It seems fine.'

'How would you know?'

'Look, we have to cross,' Irina said, 'and the longer we stand here talking about it, the worse it's going to feel. I'll go first, if you're nervous.'

'I'm not—'

Irina stepped onto the bridge.

She regretted it at once. It dropped, just a little, as the ropes took her weight. She grabbed the support ropes immediately, heart racing. This was normal, she told herself, edging forward and taking deep, slow breaths. It was a rope bridge; it was bound to have some give in it. She shuffled forward, the silver water spinning and flowing beneath her. Her hands were covered in sweat.

'How is it?' Stefan called.

'Great!' Irina yelled. 'So great!'

'Liar!'

Irina shuffled further out over the river. 'I'm a liar on a rope bridge, so shut up, please!'

Taking slow, deep breaths, she inched across the river. The bridge bent and swayed with her every step, the weight of her taking it closer to the surface of the water. It was still far, far below, but now, the splash and roar of the river echoed all around, enveloping her in noise. If she slipped through the sides and fell, she would go crashing into it. How far and how fast would the water carry her away? How long would it be before she found Catalina if she fell into the river?

Would she ever see her again?

The thought slammed into Irina with all the force of an arrow loosed from a hunter's bow. Catalina was so young, and there was no one in the land of the dead to care for her. She was lost, alone – God only knew what kind of trouble she was in with the guardians. What if Irina never found her at all? The land of the dead was vast and unknowable, filled with strange and unsettling things. How could she ever hope to cross it and find her sister safe? And that was saying nothing of their parents. Eventually they would realize that Irina had not gone back to work in Timișoara, and would find the little house at the edge of the woods. How long would it be before they came looking for her? Or maybe they wouldn't even come at all. How could she have left them to go tearing into the underworld on a fool's errand, and deprived them of another daughter?

'Irina?' Stefan called. His voice sounded so far away.

Irina clung to the support ropes, her vision blurry with tears. The silver water of the river suddenly seemed closer than it had done before, the other end of the rope bridge high over her head. It was so long, and she was already exhausted. Surely it would be better to stop for a while, to wait in the middle of the bridge until her tears had dried.

But then, she thought, Catalina was waiting. Her sister needed her. Irina would not let her down.

She took a deep, shuddering breath. Tears were coursing down her cheeks. Slowly, Irina dragged herself forward, hauling herself up towards the other end of the bridge. Her body felt leaden, and all she wanted to do was lie down on the ropes and cry her heart out. But, she reasoned, as she forced one foot in front of the other, she would do that on the other side. The far end of the bridge drew nearer, the ropes flexing underneath her feet as she climbed towards it, and finally, she was on solid ground again. Irina collapsed onto a shelf of grey rock much like the one on the other side of the bridge, shaking all over.

'Irina?' Stefan called. 'Are you all right?'

She nodded, and then remembered that he probably couldn't see her clearly from the other side of the river. It was just as well; her face was wet with tears. 'Yes,' she called. 'Be careful.'

There was a creak of ropes from the other side of the gorge, and a distant swear word echoed across to her. Stefan was crossing the bridge.

Irina turned away and wiped her eyes, flapping her hands in front of her cheeks. She didn't like the thought of him seeing her cry. It felt selfish, after everything that had happened with Danil. She was sure Stefan would not think so, but still, she did not want to be another burden for him to carry. He had died; he had been through enough. She took a moment to compose herself, shaking out her skirts and pressing the cold heels of her hands under her eyes. He could not tell that she had been crying now.

There was a creak. She turned around. The bridge was sagging into the depths of the gorge. Nothing was broken – the posts were not straining against the rock, the ropes were not fraying – but somehow, the ropes were stretching dozens of feet down, almost brushing the surface of the river. Stefan was at the centre, a dead weight pulling everything downwards. The Grey River rushed beneath him, silver-and-steel water splashing close to the soles of his blackened feet. He did not appear to notice. He was slumped forward, almost on his knees, arms draped across the support ropes like a discarded marionette.

Too late, she realized what was happening. The Grey River was the river of sorrow. Cross it, and your sadness would weigh you down.

She rushed forward, peered over the ledge. 'Stefan?' she yelled.

He did not answer. He did not move. Panic blazed through Irina like a comet.

'I'm coming to get you!' she called. 'Stay right there!'

As soon as she placed a toe onto the footrope, pain burst across the soles of her feet. Irina shrieked, stumbling back. The smell of burned leather was emanating from the bottom of her shoes. She checked, and on the tip of her shoe was a small, singed patch. Irina started forward anyway – if she was quick, it would not matter – but then, she noticed the smouldering patch of rope. Fear froze all her thoughts. If she went back down the bridge, she could burn right through it and kill them both.

'I can't come and get you!' she shouted. She had no idea if she should tell him she had set the bridge on fire: would panic propel him to safety, or would it only make it worse? 'Stefan, you need to keep moving!'

The ropes sagged. The bridge dipped a little lower. He was inches away from the surface of the water now. One surge, and the river would take him. Panicking, Irina shook out her damp and bloody handkerchief and slammed it over the smouldering patch of rope. There was a quiet *hiss*. A plume of smoke. She waited. No sparks flared, no linen crackled into flame. When she drew back the handkerchief gingerly, there was no sign that the fire had ever been there; instead, there was only a small clutch of red peonies, their stalks growing over and around the burned patch of rope, holding it in place. Hope burst into life. She could not cross the bridge, but she could touch it.

She had an idea.

Irina dropped to her knees. Scrambling forward, she knelt on the ledge and grabbed the footrope in both hands, clutching it to her chest and lifting it as high as she could. From far below, she heard Stefan swearing as the rope beneath his feet shifted upwards.

'You have to keep going!' she yelled. 'I can help from here, but you have to keep moving, or you'll fall into the water!'

At last, he spoke. His voice sounded thick. 'Did you pick up the rope?'

'Come up here and find out!'

Silence. The footrope swayed in her hands. Then, it twitched, and twitched again, as Stefan's footsteps finally resumed. Irina's arms were throbbing. Her hands were starting to cramp. Wider than her torso, the footrope was heavy enough on its own, without the weight of a young man crossing it. But she held on, sweat beading across her scalp, her whole body aching. She wouldn't let go. Not until she saw him well clear of the water.

At last, he came into view. His face was completely stricken, his hands shaking, but he was only a few steps away. Slowly, Irina eased the footrope back into place. It bounced. Stefan's hands tightened on the support ropes, knuckles gleaming grey under the purple-black skin. She staggered to her feet, arms throbbing, and held out a hand.

The footrope settled. Stefan charged across the last few feet of the bridge. His feet landed on solid ground, his fingers closed around her hand. The moment he touched her, he fell to his knees, trembling.

'Move away from the bridge a little,' she said, crouching down beside him, 'you'll feel better. You did really well, Stefan, you did so well.'

He didn't move. Irina slid an arm around his shoulders and shuffled him a few inches away from the bridge posts as best she could. He wouldn't stop shaking.

'Stefan?'

He buried his face in his hands. He shook his head.

Tentatively, Irina placed a hand on his arm. 'It's all right,' she said. 'We made it.'

'He left me.'

Stefan's voice was ragged, his face still buried in his hands, and

Irina had to lean forward to hear him speak. 'Danil?' she asked.

Stefan shook his head. 'He *left*,' he whispered, 'he just . . .'

'Who?'

'My father.'

He looked up at her then. Tears were streaming down his face. Every blood vessel in his eyes was red and, for a moment, Irina wondered if they were going to bleed. He did not need to breathe, of that she was reasonably sure, but he was gasping, clutching at his elbows as though he was afraid he was going to come apart.

Irina shuffled a little closer, laid a hand on his knee. 'Stefan,' she said, her voice gentle, 'what happened with your father?'

Stefan wiped his eyes on his sleeve. 'There was a widow he had his eye on,' Stefan whispered. 'She had good land, and money. But she was young – closer to my age than his. He got suspicious when I snuck out to see Danil. Marta was convinced it was her I was seeing and told anyone who would listen, and I let her, so my father wouldn't find Danil. I never told him where I was going – he never found out, thank God – but after what Marta spread around the village, he thought I was with the widow. We fought. We . . . we always fought. Ever since I was a child. Everyone knew.'

Dread crawled across Irina's thoughts, freezing everything it touched. Marta was one of the people Stefan had killed – her, Eugen and Anton. 'When you say you fought . . .'

Stefan pointed to a scar on his elbow that she had not noticed before. 'Everyone knew,' he spat, 'every single one of them. I learned how to defend myself, and they knew that, too. He couldn't beat the truth out of me – couldn't even get near me. But that wasn't . . . it couldn't . . .'

'It's all right,' Irina soothed, 'it's all right.'

'It's not all right!' Stefan snapped, knocking her hand away. 'Do you know what he did when he realized he couldn't hit me any more? He waited. He waited until summer turned to autumn and then he took me out with the flock on the hills when the sun was still high. He sent me looking for a lost lamb up near the forest, persuaded me to give him my coat and winter boots. He said I wouldn't need them on the climb, that he'd look after them for me. Eugen was there, too, told me a real man wouldn't need to be bundled up like a child for such a basic task. So I let him take my things. I let him do it, Irina! And when the snows came, all I had was this,' he said, plucking at his thin linen shirt.

'But . . . but you'd freeze.'

Stefan let out a mirthless laugh. It sounded more like a sob. 'He knew I would. He knew a storm was on its way; he could always tell. But he *left me* there, Irina. He left me there to die. And . . . I did.'

Irina's hand flew to her mouth.

'But I came back,' he snarled. 'I came back and I saw him through the window, slumped over a bottle and pretending to the neighbours that he needed to be consoled. And when they left, I heard them talking – Eugen and Anton. Anton had been asked to search for me when the storm came, did you know? He wouldn't do it. He said he thought I'd run off, and he didn't even sound guilty when he confessed. They said it had only been a matter of time before something like this,' he said, gesturing to himself, 'happened, considering what went on in that house. They knew. They *all knew*. And they did nothing.'

Horror had Irina in its claws. 'What did you do?'

'I killed them.'

She had known it was coming. He'd made no secret of what he did. And still, the words felt like a cold hand on the back of her neck.

'Him first,' Stefan said. 'I made him suffer. Scratched at the window for weeks, whispering his name. He burned all my things in the courtyard to make me go away, but it didn't work. Then I moved on to the rest of them. Every single person in that village knew what he did to me. None of them did anything. I lived there for my whole life, Irina, and none of them lifted a finger to help me – not once, in nineteen years! They were all of them guilty. So I punished them.'

Irina wished she could say that it made no sense to her, that she couldn't imagine anyone doing anything so horrible. But she knew that they could. The villagers had been so eager to give her to a monster. She had only been there for a few weeks before they'd asked her to participate in the wedding of the dead, and she was not the only unmarried girl in the village. They could have sent Stefan one of their own. But they hadn't. They'd let him go on killing, until a stranger with no family to speak for her arrived on their doorsteps. It was no surprise at all that they had turned a blind eye to what his father had done.

'They dug an empty grave and said it was mine,' he spat, 'but they don't even know where I fell. They never had the guts for a real search of the forest or the hillside, never cared enough to try and give me a real burial. They shut themselves away in their safe little houses, like they always did, rather than face me and face what they'd done! I had to do it. I had to make them see – and they still won't, because they sent you to fix their problems instead. You! You know nothing about my life, or my father, or my death, and still they sent *you*? Why? What do I have to do to make them see?' He slumped forward, burying his face in his hands. 'What is it about me that made it all right for them to ignore everything that happened? What's wrong with me?'

'There's nothing wrong with you,' she said.

'Then why didn't they—'

Irina grabbed the back of his neck, forcing him to look up

at her. 'There's nothing wrong with you,' she repeated. A lump was swelling in her throat. 'Nothing.'

'Then why—'

'Because they're bad people!' she yelled, her voice breaking. 'They're bad people and they shouldn't have let your father hurt you or leave you to die – they shouldn't have let any of this happen!' Her hand curled into a fist, the fine strands of hair at the back of his neck tickling her skin. 'You didn't deserve it!'

His mouth fell open. He was staring up at her, his dark eyes shining with tears. Desperate hope was scrawled across his face when he looked at her, but still, there was a glimmer of mistrust in his eyes. 'I killed people,' he said quietly. His tone reminded Irina of a man testing old wooden steps, looking for the ones that would snap underneath his feet.

'Would you have done it if you weren't hungry?' she asked, her temper rising. 'If you hadn't been left for dead? If you were a living man, would you have killed all those people?'

He shook his head. 'I still—'

'No,' Irina snapped. 'Whatever you were going to say: no. Yes, you killed people. No, you shouldn't have done it. But this was not written in the stars because there is something wrong with you, Stefan. You are the way you are because other people failed you. You didn't deserve to be treated like this!'

Her hand drifted around to his cheek, ruffling through his hair. He was looking at her as though she was something to be prayed to. One hand reached out, gently taking hold of her skirts, he touched it like it was cloth of gold.

'You deserved better,' she said.

Tears poured down his face. Irina put her arms around him and let him cry, cradling his head against her chest. Juddering sobs wracking his whole body, he clung to her and wept.

PART THREE

They did not speak on their way down the mountain. Stefan seemed embarrassed. Irina caught him turning away from her far more often than meeting her eyes. Once or twice, she thought about puncturing the silence. But when she thought about what to say, all her words curdled in the back of her throat. What could she say, after finding out that Stefan had been murdered by his own father and, in some twisted way, considered himself responsible for it? She couldn't exactly talk about the weather, after learning something like that. There wasn't any weather, for a start.

Her feet crunched over loose gravel. The path was steep and winding, and her knees were aching. In fact, her whole body was aching. Picking up a rope as wide as her own body had not been a good idea. More than anything, Irina wanted to lie down and sleep. But after vines had curled themselves around her throat the last time she'd tried to sleep outside, the rocky ground was looking even less inviting.

Stefan cleared his throat. 'Are you . . .'

'Mmm? I'm fine. Just a little tired.'

He made a sceptical noise but said nothing.

'We can't stay up here, it's too exposed,' Irina said, taking off the necklace and holding it up again. 'Let's just . . .'

Nothing was happening. Her words strangled themselves in

the back of her throat. The necklace wasn't moving at all. Panicked tears sprang to her eyes. How could it not be working? What had she done? Had she broken it? Irina shook the necklace frantically; it jiggled, and then hung still. Why wasn't it working? How would she find Catalina now?

Suddenly, it moved. The beads twitched feebly, pointing down the mountain. Irina clapped a hand over her mouth, trying to hold back a sob of relief. It wasn't broken. She wasn't alone.

Stefan laid a hand on her shoulder. She flinched; it was always a shock to remember he could move so quietly. 'Are you all right?'

'Yes,' she lied, shoving the necklace back on and praying no tears had actually fallen. 'Yes, I'm fine. It's that way.'

Gradually, the path began to flatten beneath their feet. The forest thickened around them, and though there were pines clustering close enough to touch on either side of the path, Irina could smell no sap, hear no rustling needles. She knew she ought to be relieved – that meant the beast had not caught up with them – but it was unnerving to see no signs of life at all. Further down the mountain there was only a vast green sweep of pine, a thin grey ribbon of a path, and the same cold grey sky. The only thing she noticed was a pulsing, thumping headache at the back of her brain, throbbing with every step, and when she realized what it meant, she groaned.

'I think there's another door,' she muttered.

Stefan swore, then turned on the spot three times. 'I hate these damn things.'

Irina shot him a sideways glance. '*You* hate them?'

'I don't enjoy watching you scream in pain, you know,' he said, sounding a little offended.

Irina spun around too. When she came to a halt, a slice of

the world had torn away in the direction the necklace had been pointing, revealing another layer beneath it, and another gate her sister had passed through. The world they were staring into had trees cut far back from a wide road, fanning out into a well-swept street. It was twilight there, the sky a rich, deep blue. A small cluster of wooden buildings sat on either side of the road, each one with gentle golden light at the windows. The largest building was a whitewashed inn, two storeys tall and with strong, high walls. An arched doorway was cut into the wall, wide enough for a cart to drive right through it; two vast wooden doors were held open on either side with ropes as thick as her arm. Irina glimpsed a cobbled courtyard through the arch, heard laughter and music spilling into the dusk, and made up her mind. She just knew the beds would be soft.

'So do you want to run straight through, or . . .' Stefan asked.

The door was about twenty yards away from them. Running might work. She was far away enough to build up momentum before the worst of the pain hit. If she was lucky, her legs would not crumple and she could still keep moving – and at least it would be quick.

Irina ground her feet into the dirt. 'Yes.'

Stefan nodded. He walked through the door – *so easily*, Irina thought, with a burst of envy – and stopped just inside it, turning and holding out his hands to her. 'Just in case,' he said, when she gave him a questioning look. 'If it looks like you're about to trip, I'll grab you.'

Irina took a deep breath. The headache thumped with every twitch of her pulse; she could feel it getting faster. She gave Catalina's necklace a quick squeeze, half-tempted to press it to her lips like a rosary. An animal anxiety was stalking through her thoughts. It was going to hurt so much. The memory of the pain was seared into her, blistering under her skin. Was she really going to force herself through it again? How many more times was she going to do this to herself?

Even as she thought it, she knew the answer. *As many as it took.* Irina curled her hands into fists. Then she sprinted for the door.

Agony slammed into her. Her bones felt like they were boiling, her limbs suddenly loose as rubber. She staggered but kept going. She could feel the impact of every footstep in her teeth, rattling in her jaw. Nausea rose at the back of her throat. Her skin felt like it was being seared away, but still she kept going, forcing herself forwards. The door was only a few steps away. She couldn't give up, she had to keep going . . .

Her knees buckled. She staggered, slowed. Stefan reached through the door with both hands, grabbed her by the arms and pulled her through. Red-hot pain washed over her. A scream died in the back of her throat. And then, it vanished. Loose-limbed and shaking, Irina lurched forward, feeling like most of her body had been burned away as, out of the corner of her eye, Stefan closed the door.

He put an arm around her shoulders, letting her lean into him. 'Are you all right?'

Irina nodded.

'Liar,' Stefan said matter-of-factly.

Irina nodded.

He let out a low laugh, giving her shoulder a squeeze. 'Let's get you inside,' he said. 'I can't sit you down for a drink or a hot meal, so sleep is the only thing that might actually make you feel better here.'

'But what about the beast? We need to keep moving.'

'Irina, please,' he said, clearly trying to hide his frustration. 'Do you really think you're going to get far like this?'

'Fine,' Irina rasped.

They set off, heading for the inn, the candles in its many

windows gleaming like trapped constellations. Through the darkness, she could see the shapes of the houses clustered around the sides of the road: pale, whitewashed buildings criss-crossed with dark wooden beams. There were no fields, no animal pens, not even a well at the centre of the little settlement. By all rights, there should not be a village here at all, let alone a thriving inn. There was nothing to support it. But all the same, the inn was brightly lit and ringing with music, carts and wagons trundling into the courtyard, laughter spilling into the street.

'What about the people?' she whispered, her voice still hoarse. 'It looks busy.'

'I won't let anyone get near you,' he promised.

She shook her head. 'We should keep going.'

He kept steering her towards the inn. 'And we will. After you've slept. You look like you're about to faint.' He caught the look on her face and paused. 'I can ask around while you're sleeping. See what I can find out. But I can't let you try and keep going. You'll hurt yourself.'

Every part of her was itching to keep moving, to set her feet on the road and follow the necklace while it still worked. But she felt as though she had been hauled out of a fast-flowing river: weighed down and trembling. As much as she wanted to keep moving, she knew she was no good to Catalina like this. With a sigh, she nodded.

Stumbling over the cobbles, Irina stepped into the courtyard. It was enormous, packed with brightly coloured wagons, lacquered coaches and simple wooden carts. There were no horses in sight, although there seemed to be a stable on the far side of the courtyard; Irina was torn between wanting to take a closer look at it and dreading finally seeing whatever unseen things had been pulling all those wagons. Around the edges of the courtyard, covered wooden staircases and walkways led up to the rooms, each one with a heavy wooden door. A steady stream of people was heading to the left and into a brightly lit room; the sound of clinking cups, music and laughter made it clear that this was the main taproom.

They pushed open the door.

Irina had to remind herself that all the people she was looking at were not alive. Talking, laughing, joking, singing – it did not matter how full of life they seemed – every single one of them had met their death. They seemed perfectly ordinary, huddled over bowls of stew at little wooden tables, clambering over benches to speak to their friends, guiltily mopping spilled beer off the plastered walls with their sleeves before the landlord noticed. Stefan and Irina picked their way between the tables, Stefan's arm clamped around Irina's shoulder, until they reached the bar. Behind the wide, wooden bench was a middle-aged couple who moved around each other so easily that Irina was sure they were husband and wife.

'Do you have any rooms for the night?' Stefan asked.

The woman looked them up and down, her eyes lingering on Irina's uncovered hair and Stefan's torn clothes. 'Ground floor suit you?'

Stefan grimaced. 'I was hoping for something a little more private,' he said. 'We're newlyweds, so . . .'

Irina went bright red. Quickly, she looked at Stefan, so she didn't have to see the expressions on the innkeeper and his wife's faces. It did not work. She could *feel* their eyebrows waggling.

'Top floor, at the back?' the woman asked, grinning.

'Yes, please.'

She snorted. 'All right. Follow me.'

She led them back into the courtyard, snickering. Irina shot Stefan a hard look; he gave her a syrupy smile in view of all the other guests. Footsteps creaking on the wooden staircase, the landlady showed them up to the top floor, explaining the rules as she went.

'The bar is open late. We can do you dinner if you've not eaten, and breakfast. A bath will be extra, and so will laundry, but if I may be frank with you both, that's a cost you should consider. You can look at the room now, but I'm not handing over the key until I've been paid.'

They were nearly at the back of the building now. There were three rooms on this side, each one locked. The landlady took out a heavy iron key and opened one of the doors to reveal a small, whitewashed room with a wooden floor, a narrow bed, and a table with a pewter washbasin on it. It was spotless, lit by a single dribbling candle and the last blue light before true night fell. Irina only saw the bed. The blankets were heavy white wool, striped with patterns in red, green and black, and there was a deliciously soft-looking pillow that was all but calling out to her.

The landlady held up the key, an expectant expression on her face.

'How much?' Stefan asked warily.

'Tell me how you met,' she said, her eyes shining. 'There's a story there, I know it.'

Irina cleared her throat. It felt full of splinters. 'We were—'

The landlady looked at her, alarmed. 'You're not sick, are you? I won't have you in my inn if you're sick.'

'No,' Stefan said quickly, 'she's just . . . really hoarse. From . . . well . . . we are newlyweds, so . . .'

Once again, Irina went scarlet. The landlady let out a filthy laugh. 'I should hope so!' she said, as Irina covered her face in her hands. Why did everyone have to be so interested in what people did to each other in the marriage bed? She felt like she was about to catch fire, she was so embarrassed.

'You said you wanted to know how we met?' Stefan blurted.

'There's not much to it. She's from the next village over; we saw each other a few times growing up. I never thought she'd look at me twice, so I never looked at her. But . . .' he said, his voice beginning to soften, 'I started seeing her differently. I realized how kind she was. She can be so gentle, but there's a core of granite to her. Everyone else just . . . faded away.'

Stefan's hand was motionless on Irina's shoulder. It was not warm – it never had been – but it was very, very gentle. It was as if he was afraid she was as fragile as a soap bubble that could pop under his hands with one wrong move.

He cleared his throat. 'Anyway. We were in love, we eloped. I'm not good enough for her, so her family wouldn't have . . . anyway. Now, we're married. We're heading off to meet our families first thing in the morning, so if this is everything you need, maybe we could get into the room now?'

The landlady was beaming at them. 'I *knew* you eloped,' she said. 'A ragamuffin like you, and her in those pretty clothes, without so much as a headscarf? Of course you eloped.' She handed over the key. 'You'll want a bath and laundry if you're going to persuade her family you didn't steal their little girl away,' she said with a grin. 'I could even be persuaded to give you some of my husband's old things, if you tell me what's wrong with your hands.'

There was a pause. Irina was certain the truth – that his hands had changed colour after his own death – would buy them far more than a wash and some old clothes. However, she was also certain that was a secret better kept than shared.

'I'm a dyer,' he said. 'Can't get the colour off.'

The landlady frowned. 'How did it get on your feet?'

Stefan didn't hesitate. 'I dropped it.'

She looked disappointed. 'I'll have someone bring up a tub and hot water,' she said grudgingly, 'but the pair of you are to keep your clothes on until then. I won't have one of my girls seeing something they shouldn't.'

Irina fled into the room, face burning. Stefan followed and shut the door behind them. 'Before you say anything,' he said, as Irina flopped onto the bed, 'I panicked.'

'Couldn't you just have told her I needed a glass of water?' she rasped, staring up at the wooden ceiling.

'Then she would have brought you a glass of water,' Stefan snapped, 'and you aren't supposed to eat or drink anything here.'

Irina groaned. 'It would've been fine. I'm not even thirsty.'

He blinked at her. 'You aren't?'

'Not really. I was, but it went away.' She still wasn't thirsty now, even though it had been days, perhaps, since she had last drunk anything. Unease prickled at the back of her neck.

Stefan was frowning at her, pulling at his bottom lip as he thought. His pointed teeth gleamed. 'You said you weren't hungry, either.'

Irina propped herself up on her elbows. Silence was emanating from Stefan, and it was worrying. He was leaning against the windowsill, plucking at everything within reach – his mouth, the collar of his shirt, the lobe of his ear, his hands fluttering like crows.

'And it's been like this the whole time you've been here?' he asked. He spoke as if she was an animal he did not want to startle, and it was that, more than anything, which frightened her.

Irina sat up properly. The palms of her hands prickled with sweat. 'No,' she said. 'I was hungry when we came in. And thirsty. It's been getting better. I suppose I've just got used to it . . .'

She trailed off when she saw the look on his face. Bad news was poised on the tip of his tongue.

'Are you sure?' he whispered.

There was a knock at the door. They both flinched. Two

teenage girls in white linen dresses and matching black-and-red aprons came in, lugging buckets of hot water and a tin tub with them. They were sniggering, glancing between Irina and Stefan and clearly hoping to stumble across some gossip. They filled the bath, still whispering to each other, and when the door closed behind them, they burst out laughing. It was strangely comforting. Irina's pride was smarting a little, but judgemental teenage girls whispering about her choice of man seemed so normal. A little of her unease faded.

'I'm sure it's fine,' she said, with more certainty than she felt. Stefan looked so worried. 'It'd be worse if I was hungry or thirsty. The temptation isn't there.'

Stefan was shaking his head. 'But that's the problem. People don't want for things here, Irina. Whatever they need is just given to them.'

'How do you know?'

He ran a hand through his hair. 'I don't, but . . . it's like how people get around this place. Have you heard anyone we've met complain about being hungry or thirsty? People – *living* people – talk about that all the time.' He pointed at the door. 'They don't. Maybe that's why you couldn't bring the food of the living down here.'

'They still eat, though—'

'That's not the point,' he snarled, his voice suddenly rough. 'Hunger and thirst are parts of life, but they're not parts that bother you any more! Don't you see? You're becoming like them!'

Irina's hand flew to her mouth. Dread had her by the throat. 'You think I'm dying?'

'No,' he snapped. 'No, I don't.' He sighed, and sat next to her on the bed. 'I just . . . I think this place is bad for you. Between this, the gates, and what you can do to people . . .'

Irina hugged her knees to her chest. 'I'm not sure if this place is bad for me, or if I'm bad for it.'

'You could never be bad for anyone,' he said, staring at the far corner of the room. He rubbed the back of his neck. 'I know you want to find your sister, but for God's sake, Irina, be careful. I don't want to see you hurt. We can always turn back.'

'Not without Catalina.'

'I . . . of course. Not without Catalina.' Before Irina could say any more, he was on his feet and heading for the door. 'Have your bath,' he said, avoiding her eyes. 'I'll go and see about those clothes.'

Irina sat in the bathtub, cupped hands full of steaming water. She felt no urge to drink. It was only when she stared at the water between her fingers and concentrated, forcing herself to think about how dry her mouth was, that she felt anything at all. She recoiled. When had she started needing to force herself to feel hunger or thirst? How had she not realized?

Fear sent her lurching out of the bath, water dripping across the floor. Her soaking hair felt like a snake against her back. She squeezed it out over the tub, suddenly desperate to be dry, to be safe. She could not drink any of the water here, even a drop. She'd changed enough already. If even a single droplet passed her lips, she'd be – she didn't even know what she would be.

But though her hands were shaking, her thoughts all but crushed under the weight of her fear, her eyes still ached to close. She was so tired. It dulled the edges of the dread scraping at her thoughts. She wrapped up her hair in a piece of linen and crawled into bed, burying herself under soft sheets and thick woollen blankets. For a moment, she wondered where Stefan would sleep, but then her head hit the pillow and she was gone, lost in dreams full of the sound of wings.

When she awoke, she felt groggy, weighed down. Someone had placed a thick, brown fur on the bed. She sat up, the muscles in her arms twingeing, and the moment she started to move Stefan yelled, 'I didn't see anything, I *swear*.'

Irina yelped and dived back under the blankets, face burning. Too late, she realized that the night before she had got out of her bath and into bed, without bothering to do anything so unnecessary as putting on clothes. This would've been fine if she hadn't been sharing a room.

Stefan had been sitting on the floor; now he'd sprung to his feet and was heading for the door, one hand covering his face. 'I promise I just got you another blanket,' he was saying, 'I didn't see anything. Um . . . your clothes are clean, they're over here, so I'm going to . . .'

He bolted out of the door, slamming it behind him. Irina groaned, pulling the blankets over her head and wondering, briefly, if she could stay there forever. But then she hauled herself out of bed, dressed in her clean and mended wedding clothes, and wondered exactly how red in the face she was. She was sure she looked like a poisonous mushroom; she only ever blushed blotchily.

She was unwrapping her hair and shaking it out when something made her stop. Stefan had lined up all her snowdrops along the windowsill, in order of size. The things that had been in her pockets were neatly laid beside them: a tidy tower of pfennigs; her handkerchief, now cleaned and sat in a perfectly pressed square; her beaded choker and Catalina's necklace. Each had been laid out carefully, the long loop of wooden beads encircling the choker in a ring. Every single thing that Irina had carelessly shoved into her pockets was laid out, waiting for her. It was oddly touching to think of him taking such care over her things. It made her wish she'd taken better care of them, too. What had he thought, when he'd seen there were only pfennigs in her pockets, or eyed the rushed edges of her handkerchief? She laid a careful finger on the linen, a doubt she'd never entertained before creeping into her mind when she looked at the wide stitching. Had he noticed and thought her careless?

Blushing, she crammed everything into her pockets apart from the necklaces and the flowers. Fastening her jewellery around her neck, she went to open the door.

Stefan was waiting outside, staring determinedly at the floorboards. He started when he heard the hinges squeak, whirling around with eyes full of guilt and panic. 'I promise I—'

'I believe you,' Irina said, holding the door open. He scuttled back inside, and it was only then that Irina registered his clothes. Clean, well-fitting, and with no suspiciously claw-like tears in the material, they made him look like a new person. He was holding himself differently in his fresh linen shirt: no longer half-hunched and ready to spring, his shoulders were set back to show off the line of red-and-black embroidery running down the centre of his chest. She could see the line of his shoulders underneath his embroidered black vest, notice the shape of his waist defined by his broad leather belt. He even seemed to be standing a little taller – but he was, she realized; his new linen trousers were tucked into a pair of high black boots, worn but supple. The last traces of blood were gone from his face, and as he turned to look at her, nerves writ large across his face, for the first time she saw what they had been trying to make everyone else see. With clean, new clothes and an anxious expression, he looked like a groom waiting at the altar. Only his hands gave him away. He'd rolled down the sleeves of his new shirt, buttoning them at the wrist. At a distance, they might have passed for black gloves; close to, there was no ignoring the purple-black of his fingers, or the ink-dark veins on the back of his hands. Irina was struck with the sudden urge to take his hand in hers. He looked so nervous.

'You look nice,' she said.

He smiled sheepishly, rubbing the back of his neck. 'I think I'm just clean.'

'No, I mean it,' Irina said. She gestured to his clothes, ignoring the blush creeping into her cheeks. 'This suits you.'

She turned away, twisting her hair into a braid. Why was it suddenly so warm in here?

'So do you,' Stefan said, his voice quiet.

'I'm sorry?'

He cleared his throat. 'Not that you suit me, I mean – although you do, of course, but that's not what . . . it was the first part. The nice part.'

Irina's hands stilled halfway down her plait. Was there a compliment buried underneath all of that, or was she reading too much into things? She pushed a little further. 'I'm just wearing the same thing as always.'

'It's nice,' he mumbled. 'It's always nice, you always look . . . you're just – your hair is . . . good.'

Irina blushed. That definitely was a compliment. If it had come from a stranger, she would have batted it away or changed the subject; compliments had only ever led to awkwardness, in her experience. But, coming out of his mouth, compliments sounded different. They sounded like something she might want to listen to.

'Well,' he said, too loud, 'should we go?'

'Yes,' Irina blurted, cramming the snowdrops into her pockets.

They left the room, creeping towards the wide wooden staircase. Footsteps creaking on the floorboards as they stole down the stairs and into the courtyard. No sound came from the bar below. Overhead, the sky was the same rich blue as it had been when they arrived. Irina had no idea if it had changed while she had been sleeping. The only sign that time had passed at all was the quiet, and the fact that the double doors leading into the courtyard were now closed.

'Where to now?' Stefan whispered, when they were in the centre of the courtyard.

Irina took off Catalina's necklace and held it aloft. It shifted slightly to the right. Was that enough? Had she accidentally moved it herself? 'That way, I suppose,' she said. She headed for the double doors.

'That can't be it, can it?' he asked, staring at the necklace. 'It used to move much more.' He paused, biting his lower lip; Irina's eyes snagged on it. 'Is it still working?'

'Of course it's working,' she said, reaching for a confidence she did not feel. 'Look, it's moving.'

'Not like it used to.' Stefan put a hand on her arm. 'Why don't we try and find that doctor? He seemed to know his way around. If the necklace isn't working, maybe he can tell us where to go.'

'I mean,' Irina whispered, 'if we run into him, that'd be nice, but—'

She hauled open one of the doors. Stefan threw out an arm in front of her before she could walk through it. 'Wait.'

'What is it?'

He crouched down, peering at the ground. He was leaning so far forward that Irina wondered if he was going to sniff at the soil like an animal. Then he went still. Moments later, Irina saw what he was looking at, and panic caught her by the throat and squeezed.

Tracks. Vast tracks, pressed into the dirt outside the courtyard. They were enormous, each footprint easily as long as Irina's thigh. Long, pointed, and ending in three toes, they were bookended by divots in the soil, deep as Irina's finger. She dreaded to think of the claws that had sunk that deep into the earth.

The tracks were crossing over each other, just outside the

double doors. She could picture it now: some gigantic, claw-footed thing sniffing around the courtyard while she slept. They scratched up the dirt in a wide ring around the inn, disappearing behind one corner and reappearing around another. They were not the tracks of the beast they had seen earlier: neither the wide, smooth trail of the snake's tail nor the padded, four-toed tracks of a wolf's paws had any resemblance to these. What *was* this thing? How long had it circled the walls, snuffling at the ground to catch her scent?

Gently, Stefan reached over and closed the door. He caught Irina's eye and shook his head. Fear swiped a claw across her thoughts. Was it still out there?

'We can't stay,' she mouthed.

'We can't leave, either,' he muttered.

Irina retreated to the taproom and pushed open the door. The bar was empty but for the landlady. She was sitting in a wooden chair by the fire, her feet propped up on a stool. She gave them a lazy wave as they entered.

Fighting the urge to look over her shoulder, Irina went over to the landlady. 'Excuse me,' she said, 'you didn't hear any strange noises last night, did you?'

The woman snorted. 'Strange noises, is it?'

Irina flushed. 'Not from – come and look. There's funny marks outside the door.'

The landlady eased herself out of her chair and went to the door, rubbing her back. She peered outside. 'I'll be damned,' she muttered. 'I thought you were being coy.'

'Do you know what left them?' Irina asked.

She shook her head, frowning at her doorstep. 'Must've been quite a beast that did it.' She looked up at them sharply, all her tiredness gone. 'You're not planning on walking, are you?'

'Well—' Irina began.

'Absolutely not,' Stefan cut in.

'Smart boy,' the landlady said. 'My nephew Vasile is heading for the city with his wagon. You can ride with him, if that's where you're going.'

'What's in the city?' Irina asked.

The landlady shut the door and motioned them over to the fire. Close to, Irina noticed that, just as they had been in the hunters' camp, the flames were all moving in the exact same way: a slow, wide swoop to the left, a quick snap to the right. It reminded her of the monotonous way those wide-eyed animals had been staring at her, chewing. She shuddered, remembering the grinding of teeth.

'There's all sorts in the city,' the landlady said, easing herself back down into her chair with a groan as they pulled up a bench beside her. 'There's the dance, of course. You'll want to go to that. A coffee house or two, near the university. Markets, theatres, taverns – none so fine as this, mind you. What are you looking for? Somewhere to meet your parents?'

Irina and Stefan exchanged a glance. A university could be useful: if Doctor Emil was anywhere, he would be there, and with the necklace starting to fail he could be their only chance at navigating the land of the dead. Stefan sat up a little straighter and tried to look earnest. 'Yes, but I thought I'd see about studying something as well,' he said. 'Improve my prospects, now I'm married.'

The landlady gave him a sidelong smile. 'Make sure you're worthy of your wife, is that it?'

He looked away. Silence rolled over them all like thunder. Irina was already reaching for him, ready to lay a hand on his shoulder, when she froze, doubt locking her muscles in place. He was so proud. Would he even want her pity? She didn't want to make things worse. Besides, laying a hand on his arm in front of the landlady, feeling the muscles in his forearm twitch underneath her fingers as he clenched and unclenched his fists, would be unbearably intimate.

The landlady sighed. 'I was only teasing. I'll sure you'll make a fine scholar.'

He still didn't say anything. Irina cleared her throat; relief flashed across the landlady's face. 'I was wondering,' she said, 'those tracks outside the door . . . they wouldn't be from the guardians, would they?'

'No guardian I've ever seen,' the landlady replied. 'The ones that brought my Iulia were much more—'

Irina nearly fell off the bench. 'You've seen them? They brought your daughter home? What were they like?'

The landlady sniffed. 'Granddaughter, actually, but I'll take a compliment when I get one. They were . . .' she paused, rotating a hand as if she was trying to waft a cloud of steam towards her. 'Tall? I think they were tall. Or were they short? I don't know. There was a lot of light, I didn't get much of a look.'

Irina leaned forward. 'How did you know they were the guardians?'

'They brought Iulia,' the landlady said. 'And . . . there was something about the way they moved. It wasn't right.'

Stefan laid a hand on Irina's arm just as she was gearing up to ask another question. The landlady's face was screwed up, her eyes focusing on somewhere in the middle distance. Concern had started to trickle into her expression. If they pushed her for details, would she remember the face of the thing that had brought her granddaughter back to her? Or would she remember the truth of where she and her family were?

'Why are you asking about the guardians, anyway?' the landlady said, her voice disconcertingly slow. Irina tensed. She couldn't realize the truth. Not before they left on her nephew's wagon.

'We're looking for my sister,' Irina said. 'I thought if we could find her before she's delivered to my family – if Stefan could bring her back instead – then maybe they'd look a little more kindly on us.'

The light of gossip gleamed in the landlady's eyes. Suddenly, she was herself again. 'You crafty little thing,' she said, with relish. 'Meeting your parents with a smartly dressed husband *and* the prodigal son. Well, daughter, in your case. Oh, no wonder you eloped! A girl like you isn't going to let anything stand in the way of what she wants.'

Stefan snorted. Blushing, Irina resisted the urge to push him off the bench. 'So there's really no way to find them?' she asked.

'None that I know of. They find you, in my experience,' the landlady said. Irina shivered. After seeing those tracks, she had no desire to be found by anything. 'I'll tell you one thing, though. They left behind a little something, when they brought back Iulia.'

'What is it?' Irina asked eagerly.

The landlady nodded to the mantelpiece. 'Up there.'

Irina sprang off the bench for a closer look. The long mantelpiece above the fire was crowded with pewter tankards and steins, so well polished that Irina suspected they were only for show. But lying in front of them, flat against the wood, was a single feather.

'May I see?'

The landlady nodded. Irina snatched it at once, desperate for a closer look. The feather was long and thin when she held it one way, and when she pinched it between thumb and forefinger and rolled the quill, it spun into a shorter, fatter shape. Sleek, then downy; white, then black; coarse, then smooth as silk. The slightest movement sent it twirling into another shape entirely. Just looking at it made Irina's head ache. She was only holding one feather in her hand, but somehow, she was staring at a whole fistful flashing past one at a time.

'How is that possible?' she whispered.

The landlady shrugged. 'Who knows. Wiser folk than I might have an answer for you, though. If you visit that university, you can ask them about it.'

The landlady would say no more about the guardians, and Irina did not want to ask her. She was still wary of that empty look that had crossed her face. Drawing attention to herself now would be a mistake. So she sat on the bench with Stefan while the landlady went to fetch Vasile and his wagon, wondering about the creature that had been outside the tavern door, and the guardian that had left behind a feather that seemed to be every feather she had ever seen – and the dream she'd had the night before, which had left her with nothing but the memory of the sound of wings. She shivered, and edged a little closer to Stefan. After a little pause, he slid his arm around her shoulders.

Vasile was not much older than Stefan, with a broad, friendly face. He was wearing a sheepskin coat that was so enormous, all she could see of him were his hands, face and feet. He agreed to give them a lift into the city in exchange for a flask of țuică, which Irina paid for with an extravagant lie about the night she and Stefan had eloped. Before long, they were sitting in the back of Vasile's cart, watching the inn roll away from them. Irina tried to ignore the distinct lack of hooves ringing out across the road as the wheels turned underneath them.

For a while, they sat in silence. The sun had not risen, because there was no sun, but the sky was the delicate duck-egg blue that Irina always associated with early morning. Away from the inn, the countryside flattened out into a wide, grassy plain. Nothing moved. Sheets of gold and green grass stood perfectly still, looking more like the nap of a fine velvet than any plant Irina had ever seen. Occasionally they would pass by a lonely mill, dark against the grass, the blades unmoving. She wanted, badly, to check the necklace and make sure they were going in the right direction, but the thought of watching it hang still made her want to cry.

'Your flowers,' Stefan said suddenly.

'What?'

He gestured to her hair. 'You aren't wearing them.'

'Oh. They're in my pocket.'

'Do you want me to . . .'

Irina had never got a look at her hair after Stefan had fixed it for her the first time; she had no idea if he'd done a good job. But she remembered the gentle tug as he had tucked the first flower into her braid, the soft brush of his hand in her hair, and the word 'Yes,' was out of her mouth before she knew what she was saying.

He shuffled back in the body of the wagon, making space for her. 'Sit here.'

She did, fishing out the handful of snowdrops from her pocket and dropping them into his hand. She was careful not to touch him. Something felt different, and she was terrified that if her fingertips brushed against his, even for a moment, she would know what it was, and never be able to remove that knowledge from her mind. Irina turned around, staring at the road behind them, nerves rolling through her like storm clouds.

For a moment, nothing happened. Then she felt Stefan's fingers whisper across the top of her braid, and she flinched.

He stopped at once. 'Sorry. Did I pull?'

'No, no,' she said, heat rising in her cheeks. 'Just . . . wasn't expecting it.'

'What were you expecting?' he said, a smile gilding every word. 'I told you I was going to fix your hair.'

'Just . . .' She trailed off.

What *had* she been expecting? Why did she feel like a fledgling perched on the edge of its nest, wondering if she was going to hit the ground or soar into the sky? It wasn't anything new. He'd done this before. Other people had done this before too; her mother, and Catalina, and half the girls in the village. But all she could think about was his hands in her hair.

'Well, don't flail around so much,' Stefan said, after a pause. 'If you knock one of the flowers out of my hand, I'm not jumping out and getting it for you.'

Very carefully, Stefan laid a hand on her hair. Threading the first snowdrop carefully into place, he was quiet, gentle. Irina could feel every twist and flex in the plait as his long fingers worked the flowers through her hair. Her face was burning. Under his hands, her hair felt like a living thing, sensation travelling all the way up to her scalp and prickling across her skin. When he took his hands away, it did not fade. All she could think about was the fact that he was sitting at her back. Was he looking at the slope of her shoulders and trying to read the tension there? Or was he staring at his own hands and thinking about how they had been buried in her hair?

Irina couldn't turn around. She stared straight ahead, barely seeing the road they'd travelled. Why did this matter? What did she care if he was looking at her now, and wondering what kind of expression was on her face? He was her guide, her bodyguard – and, she realized, her friend. It had settled on her like summer, the warmth of it building up so slowly she could hardly have said exactly when she'd set her animosity aside. But those weren't reasons to avoid his eyes. There was no reason why she couldn't turn around and face him right now, no reason at all. Yet here she sat, paralysed. Viscerally aware of the set of her shoulders, the slope of her back, and every hair on her head, Irina could feel him looking at her. If she turned around now, everything would change.

'Irina?' he asked. 'Are you all right?'

She nodded, her cheeks bright red. 'Just looking at things.'

There was a moment's silence. Then he shuffled forward and sat beside her, staring at the open road. The dusty brown track cut through a swathe of emerald-green grass, flecked with gold. Copper-leaved trees grew further back from the road, bright against the purple shadow of the distant mountains. Every colour looked as though it could have been pulled straight from a tapestry, or a mural painted on a monastery wall. No blades of grass were trampled at the sides of the road, no leaves fell from the trees. But Stefan's hand was inches away from hers, the side of his palm not quite brushing her fingertips, and somehow that was the only thing she could think about.

'It's quite a view,' he murmured, after a long moment.

Irina kept staring straight ahead. She could just see him out of the corner of her eye, and in one heart-stopping moment, she wondered if he was looking at her.

Then, she knew.

'Yes,' she whispered, cheeks burning. 'It is.'

The city had spilled out ahead of its own walls, like frost that could not be contained to one windowpane. As such, Irina had plenty of warning when they were drawing near. The cart slowed. The trees straggled back from the widening road. The grasses were cut short, hay piled into vast stacks. Wooden fences marked out plots of land; a steady stream of people in carts and on foot trickled in from either side; the wheels ran over the first cobblestone with a loud rattle. By the time Irina and Stefan turned to look ahead, the walls of the city were already looming over them. They were covered in bright white plaster, with glimmers of stone peeking through. Now that she knew what to look for, Irina could see the faintest shadow of the inscriptions on the stones. *Sacred to the memory of, beloved wife, devoted son* . . . She shivered and forced herself to stop reading, staring up at the enormous turrets crowning the walls instead, each one with a roof built to a wickedly sharp point. The wall stretched as far as she could see in either direction, the red-tiled turrets sticking up like bloody fingers. This city was far larger, and Irina could not help but think of how much harder it would be to leave it in a hurry if something went wrong. There was so much ground to cross.

She looked around, checking for moats, drawbridges – anything that might cause a problem if she and Stefan needed to flee. But there was nothing. Nothing at all to defend a vast city rich enough to house a university and call swathes of the dead to its doors. Why? Irina thought back to what Stefan had said in the inn: that the dead did not hunger. What was it like, to exist without that drive? Did that mean they did not fight, either?

There was certainly no sign of conflict in the crowd. The city gates were thronged with people, who all seemed cheerful, if a little distracted. A group of soldiers in loosely buttoned uniforms were laughing and shoving each other as they passed through. Serious-looking students followed after them, talking animatedly and waving ink-stained hands. A Jewish family stood off to one side, the mother kneeling down and tugging her children's shirts straight, the father brushing something off his son's embroidered waistcoat. Roma wagons trundled past. Three veiled women strolled by, gold bangles on their arms. A blind man's cane skittered over the cobbles as he passed; a chubby toddler went haring past him, and he shouted for her to come back and behave herself in front of all the people. Farmers, soldiers, sailors, servants, midwives, physicians, shepherds, beekeepers; all of them were passing through the archway. Irina shifted further into the cart, making sure no part of her was in reach of the crowd. What, exactly, made this city so special? There were so many people here. What was drawing them all down these streets? Was it simply the dance?

'I probably should've said this earlier,' Stefan muttered, as the cart crawled towards the archway, 'but I need to eat.'

'Can it wait?'

'Until we get into the city, yes. But after that . . . I might not be myself.'

His jaw was tightly set, his fists clenched. He was holding himself far away from her, and a chill stole through her thoughts when she wondered what that might mean. Was he afraid he was going to hurt her?

'All right,' she whispered. 'We'll find somewhere quiet.'

The cart rolled towards the entrance. Stefan sat as far away from her as he could get, gripping his elbows. Irina was grateful there was no door to pass through here. It would be cruel to cling to him now, when he was so hungry and there were so many people. She shouldn't. It was unfair to want his arms around her, to dare him to do something with all that hunger.

She blushed.

She was soon distracted. A quick glimpse of the city was enough to intrigue her: even through the arch she could see minarets alongside steeples, black-beamed houses sitting next to wooden cabins and marble facades. There was glass in every window, wrought-iron balconies next to ornately painted shutters, dormers in the roofs that looked like eyes about to blink at her. It seemed as if handfuls of the world had been scooped up and set down here.

When they were finally through into the city proper, and free of the crowds, Stefan jumped down from the cart. They had trundled into a wide cobbled square, surrounded by houses in turmeric yellow, cobalt blue and rich terracotta; in the next street she could see white plaster and black beams, in the next, the sandstone facade of a smart townhouse. Large pots stood outside some of the houses with nothing growing in them, and a steady stream of people passed them by, filing into houses or chatting as they walked up the street.

Stefan reached for her, looking pained. She scrambled over to the edge of the cart and let him lift her down, catching him swallowing when he put his hands on her waist. She barely had time to thank Vasile for the lift before Stefan had grabbed her hand and was all but dragging her away, heading for a quiet, dark street branching off the opposite side of the square. Irina kept her elbows tucked in, keeping well out of the way of the crowd, spinning and lurching like a broken marionette whenever anyone got too close. When they finally slipped into the little street, she sagged with relief.

He still had not let go of her hand. Perhaps it was the quiet, or perhaps it was the gloom of tall buildings pressing in on either side, or perhaps it was simply that now, she understood. Whatever it was, it felt different to be standing in the dark with her hand in his. He gestured to her necklaces. 'Could you . . .'

She took them off, cramming the beads into her pockets. The memory of his fingers was still curled around her palm. Adjusting the collar of her shirt to give him better access, she was suddenly gripped by uncertainty. What the hell was she supposed to do with her hands? Hold him? She flushed, heart beating very fast. It would feel so intimate in this quiet, dark street. Not that anyone would know. There was no one to see them, here.

Stefan took a step forward, reaching for her. Irina's back bumped against the wall. One cold hand curled around the base of her neck, thumb pressing against her cheek. She tilted her head up and to the side, trying to tell herself she was not leaning into the palm of his hand. His other hand had settled on her shoulder, delicate as a bird. Lips parted, teeth gleaming, he drew closer.

That was when she saw him. Vasile, standing in the mouth of the alleyway. He was staring at them, eyes wide.

'Wait,' she muttered, 'Vasile's back.'

Stefan stopped, a growl of frustration lodged in the back of his throat. The moment she heard it, Irina knew she was going to spend a lot of time thinking about that noise. 'Is he watching us?' he murmured.

She nodded. A sudden clarity settled on her. She placed a hand on Stefan's cheek; his eyes widened.

'You don't have to—'

'I know,' she said, and kissed him.

It was as if, in a clashing scrum of noise, she had suddenly heard the refrain of a familiar song. Stefan's lips were soft and cool on hers, as if he'd been drinking ice-cold water. Her fingers brushed against the fine hairs on the back of his neck. There was none of the uncertainty she'd felt when she'd kissed the boys she barely knew, none of the impatience for it to be over. She was exactly where she wanted to be.

She pulled away. Doubt flickered through her. Had it been good? What if she really had been doing it wrong? But then she saw his face. It was lit up, a slow, disbelieving smile spreading across his face like a sunrise. Her breath caught. He was beaming at her, his tea-coloured eyes darting between her lips and her eyes, stroking her cheek with a thumb, and all those love songs that had never seemed to apply to her suddenly made sense.

'I thought . . . I thought you didn't like doing that.'

Her hand slid down his chest, the ridges of embroidery on his waistcoat running down her palm. 'I didn't, with strangers.' She dragged her eyes away from the lines of his throat, disappearing into the linen collar of his shirt, and met his gaze. 'It feels different, with you.'

He stepped forward, leaving nothing between them but their

clothes. One hand slipped into the curve of her waist. 'Oh, *good*,' he murmured, and kissed her again.

This kiss was different. Urgent, hungry. She could not have said exactly when her lips parted and his tongue slid into her mouth, but when it did, she realized how long he had wanted her. The arms around her shoulders, the hands in her hair, the fingers curled around her own – all of them seemed free of a restraint that had suddenly been lifted. He had been handling her as though she was carved from ice, delicate and cold, and now, at last, she was melting under his hands.

When they pulled apart, Irina was pressed against the wall, breathless, one hand tangled in his hair. Too late, she realized she must've been pulling. She let go at once. 'Sorry.'

Stefan's arms were wrapped around her, pressing her against him. 'Don't you dare apologize,' he whispered, and Irina flushed.

Quickly, she peeked over his shoulder, and caught a glimpse of Vasile's retreating back. 'I think he's gone now, if you want to eat,' she said.

'Not just yet,' said Stefan, as he leaned in for another kiss.

They emerged from the side street guilty, flushed, and giggling. Vasile had not been the only one to interrupt them – the moment Irina had pulled Stefan in for another kiss, their little side street had suddenly seemed to become a thoroughfare. But now, Stefan's fingers were threaded through Irina's. He couldn't stop looking at her. As they crossed the wide, cobbled square, she caught him giving her greedy sidelong glances. Irina squeezed his hand, smiling a small, secret smile; he saw, raised both their hands to his lips, and pressed a quick kiss on her gloved knuckles.

'I suppose we should try and find the university now,' Irina said.

'I mean, we *could*, but we could also find somewhere quiet and just . . . well . . .'

Irina bit her lip, tempted. Stefan swallowed. 'We probably shouldn't,' she said. 'Well, not now, anyway. And you still need to eat. But maybe there'll be somewhere quiet near the university.'

Stefan smirked at her. 'That's what I like about you. You're such an optimist.'

Hand in hand, they went deeper into the city. No one gave them a second glance. In his new clothes and with his high boots, his purple-black hands looked like he was also wearing gloves. It was easy to find their way to the university: a steady stream of scholars was filtering through the streets, all heading in the same direction. Stefan and Irina simply slipped into the crowd. Feet picking over well-worn cobblestones, they filed past white-plastered houses with heavy, dark beams set into the upper storeys; ducked under wide, terracotta-coloured archways with low-ceilinged rooms built above them; stared at walls of perfectly carved sandstone. They passed by a market, bubbling vats of blueberry jam, mămăligă, țuică and sour soup rippling gently under the sounds of dozens of voices haggling, bartering, and chatting. Irina barely registered the smell of frying jumări; when she noticed it, and registered her lack of hunger, her hand tightened on Stefan's. He pulled her a little closer.

Carts trundled past them, laden with barrels; Irina saw them turn towards a tavern, and the smell of spilled wine and cherry brandy suddenly assailed them as the door opened. Palatial estates with fine marble pillars rubbed up against long, low barracks. Painted shutters swung open opposite balconies so delicate they looked like they had grown out of the buildings like ivy. Students staggered past them, arms full of books. Children laughed and looked for things to throw. Stallholders pushed carts of pots and pans, or old clothes, or piles of wicker baskets towards the market. Parents shouted after children; couples strolled arm in arm. With her hand in Stefan's, Irina could have believed that this was an ordinary city, full of ordinary people. Their eyes were bright, their smiles were easy. It took real effort to remember they were dead.

It soon became clear that the university was close. First came the smell of the coffee houses: bubbling coffee, hot meat pies, the press of too many people in a small room, debates bursting into life every time the doors swung open. Then she saw the booksellers. Cheap political tracts were piled onto tables alongside historical pamphlets and sensational novels. A glass-fronted shop with scrolls stacked in the window, some as small as her finger, others far taller than her. Students staggered out, their arms full, and as the door shut behind them Irina caught a glimpse of a room so full of colourful books that it looked like a jewellery box. Then, at last, the city made way for the university itself, buildings edging back like heralds making way for a king.

Rolling out like a carpet, a spotless expanse of grass. A fountain, with a faceless figure shooting water from an outstretched hand. And behind it, the university itself. It was easily the largest building Irina had ever seen, made of pale stone and with more windows than she could count. It stretched wide across the lawn, every surface shining. People scurried in and out of its many doors like ants chipping away at a fallen piece of fruit. If she had not known better, she would have said it was a palace rather than a place of learning. Certainly, the people filing in and out of the doors looked more like courtiers than she and Stefan did. Here, the students favoured the suit and britches of the Austrian court over the high-necked linen shirt and wool waistcoat that Stefan was wearing. Irina wished she had a headscarf; walking around so many smartly dressed people with her hair uncovered was making her feel decidedly underdressed.

'This is incredible,' Stefan breathed. 'What do you think they've got in there?'

'Doctor Emil, hopefully. Or someone else who can help us find our way around.'

'Right, yes. Sorry. Where do we start?'

Irina scanned the crowd and picked on a nervous-looking young man whose white stockings were starting to slip. 'Him,' she said, and strode over.

Behind her, Stefan was protesting. 'You can't just—'

Irina ignored him. Her smile was already in place. 'Excuse me,' she said, feeding helpfulness into every word, 'I don't know if you've noticed, but your stockings aren't staying up. Would you like me to hold your book while you fix them?'

The young man started. 'Oh! Oh, I . . . er . . . yes, please.' He passed Irina an enormous book as though he were handing her a baby, and Irina palmed it off on Stefan as soon he caught up to her.

'I'm Irina, by the way,' she said. 'This is Stefan. We're looking for Doctor Emil Nicolescu. Is he here?'

'Doctor Nicolescu?' the student repeated. 'Yes. I've just come from his lecture, actually. If you hurry, I'm sure you could catch him before the next one.' He pointed over his shoulder towards the palatial building behind the fountain. 'Ground floor, turn left, fourth door on the right. You'll know it, I'm sure.'

Irina blinked; she hadn't expected it to be that easy, but if the dead really did find themselves in places similar to those they'd loved in life, she supposed it made sense that Doctor Emil had ended up at a university. She thanked the student while Stefan handed the book back, and the two of them set off across the lawn. Irina had the vague sense that she was not supposed to walk on the grass, even though there were several students lounging on it; it felt a little like walking on green velvet. The feeling only got worse when they stood in front of the building itself. The doors to the university were propped open; standing nearly fifteen feet tall and made of heavy, carved wood, they must have taken four people to push them open a crack. Beyond them was a tiled marble floor and a sweeping staircase flanked by more faceless statues. A vast corridor stretched out on either side, lined by tall and immaculately polished windows, and as Stefan and Irina turned left and headed for Doctor Emil's lecture theatre, their footsteps rang down the corridor like stones bouncing down the mountainside.

'What are we going to ask him?' Stefan muttered, as they paused outside the door.

'How to get around,' Irina replied. 'If we can't use the necklace as much, we need to know where to go. Obviously we can't tell him we're in the underworld on this side of the river, but that book he liked – the *Aeneid* – seemed like it was similar, so we can ask how they found their way in that. And if it mentioned any guardians. But . . . wait,' she said, as an idea struck her, 'do you think he's got a copy? Would he show us?'

Stefan chewed his bottom lip, thinking, and Irina was briefly transfixed. 'That would be good, but would this place even allow it?'

'It's a university, isn't it? They love books!'

'No, I mean this *whole* place,' he said, sweeping an arm at the general area. 'You know,' he whispered, glancing up and down the corridor, 'the land of the dead. If it was up to me, and I knew there was a book floating around that would tell everyone exactly how this place works, I'd have it under lock and key.'

Irina could feel her enthusiasm deflating. Stefan noticed and slipped an arm around her shoulder.

'We can always ask and see,' he said, his tone suddenly soft. 'It'd certainly be useful. And even if it isn't here, odds are Doctor Emil will tell us all about it anyway.'

Irina gave him a small smile and knocked on the door. Moments later, a voice called 'Enter!'

Doctor Emil's lecture hall looked more like a drawing room than anything else. The walls were hung with tapestries and statues stood in every corner. A wall of windows looked out onto another spotless lawn and velvet-upholstered chairs stood in neat rows on top of a beautiful Turkish carpet. It was only the wooden lectern at the front that stopped it from looking like some kind of receiving room. Doctor Emil was standing there, leafing through a sheaf of notes. He waved at the chairs without looking up.

'Sit down, sit down. You're a little early, so if you'll excuse me while I review the—'

'You were expecting us?'

He looked up sharply. The moment he saw them, his face split into a smile. 'How delightful!' he said, setting his notes aside. 'What a pleasure it is to see you both again. Are you enrolled? Oh, this is marvellous news, just *marvellous*.'

Irina found herself smiling too. 'Only passing through,' she said. 'We enjoyed your conversation so much we had to drop by.'

'My dear, you are a shameless flatterer,' said Doctor Emil, waving them into chairs, 'but luckily, you are also a very good one. Now tell me: have you found yourself a copy of the *Aeneid* yet?'

'Unfortunately not,' Irina said, sitting down beside Stefan, 'they're so expensive.'

Doctor Emil leaned forward. 'Do you mean to tell me there's a copy of the *Aeneid* in the market? Where? Can you remember?'

Irina floundered. From his eager eyes, she was sure that Doctor Emil was going to go looking wherever she described next. 'Well . . .'

'My dear girl,' he said, 'complete copies of the *Aeneid* are like gold dust in this city. The library in this university is woefully understocked, you know. Not one copy! I daresay all the funding goes to the *sciences*,' he said, loading disdain onto the word, 'but we classicists must have our fair share of – but I'm getting carried away. The point is that if you have found a copy, you simply must tell me where.'

Irina opened her mouth. Absolutely nothing came out. She had no idea what to say. If she made up a description on the spot, what would she do if it matched someone already here? What if he realized they were lying?

'Very suspicious seller,' Stefan chimed in. 'I didn't like him.'

'So it was a man?' Doctor Emil asked, neatly crossing his legs as he sat down. 'What makes you say he was suspicious? Were the books stolen?'

Stefan faltered. He was looking even paler than usual, Irina noticed. 'Just . . . just very suspicious. He was . . . er . . .'

'Oh yes,' Irina jumped in, 'very suspicious. Cagey, you know. Wouldn't let us look through things. And . . . and . . .'

'And he was flirting with Irina,' Stefan said.

Irina was completely thrown. 'Was he?' she blurted, turning to look at him. There was a mischievous smirk playing around his mouth, and she realized what he was setting her up for. 'I don't think he was,' she said, trying to communicate *do not call me the stupid joke pet name in public* using only her eyes.

Stefan ignored her. 'Not that I blame him, of course,' he said, his smirk widening into a grin. 'Anyone would want to flirt with my little cauliflower.'

Irina held in her sigh. Then he winked at her. She blushed, and that was extremely unfair. If she ended up liking the stupid cauliflower thing, she was going to be really annoyed about it.

'Well,' Irina said, turning back to Doctor Emil, 'seeing as we can't find a copy of our own, I thought perhaps you might be able to tell us more about it? If it's not too much trouble, of course. It's just that it was so interesting! Book Six in particular,' she said, wondering if it was safe to mention the word 'underworld' in Doctor Emil's presence. 'I'd never thought that rivers could be made of concepts, so I'd love to . . .'

She trailed off, waiting for the glazed look. To her relief, it did not come. Evidently, talking about a story was not the same as talking about the thing it was based on. Nor did Doctor Emil look as though he was teetering on the brink of a shattering revelation. His eyes had lit up with enthusiasm, and he was rubbing his hands together like a musician warming up before a performance.

'You're quite right to be so taken with it,' he said. 'It truly is a fascinating insight into how the ancients viewed the world. And so refreshing, too, to come into contact with a mythos that is so very different from our own.'

'Oh yes,' said Irina, 'very refreshing. I was wondering, is it possible that a scholar might have tried to map it all out? It sounds so vivid when you talk about it, I'd love to see it drawn up.'

Doctor Emil's eyes were sparkling. 'What an intellectual exercise that would be! Oh, I would give my right eye for such a map! I suppose it must be possible – there are rivers mentioned in the text. Acheron, the river of sorrow; Styx, the river of unbreakable oaths; Lethe, the river of forgetfulness.'

Irina and Stefan exchanged glances. Remembering the rope bridge sagging into the depths of the Grey River, and how she'd wept as she'd been weighed down, Irina fought off a shiver. A haunted look came into Stefan's eyes; she took his hand.

Doctor Emil did not appear to notice. 'But you know about those, of course,' he continued, 'we discussed them back at the . . . at the . . .'

'Oh yes, I remember them very well,' said Irina, trying to chase away the lost look creeping across Doctor Emil's face.

'Are there other landmarks mentioned? Mountains, forests, anything like that?'

His attention snapped back onto them. 'Well, there's a certain amount of descriptive language, of course. I'd have to check my copy, but I don't recall much. Apart from what Anchises and Aeneas discover, of course, but truth be told that only sticks in my mind because of the sheer drama of the scene.'

'What scene is this?'

'Towards the end of Book Six, there's a marvellous passage. It's so emotive. Anchises and Aeneas come upon the shores of the River Lethe, and find a crowd of souls there about to drink its waters. When they drink, you see, their memories will be erased and they can proceed to the deepest level of Hades, where their souls can leave the underworld and be reborn again on earth.'

Irina's breath caught. 'So they'll come back to life?'

'Not quite, it is a little more complicated. Once they pass through that point they are reborn into new bodies, as completely different people. It really is a marvellous passage. I count myself very lucky to be able to study such different beliefs from our own, you know. In days gone by—' He stopped, his eyes suddenly focusing on Irina. 'But, my dear, are you quite all right?'

Irina was trembling. An awful, creeping fear had blossomed across her mind like mould. Had Catalina already reached that point? Was that why the necklace wasn't working? Was she already too late?

'Yes,' she said, her voice small. 'Reborn. Right.'

Stefan gave her hand a squeeze. 'Thank you, Doctor,' he said. 'We'll be sure to come back and let you know if we find that seller.'

'Please do,' he replied, his eyes still on Irina. 'Oh, dear. I hope I haven't upset you. Do let me know if you find a copy. You must come back and discuss it with me before either of you are tempted to go to the dance.'

'What dance?' Stefan asked.

Doctor Emil waved his hand. 'Oh, that tawdry little affair they call the Totentanz. Rather morbid, if you ask me, but I suppose that draws a crowd. That dance is the bane of my existence, you know. It runs every night, making *such* a racket, and whenever one of my students takes it into their mind to attend the damn thing, I never see them again. Quite the distraction from their studies. I do wish they'd move it along. You're sure you're all right, my dear?'

Irina screwed her smile back into place. It felt like it could splinter at any minute. She nodded. There was a lump in her throat. If Catalina had already moved on – if they were already too late – she would never forgive herself.

Stefan slid an arm around her shoulders. 'Come on,' he murmured, 'let's go.'

They stood up. Doctor Emil got to his feet too, nervously polishing his glasses. 'I . . . I hope I didn't . . .'

Irina cleared her throat, blinking fast. She didn't want to leave the doctor like this. He'd been nothing but kind. 'I'm sorry,' she said, her voice a little thick. 'I was just thinking of how much my sister would enjoy talking to you.'

Sympathy unfolded itself across the doctor's face. 'You miss her very much, I take it?'

Irina's throat closed over. Tears burned in her eyes as she nodded.

'She'll turn up,' he said, 'I am quite sure of it. There seems to be something in the air, here; you would not believe how many reunions I've witnessed. You won't be waiting long.'

'Thank you,' Irina whispered.

Stefan steered her towards the door. 'Yes, thank you, Doctor. I hope we haven't taken up too much of your time.'

'Not at all, not at all. Do let me know about that seller. And when you find your sister, I should be delighted to meet her.'

Stefan led Irina out of Doctor Emil's room and back onto the velvety lawn. He headed straight for the fountain, sitting Irina down on the wide stone rim, the faceless statue looming over their heads. He knelt in front of her, both of her hands clutched in his.

'What if she's already—' Irina began.

He cut across her. 'She's not.'

'But—'

'She's not. I promise you,' he said, his voice quiet. 'She's living. If she's been picked up by the guardians, they wouldn't push her soul through to a whole new life just to get rid of her. That's only something that can happen to the dead.'

Irina sniffed. 'How do you know?'

He didn't say anything. Fear lurched through her. 'Well,' he said, 'you still have your necklace, don't you? It's been leading us to her, showing the doors she's been through. If she wasn't here, it wouldn't work.'

Irina fumbled for the wooden beads. With trembling hands, she lifted it over her head and pinched it between finger and thumb, waiting. There was a second of terrible stillness. She waited. There had been stillness before. The necklace had always sprung into life. Always. She just had to wait. It was not moving now, but it would, soon, she thought; it had to move soon, it had to, why wasn't it moving, *why wasn't it moving* –

Stefan cleared his throat. He was staring at the motionless beads. 'Well – that could mean anything . . .'

The beads were all Irina could see. Her breath was snagging in her throat. Her eyes ached from staring and still, they were not moving. 'We're too late,' she whispered.

'No,' Stefan said at once. 'No, we can't be.'

'But they aren't moving. They would be, if she was still here.' Tears choked her. 'We're too late. She's . . . she's gone.'

Cold fingers closed over hers. Stefan guided her hand into her lap, but she still could not stop looking at the unmoving necklace. 'Listen to me,' he said. 'We're not too late. We can't be. If the necklace just points the way to the last door she went through, then all that means is that she's nearby. We can still find her.'

'How do you know?' Irina whispered. 'If it's her the necklace points to, and not the doors, then it means . . . it means she's . . .'

'Irina,' he said, tilting her chin up and forcing her to look away from the necklace, 'I don't know. But one of those options means you give up and stop looking for her altogether. Are you really going to do that, after you've come so far?'

Irina took a deep, shuddering breath. He was right. She was further into the land of the dead than she had ever thought she would get. What was she going to do – turn back? Go home, with the knowledge that Catalina could have been right there and she had chosen not to look for her? Give up? It was unthinkable. How could she live with herself if she turned tail and ran when she'd got this far?

'All right,' she said, pressing the heels of her hands into her eyes and willing the tears away. 'The necklace doesn't work. We'll ask around. If her journey has been anything like mine, she'll have left a trail.'

Stefan sat behind her on the edge of the fountain. 'But we'll do it carefully. If we need to search the city, we can't get chased out by the dead, or that beast.' He slid an arm around her shoulders. 'We'll find her. I promise.'

When Irina had composed herself, they started searching. Away from the university, through cobbled streets and past houses painted sage green or cobalt blue, they asked anyone who would stop and talk if they had seen a blonde girl in the company of some guardians. They passed stately carriages and simple wooden carts, children chasing each other while their parents looked on, featureless statues presiding over bustling squares, craning their necks to catch a glimpse of Catalina's face. Nothing. Through it all, Irina kept her arm threaded through Stefan's. Even though she had her gloves, she still did not like walking with her hands swinging free. It was asking for trouble. Besides, it kept her from reaching up to touch the necklace. Knowing it would no longer help her, it felt like a millstone around her neck. Every clatter of the beads was another reminder: she had nothing to guide her to her sister. Stefan seemed to hear it too; the slightest little sound made a muscle in his jaw twitch.

Eventually, they stopped beside an enormous square with absolutely nothing in it. It was easily as large as a field, cobbled, and surrounded by a wide arc of high, white houses. Their shutters were all closed, their balconies empty. The square was so large that Irina could not see all the way across.

'Let's go,' she said, 'Catalina could be on the other side.' She stopped. Stefan was lagging behind, rubbing the bridge of his nose. 'Are you all right?'

'Yes. It's just really bright. Where are we going?'

She frowned; the light hadn't changed at all. 'Across the square. Come on,' she said, leading him by the hand.

'Excuse me! Excuse me!'

She stopped. A short man in breeches and a flapping blue coat was hurrying towards them. Behind him was a large group of people filing into the square, some pushing carts laden with pots and pans, others with cobza slung over their backs and drums balanced on their hips.

'I'm terribly sorry,' the man said, ushering them away from the square, 'but we're still setting up. I'm going to have to ask you to wait.'

'Wait for what?' Irina asked.

The man stared at her. 'For the dance, of course! Isn't that why you're here?'

'Actually, I wanted to cross the square. We're looking for my sister. She's seven years old, blonde, with a chipped tooth just here,' Irina said, tapping a canine. 'Have you seen her?'

He thought for a moment. 'Some guardians passed over not too long ago with a little blonde girl, but I didn't get a good look.'

Irina's heart leapt. 'When? Did she say anything? Where did they go?'

'Oh, they passed over at the last dance,' he said, gesturing vaguely at the sky, which was a perfect robin's egg blue. 'As for where they went, I couldn't tell you. They flew overhead to about the middle of the square, and then vanished. I suppose I could've lost sight of them, but everyone knows they don't have to travel the same way as the rest of us. Perks of the job, I suppose.'

She seized his arm, gloved hands scrunching the sleeve of his coat. 'You're sure? You definitely didn't see them leave?'

'Of course,' he said, shaking her off. 'Nobody leaves the dance. Why would anyone want to?'

Irina's heart was pounding. She set off for the middle of the square, but the man threw an arm out in front of her. 'Didn't you hear me? We're still setting up. The way is closed until the dance begins. You're going to have to wait until this evening, just like everyone else.'

She plastered on a smile. 'Could you make an exception? We're newlyweds and we were supposed to be looking after her, so maybe you could—'

'Irina,' Stefan said. Something in his voice made her stop. His hands were trembling.

'All right,' she said, leading him away and calling over her shoulder to the man in the blue coat. 'Thank you, we'll come back later.'

They ducked into a side street. It was long and narrow, partially covered by overhanging houses. A steady stream of people was heading in the opposite direction. All of them were dressed in their best: spotless linen shirts, polished black boots, hair carefully braided under artfully draped headscarves. They would be attending the dance, Irina was sure. The further they walked, the fewer people they encountered. The road was long and straight, going past the high wall of the square. Soon, the houses they passed grew dark, cold chimneys and unlit windows on every side. Plaster dust began to drift down over their heads, and when she looked, Irina could not quite fix on what lay underneath the patches in the plaster. The black beams of the houses faded to grey, the patterns on the shutters flaked off. Doors with no handles, windows with no glass – the further they walked, the more it seemed that someone had simply forgotten to fill in the rest of the details. But still, the street stretched in front of them, as endless as if they were tightrope-walking along the horizon.

When the last stranger was out of sight, Irina turned to Stefan, bursting with impatience. 'He saw her! He *saw* her, Stefan, he actually – are you all right?'

Stefan's skin was tinged with grey. His hands were shaking and he seemed to be looking at her from the bottom of a deep, dark pit. Too late, she remembered what he had told her when they entered the city: he was hungry.

'Hold on,' she said, trying the nearest door and stumbling inside. 'Let's get out of sight.'

It was clear that the house had not been lived in for some time. There was almost nothing in it, for a start: wooden walls, wooden floors, and very little else. The only furniture was a pile of old furs on the floor. Irina inspected them. Sable, rabbit, fox, bear, even a wolf pelt – all lay tangled together in a heap, thick and soft. Cold to the touch, they were in good condition, although Irina had no idea what that meant. They could have just been put down; they could have been lying there for years, safe in a land free of moths and dust.

Stefan was clutching his own elbows, as though afraid he was about to come apart. 'Go back outside,' he rasped, his voice hoarse. 'You're not safe.'

Irina shook her head. 'That won't solve anything. You need to eat.'

'I don't want to hurt you.'

'Then don't hurt me.'

'It isn't that simple. I . . . I'm so hungry . . .'

For a sliver of a second, she could see it: the monster that had terrified the villagers back in the land of the living. He was hunching over, curled around his hunger as though hoping that would hold it in. There was a faint ripping sound; he was gripping his own arms so tightly his sleeves were tearing under his fingers. But she could see the real him too, peeking through the hunger. It was in the way he was holding himself back, in the way he turned his face from her, in the way he had refused to take another step towards her. Everything in him was devoted to keeping her safe – even from himself. Pity and fear tangled together like vines. Irina took a deep breath. She couldn't let him know she was afraid. It'd break his heart.

'Stefan,' she said, keeping her voice low, 'everything is going to be all right. Just listen to me.'

He nodded.

'Here's what we're going to do,' she said, unravelling the makeshift bandage on her wrist. 'I'm going to feed you. Just so you're yourself again. And then I'm going to stop. When you're feeling yourself again, you can have some more. We've got to do this slowly.'

'Go,' he said, doubling over. He looked like he was about to spring. His whole body was shaking now, his sharp teeth glistening. 'Run. Irina, you have to go. I don't want to hurt you.'

'Don't tell me what to do.' She tried for a smile. 'This whole thing was my idea, remember? That means I'm in charge. Now, get on your knees.'

For a split second, he stopped shaking. 'Excuse me?'

'You look like you're about to jump at me. That'll be harder if you're kneeling. Go on.'

'It's not that easy.'

She put some authority into her voice. 'Yes, it is. You're still yourself, aren't you?'

He nodded.

'Then prove it. Don't listen to your hunger. Listen to me.' She took another deep breath, softening her words. 'It's just you and me. Nothing else matters. Just do as I tell you. You don't need to worry about anything else.'

Silence billowed around them. Then, after a long, long moment, Stefan fell to his knees. Hunched over and trembling, he looked like he was about to faint, but still, he had listened to her. There was enough of himself left to hold his hunger back.

The wound on her wrist had scabbed over; Irina reopened it. Blood oozed from the cut. Stefan stopped shaking. He raised his head, staring. It was as if it was the only thing he could see. He started forward, getting to one knee and reaching out a hand.

'Stay where you are,' Irina snapped. 'I didn't tell you to get up.'

He froze. The power in him was clear, in the tensed muscles of his legs, in his strong hands, in his glistening teeth. Slowly, he drew back his hand, settling back onto his knees. Irina watched every curl of his fingers, every shift in his stance, and her mouth went dry.

'That's better.'

She walked towards him, slowly, deliberately. Her every step seemed to ring out across the room. All his attention was focused on her; she would have known he was staring at her even if she had been blindfolded. She had never felt so powerful, nor so vulnerable. Her control was spun from spiders' webs, and at any moment, he could brush them aside. But he did not want to. She could see it in his face. In this moment, he would have done anything she asked him to.

She stopped in front of him. He stared up at her, eyes wide, lips parted. Irina felt like a storm: powerful, dangerous.

She held out her injured hand.

'Drink,' she said.

His fingers found hers; she could feel them trembling. He pressed his lips to her wrist, soft as a kiss, and the urge to take his chin in her hand and make him look at her struck Irina like lightning. But he was already drinking, and as the blood was pulled from her veins Irina felt almost giddy. The tips of her fingers were brushing against the soft place underneath his jaw, and she could feel his throat working as he swallowed.

'That's enough,' she said, her voice hoarse.

He pulled away with a gasp that made Irina blush to the roots of her hair. Holding her hand in both of his own, he stayed kneeling for a moment longer, fingers caressing the back of her hand. When he looked up at her, Irina felt like a queen in front of a supplicating knight.

'You're blushing,' he said.

Irina's cheeks were burning. 'No, I'm not,' she said instantly.

Stefan grinned at her, and her mouth went dry. 'Can I get up now, or are you going to make me wait again?'

For a brief, dizzying second, Irina thought about what, exactly, might happen if she told him to stay on his knees. But then she remembered what she was here for. She cleared her throat. 'Um. Now is fine. You can . . . I'll be over here.'

She fled across the room, still blushing. Fanning her face frantically, she stared at the wall as Stefan got up behind her, trying to pull herself together before she had to turn around and look at him. She felt as though some part of her had come suddenly unstuck, like a horse that would not pull a cart until the moment that it wanted to, and now that it was finally moving, she had to work out how to slow it down. If this was how other people felt all the time, she thought, it was an absolute miracle that anybody got anything done.

'Irina? Are you all right?'

'Yes!' she squeaked, face still burning. 'Yes, I'm fine.'

There was a moment's silence. Then, 'I didn't scare you, did I?'

She turned around. Something about him seemed to have wilted. 'What? No! Of course not.'

'I'd understand,' he said, avoiding her gaze. 'I know I'm not . . . I know I can be . . .'

She went to him at once. 'I'm not afraid,' she said, taking his hands in hers. The all-consuming focus in his face had vanished, but now he would not look at her. Gently, she reached up, cupping his cheek. 'You stayed yourself, all the way through. You did really well, to keep that kind of control.'

'Then why did you run like that?'

'Oh,' she said, all the blood rushing to her cheeks. 'It felt like things were getting a little . . . you know . . . heated. And we have things to do, so I – I just . . . went.' She swallowed; her mouth felt dry as dust.

'Well,' he said, giving her a small smile, 'if that was something that you wanted . . .'

Irina's heart was beating fast. There was a distinct wedding-night feeling to this situation, and she wasn't sure what to make of that. On the one hand, she liked Stefan, and they were technically married, so a wedding night would be appropriate; on the other, it felt like she was plummeting forward at the same pace as someone falling off a cliff. Intimacy was something that Irina was interested in as a concept, but she wasn't sure if she was ready for the practical business of it all just yet.

'Maybe not right now? Someone saw Catalina, so I don't think this is the best time—'

'Wait,' he said, 'someone saw her? When?'

Quickly, Irina filled him in on what the man in the square had said. Judging from the expression on his face, even though he had been standing next to her he had not taken in much. Guilt twinged like an old wound. His hunger must have been terrible. With a start, Irina realized that her own hunger had all but vanished.

By the time she had finished talking Stefan was frowning, lost in thought. They were both sitting on the pile of furs and he was plucking absent-mindedly at the bearskin beneath them. He had torn off a part of his sleeve for her bleeding wrist and she was staring at the loose threads, feeling vaguely guilty that he had ruined his fine new clothes for her sake. He had so little, and yet still he was prepared to give it to her.

'Let me see if I've got this right,' he said. 'Catalina was seen flying over the dance with a guardian, and they disappeared about halfway across the square. We also know that no one comes back from this dance, and that man said no one ever leaves it. So unless you're stuck in the dance forever – which can't be right, because there was no one in the square when we went earlier – there must *be* a way to leave the dance, but it's not through the main entrances or exits otherwise it wouldn't have this reputation.' He stopped pulling at the bearskin. 'There's got to be a door in there.'

'But Catalina didn't go through that door,' Irina said. 'The necklace would've moved if she had.'

'I'm not sure about that,' Stefan countered. 'Didn't the man running the dance say guardians don't travel like everyone else? They clearly went somewhere, otherwise they wouldn't have disappeared into thin air. Think about it. Maybe the trail has been going cold because she isn't passing through the doors in the same way that everyone else has to.'

Desperate hope sparked up in Irina like a firework. 'So she hasn't been forced to pass on? Doctor Emil was wrong?'

'I don't know for certain,' he said, avoiding her gaze. 'But I do think it's worth searching the dance – both for Catalina, and to see if there's a door in the middle of it.'

'That makes sense. But we probably shouldn't stay much longer,' she said. 'Whoever left these furs could be back any minute.'

'Do you really think there's someone living here?' he asked, gesturing at the empty room. 'There's no . . . stuff.'

'Not someone *living*, no,' she said, with a smirk. He pulled a face at her; she ignored him. 'I suppose you don't need much when you're dead. No food, no drink – and I suppose no . . . no drive, either. Everyone's so calm here.'

Stefan nodded. He was starting to look worried. 'Maybe it's the same thing that's happening to you. The longer you stay here, the less things you need, until finally you're ready to – I don't know.'

A horrible thought occurred to her. 'You're . . . you're sure I'm not dying?'

'No,' he said immediately. 'No, you can't be. I can't feed off the dead.'

'What about the dying?' she asked, her voice quiet.

'You're not dying,' he said, his voice suddenly rough. 'You can't be.'

Irina studied him. The ties at the collar of his shirt had loosened, revealing a thin triangle of chest. It was dragging her eyes downwards. She flushed. She might not be ready for a whole wedding night, but some kind of wedding evening situation was starting to seem more and more intriguing. But would he want that? It was one thing to tell people that they were husband and wife, even if it was true, and another to insist that they treated this as a proper marriage. Would Stefan have chosen her if she wasn't keeping him alive? Would he keep choosing her if she really was dying, and her blood could no longer keep him upright? *Could* he choose her if her blood ran dry and all he was left with was his hunger, and nothing to keep that monster at bay?

'But you're still hungry?' she asked.

He gave her a sad smile. 'Always.'

Sadness settled on Irina like frost, but then, a thought occurred to her. Whichever way she looked at it, that did not make sense. After spending time in the land of the dead, she was losing her appetite, though her heart was still beating. Why was nothing changing for Stefan? Surely if she no longer felt hunger, the same should be true for him – more so, perhaps, because the land of the dead seemed to be designed to make the dead forget the wants and needs that drove them through life, and he was actually dead. She opened her mouth, ready to argue, and caught herself when she saw the expression on his face. Regret, longing, sadness, fear – and, underneath it all, the hunger.

'What is it?' he asked.

'Nothing. Here,' she said, moving her hair aside and removing her necklaces. 'You should eat again, before we search the dance.'

'Are you sure you'll be all right?'

'Of course. That square is big enough to hold a crowd; I want you to be ready if anything happens. Besides,' she said, smirking a little, 'I'll tell you when to stop.'

'There's something I have to do first,' he said, shuffling around to face her.

'What is it?'

He smiled. 'I love it when you set it up for me,' he said, and kissed her. His mouth was soft, cool.

Irina smiled into the kiss, winding her arms around his neck. 'How long have you been planning that one for?' she breathed, when they pulled apart.

He planted a kiss at the corner of her mouth, another on the line of her jaw. 'I don't have to answer that,' he murmured, the words brushing against her skin.

Irina opened her mouth, ready to say something clever, even if she wasn't sure what that would be. But then Stefan kissed the soft place beneath her jaw, and any kind of smart comment was swept away in the whole-body *oh* that rushed over her. She leaned into the kiss with a shiver, stretching out her neck and closing her eyes. Another kiss, right on her fluttering pulse. Her fingers slid up the nape of his neck and tangled in his hair as he wound his arms around her. When the scrape of teeth finally came, she was ready. There was a brief pulse of pain as he bit down; her hand curled into a fist. It did not feel too different from a kiss: there was a sting to it, but also a throb that sent sensation rippling through her. He held her close, one hand sitting in the curve of her waist. As he drew the blood from her veins, she relaxed, fingers tracing meaningless patterns in his hair.

He pulled away, mouth bloody, not quite breathless. For a moment he looked at her, his tea-coloured eyes darting all over her face. '*God,*' he breathed, and kissed her again. He pulled her closer, and Irina tasted blood on his tongue.

'We should – the bleeding—' Irina said, in between kisses.

He stopped at once. 'Oh! Yes. Sorry.' She fumbled for her handkerchief, holding it over the bite, and when it was in place he covered her hand with his. 'You've got a little . . .' he said, gesturing to her mouth.

'Where?'

He ran a thumb along her lower lip. Crimson blood was smeared across the tip; he licked it off, and Irina flushed. He noticed, and grinned. 'You've got a little more here,' he said, wiping a lazy finger along her collarbone. 'Let me just . . .' He raised the finger to his lips and, without breaking eye contact, put it in his mouth.

'You're doing that on purpose,' Irina blurted.

'Yes,' he said. 'Yes, I am.'

Irina groaned. She tried to make herself sound annoyed. 'You know that makes it worse when you admit it, don't you?' she said.

'I don't know what you mean,' he said, grinning.

They cleaned themselves up as best they could. The bite on Irina's neck stopped bleeding, and she put the necklaces back on as Stefan cleaned the blood off his chin. After a few moments' work, they looked respectable, if a little rumpled. When they stepped back outside, the colourless sky had turned to a deep blue. From the other side of the wall came conversation, laughter, the sizzle of food hitting a hot pan, the plucking and scraping and piping of musicians tuning their instruments.

Irina grabbed Stefan's arm. 'The dance,' she hissed.

He nodded, his face suddenly serious. He gave her hand a quick squeeze, and the two of them started walking back towards the main square, the houses alongside them growing richer and more detailed as they passed. Soon, they found themselves in a steady stream of people leaving the houses and filing into the square, all of them laughing and chatting in excited voices. Irina tucked her elbows in and held Stefan's arm a little tighter.

'Promise me you'll be careful?' he whispered, as they left the side street. The vast square was lit up before them, sparkling with torches and already thronged with people.

Irina touched Catalina's necklace. Nerves roiled in the pit of her stomach. The key to finding her sister could be in the dance. She would be careful if she needed to be.

'I will,' she said.

Stefan gave her a quick smile, and the two of them stepped into the square.

It was difficult, at first, to see much of the square. People thronged on every side as they passed through the archway: excited children clinging to their parents' hands; gaggles of students and teenagers, shrieking and laughing and shoving each other; couples holding hands and pointing to familiar faces in the crowd. Irina kept close to Stefan as she peered into every face. She'd be fine, she told herself; she had her gloves. Her face and neck were the only uncovered skin on show, and no stranger was about to touch those with Stefan's arm draped possessively around her shoulders. If someone bumped into her, they wouldn't start to rot before her eyes – unless they smacked directly into her face. They'd apologize, move on with their evening, and no one would ever need to know that she was the only living person in this crowd. Still, her heart was pounding. Every little nudge against her shoulder sent panic fluttering through her, every foot stepping too close to hers made her want to turn and flee. But it would be fine, she told herself. All she needed to do was to get through the square.

A Steep and Savage Path

The crowd fanned out, milling around in the vast empty area that had been cleared for the dance. When the press of people loosened, Irina could breathe again. Stefan gave her shoulder a little squeeze. 'All right?' he whispered.

She nodded and led Stefan off to the side, surveying the square. Flaming torches glimmered around the edges of the square like fireflies, heavy iron braziers dotted around the square emitting a reddish glow. Heavy, sweet smoke hung in the air, more like the fug of stale incense than the clean burn of woodsmoke. She and Stefan were standing not too far from a long row of food stalls, set up against one wall of the square. A thousand different dishes sizzled and spat and bubbled: jumări, heavy with salt and paprika; cabbage leaves oozing with pork and rice; a huge sheet of golden-brown baklava; cozonac, studded with poppy seeds and rich with the smell of sweet walnuts. At the sight of them, Irina felt nothing. Pushing down the spike of panic – it had been *days* since she'd eaten or drunk anything, how could she not feel hungry? – she focused on the opposite side of the square. On a small raised platform were a group of musicians tuning their fiddles and plucking at cobza strings, while a man seated at the back of the stage tried not to tap his fingers against the skin of a double-headed drum. Everywhere she looked, the square was crowded with people, but she could see no sign of Catalina, the guardian that had taken her, or the way that might open on the other side of the dance.

'Let's see if we can search the square before the band starts playing,' Irina whispered.

Stefan nodded, his eyes scanning the crowd. 'We'll stay near the edges,' he replied. 'I won't let anyone near you.'

They set off, heading past the row of food stalls. Irina caught snatches of the secrets people shared to pay for their food – the affairs they'd had, the things they'd stolen, the lies they'd told. A woman in court dress and a wig nearly a foot high was telling a salacious story about a duke in exchange for a dozen sweet cheese pastries, steaming in a paper packet; a child of no more than seven confessed to stealing three eggs in between mouthfuls of sausage; a priest in a plain black robe was struggling to come up with something good enough to pay for the apple pastry he'd already taken a bite of. Irina let the secrets wash over her and tried not to think about how her stomach was not rumbling.

A long, low note from a violin swooped over the heads of the crowd, as smooth as the sweep of a raven's wing. There was a murmur of excitement. Half the crowd at the food stalls abandoned their wait, peeling off towards the musicians instead. A short man in britches and a blue coat barged past Irina, knocking her into Stefan; he stopped when he realized what he'd done. 'I'm so sorry – oh, hello. Did you find your sister?'

Stefan bristled, but Irina laid a hand on his arm with a smile; this was the same man that had chased them out of the square earlier. 'Not yet,' she said, 'we're just passing through.'

The man looked shocked. 'You're not dancing? But you're newlyweds!'

'Oh, I . . .'

'We're already—'

A steady stream of people was moving towards the musicians. The man looked mortified. 'Please don't let my clumsiness put you off,' he said.

A delighted gasp came from somewhere behind Irina. She turned, dread ballooning inside her, and saw an eight-year-old girl clutching her mother's hand, her face lit up. 'Is this a wedding?' she asked. 'Mama, is this a *wedding*?'

'No,' Irina said quickly, 'not our wedding. Look, I haven't got a bridal crown, so it can't be a wedding. We were actually going to watch the dancing for my sister, so if I could just squeeze past—'

The girl's mother laughed. '*Watch* the dancing? Listen to me, my girl. You're no old maid, just because you've been wed. Go and enjoy yourselves! Honestly. A new bride, *watching* the dancing.'

Stefan's hand was clamped around her shoulder, squeezing. Irina glanced around. They'd attracted a small audience: not just the man who'd walked into them and the girl and her mother, but a small group of apprentices milling around the papanași stand were looking over too, and three sisters in identical white headscarves were whispering behind their hands and glancing in their direction. The back of Irina's neck itched. How had they drawn so much attention already?

She turned to Stefan. 'Maybe one couldn't hurt?' she said, glancing meaningfully at the crowd around them.

The woman clapped her hands together. 'That's more like it!' she said, pushing them towards the music. 'You two have fun. It's a party!'

A rhythm like a heartbeat was rolling out over the crowd. The dancers were getting into position, couples lining up alongside each other and grinning. Stefan bent to whisper in her ear. 'This isn't a good idea.'

'What was I supposed to say?' Irina hissed.

'No!'

They joined the lines of dancers standing opposite each other. 'Do you really think that would've worked?' Irina muttered. 'We need to get through this without people paying too much attention to us, and we were already causing a scene.'

They faced each other. Stefan glanced up and down the line of dancers, like a wolf picking a lamb to pounce upon. 'I don't like it.'

'I know,' she said, catching his hand. 'Neither do I. But we'll only stay for one. We can say we're hungry after this, or that I twisted my ankle—'

The drumbeat blurred into a roll, then stopped. A hush fell over the dancers. Another long, low violin note snaked over the crowd. A second fiddle joined it, high and a little scratchy, and with the first clap from the dancers, the two wove themselves into music.

Irina had danced before. At every wedding in the village, every festival, every christening, she had been spinning and clapping and stamping her feet alongside her neighbours. One way or another, she usually ended up laughing. This was different. Feet stamping on the cobbles made her flinch. Hands clapping by her ear sounded like gunshots. She moved with her elbows tucked in, desperate not to brush against the other dancers. But then, as the men stepped forward to spin their partners across the square, Stefan took her hand.

'It's all right,' he mouthed.

He raised his hand. She spun – once, twice, three times – and came to a staggering halt against his chest. He smiled. Then his hand was on her waist and he was dancing her across the square with the rest of the partygoers, and as her feet skipped across the cobblestones Irina felt like a dragonfly skimming over the surface of the water. The seed of a laugh was blossoming inside her; it was so easy to forget the danger, in his arms. She turned – and there, out of the corner of her eye, she saw a slice of pale grey torn away from the dark blue sky.

'Stefan,' she hissed, 'the door.'

'Where?'

The couples separated into two long lines. Standing opposite him, Irina shot a meaningful glance in the direction of the door.

He looked over his shoulder. 'Should we—'

A Steep and Savage Path

The line of women split. Irina was dragged into a circle of giggling girls, holding hands. A stranger's fingers closed over hers. Panic fluttered through her. She turned to the girl beside her, dread lying thick in her throat – and saw a young woman a few years older than her, smiling excitedly. Irina sagged. Nothing happened. The gloves had worked.

The circle started turning. Irina craned her neck, looking for Stefan. The men's line was circling around the groups of women, and Stefan was somewhere off to her left. She caught his eye and watched the panic roll off his face. She jerked her head in the direction of the door; he nodded. The men's line moved on, Irina's circle split and followed it, and suddenly, she was face to face with another stranger. A student, from his sombre suit and britches, perhaps a few years older than her; from the brief glimmer of recognition in his eyes, he'd heard her protesting before she joined the dance.

'So you're the bride,' he said. 'Congratulations!'

'Where's—' Irina began.

The student took her hand and twirled her around. 'He'll turn up!' he said cheerfully. He grabbed her around the waist and danced her across the square, laughing. All Irina's lightness had vanished. Her feet felt as unsteady as blades of grass.

They came to a halt and separated into lines of men and women again. Stefan was nowhere to be seen. Irina took a deep breath as two strangers took her hands and pulled her into another circle. She would be fine. Nothing was going to happen. She had her gloves. She'd get through the dance, find Stefan as soon as it was over, and the two of them would get through that door.

The beat was getting faster now, the violins frenetic. Every stamp of her feet or clap of her hands felt like it would burst something. A stranger pulled her into another line. Face to face with a soldier with a scar across his face, he gave her a quick once-over before grabbing her hand and spinning her like a top. Skirts flaring out around her, she spun into him, and he grinned at her as he danced her across the square.

'Where's your—'

Irina yanked her hand out of his grip. Another circle; another stranger. She was spinning faster and faster. Something went *plink*. The drums were a racing heart, the violins blurring together so fast the notes felt like one long scream. Another partner – an old man, half her size. She spun, looking for Stefan. Nothing. They danced across the square, Irina scanning the crowd. Where was he? They were in the same dance. How had they been separated so quickly?

At last, the music came to an end in one long wail from the violin. Irina stepped back and applauded, breathless. She had stopped spinning; no strangers were snatching at her hands. She could find Stefan. It was going to be all right.

The old man patted her hand. 'Many congratulations,' he said, and wandered off, unconcerned. A slice of cool air wormed its way across Irina's wrist. Fear tore into her. She turned her hand over and saw that the button that secured her right glove in place had fallen off. The only skin showing was a sliver of her wrist between the cuff of her glove and her sleeve. Irina cradled her hand to her chest at once, heart pounding. She *had* to find Stefan.

People ebbed and flowed across the dance floor. Irina squeezed between old couples and young, craning her neck. Nothing. Where was he? To her left was a gaggle of apprentices, to her right, a group of five girls sizing them up. Families rushed past, students talked in low voices, exchanging nervous glances, grandmothers led children into the dance by the hand. There was no sign of Stefan. How could she search for Catalina, with a broken glove and no one to keep the crowd away from her?

A Steep and Savage Path

Irina's heart was pounding. Her breath came fast and sharp. She dithered on the edge of the dance floor, staring into the crowd. Where *was* he? Had he been pulled into another dance? She peered around, clutching her hand to her chest, and saw the door. It was the only way forward; if she couldn't find him in the crowd, he could meet her there. Besides, if Catalina and the guardian had gone through, that was exactly where she needed to be.

Drumming rang across the square. Irina flinched. She scrambled off the dance floor. There were complaints – 'Oh, come on!', 'We don't bite!', 'Mihai, you'll dance with the bride, won't you?' – but she ignored them. People could tut all they wanted. They'd have to drag her back onto that dance floor.

She pushed through the crowd with her left hand, keeping her right close to her heart. It was only a sliver of skin showing, but she felt it like an open wound. All it would take was one touch, and she'd be discovered. Irina squeezed past a line of people queueing for țuică. All she could imagine was the collapse of their rotting faces, if one of them was to reach out and grab her by the wrist. She shuddered.

The door was shining ahead of her, pale grey light gleaming like a mirror. Nobody else seemed able to see it. The tell-tale headache was starting, buzzing at the back of her brain. Her palms began to sweat. She panicked; what if the gloves slipped off? How would she hide the agony of approaching the door in a crowd full of people, with no one to hold her upright? Irina gritted her teeth. There was no question of how. She simply had to.

The violins had started up again. The scrape of the bow on the strings reminded Irina of wolves baying in the forest. Another group of dancers was up ahead; one of them spotted her and waved her over, making a space in their circle. Irina smiled and shook her head. She gave them a wide berth, skirting the edge of the dance floor. As long as no one came too near, she would be fine.

'Hey!'

Irina glanced over her shoulder. The soldier she'd danced with had spotted her. He was shouldering his way through the crowd. Stocky, and with that long scar running down the side of his face, he was about ten years older than her. Irina's heart sank. She walked a little faster, twisting through the crowd.

'Hey!' he called, matching her pace. 'Where's the groom?'

Irina ignored him. Shouldering past a bearded man holding a bawling toddler, she kept the door in her sights. The buzz in her head was blossoming into a whine. Nausea was sloshing around the pit of her stomach. She was getting close.

A hand descended on her shoulder. Irina yelped. She tried to wriggle away, but she was wrenched around before she could get out of his grip. The soldier was smiling at her, the thrill of the chase glinting in his eyes.

'Slow down, sweetheart,' he said, grinning. 'Where are you off to in such a hurry?'

Excuses fluttered through Irina's head like birds. 'I have to go,' she blurted.

The soldier's smile faltered. 'Go where?'

Irina gestured vaguely behind her, already stepping back and turning away. 'I should go.'

He snatched her hand – the hand with the broken glove. Irina was drenched in fear. His smile didn't flicker. He had her fingers in his grip, not her wrist. She still had time. She could still get away.

'Your groom left you all alone, has—'

Irina yanked her hand out of his grip. Material slid across her fingers, and then, cold air. She stepped back, horrified, as her hand slid out of the glove.

'Give it back,' she whispered. 'Please, give it back!'

'I'll give it back if you dance with me,' the soldier said, with a wink.

Irina staggered back, clutching her naked hand to her chest. Panic jolted through her like something rattling the bars of a cage. 'You don't understand. You don't understand, I need it. Please, just give it back!'

The soldier's smile vanished. 'Why are you making this so difficult? It's just a dance. Don't I get a dance with the bride?'

People were staring now, whispering behind their hands. Even some of the dancers were glancing over their shoulders. A woman reeking of țuică yelled 'Go on, love, you could do worse!' and laughter spilled across the square.

'I don't – I can't—' Irina stammered, backing away. Where was Stefan? Was he doubled over again, hunching around his hunger? Had her blood failed after all?

The soldier's lip curled. 'Keep your damn glove, then,' he said, and threw it into the dance. It sailed over the crowd, dropping into the middle of a circle of dancers. Irina bolted after it, running around the edge of the dance floor to keep out of the crowd. The dancers called to her to join in, but she ignored them. She waited at the edge of the floor, eyes trained on the glove. Charging into the middle of the dance would only put her in danger; as much as every nerve was screaming at her to get the glove, she had to wait. A shining black boot trampled it, scuffing it over to the left. A pair of opinci skidded on it, kicking it further into the dance. Irina didn't move. Heart pounding, she watched the glove like a cat stalking a mouse.

The song ended. Applause rang across the square. The dancers separated, and Irina darted forward, sprinting across the square and snatching up the trampled glove. She crammed it onto her hand, shaking so badly it took her three tries to get her fingers in the right holes. The moment it was on, she could breathe easier. All the buttons had been snapped off, and the fit didn't feel like it had before, but that was all right. She had it. She could find Stefan, and together, they could work out where Catalina had been taken.

The drums started up again. People flowed onto the dance floor in a wave. Irina ran for the edge of the dance floor, ignoring the protests. A hand snatched hers, spinning her around as the fiddles struck up a tune. It was a girl around her own age, smiling.

'Where are you going?' she said. 'Come and join the—'

She stopped. Her eyes widened. The smile slid off the girl's face. So did the flesh. As the drums pounded and the violins blurred into a whirl of sound, the girl's face began to wither. Fear splashed over Irina. How? She had her gloves. This shouldn't be happening. The stranger's face was contorting, crackling, patches of charred skin crawling down her throat.

'Oh God,' the girl rasped. 'Am I . . . I didn't . . .'

Irina yanked her hand away. Too late, she saw what she had missed: a tiny tear, right on the fingertip of her glove.

Someone screamed. Irina ran, tearing through the dancers.

'Wait!' the girl howled. 'Please wait! I have to know – did they get out?'

A spinning couple barrelled into Irina. She staggered sideways. Shoving them out of her way, she kept moving – but she'd caught the man's bare forearm, and now his face was swelling, all the colour leaching out of his skin as water poured from his horrified mouth. His dance partner screamed. Irina kept running.

'Wait! Please, wait!'

'Oh God. Where . . . where's Nadia?'

Someone snatched at her hand. The glove slipped away. Irina's feet pounded over the cobblestones. The buzz of the approaching door was getting louder. So were the screams. She had to keep going, she had to. She couldn't let them catch her, couldn't turn and see what she'd done . . .

A man in a soldier's uniform stepped in front of her, arms outstretched. 'What's all – good *God*,' he said, his face slackening as he saw the dead behind her. 'Get—'

Irina tried to dart around him. She was already veering off to the side. But he caught her bare hand and hauled her out of the path of the dead, and the moment his skin touched hers black blood bubbled up from his mouth, oozing through the front of his white shirt. Staring at her, his bloodstained mouth falling open, he would not let go of her hand.

'You . . . you . . .'

Irina tore her hand away. 'Stefan!' she yelled.

'What have you done?' the soldier gurgled.

All Irina could hear was screaming. The door gleamed in the distance. She darted towards it. A hand closed over her wrist, yanking her back. The soldier's bloodstained face was white, and full of terror.

'*What did you do to me?*' he rasped, the words bubbling up through black blood.

'Let go!'

'Hey!' A few apprentices were barging through the crowd, intent on pulling them apart. 'Leave her—'

A hand descended on her shoulder, hauling her back. The side of a finger caught the bare skin of her neck. Flesh withered against her skin. The grip tightened. The screams grew louder. Irina tried to shrug off the hand, but the soldier was still hanging onto her wrist, and the drowned man and the burned girl were catching up to her, reaching for her.

'Please,' the apprentice said, dragging her around to face him. His eyes were bulging, his tongue swollen, a collar of bruises around his neck. 'You have to tell them I'm sorry.'

'Nadia!' the drowned man was shouting. 'Have you seen Nadia?'

Someone grabbed the soldier's hand and tried to prise it away. Irina's sleeve tore. She watched a grandmother's face fade into greyness, horror dawning across her wrinkled face. 'The children,' she breathed, 'who's looking after the—'

Three people were holding her fast. Irina attempted to wriggle out of the apprentice's grip. Someone tried to haul her away from him, caught a handful of her collar and tore it. She felt like an animal in a trap. Cold fingers withered against the back of her neck. There was a whimper, right by her ear.

'Get away from me,' she protested, kicking at anything she could reach. 'Please, you have to get away from me!'

Hands clawed at her. Each new touch came with the crack of bones breaking, the whispering of flesh withering. Fingers snatched at her hair, her clothes. Linen tore. And, on all sides, the begging.

'Please, I have to know if they're all right . . .'

'Just tell me if they got out, that's all I want . . .'

'You must have seen her! What happened to—'

'They're so young, I have to know if—'

'What have you done? *What have you done?*'

One hand pulled her back; another pulled her forward. Something wrenched in her shoulder. Irina screamed. She tried to break free, but a dozen different hands held her in place, all of them rotting. Faces pushed in on every side: burned, drowned, bloody; riddled with sores and with pits where the noses should be; caved in and crushed on one side, glittering with fragments of bone. Horror pulsed through her. There was nowhere to run. Nowhere to hide. There was only the dead, clawing and begging and pleading and all she could do was kick and scream . . .

A hand was torn away from her. Not away, she realized, as

something sailed through the air. Off. A scream of pain, as a woman was yanked backwards into the crowd. Bone, crunching. A man howled into her ear, and another pair of hands vanished. The rip of cloth and the tear of flesh. The drowned man screamed. Teeth sank into his neck. A pair of purple-black hands threw him aside.

'Stefan?'

He spat out a mouthful of blackened blood and waterlogged flesh and snarled at the ranks of the dead. Shoulders hunched, eyes wide and feral, his arms were slick with gore. Irina froze. She'd never seen him look so monstrous.

'*That's my wife*,' he snarled.

He launched himself at the soldier, tearing the man's hand away from her with a sickening *crack*. The soldier scrabbled for his knife. Stefan lunged at him, teeth bared. Irina screwed her eyes shut. Something tore. The soldier screamed. Irina risked a peek. The soldier was staggering backwards, clutching his face, blood oozing through his fingers like tar. Someone tried to haul Stefan away from her. He rounded on them, snapping at their fingers like a wild beast. There was a crunch, and the stranger's hand came away bloody.

Irina shut her eyes again. Something slammed into her back. There was a crunch, a scream, and a sound like wet cloth tearing. A hand was torn away from her. She staggered sideways; someone was trying to drag her. Growling. Gurgling. Screaming. Fingers digging into her arms. A voice in her ear, whispering 'Call him off, call him off, I just want to know if—' and then, a strangled cry. Fingers broke against her body. Nails sliced her skin. Her arms throbbed as, one by one, the hands of the dead were torn away. And then, at last, cold fingers curled around her shoulder and wrenched her free.

Her eyes flew open. Stefan was covered in blood, teeth bared.

He was snarling at something behind her as he pulled her towards him. She stared up at his inhuman face, horror and relief whirling through her like a storm. He glanced down at her. Pain flickered in his eyes. Then, he grabbed her hand.

'Door?' he growled.

'Door,' she said.

Hand in hand, they sprinted for the slice of sky. The crowd peeled out of their way, horrified. Behind them, the dead hauled themselves back upright on broken legs, clutching torn necks with crushed hands. Irina glanced over her shoulder. They didn't look like corpses. Corpses were still shaped like humans. These things looked like meat. Still, they reached out to her, and horror seized her by the throat.

'Wait!'

'Please!'

'Come back! I only want—'

Stefan's hand tightened over hers. Irina's attention snapped back to the door. Feet pounding into the cobbles, they hurtled towards it. Pain slammed into her with every step. Her head felt like it was about to burst. Lungs burning, chest tight, every breath felt like a slice. The door was close now, only a few yards away. She faltered. Slowed. Agony splashed across her skin. Stefan was pulling ahead, but her every step felt loose, joints rattling as though they could tumble free at any moment. Her hand spasmed. The dead grew louder. Fear swept through her like wildfire. She wasn't going to make it. She tried to speak, but all that came out was a strangled whimper.

Stefan heard it. Despite the screaming, the pleading of the dead, and the last lingering strain of music, he heard it. He glanced over his shoulder, animal panic scrawled across his face. He stopped. Irina went flying past him, carried by the force of her own momentum. She staggered. Hands snatched at her – they'd found her, she thought in a rush of panic, *they'd found her* – and suddenly, her feet were not touching the ground any more. Stefan had scooped her up like a ragdoll and started running for the door again. Irina clung to him and screamed, eyes shut tight, as white-hot pain burst across her skin. There was a burst of pressure, agony so intense it felt like her eyes were going to boil right out of her head – and suddenly, they were through.

The silence was deafening. After the gloom of the square, the cold grey light seemed unbearably bright. Stefan staggered to a halt and dropped to his knees, still holding her. Carefully, he let go of her, then sprang back up to close the door behind them. When he was done he gathered her to him, shaking, holding her so tight against his chest she half-wondered if she was going to feel a heartbeat.

'I'm sorry,' he muttered, 'I'm so sorry.'

Irina felt numb. There was a gulf between her body and her mind: she could feel herself shaking, heart thrumming against her ribs, but the part of her that felt anything more than the physical seemed to have floated away. A part of her knew that she should be frightened by that, but it was very distant.

Stefan loosened his grip. He held her at arm's length, eyes travelling over every inch of her. He looked completely stricken, his mouth a mess of gore. Spattered with blood and dark fluids she didn't want to think about, his clothes were torn and covered in handprints. His blackening hands were sodden, trembling against her skin. Her skin, she realized, because her shirt was torn, the sleeves all but ripped away and the neckline nearly slashed open. Her hair had come loose too, the last of the snowdrops lost. The more he looked at her, the more fear and shame and guilt swirled across his face.

'I'm so sorry,' he said, his voice breaking. 'Are you . . . did they hurt you?'

Irina opened her mouth. Nothing happened. Throat raw from screaming, it felt like her voice had been torn out of her, and words seemed so small next to what she'd just seen.

'Irina,' Stefan said, every word meticulously placed, 'please talk to me. I need to know if they hurt you.'

What could she say? There were scratches and bruises all up her arms and her shoulder pulsed with pain, but that was nothing. She felt like a cracked egg: something vital was oozing out of her. Would she ever be herself again, after what she had seen?

Stefan's eyes were desperate. His hands tightened on her shoulders. 'Please,' he begged, 'just tell me if you're all right. *Please*, Irina.'

There was the briefest burst of pain at his touch. It was like striking a match. She rocketed back into herself, into all the terror and guilt and despair. Her throat was tight. Her eyes burned. She drew in one gasping breath, then another, and suddenly she was sobbing.

Stefan wound his arms around her. Pulling her close, he cradled her against him as she howled into the crook of his neck. His hands shook against her back. 'I'm so sorry,' he murmured, 'I'm so, *so* sorry.'

It took Irina a long time to uncurl herself from Stefan's neck and dry her eyes. By the time she had cried out all the horror, she felt like something had been wrung from her drop by drop. She got to her feet on shaking legs and wiped her eyes with bruised fingers. Stefan looked a lot worse – he was covered in blood – and every time she saw him out of the corner of her eyes, Irina flinched, panic rippling through her. She had to remind herself that the blood was not his. It was much easier not to look at him altogether. When the shock and fear began to fade, a question was burning in her mind: where had he been?

Now that she no longer felt like a mouse fresh from a trap, Irina could look around. They were standing in what looked like a vast, colourless cave. Everything around them was painted in shades of grey. The floor was perfectly flat, the walls perfectly smooth. There were stalactites and stalagmites, but they were shaped more like long strands of honey oozing off a spoon than living rock. There was no light, and no shadow. Everything else had been wiped away.

She cleared her throat. 'So what happened?' she rasped.

'Excuse me?'

'At the dance. I looked for you, after we first got separated, but I couldn't find you anywhere.'

'I looked for you too,' he said at once, 'but there were so many people I couldn't see you. You're quite short, it's hard to spot you in a crowd.'

Her temper flared. 'This didn't happen because I'm short, Stefan!' she snapped.

'No, I – I'm sorry.'

The miserable look on his face punctured Irina's anger. 'Don't apologize,' she sighed. 'If I'd known I wouldn't be able to find you after that first dance, I never would've agreed to it. We were always going to lose each other.'

He went still. 'What do you mean?'

'In a crowd that size. Why do you ask?'

'It's nothing. But I am sorry,' he repeated. 'You . . . you shouldn't have had to see that.'

'You shouldn't have had to do it,' she said. 'If I'd been more careful . . .'

He shook his head. 'This isn't your fault.'

'It isn't yours, either!'

'Irina,' he said, finality ringing in every word, 'I never want you to see me like that again. You . . . you deserve more than a monster.'

She reached for him. 'You *aren't*—'

'Please, don't,' he whispered, pulling away. 'Let's just . . . let's just keep going.'

She grabbed his hand and squeezed. Tears brimmed in her eyes as she glared up at him. 'You are *more* than a monster,' she said, her voice fierce. 'You're *you*. That's enough.'

He gave her a smile that looked like it was about to shatter. 'You deserve a lot more than just enough.'

A spark of anger blazed in Irina's belly. 'And you think you get to decide what that looks like?'

'No, but . . .'

Irina ground her teeth. It was almost a relief to feel something other than fear. Still, she knew it would not serve her. 'Look,' she said, forcing her temper back under control, 'I've made my choice. It's you. You can make a choice too, if you want. But don't tell me that I've made a mistake, or that I don't know what I'm doing, because you don't see yourself the way I see you.' She stepped forward, brushing a strand of hair out of his eyes. 'It wasn't you I was afraid of back there.'

He fixed her with a look that pinned her in place. 'Are you sure?'

Irina's breath snagged in her throat.

'I saw the look on your face,' he said, relentless. 'I saw the fear in your eyes. You—'

Irina tore her hand away. 'Don't tell me how I feel!' she snapped. 'Yes, I was afraid, but I wasn't afraid of you! *You* weren't the one about to tear me into pieces!'

'I could have! If I'd lost control—'

'But you didn't!' Irina yelled. 'You were in control – you still are! Why are we fighting about something that didn't even happen?'

A muscle twitched in Stefan's jaw. His hands twitched, as if he wanted to grab her by the shoulders, but he held himself back.

'Do you know what I feel, when I look at you?' he asked.

Irina shook her head.

For a moment he paused, his face softening. 'So many things,' he murmured. 'There's so much life in you, Irina. And hope, and drive, and self-belief – you have them in fistfuls. It's like there's some vast well of possibility in you, and whatever happens, you can dig deep and come up with a handful of something that will carry you through. I don't have that.'

A lump settled in Irina's throat.

'What I have is hunger,' he continued. 'It's like a song I can't stop hearing. It is in everything I do, everything I say, everything I think. Even when I look at you, I hear it. I can't let go. I can't lose control, even for a moment, or I could hurt you. Back there . . . I came close. I saw them clawing at you, tearing at your hair—' He paused, took a breath he didn't need. 'I can't come close again.'

'What are you saying?' she asked, her voice suddenly swollen.

His eyes were bright with tears. 'I envy you. I adore you. You make me remember what it means to be alive – how wide open everything seemed. But that won't stop the hunger. Sooner or later, I'll snap. I don't want you to be there when I do. Not again.' He tried for another smile. 'I think you might've been right, earlier. We were always going to lose each other. But if I'm going to lose you, I don't want to lose you to that.'

Irina's hands curled into fists, her eyes burning. A thousand sharp and spiteful things clamoured in her head. They whirled through her like wind in a storm – he'd given up without even trying, he envied the thing he was taking from her, he wasn't *listening* – and part of her wanted to hurl them at him, to let them loose so they would not crowd out her thoughts. But those would be wounds that would not heal, coming from her. They were both hurting, in their different ways. If she made sure one of them hurt more than the other, that would not make the pain any less.

Irina barged past him. She did not know where she was going or what she intended to do next: she just needed to move. Her vision blurred. The smooth grey landscape of the underworld seemed somehow cruel. She wanted colour. She wanted sharp edges. She wanted something she could sink her fingers into. After the things Stefan had said, she longed for something – anything – that would serve as a distraction. But in this flat, featureless corner of the land of the dead, there was nothing.

After a long moment, Stefan's footsteps rang out behind hers. Part of her did not want them to – if he was going to distance himself from her, let him do it properly and leave. Surely that would be better than the two of them skirting around the things he'd said for the rest of their journey. But the thought of going through the land of the dead on her own was like snow: the chill of it settled over all her thoughts, erasing everything underneath. Her arms were mottled with bruises, a few stray cuts still oozing; a lone red flower blossomed in her wake where a drop of blood had hit the floor. She shivered. How long would she feel the cold fingers of the dead on her skin, when she closed her eyes?

The featureless landscape was growing brighter. From somewhere far up ahead came a small, quiet sound, a little like rustling. For a moment, Irina was confused – there was nothing to rustle in this expanse of smooth rock – and panic flashed through her. Had the beast come back? But then, she realized what she was hearing. A river.

Irina quickened her pace. Soon, she could see it, too: a bright ribbon of light shining up at the ceiling. Even at this distance, it was almost blinding. It curled through the rock like a snake and, as she drew closer, Irina could see the water. Her breath caught. It was the most beautiful thing she had ever seen. At first, she thought it was pure white, glowing like the moon. But then, as the water moved, she saw flashes of colour: pink, turquoise, gold, lapis. Each new roll and tumble of the current revealed a new flash of colour, gone as quickly as it came, like someone was turning an opal over and over in the palm of their hand.

'Oh,' Irina breathed. 'Isn't it beautiful?'

Stefan came up beside her, examining the banks. 'How do we get across?'

Irina drew closer to the water. A thousand colours winked up at her from the depths. Unlike the Blue River, there was no sign of a boat or jetty. There was no bridge that she could see, no convenient rope that they could sling across the water. She could not tell exactly how wide it was – the bright white light made it hard to see the opposite bank – nor could she tell how deep. But the current was slow, gentle, almost inviting.

'Can you swim?' she asked.

'Are you serious?'

Irina's temper flared. 'Well, how else are we going to get across?'

Stefan cast the river a wary look and put an arm around her shoulders, trying to lead her away from the water. 'You realize what river this is, don't you?'

Irina tried to look as if she wasn't rifling through her memories of everything Doctor Emil had told them at speed. They'd already crossed the Styx and the Acheron; the other three rivers were rivers of fire, screaming and forgetfulness. With no smoke or shrieking, there was only one thing it could be. 'The River Lethe,' she said.

'Exactly,' said Stefan, pulling her away from the bank. 'The river of forgetfulness. Irina, you can't get near that water. You'll forget everything.'

A dozen different hands on her skin. Faces, rotting in front of her at a single touch. The crackle of a withering hand against her cheek. Horror, blossoming in hundreds of hollow eyes. Irina stopped. Her heart was pounding.

'Everything?' she whispered. 'Or just . . .'

Stefan stared at her. 'You can't be serious.'

Irina stared back at the river. 'We don't know that it'll take everything,' she mused. 'There's no way of knowing that—'

'But we *do* know that you have to drink it for it to work – that's what Doctor Emil said. You can't eat or drink anything here, or you're stuck. You know this! Why are you even thinking about—'

'Maybe if you wanted to forget everything, you have to drink it,' she said, eyes fixed on the sparkling colours. 'Maybe if you want to forget one specific thing, you just have to touch it. Maybe as long as I don't drink it, I'll be—'

Stefan grabbed her by the shoulders. 'Irina, this is insane! You can't seriously want to stick your hand in there, just in case something—'

'Oh, it's insane, is it?' she snarled. 'It's insane to want to forget one of the worst moments of my life, Stefan?'

'Yes! I mean, no!' he said, when he caught sight of the look on her face. 'It's not – you can want to forget, of course, but you can't plunge your hand in and hope for the best! You don't know how it works – what if you can't control what you forget?'

'We won't ever find out how it works if we just stand here!' Irina snapped. 'We have to cross the river. There's no bridge, there's no rope, there's no boat. We wade across or we swim, and we might as well find out what the water does before we jump right in—'

Stefan's eyes were desperate, cold fingers digging into her skin. 'What if you forget Catalina?' he said, as Irina tried not to remember the faces of the dead collapsing in on themselves on every side. 'What if you forget why you're here, or the things that keep you safe? What if . . . what if you forget me?'

The words slipped out before she could stop them. 'Didn't you just say that I saw a part of you that you didn't want me to see?'

Silence cracked over them like a whip. Stefan's hands twitched on her shoulders. Pain and possibility swirled in his eyes. He looked as if the words had punched a hole through his chest; he looked as if he had realized they were the key to a door he had been yearning to open.

'No,' he said, slowly. 'We . . . we shouldn't. It isn't worth the—'

A breeze ruffled his hair. Wind roared around them, lifting Irina's curls. And then, the snap of wings. Stefan's eyes widened, fixed on a point high over their heads. He threw out a hand towards her.

'Get—'

Something slammed against her side. A three-pronged, scaly foot closed around her, bigger than her torso. Talons scraped along her arms as the thing tightened its grip. Irina had time for a split second of panic. Then she was hoisted off her feet and into the air.

She tried to scream. Stefan yelled something, many feet below. But all Irina heard was screeching, coming from somewhere high over her head. It sounded like the scrape of metal on bone. In a rush of wind and a flex of wings that snapped out like a thunderclap, the beast flew higher. Stefan reached out a hand, fear in his eyes. There was a flurry of feathers, a *smack*, and another vast claw snatched him around his middle. Irina caught a glimpse of a huge, feathered flank, stretched out far longer than that of any bird, a hunched back corded with muscle, and a handful of feathers falling to the ground, each one changing as they turned. Then, the thing carrying her banked to the left, rising higher and higher, its massive wings cracking like a whip.

The guardians, Irina realized. They'd found them.

The white river shrank to a ribbon as they climbed higher and higher. Air rushing around her, all Irina could hear was shrieking. There were easily a dozen of the creatures, all of them keening and wailing as they swooped past. Too close to see them in their entirety, Irina saw them in snatches: a massive claw with gleaming talons; the span of an enormous wing that, somehow, reminded her of a diaphanous dress; an unnaturally elongated head in profile, shaped like the blade of a scythe. A patchwork of the underworld passed underneath them, flashing past under the swoop of dozens of wings. A burning river. A dark, screeching pit. A serene patch of light, glowing like a pearl. Then the scenery fell away. Shadows spilled across the ground like ink. For a moment, Irina could see nothing at all. There was only the keening of the creatures, the rush of the wind, and the talons cutting into her skin.

Something greenish-grey glimmered in the darkness. A light – and, moments later, another. The creature carrying Irina banked right, and in a rush of wind and wings, they sailed past a vast, dark fortress. All Irina could see of it were the glimmering, grey-green lights, and glimpses of smooth stone walls. The slope of a turreted roof. Gleaming iron spikes. The curve of enormous towers. Links of a chain as thick as her thigh. And, hurtling towards them like an arrow, an archway.

A Steep and Savage Path

The thing carrying her dropped like a stone. Irina screamed, lost to the wind. The ground came rushing up to meet her. She screwed her eyes shut. A *snap* of wings. Irina was jerked back. She opened her eyes to see she was hurtling through the archway, barely five feet off the ground. With a shriek, the creature sped through an enormous hallway made of something black and shining. Irina glimpsed torches burning green, gigantic columns, the dark glint of sharp iron. A pair of doors creaked open with a sound like a tree about to fall. They hurtled through, skimming closer to the ground.

The claws released her and Irina went tumbling down, slamming into the floor. She rolled, spinning in a tangle of limbs and torn linen. The echoing shrieks of the things that had snatched her and Stefan rang out all around them. There was a grunt from somewhere behind her, a muffled swear word, and as Irina came to a halt she heard the *thump-thump-thump* of Stefan landing.

She sat up, her whole body throbbing. The shrieks of the guardians wheeled away. A *whump* – a little like cloth falling – came from either side of her, then another, then another. The shrieking stopped. Stefan tumbled to a stop, his foot catching her in the hip. Trembling, Irina squinted into the darkness. Flickering green light cast shadows across the gleaming black floor, coming from pairs of torches lined up on opposite sides of the room. There was a pillar of darkness between every torch, and she could not see what stood in the shadows. The end of the room was lost to the gloom; all she could see was the distant glimmer of the torches, like green stars.

For a moment, there was quiet. The only sounds were the crackle of flames, the soft rustle of feathers reaching the floor, and a muffled groan from Stefan as he sat up. Then came the loud *thump* and *click* of several things hitting the floor in perfect unison. Irina flinched. Silence spilled across the room like ink.

A quiet *tap* echoed around the room. The furthest pair of torches winked out. Another *tap*, slow and measured. A hiss, as the next pair of torches was extinguished. Another tap; another two lights snuffed out. Irina scrabbled for Stefan's hand. The darkness drew closer. The tapping grew louder, and as it echoed all around them, shadows spilling out towards them, Irina finally realized exactly what it was she was hearing.

Footsteps.

Dread coiled itself around Irina and squeezed. She knew what was approaching them from the other end of the hallway, as sure as she knew her own name. The spectre of it had hung over her since the moment she'd set foot in the land of the dead, since the moment Stefan had pushed open the door of the little cottage, since the moment she'd seen Catalina fall.

Death.

PART FOUR

When Irina had been six years old, a bear had started wandering into her village. After the sun went down, it lumbered out of the forest and up towards the houses, cracking open beehives and tearing the doors off the chicken coops. For the two months before the trap finally worked, her parents had kept her within arm's reach at all times, hurrying her indoors the moment the sky began to darken. Irina would lie in bed with the blankets pulled up to her chin, listening to the bear pad past the house, snuffling around the fence. Occasionally, she'd hear the squawk of an unfortunate hen, or the screams of a goat not taken in for the night, followed by the crunch and tear of bone and flesh. Tears pouring down her face, she would stare up at the ceiling, little hands gripping the blankets, and wait for the roar. It never came. Now, as the shadows stalked towards her, she remembered the waiting in the dark. Death's slow, measured footsteps reminded her of claws scratching at the dirt, the pause as the beast scented the air, the long, slow wait as, on the other side of the wall, it chose which defenceless animal would have its throat torn out by its powerful jaws.

The footsteps stopped. Silence unfurled like a roll of black velvet. Irina's heart fluttered. She stared into the dark. Nothing. It was as if she'd been blindfolded. The only exit was at her back, at the other end of the vast room. She'd never make it, not when Death could move faster than snuffing out a light. This was it. Stefan squeezed her hand. His fingers were trembling.

The voice, when it came, was like the gentle pad of a predator at Irina's back. Soft, measured, and far closer than she would like; Irina could hear the claws in it.

'Children,' said Death. 'All this trouble has been caused by a pair of children.'

'I—' Irina began.

A cacophony of screeching rang through the hall. There was a sudden rush of wind. Long after it ended, it echoed around the room.

'I have no need of your opinion,' said Death, the tone of their voice as smooth as bone. 'You will speak when I tell you to speak.'

The last of Irina's courage shrivelled. Stefan's hand was like a vice on hers.

The footsteps started up again, prowling around them. There was something hard to the sound, like metal or bone tapping against the rock. Behind them, a slow, steady hiss that was halfway between something dragging and something slithering across the floor.

'I do not expect you to know what is required to keep my realm balanced,' said Death, no trace of emotion in their voice. 'If either one of you had demonstrated the slightest regard for the dead, or the intelligence and foresight to orchestrate that kind of planning, you still would not know it. But that is not an excuse for the trouble that you have caused.'

There was still no anger in that voice – no disappointment, no frustration. Dispassionate and detached, each word was delivered with the precision of someone assembling a mosaic.

A Steep and Savage Path

Dread had Irina in its claws. She may as well plead her case with the surface of the moon.

'It takes time for a soul to move on,' Death intoned. 'For a soul to be reborn, or to pass into the true afterlife, it must leave many things behind, and life has a way of leaving its marks. Nothing can move on while the mark of life is upon it – but given time, those marks fade. They forget their deaths. They forget their fears. They atone for their sins, and forget those too. At that point, a soul reaches a state of perfect peace. It can go anywhere, become anything, when it is finally free of those last few bonds.

'Seventeen people are living corpses in my realm,' Death continued. 'One hundred and eighty-six more have seen them, and been reminded of mortality. Three hundred and twenty-four more have heard the commotion you caused, and been reminded of fear. Five hundred and twenty-seven souls cannot move on because of your actions. Explain yourselves.'

The sudden silence was like a slap. Every argument, every reason, every plea, had gone from Irina's head. What on earth could she say in her defence, when her sins were so thoroughly accounted for?

'Will they be all right?' she whispered.

There was a pause. 'In time,' Death replied.

'I . . . I'm really sorry. I didn't mean to—'

'That does not matter,' Death said. 'Explain yourselves.'

Irina licked her lips. Her mouth dry as dust, her pulse skittering like a frightened animal, she wondered where to begin. Stefan's hand was still locked around hers, icy cold and slippery with her own sweat.

'It's my fault,' she mumbled, 'not Stefan's. This was all my idea, I just made him come along. I . . . I'm looking for my sister.'

'If your sister is dead, then you have no business looking for her. Mourn, with your living family, and let her move on. It is no kindness to make her remember her death.'

Panic flooded through her. 'She isn't dead,' Irina yelled, 'I swear she isn't! She hit her head and the witch said that knocked her soul out of her body and if I could get it back then she'd be all right. I know she's here; I know the guardians found her. Please, she's seven years old and she isn't dead, she can't be dead . . .'

Irina's breath was snagging in her throat, her eyes burning. Had the witch lied to her? Had she really come all this way for nothing?

'How did you think to find her?' Death asked.

'I have her necklace,' Irina said, voice thick.

'Show me.'

Irina hesitated. Would it hurt Catalina if she handed Death her necklace? It was only a few wooden beads. Slowly, she lifted the necklace over her head and held it out, beads rattling as her hand shook.

It was lifted out of her fingers. She reached for it, despite herself. There was another pause, and then the wooden beads were placed delicately back into her hand. The chill touch of bone brushed across Irina's fingers.

'She is not dead,' said Death, and Irina let out a sob. There was a sigh like wind whistling through gravestones. 'Follow me,' said Death. 'It appears we have more to discuss.'

Irina scrambled to her feet, hauling Stefan up with her. Death's footsteps began to recede. Irina scurried after them, still clutching Stefan's hand. She had travelled perhaps a dozen paces into the darkness when the sound was deadened. The echoing of ringing steps was snatched away, replaced with something warm and familiar. Then, a creak. A thin slice of bright light. Irina caught a glimpse of a shadowy figure swathed in rags, famine-thin and impossibly tall. Then the light became too bright and she had to shield her eyes.

'Come in,' Death said. 'Sit down.'

Irina opened her eyes. The glittering black hall had vanished. Instead, they were in a room that looked a lot like her mother's kitchen, but on a scale far bigger than she had ever imagined. It was enormous, with wooden floors and walls, each plank wider than Irina was tall. Vast beams spanned the ceiling, and striped hangings bigger than the side of a church were hung on the walls. There was a stove with a crackling fire lit, a large wooden table and two benches – Irina was sure that she'd have to jump with her arms outstretched just to touch the seat of the bench, let alone sit down – and a massive window set into one wall. Irina could not help but look through it. The window looked onto an outdoor enclosure, full of birds in every shape, size and colour. Irina stared. They were the first animals she had seen in the land of the dead that actually looked real. Quail, partridge, doves, cuckoos, swifts, kites, orioles, bee-eaters and kingfishers flitted around the enclosure, fluttering from branch to branch.

A woman was striding towards one of the benches, walking with a staff. She was perhaps fifty, with a stern and haughty face and thick brows. Her hair, twisted into an elaborate knot, was liberally streaked with grey. She wore a man's shirt with the sleeves rolled up, tucked into britches and gleaming boots. It was only when Irina noticed that the staff was, in fact, a scythe that she remembered the stories and realized who the woman was. Whether it was the face of an older woman or a grinning skull, evidently Death had as many faces as the land of the dead itself.

Death glanced back at them. If it were not for her eyes, she would have looked human. They were filled with undulating smoke. She spun the scythe like a baton and, as it whirled, it shrank, the blade disappearing, until it came to a halt in the palm of her hand in the shape of a long, dark cane. The room had shrunk with it; when Irina looked up, the kitchen they were standing in was the size of any other.

'I . . .' Irina began, 'are you . . .'

'Yes,' said Death. 'I am many things, to many people. Please, sit. We have much to discuss. The two of you have been outmatched for quite some time; you must be tired. But first, allow me.'

She clapped her hands. The sound echoed, loud as thunder. The clothes on Irina's body twitched, pulsed – she scrambled back, scrabbling at her sleeves reflexively – and as she watched, the tears in her clothes were mended, the stains wiped away. It was the same for Stefan. He was plucking at his shirt and staring.

'Thank you,' Irina said.

Death waved a hand. 'All dead things are at my command. I can make – or unmake, as the case may be – all that dead hands do. Now, sit.'

They sat at the table. Death joined them, sitting opposite and laying her cane neatly on the bench. In the corner of the room was a small basket, with something that looked stuck halfway between a dog and a snake curled up inside it. With a jolt, Irina counted three heads, only two paws, and saw its scales were the colour of dead things.

Death put her elbows on the table and steepled her fingers, staring over the top of bony hands.

'I would ask you to tell me everything,' she said, 'but I do not need you to. You,' she said, nodding to Irina, 'are a living woman. I want you out of my realm as soon as possible. And you,' she said, turning to Stefan, 'are undead. Your being here is an affront to me. Neither one of you has a place here in your current state. But nor, it would seem, does your sister. Despite the considerable trouble you have caused me, I am willing to be merciful.'

Stefan shifted in his seat. He was clutching Irina's hand so tightly that her fingers were starting to go numb.

'First, tell me this,' said Death. 'Has either one of you eaten or drunk of anything in my realm?'

They shook their heads. 'What would have happened if we had?' Irina asked.

Death turned her swirling gaze on Irina. 'You would have stayed in Death, for as long as necessary to atone for what you took. But if you have not eaten of the land of the dead, then it has no claim on you.'

'Has Catalina?' Irina whispered, voice suddenly hoarse.

'No,' Death replied. 'My guardians brought her here before she could.'

Irina sprang to her feet, looking around wildly. 'She's *here*?'

Death pointed to the window. It swung open with a creak. Irina scrambled over to it, peering out into the enclosure. She couldn't see any sign of Catalina, amidst all the fluttering birds. Where was –

Irina stopped. She looked over her shoulder. Death was still watching her, no expression at all on her face. Stefan was still sitting at the table, completely frozen, looking as though he wanted to bolt out of the window and join the birds.

'This is a test, isn't it?' Irina asked.

'Of course,' Death replied.

'But she's not meant to be here! Can't I just take her home?'

Death's face was implacable. 'I have only your word for that, and after the trouble you have caused me, I am not inclined to take that on faith.'

'Can I—' Stefan began.

Death raised a hand, without looking at him. 'Stay where you are.'

Irina turned back to the window. She took a deep breath, staring into the flurry of feathers. Why did Death have all these birds in the first place? It seemed unlikely that Death would keep pets just for the sake of having them. She suspected that the thing in the basket might have been the beast that had tracked them through the woods, but that creature had a purpose. What were these birds for? And why were these animals different to those she'd seen in the land of the dead thus far?

A little yellow oriole flitted past, hopping onto a branch. A flash of blue, and it was joined by a kingfisher. It was strange, thought Irina, that the two birds were sitting together. All the kingfishers she had seen hunted along the riverbanks, while orioles kept hidden among the trees. Yet there was no water in sight – and, she realized, no food.

Irina's breath caught. The truth felt like it had reached into her chest and wrapped its fingers around her heart.

They were not birds. They were souls. And there were thousands of them, she realized, despair seeping into her like floodwater. How was she supposed to work out which one was Catalina?

She turned back to Death. 'Can I go inside?'

Death waved a regal hand. Irina climbed out the window and landed in the dirt, wincing as her hip caught the window-sill on her way down. She went still, listening for something like sniggering. If Catalina had seen Irina fall out the window, she would be laughing about it.

Nothing.

Irina took a cautious step into the enclosure. Birds of every size and shape flitted over her head in flashes of brown, red, blue, grey, black. Irina caught herself looking for familiar colours – a wing the colour of Catalina's blonde hair, a feather the same red as her apron. Lost on a rising tide of panic, she stared around the enclosure. There had to be something that would reveal her sister to her. She took off the necklace. It did not move. It was never going to, she told herself, as anxiety slashed at her. Catalina had passed through no more doors; there was nothing else to point to.

Taking a deep breath, she forced herself to calm down, to think. Off to the left was a group of about four or five birds sitting on the branch of a tree she could not identify. Two crows, a mangy-looking pigeon, an oriole and a kingfisher all sat in a line, looking at her. Or rather, at the necklace in her hand.

Irina was not sure what to do next. If she grabbed a random bird, would that mean Death assumed that she had made her choice? Or was she supposed to do something else once she'd caught one? She risked a glance back over her shoulder; one look at the lack of amusement on Death's face told her she would get no answers there. This was a puzzle she would have to figure out on her own.

She turned back to the birds. The crows and the pigeon had taken off, startled by her movement, but the oriole and the kingfisher were still on the branch, looking at her. She put Catalina's necklace back on, still thinking, and saw the little yellow bird following the movement of the beads.

Her heart jolted. Catalina always hated people touching her things.

With shaking hands, Irina lifted the necklace of wooden beads over her head. The kingfisher ignored her; the oriole ruffled its feathers.

She took a cautious step back, holding out the necklace. 'If you want this,' she said, retreating to the windowsill, 'then you'll have to come with me.'

The little bird flew over. It settled on the windowsill. Its dark eyes peered up at her, curious. Though it was small enough to fit into the palm of her hand, it did not seem afraid of her. Riddled with nerves, Irina shuffled a little further back, brushing up against the wall of Death's home. The strength of her own hope felt like a boulder about to crash down a mountainside. If she was wrong, and she failed Death's test, she would break.

Desperate not to startle the bird, Irina laid the necklace carefully on the windowsill. It hopped closer; once, twice. It peered down at the necklace, tilting its tiny head, and pecked it. As it drew back, it kept moving, stretching, growing, the feathers falling away, until Catalina was crouched on the windowsill like a goblin, staring at her.

Irina froze. Hope and fear had her by the throat. Was this part of the test? Was this not Catalina at all? It certainly looked like her sister – the same blonde hair, the same narrow face, the same gangly limbs. She was even dressed in the same clothes she'd been wearing when she'd taken her fall: a white shirt and skirt embroidered with flowers, and a long red apron. But she was saying nothing. Her head was still tilted like the bird she had been moments ago. One hand was touching the wooden necklace, splayed across the beads like a claw. And there was nothing in her face, nothing at all. Tears burned in Irina's eyes. Had she failed?

The little girl on the windowsill frowned. She glanced down at the necklace and looked back up at Irina, her eyes narrowed.

'Were you wearing my necklace?' Catalina asked.

Irina caught a glimpse of Catalina's chipped tooth, and the faint tone of suspicion in the words was as familiar as a song. She could see the argument waiting to be started; feel the impulse to lie and say no even though Catalina had seen the beads around her neck. It was that, more than anything, which melted Irina's doubts.

'Catalina!' she yelped, and burst into tears. Throwing her arms around her sister, she sobbed into her shoulder, all but pulling her off the windowsill. Catalina was squirming, her knees knocking Irina in the chest, but Irina wouldn't let go. She was terrified that if she did, Catalina would shrink back into a bird and fly away.

Sniffling, Irina held her sister at arm's length, beaming at her through her tears. 'Are you all right? Did anyone hurt you? God, Catalina, I've been so worried . . .'

Catalina rolled her eyes. 'I'm not a *baby*, Irina. I can take care of myself.'

'You're seven—'

'Yeah! I'm *seven*. That's old enough to take lunch up to the shepherds *and* to make cornbread. I bet *you* couldn't – why are you crying?'

Irina sat on the windowsill and pulled her into another hug. This time, Catalina didn't wriggle.

'Let's go inside,' Irina said. 'I'm here to bring you home.'

Catalina looked up at her, all the petulance gone from her face. Her eyes were full of worry. 'Have I been gone for a very long time?' she asked, her voice small.

Irina sniffed, smoothing back Catalina's hair. 'A little while, yes. But it's all right.'

'I didn't mean to be,' Catalina said, her voice starting to wobble. 'Are . . . are Mama and Tata cross with me?'

Irina shook her head. 'Not at all. They'll be so, *so* happy to see you. Now let's go inside, all right?'

Irina climbed over the windowsill and back into the kitchen. Instead of swinging her legs over the windowsill and climbing down, Catalina tried to hop straight off, lifting her arms as she did so. She crashed onto the floor in a heap of limbs. It did not appear to hurt her. Grabbing onto Irina's skirts, she hauled herself upright.

'Sorry,' she said to the room at large, when she was standing on shaking legs. 'I was a bird.'

'Do you want me to—' Irina began, putting out a hand.

Catalina was already sliding her feet across the floor like an ice skater. 'I can do it myself,' she grumbled, as she slowly sank into the splits. She caught sight of Stefan, and stopped. 'Who's he?'

Irina blushed. 'This is Stefan,' she said, unable to look at anyone in the room. 'He's . . . he's my . . . um . . .'

Catalina's eyes narrowed. She was assessing Stefan with the kind of look she usually reserved for tripe soup, or for a mess she did not want to clean up. She took in his frozen posture, his purple-black hands, and the awkward look he kept directing at Irina. Clawing herself into a standing position using Irina's elbow, she rounded on her sister.

'Have you been kissing?' she accused.

Irina felt herself go scarlet. 'I . . . what?'

'Have you been kissing?'

'I . . . I don't see how that's any of your business,' Irina tried, groping for the last shreds of her dignity.

At the table, Stefan put his head in his hands and groaned.

Catalina recoiled. 'Irina, that's disgusting!' she cried. 'I can't believe you've been kissing, with your *mouth*. That's where the spit goes!'

Death was watching them with no change on her expressionless face. For a moment, Irina was grateful that there was one person in the room who could not understand exactly how embarrassed she felt. But then, with the slightest curl at one corner of her mouth, Death said, 'That is where the spit goes,' and Irina wondered if there was any chance that Death would turn her into a bird too, so that she could fly out of the window and far, far away from everyone who had just heard what her little sister had said.

'Let's sit down,' Irina said, guiding her sister towards the table. Catalina tottered onto the bench, clearly resisting the urge to simply jump onto it with the aid of wings she no longer had, and Irina sat beside her. 'What happens now?' Irina asked. 'Can we go home?'

'Yes,' said Death.

'How?'

'You will be escorted back to the border with Life,' said Death. 'I have no desire to see the chaos you would cause should you make your own way back. You will cross the Blue River, pass through the first gate, and anyone who passes with you will be restored. All you will need to do is walk back into Life, and everything will be as it was.'

Stefan cleared his throat. 'And she'll be all right?' he asked. 'She won't be . . . faded?'

Catalina sat up straight, her eyes wide with panic. 'Faded? What do you mean, faded? Irina, are you sick?'

'In a sense, yes,' said Death. 'This place is not meant for those with a living body. The longer you stay where you are not meant to be, the more you shall wither. In the land of the living, you will be restored.'

'You're sick?' Catalina breathed, her hands over her mouth. 'You're sick and you still came looking for me?'

Irina ruffled her hair. Catalina tried to push her hand away, but missed. 'Of course I did,' Irina said. 'Don't be—'

'A word,' said Death. She stood up, scooping up her cane, and nodded to the window. It stretched, the bottom windowsill falling away until the window was transformed into a door. 'Outside.'

Irina got up, nerves squirming. 'Get to know each other,' she said to Catalina and Stefan, 'I won't be long.'

Stefan caught her hand. 'Be careful,' he said, giving her fingers a quick squeeze.

'I always am,' she said with a smile.

Catalina pulled a face. She eyed Stefan with a mix of distrust and disapproval as Irina extricated herself from the bench and followed Death back into the enclosure.

The floor was littered with stray feathers. At the sight of them, Irina felt a little stab of panic, thinking of the guardians. She poked a feather with the tip of her shoe; it stayed resolutely long and grey. A kingfisher flashed past in a blur of blue; a cluster of ravens sat like shadows on a crooked branch. Death was waiting for her at the end of the enclosure, leaning on her cane. Birds fluttered around her head as easily as if she were a tree sprouting in their pen.

Irina joined her, staring around at the birds. 'Is every one of these like Catalina?' she asked.

Death nodded.

'What happens to them?'

'Sometimes they return to the land of the living,' Death said. 'Sometimes they do not. They do it of their own accord; rarely does someone walk into my realm to ask for their return. Understand me: this generosity is a gift you will not receive twice. And, child, it is a gift with limits.'

Fear curled through Irina's thoughts like smoke. 'What do you mean?'

Death raised a hand. A finch settled on her bony fingers. For a moment, she examined it, her face dispassionate, her hand steady. With a shiver, Irina wondered if the soul within that bird understood where it had alighted, or could hear its own condition being discussed so freely.

A Steep and Savage Path

'Two of you walked into my realm,' said Death. 'Two of you will walk out.'

Her tone was calm and reasonable; the little bird was still perched on her fingers, its tiny claws curled at her first knuckle. She looked so peaceful, so gentle, that it took Irina a long moment to register exactly what she had said.

'What?' Irina whispered.

Death gave her a long, cool stare. 'Two of you entered. Two of you will leave.'

Irina's chest was growing tight. Every breath felt like it was stolen. 'But . . . but . . .'

'You forced your way into my realm before your time,' said Death, 'dragging with you a soul that should have come to me months ago but instead, feeds off the living like a parasite. That alone is insult enough. But then there is the question of your behaviour. You tried to bring the food of the living into my realm. You crossed my rivers. You crashed through my doors and tore holes through the barriers I put in place to keep my charges calm. You did untold damage to five hundred and twenty-seven of the souls I watch over. You did not eat or drink the food of the dead, and so I have no claim on you, but that does not mean you will not be punished. It is no justice if you do not bear some part of the pain you caused. The balance must be redressed.'

Death brought the little finch close to her face. It made no attempt to fly away, sitting contentedly on her finger. But in the surface of her smoke-filled eyes, Irina saw faint shapes flickering. A woman, running. Bears retreating into the woods. An old man weeping over a narrow bed. A detached part of her floating above her own panic wondered if the little bird could see them too, and knew what they meant.

'I will allow you and one other companion to leave in safety,' Death said, staring over the impassive head of the finch. 'You will both be restored, in every sense of the word. Your sister's soul would be reunited with her body the moment you crossed the border; your lover would become a living human man. When your time truly comes, and you pass away, you and your companion will be welcomed into Death as any other souls would be. But you must choose who you take into Life, and who remains behind.'

The finch had frozen on Death's finger. It was staring up into her face, watching the ghostly images flickering past on the surface of Death's eyes – forests, roads, a monastery, mountains, a sewer. Irina felt as though the little bird's claws had been wedged into her heart.

'But isn't there an arrangement we can come to?'

Death's eyes glittered like a snowstorm. 'There is not,' she said. 'Do not make me regret my generosity, child. It goes this far, and no further.'

Irina swallowed. Wings fluttered past her ear. They felt like an arrow darting past, and she flinched. 'What will happen to the one that stays behind?' she asked, her voice a scraping thing.

'They will die,' Death said, 'truly die. Their soul would be judged like any other, and when their wants are forgotten and their sins are atoned for, they will move on to whatever awaits them. The reverse applies to whichever soul accompanies you into Life: they would truly live. I would relinquish any claim I have on them – until, of course, their time comes for them to join me once again. I give you my word.'

The little bird still hadn't moved. The images were still flickering past, too fast to see. Its claws were digging into Death's finger, snagging and tearing the skin. There should have been blood. There was not.

'What if I stayed, instead?' Irina asked. 'Would you take me, and let them both go?'

Death considered her for a moment. The finch's claws were pulling at her finger, peeling back fragments of skin. She did not appear to notice.

'I have no claim on you,' she said, at last. 'One living soul and one between life and death came in; the same must be true when you go out. You must make the choice. You have transgressed against me, and this is the price you must pay. But I will grant you one small kindness.'

She raised a hand, pinching her thumb and forefinger together. At the movement, the finch exploded into life, rocketing away from her with the force of a musket ball. Its claws tore away a chunk of flesh, exposing the bone beneath. Death did not even wince. As if nothing had happened, she pulled her raised hand down in a straight line. A small vial of opalescent water was pulled out of the air and into Death's hand, half the size of Irina's little finger.

'This is water from the River Lethe,' she said. 'It will allow the drinker to forget. It is not for you. Should this pass your lips our bargain will be broken, and I will visit torments on all three of you as recompense for your treachery. You *will* bear the burden of your choice, and the things you did to make it. But the one you leave behind need not.'

Death held out the vial. Glimmers of a thousand different colours swirled behind the glass.

'Whoever drinks this will forget you,' said Death. 'They will not remember you leaving them behind. It will be as if you never came here – as if they never knew you at all.'

Tears burned in Irina's eyes. 'Will that make it easier?'

'For them? Certainly. It is not their punishment.'

Irina turned back towards the house. For a moment the walls blurred, then settled into the sides of a large wooden house, the kind Irina had seen throughout the village. Catalina and Stefan were still at the table, making awkward small talk. Stefan was sitting up painfully straight, clearly trying to seem responsible. Catalina, by contrast, was crouched on the wooden table like a goblin, peering at him suspiciously, her head cocked in an almost avian way. Irina wanted nothing more than to put an arm around each of them and hold them tight. She couldn't even imagine letting one of them go.

Death came and stood beside her. 'Make your choice at the Blue River,' she said, pressing the vial into Irina's hand, 'and do not look back.'

Stefan, or Catalina. Catalina, or Stefan. Choosing between them would be like choosing between her lungs: whatever choice she made, something was going to be ripped out of her chest. How could she pick? Didn't they both deserve a second chance at life?

As she walked back into the house, Death loping along beside her, Irina tried to pretend that nothing was wrong. She smiled. She stood up straight. She failed. Stefan was half-out of his seat the moment he saw her, eyes darting between her and Death. Catalina saw him move and turned in a strange half-hopping, half-twisting motion. She jumped off the table, landing in a heap, and hurried over to Irina at once, moving as though she was repressing the urge to jump with both feet instead of walk.

She lowered her voice. 'Did you get told off?'

Her sister's eyes were large and full of sympathy. She'd spent so long in bed since her accident that Irina had forgotten how tall she was; the top of her head was nearly level with Irina's armpit. Had her body kept growing, while her soul was elsewhere?

There was a lump in Irina's throat. She nodded, not trusting herself to speak.

Catalina patted her arm. 'One time, the witch told me off for splashing mud onto her linen when she was bringing it in, and she shouted at me for a *whole hour*. Maybe two. And she did a funny thing with her hands,' said Catalina, imitating a rude gesture Irina hadn't realized she'd learned. 'I think she was trying to put a curse on me.'

Irina put her arms around her sister and gave her a tight squeeze. It was much, much easier than looking at her. 'That sounds horrible,' she said, her voice thick.

'It didn't work. I ran away.'

Stefan came over and laid a hand on Irina's shoulder. 'Are you all right?'

Irina had no idea what to say. The weight of his hand on her shoulder was cool and strong. Once, it would have felt like a manacle about to clamp around her neck. Now, it seemed like something softer, stronger, a safe house on a lonely road. He'd changed so much. Could she abandon him? But if she didn't, that would mean abandoning Catalina. Catalina, who had trusted Irina for all her life. Catalina, who was the reason why Irina had come here and wrought such destruction in the first place. Catalina, who had done nothing wrong. Irina recoiled from herself at that thought. She was no judge. Had she really started weighing up their worth so quickly?

Death stood at a distance, watching them and leaning on her cane. Bone glimmered on her wounded finger like the glint of a ring. She waved a hand, and the door they'd entered through opened. But instead of leading into a cavernous hall filled with black and green shadows, it led into a courtyard. Wide blue sky stretched over their heads, and gently rolling hills sloped across the horizon. A neat wooden fence surrounded them, and a carefully carved gate was set into it.

'You must go,' said Death. 'You have tarried in my realm long enough. My servants will see you home.'

Still half-listening for the echo of their footsteps on stone – surely that hall had to have gone somewhere – Irina and Stefan helped Catalina out into the courtyard, kicking up the dirt under their feet. Death followed them. When they were all outside she raised her cane and drew a wide, sweeping curve in the dirt with its tip. As the point traced the arc through the soil, the ground started to shake. Six points of dust started to whirl on the spot, spaced out in a wide curve. They grew larger, stretching and bulging as they spun. Dust and dirt were drawn in, whipping past the backs of Irina's hands, until all six stood far higher than her head. The dust clarified, settled, and when the wind stopped blowing, Irina was looking at six women.

She could not have said exactly how old they were. There was an ageless quality to the cast of their faces: from some angles, they seemed little older than her; from others, they seemed burdened with the wisdom of centuries. Their hair was long, uncovered and floating around their heads like pondweed. Each one of them was clothed in floaty diaphanous material, cut somewhere between a dress and a robe. Their sleeves hung from their arms like wings.

'Oh, hello,' said Catalina, as though it were perfectly normal for women to spin themselves out of the earth in six tiny whirlwinds. 'Did you bring Anca her cake?'

One of the women nodded. It took Irina a moment to register; when she did, the exchange shocked her out of her despair. 'You know these women?' she asked her sister, lowering her voice.

Catalina nodded. 'They brought me here. I wish they'd told me I was going to be a bird, though. They could've given me some tips.'

'What do you mean?'

Wriggling with glee, Catalina shook her head. 'It's more fun if it's a surprise,' she said.

'Catalina,' Irina whispered, alarmed, 'what's going to happen?'

Catalina shook her head harder. 'I'm not telling you. I don't want to ruin it – but it's a nice surprise, I promise. You'll forget all about being told off.'

Death gestured towards the six waiting women. 'They will see you to the Blue River, and no further. The ferryman will take you over the water, and you will walk back into Life. From there, your path is your own.' She gave Irina a long look. 'As are your choices.'

The six women walked forward. Two of them stood on either side of Irina; two flanked Catalina; two surrounded Stefan. Beside the two strangers, Irina longed for a familiar hand in hers. When they each placed one hand on her shoulder and one on her wrist, she felt like she was going to be torn in two. Stefan looked equally uncomfortable – he had the air of a boy who had just been arrested – but Catalina was almost giddy. She was giggling, her eyes tight shut, bouncing on the balls of her feet. Irina squirmed. If her sister was excited, surely whatever happened next was at least not going to hurt, but what kind of surprise required two women standing like jailers on either side of her?

The women's grip tightened. Irina felt them tense, preparing to spring. She glanced down at the hem of their dresses. Peeking out beneath the hem was an enormous talon.

Then they launched themselves into the air. Wind whipped up around Irina's face. She screamed; it was lost to the air. Two clouds of feathers burst on either side of her. The snap of delicate cloth in the wind slowly became the flexing of wings. As she shot up into the sky like a cork popping out of a bottle, Irina heard her sister laughing. Angels? Irina wondered. But then, she saw them. The dresses had melted away. Feathers and scales on what had once seemed like skin. And, peering down at her with all the intent of a raptor scouring the field below for a mouse, was the scythe-blade face of the guardian holding her arm. Unnaturally long and ending in a point that was not quite a beak, its head was completely bald and covered in the scaly skin of a creature used to plunging its head into something else's guts. But there was still something human about it. Perhaps it was the eyes – still blue, Irina noted, from behind a sheet of unbridled fear. Perhaps it was the features – still more or less human, but stretched and pulled across an inhuman skull. Perhaps it was simply the spark of recognition Irina felt – whether this was one of the guardians that had picked up her and Stefan, she was not sure, but she was certain she had seen this creature before. Either way, for a moment horror had her in a grip so tight that Irina almost forgot that she was flying.

They had already climbed much higher than she realized. A patchwork carpet of places was spread out before them, fields and forests sitting side by side with monasteries and mines. At this height, Irina could see the stitches between them, the gathering up of the edges of reality where one place bordered another. It was as if the lines between them had been ruched.

They swooped over purple-grey mountains and saw their reflections in glittering lakes. Treetops bent underneath the ripples of wind from under the guardians' wings. The path of their flight was flattened in green and gold fields, many feet below. They passed over cities, and villages, and lonely cabins, and carts pulling themselves along the road, and farmers working in soil where nothing grew, and traders taking goods to market that they had never made. Was it easier, Irina wondered, to sing along to the echo of a life that you had once known? Was the memory of life always going to be sweeter than the thing itself? Or, with all the hard work and harder choices removed, would it only ever be a pale imitation of something with real meaning, like a wan moon next to the blazing sun?

When she left someone behind, would they be happy here?

Eyes unseeing, Irina stared across the expanse of Death below. It would be easier to leave someone behind if she knew that they would be happy in Death, and safe. With a shock, she realized Catalina would be. Irina had seen the village for lost children: her sister would have everything she wanted there. She'd already made friends, and the guardians would protect her until their parents came to join her. Perhaps, when she was truly dead, she'd even get a chance at paradise. The same was not true for Stefan. He had killed people.

She'd told him he wasn't a monster. If she left him behind, she could be condemning him to an eternity of torture. He certainly believed that was what awaited him. She could see it now: herself stepping into the boat while he stood on the shore, screaming her name, pleading for his chance while he was dragged away. She couldn't condemn him to that. Everyone else in his life had abandoned him. They'd turned away when his own father had screamed at him, struck him, and left him to die in a snowstorm. But she was different. She'd been kind to him. She'd put her trust in him. It was clear how much that surprised him, and how much he craved it. It would be different, if she was the one to leave him behind.

But if she and Stefan walked into Life hand in hand, leaving Catalina on the shores of Death, how could she ever face her parents?

The thought had her by the throat. She remembered their pale, drawn faces on the night she'd left, both of them holding each other at Catalina's bedside. Grief had already raked its claws down their faces then. Was she really going to turn those scratches into scars? Was she going to stand and watch them weep as Catalina's coffin was lowered into the earth, knowing that she could have saved her? How could she sit through her sister's funeral when it had been her choice to put her in the ground? It did not matter that Death's gift would mean that Catalina would not remember Irina leaving her behind. Every day that she spent with her parents, Irina would remember. With every tear, every fresh grey hair, every time the table was set for three, Irina would see the shadow of what she had done.

The ground was growing closer. They were still far from the Blue River; Irina could not yet see it winking in the distance. Instead, they were hurtling towards a monastery, its red-tiled roof made redder by coppery light from a sun that Irina could not see setting. The guardians swooped down, banking around the building – Irina saw a whirl of coloured figures painted on the walls as they passed. Over her shoulder, Catalina was shrieking with laughter. With less of a bump than she was expecting, they landed in front of the doors, and it was only when the wind had stopped rushing into her face that Irina realized that she had been crying. She turned away quickly. It would make everything so much worse if she had to explain.

The monastery was a large building, every inch of it painted. Irina had seen such monasteries before, covered with the faces of serene saints and placid apostles. But while the shape of the building was familiar – long, thin windows, a tall, arched doorway set behind a portico, a tower set into the pointed roof – the paintings were not. A creature was painted arching around the doorway: a snake's tail on the left merging into the body of a three-headed dog on the right. Winged women – some with human faces, some with sharp, birdlike beaks – reared up beside the columns, holding sets of scales, or swords, or sinners by the ankle. Five ribbons of colour ran through the images – cobalt blue, white, silvery grey, burning red and forest green – and towering above them with her hands outstretched, the black-clad figure of Death. At first, Irina saw her as a warrior queen, crowned with iron and draped in a robe studded with stars. But then, she turned her head, and the painting changed. Death's face was a skull, their hands only bone, the arc of the scythe curving over their head. Irina thought of the bargain she had made, and the choice she would have to face reared up in her mind, like a bear about to strike.

There was a series of *thumps* behind her. Catalina had fallen over on her way to the door, still not used to the shape of a human body. She'd hit her knee, hard, and was trying not to cry. The guardians – back in their human shapes, Irina noticed – were helping her to her feet, feathers littered around the hems of their dresses. Stefan was a little way off, looking decidedly rumpled after his flight. He was straightening his shirt and fussing with his hair. The moment he saw her face, he stopped.

Irina went over to Catalina, brushing her down so she didn't have to meet her eyes. Behind her, the guardians began filing into the monastery. 'That was quite a bang, when you fell over. Are you all right?'

'It was a lot easier when I was a bird,' Catalina grumbled. 'If I thought I was going to fall, I could just fly instead.'

'That does sound easier. But at least you'll have a good bruise.'

Catalina brightened up. 'What colour?'

'Well, how hard did you fall?'

'*So* hard. I thought my knee was going to bend the other way, that's how hard it was.'

Irina tried for a smile. 'I expect you'll get all the colours you want. If your knee doesn't fall off first.'

'I'll show Mama! And knees can't fall off, that's not how that—' Catalina stopped, catching sight of the look on Irina's face.

Stefan caught up to them, worry scrawled across his face. He laid a hand on Irina's shoulder. 'Are you all right?' he asked.

A lump swelled in her throat. Irina nodded.

He made a small, frustrated sound. 'I know you aren't. What's wrong?'

Irina shook her head.

Catalina took her hand. 'Are you feeling sick after the flying?' she asked, her voice small and full of doubt.

Irina nodded, blinking fast. With both of them trying to comfort her, the choice she had to make seemed to stalk ever closer. She didn't want to draw it any nearer by telling them about it.

'Yes,' she said, her voice catching. 'Yes, it was the flying. I just . . . I just need to sit down. I'll be all right.'

'Irina,' Stefan began, his voice low.

Catalina rounded on him, puffing up like an angry cat. 'She said she needs to sit down! That means you have to be quiet. We've all got to be quiet, and then she can rest, and then she'll be better and we can go home where Mama and Tata will look after us!'

Irina gave him an empty smile. 'I'll be fine,' she said. 'I just . . . I'll be fine.'

She set off, turning her back on the painted monastery. No one held her back.

Irina walked for a long time. It did not help. After so long in the air, her legs felt unsteady, and for a while she thought that staggering along would be enough of a distraction that the lump in her throat would finally start to fade. It did not. Footsteps crunching along a gravel path, she passed by more painted buildings, the regal faces of Death staring down at her from each one – sometimes a woman, sometimes a skull, and sometimes two people: a bearded man and a young girl, facing each other – and a large, bare patch of earth that might have been a garden cleared for planting and might have been a graveyard cleared of corpses. She quickened her pace. Up ahead were the remains of another painted building, long since collapsed. She picked her way towards it, desperate for a few moments to think.

Catalina or Stefan. Stefan or Catalina. Catalina had a loving family waiting for her; Stefan did not. Stefan could be tortured if she left him here; Catalina would not. She had to make her choice. There was no way around it. But testing the weight of their souls in the palm of her hand felt like a betrayal. Who was she to decide which of them should live or die? She was Catalina's sister; she was Stefan's wife. Didn't she owe them both loyalty? She had two hands; couldn't they each take one of her own and run headlong into Life with her?

She reached the ruins. Three walls towered over her, empty window frames large enough to stand in; the fourth had crumbled. The roof of the building was long gone, but no tiles or beams were strewn across the ground. Instead there was a vast willow tree growing in the centre of the ruined building, its leaves falling in a soft, green curtain. Vines covered the walls, but there was no sign of their roots; they looked more like garlands tangled across the flaking plaster. Irina crept closer, pushed the vines aside. The painted face of a man holding some kind of stringed instrument stared back at her, standing before the hooded ferryman. Irina's hand tightened on the vines. She didn't need another reminder of how careless she'd been, of whose heart she was about to break. Suddenly she was tearing at the vines, ripping them away in handfuls. All she wanted was a place to think, but even the damn walls wouldn't let her be. She'd drag the stupid vines over the stupid paintings and then she wouldn't have to look at them, wouldn't have to think about the choice she had to make. Better yet, she'd tear the wall down, and show Death what she thought of her cruel bargain.

A pair of purple-black hands closed over hers.

'Hey, hey,' Stefan said, his voice gentle. 'Don't do that. What if you cut yourself?'

She wouldn't look at him. Couldn't. 'I just . . . I just want them gone.'

'Why?'

Irina closed her eyes. Hot tears burned behind her eyelids. Stefan's cold fingers lifted her hands away from the vines, thumbs stroking her knuckles.

'Irina,' he said, 'tell me what's wrong.'

'Nothing,' she mouthed, her voice too tight to speak.

'I don't think that's true,' he said, and the tenderness in his words was like a lash across her back. 'You haven't been the same since you spoke to Death. She told you something, didn't she?'

Eyes tight shut, Irina nodded.

Stefan's hands froze. 'All right,' he said, his voice carefully calm, 'come and sit with me and tell me what she said.'

They shuffled over to the willow tree. There was a gap in the waterfall of leaves; Stefan held them aside for her and Irina sat down, settling against the trunk. Through the veil of leaves she could see the monastery below, all the gold paint winking in the warm light. The sky burned copper, gold, crimson. The trees beyond were already silhouettes, dark against the blazing sky. It was as if they were sitting in a little nest made from the last leaves of autumn, waiting for winter.

Stefan put an arm around her. She rested her head on his shoulder, and when she felt him press a kiss into her hair she could have broken into pieces.

'What did she say?' he asked.

Irina drew in a deep, shuddering breath. A fine mist was rising off the grass, burnished gold. It seemed unbearably cruel that she was looking at something so beautiful when she was going to break Stefan's heart.

'She isn't going to let all of us just walk out,' she mumbled, her voice thick with tears. 'I did too much damage for that. She'll only let two of us leave.'

Stefan's hand tightened on her shoulder. 'If you think for one minute that I'm letting you stay behind—'

She shook her head. 'I can't. She wouldn't let me. I *have* to leave, and . . . and I have to decide who leaves with me.'

Stefan had gone completely still.

Irina's voice snagged in her throat. 'I don't know how I'm supposed to choose,' she said, burying her face in her hands. 'Whoever comes with me comes back to life, and whoever stays here dies. I don't want to kill either of you! I want you both safe, and happy, but I have to pick someone to bring with me and it's like choosing which of my limbs to hack off and I can't do it, Stefan, I can't do it! I just – I can't . . .'

Her throat closed over. Tears were pouring down her face. She stared out at the ruins, terrified of what she would see if she turned to look at him. Would he plead for his life? Or had she broken his heart already?

'That's easy,' he said. 'You pick your sister.'

Irina froze. She stared at him, the sound of her own pulse thudding in her ears. Surely he didn't mean it. But his face was serene. The golden light had turned his brown eyes to gleaming bronze, and though his hands were trembling, he was smiling at her.

'What?' she breathed.

'Of course you pick her,' he said, his skin tinged with gold.

'She's who this has all been for. Besides, she's a child. She has a loving family. She's done nothing wrong. She . . . she deserves a second chance.'

'But what about you?'

He placed a hand on her knee, plucking at her skirt. 'Think about what would happen if you brought me back,' he said, avoiding her gaze. 'What kind of life could I give you?' He held up his purple-black hand, the veins of shadow rippling down his arm. 'You'd be married to a monster. I'd only be able to see you at night, creeping through your window like a thief. I'd kill people wherever you went – or at the very least, hurt them. Sooner or later people would realize it's you I'm following, and when they came for you, I wouldn't be able to protect you.'

She shook her head. 'Life isn't something you give! It's something you make. And you wouldn't be the way you are now. If you came with me, you'd be human.'

He stopped. His lips parted. Desperate hope blazed on his face; then, he folded it away. 'That doesn't change anything.'

'Doesn't it?' She paused, trying to speak past the lump in her throat. 'Don't . . . don't you want a life with me?'

Stefan took both her hands in his. Full of tears, his eyes gleamed like bronze.

'Of course I do,' he said, his voice thick. 'I don't think I've ever wanted something so much, alive or dead.'

'Then why?'

His throat worked. 'Irina,' he began, 'I've told you something about what my life was like. People were not kind to me. You are. I didn't know how much I needed that, until I met you. But it's not just that.' He reached out, tucked her hair behind her ear, fingers brushing along the back of her neck. 'Even when I was alive I didn't think I could ever find someone like you. I didn't think the world could have something so perfect in it.

But you reminded me that all the good things in life – hope, and love, and kindness – weren't just things that people talked about and set aside. They were real. They're in you. You're everything that life could be. A life with you . . . I know I can't enter paradise, but a life with you would come close.'

A tear slid down his cheek. Irina reached for it. He caught her hand and kissed her fingertips, closing his eyes.

'I love you,' he said, his voice thick. 'You are the most precious thing in the world to me, and I would do anything to make you happy. And . . . and that means I have to do this. Irina, I don't ever want you to look at me and see the choice you didn't make. I . . . I want you to choose me. But if choosing me would make you unhappy, then what I want doesn't matter. Not when there's something that I can do that could fix it.'

Irina's vision blurred with tears. For one wild moment she thought about clawing at the tree behind her, cramming handfuls of leaves into her mouth or carving handfuls of sap from its bark, licking it off her fingers. Then she wouldn't have to make a choice at all. They could all stay behind in Death. No one would have to stand on the shores of the Blue River and watch her sail away without them. Her parents would be distraught. One child confined to her bed, the other missing. They'd never be the same, with both their children gone. But she'd see them again, when they died. They'd be reunited eventually.

Stefan drew her closer. His face was full of tenderness. In the golden light, she might have been looking at the icon of a saint, and she knew that if she did eat or drink something just to stay with him, he would never forgive her.

'I don't have much to give you,' he said, fingers smoothing back her hair, 'but I can give you this. It doesn't have to be your burden. You don't have to make this choice alone.' He smiled, his touch lingering in the soft place just behind her jaw. 'Isn't that what marriage is supposed to be all about?'

Tears coursed down Irina's cheeks. Each one felt like the point of a knife. She wound her arms around his waist and buried her head in his chest, a sob curling around her throat like a snake. 'I don't want to leave you,' she whispered.

He lifted her into his lap, cradling her to him with one hand in her hair. 'I know.'

'I . . . I love—'

'Please don't say it,' he said, his voice rough. 'I don't think I could go through with it if I heard you say it.'

Irina looked up at him. For the first time since he'd sat down beside her, she saw the fear in his face. He was not making a leap of faith, some grand gesture with no understanding of exactly what it would mean. He knew what he was offering her, and he was terrified of it. He would watch her cross the Blue River and walk, willingly, into the darkness of Tartarus when she was out of sight. He was dreading it. She could see it in his eyes. But despite the terror so clearly visible on his face, he was still sitting here, making his offer. And he still wanted her to take it.

She said nothing. There was nothing she could say, in the face of such devotion. Words seemed far too small. Saying what she felt was like trying to paint a sunset in black and white. So instead, she curled her fingers around the torn lapels of his shirt and pulled him into a kiss.

His mouth was cool and soft on hers. The salt of his tears lingered on her lips. Pulling him closer, the life they might've had flickered through her mind's eye. Emerging from the cave, hand in hand. Taking him home to meet her parents. A real wedding, with feasting and dancing and clothes she'd made herself. A new home in a new place, with the whole world waiting to see what they would make of it. It was cruel; it was beautiful. It was the harshest punishment she could imagine; it was everything she had ever wanted. But next to what Stefan had promised her – the labour and sacrifice of real love – she could see it for what it was. A lovely, empty dream.

Irina was not sure how long they spent under the willow tree. The sun did not set. There was no sun, only the last golden moment of an evening, stretched out into eternity. Part of her was grateful. She wanted the moment to last forever. But the knowledge that it would not end was like the bite of a knife: *she* had to be the one to end it.

Eventually, they wound their way back to the monastery, hand in hand. Catalina was waiting for them. The guardians had finished their business in Death's monastery, and now Catalina was sitting with them, telling an elaborate story and waving her arms. She scrambled to her feet when she saw them approaching, lurching slightly.

'Have you been—' she stopped, alarmed, when she saw Irina's face. 'What happened?'

Irina pulled her into a hug. 'Nothing's happened,' she said, into the top of Catalina's head. 'We were just talking.'

Catalina wriggled free, scowling. 'Just *talking*,' she muttered, glaring at Stefan. 'You were fighting, weren't you?' She rounded on Stefan, drawing herself up to her full height. 'If you have been mean to my sister,' she said, with a vague stab at dignity, 'I will push you over. *And* I'll push you into some mud, so you'll get dirty and we'll all laugh.'

'No pushing,' Irina said, with a sniff.

'You don't get to say no pushing,' Catalina muttered, 'you're not Mama.'

Irina ignored her. She flopped onto the grass and stared up

at the burning sky. All her energy seemed to have been cried away. The Blue River was waiting for her. She'd made her choice; it would hurt less if she got it over and done with. But the thought of hauling herself upright and putting herself into the clawed hands of the guardians one more time felt like a mountain too high to climb.

Catalina sat down beside her, peering at her anxiously. 'That lady said you were sick,' she said. 'Is that why you were crying?'

Irina tried for a smile. 'I'm just tired. I'll be all right when we get home.'

Catalina laid a hand on Irina's forehead. It was not the soothing hand of the practised nurse; one of her fingers was all but poking Irina in the eye, and if Catalina moved her thumb in the wrong way it was going to end up in Irina's nose.

'I don't know if that's a temperature,' Catalina confessed, after a long moment. 'Mama never told me. She'll do it properly, when we get back. But do you feel better?'

'Thank you,' Irina said.

She closed her eyes. Sleep did not come; she could feel her sister looking at her.

'Irina?' Catalina asked. 'Are you awake?'

Stefan's voice, still a little thick. 'Let's let her sleep,' he said.

That had never worked once. Irina sighed, keeping her eyes closed. 'I'm awake.'

Her sister's voice shrank as she spoke. 'There's a scratch on your arm, under your sleeve. Did . . . did you get hurt?'

Irina heaved herself upright, finally opening her eyes. Catalina was crouched in front of her, looking like she was about to cry, her eyes locked on the wound at Irina's wrist. Suddenly it felt like something sharp was lodged in her throat. How could she tell Catalina what she'd gone through to get to her – what she was going to go through, so that Catalina could have a second chance at life? She was a child. It would be cruel to put the weight of that knowledge on her shoulders. If Catalina even believed her. Irina was not sure if her sister understood the full weight of where she was – and the more she thought about it, the more certain Irina became that she did not want her to. Catalina was seven years old. A part of her had been trapped in the land of the dead. How could she ever hope to have a normal life if she understood the true depths of what that meant? She had seen what waited in the afterlife. That knowledge would be a terrible burden to bear. No one would believe her. If she tried to talk to anyone about what she'd seen, they'd call her a fanciful child – or worse, mad, or a heretic. How could she thrive if she had to bear that burden alone?

A realization slid into Irina's thoughts like a dagger between her ribs. This was a burden *she* would have to bear, too. Catalina at least had the mercy of not understanding. Perhaps, in time, she'd remember the land of the dead as some strange dream, or a delirium she'd been caught in as she lay bedridden. Irina would know the truth. No ignorance would shield her, no quirk of memory would soften the blow. And there would be no one, ever, who would believe her. Death's punishment was as finely balanced as a rapier.

Stefan sat down beside Irina. He took her hand, snapping her out of her daze. 'It's been a hard journey,' he said to Catalina, 'but we're all right. And it'll be a lot easier on the way back.'

'Is that how you hurt your hands?' Catalina asked.

'I'm sorry?'

She pointed to his purple-black fingers. 'That's a big bruise.'

There was a fraction of a pause. Then, 'Yes,' he said. 'I tripped. Lots.'

'That was very silly of you,' she said, fixing him with a stern look. 'You better not have laughed when Irina fell over, either.'

'Not even if it was funny?' he said, clearly trying for a smile.

Catalina looked genuinely stumped. 'That's still mean, but if it was funny . . .'

Irina held out her arms. Catalina came in for a hug, all her anxiety gone. When they broke apart, she peered at Irina's arm, where there was a ring of bruises showing just above the cut. For a moment, Irina panicked – had she noticed the bruises were shaped like handprints? – but then, she caught sight of Catalina's index finger, drifting towards a bruise. The sight of it was so familiar, so reassuring after Catalina's long months of immobility, that Irina could have burst into tears.

Instead, she dredged up a smile and an indulgent tone, rolling up her sleeve. 'Do you want to poke it?'

'Can I?'

'Once.'

Catalina's hand jumped to the biggest, bluest bruise and prodded it. It was only sore, compared to the agony of forcing herself through the gates of the land of the dead, but Irina made a show of acting pained to make her sister giggle.

'That's nothing,' said Stefan, spreading out both his hands in front of Catalina. He rolled up his sleeves, so she could see how far the purple-black skin extended up his arms. 'See?'

'Can I poke that one too?'

'All right.'

Catalina went to poke the back of his hand. Stefan yanked it out of the way, grinning. 'Stefan!' she yelled. 'You said I could poke it!'

'All right, all right. It's just so sore, I can't—'

He snatched his hands away again. Catalina jabbed at him; he darted back. She went for him again; he moved his hands away, pulling a face at her.

'Bet you can't get me,' he said.

'Bet I can!'

'Bet you—'

Catalina tackled him. Stefan toppled over backwards with a squawk. When he was flat on his back, Catalina grabbed one of his hands, held it up and prodded it with her finger, crowing 'I got you! I got you!' while he let out theatrical groans of agony.

He looked up, caught Irina's eye. His face softened. He gave her a small, encouraging nod. With the sound of her sister's laughter in her ears, Irina wondered how, on the cusp of heartbreak, she could still be happy. The Blue River was waiting. When she closed her eyes she could see its sparkling waters, as though the blue glow was already shining at her feet. There would never be another moment like this.

Stefan held out his arm. Irina lay down beside him, cuddling into him. She laid her head on his shoulder, listening to her sister's increasingly elaborate victory chants. Despite the lump in her throat, she couldn't hold back a smile. On the brink of parting, they had found themselves a slow, perfect sunset – one last moment before night would fall and she would have to carry out the choice they'd made. She intended to make it last.

Irina was not sure how long the guardians gave them. The light did not fade; there was no sun in the sky to mark the time. But when Catalina had stopped torturing Stefan and started digging her fingers into the grass instead, suddenly they were on their feet, encircling the three of them like sheepdogs. Despair seeped into Irina like water trickling into her shoes.

'Already?' she asked.

One of the guardians held out a hand to help her up, her sleeve trailing in a gentle breeze. From the movement of the cloth, the air seemed to be rolling its way down her arm.

Stefan squeezed Irina's hand. 'We can't stay.'

Irina tried to swallow the lump in her throat; Catalina was watching them. She got up. At once, two guardians stepped forward, already reaching for her. Irina shook off her skirt, brushing off grass and dirt that she knew would not be there so she could have a few more moments without looking anyone in the eye.

The guardians' hands locked around her like shackles. Catalina was on her feet, wriggling in anticipation of the flight; Stefan was hauling himself upright, not looking at anyone. The guardians on either side of Irina tensed, ready to spring. Their hands lengthened. A faint cracking sound came from either side of her, as skin gave way to the smooth, curved point of a claw.

Then, they set off.

With a flex of wings and a giddy laugh from Catalina, they launched themselves into the air. The monastery receded, spinning away from them like a florin tumbling out of sight. High above the ground, Irina could see the stitches in the land of the dead again. The thickness of a vast forest was cut short to make way for a golden field. A wide harbour sat at the foot of a thriving town, the shimmering water slashed through by a straight line of tall, dark mountains. A church, sealed away from the rest of the world by a high, thick wall, had its neatly tended garden sliced in half by a winding dirt road. Worse, if she looked too hard at one part of the land beneath her, Irina could see the edges of it bleeding over the borders. The forest stretched across the fields; the harbour sat in the shallows of the sea; the church wall ran unbroken around the rest of the buildings. With the ground already rushing past several hundred feet below her, it made Irina feel extremely sick.

Ahead: a pool of bright white light. Then, a forest, glittering with green and pink lights. A brightly coloured clutch of houses, surrounded by a ring of haystacks. A vast plain of grass. She recognized each one as she passed over them. Her heart lurched. Soon, their journey would be done.

She looked up. Straight ahead of them were skeins of light, darting across the sky. She could not see the picture that they were forming; like looking at the back of a tapestry, all that she could make out in front of her were random streaks of colour. The tapestry of lives. She had a second to wonder what she was seeing when she looked at it from the back – the paths not taken? Decisions not made? – before the colour split down the middle and parted like curtains. Darkness spilled across the sky. They hurtled towards it, and in a burst of agony, they were through, rocketing over a black-and-white forest and the heads of an endless crowd. Blue light glimmered in the distance.

The guardians slowed. Swooping and banking to avoid the stalactites, they drifted gently towards the ground. The jetty sat on top of the gleaming river like a shadow. The boat was already waiting, the hooded ferryman leaning on their pole. Apart from them, this bank of the river was deserted.

Irina's feet settled onto solid rock as the guardians landed. With a ripple of fabric and a flurry of feathers, their avian forms melted away, beaks receding into impassive, human faces. They had touched down only a few feet from the dock. The ferryman was watching them, face hidden by the depths of their hood.

'Well,' said Stefan, his tone forced into a lighter shape, 'I suppose this is it.'

'I suppose it is,' said Irina, her voice thickening with every word. 'Will you be all right?'

They both glanced back in the direction of the gate.

'I don't know,' he said, fear sweeping across his face. 'It depends on where I end up.'

'What do you mean?' asked Catalina, appearing at Irina's

elbow. She was staring at Stefan, frowning. 'Aren't you coming with us?'

Tears burned in Irina's eyes. She put a hand over her mouth.

'No,' said Stefan. 'No, I'm not.'

'But why?'

'There's only room for two people in the boat,' he said, his voice gentle. 'I'm staying here.'

Catalina was still frowning, picking at her bottom lip in the way that she often did when she was thinking. 'But there were lots of people on the boat coming the other way,' she said. She glanced up at Irina, her eyes widening when she saw her tear-stained face. 'You . . . you could come after us, couldn't you? On the next boat?'

Stefan patted Catalina on the shoulder. 'Maybe on the next boat.'

Irina tried for a smile. It did not work; she could see the panic in Catalina's eyes. 'Could you wait by the dock for a minute? I won't be long.'

Catalina stumbled off towards the jetty, looking back with every step. In a few moments, she was back, tugging on Irina's sleeve and clutching a dark wreath in her hands.

'The ferryman said the lady gave them this to give back to you,' she said, handing over Irina's battered bridal crown. 'Did . . . did you . . . are you . . .'

Irina took it, with shaking hands. 'Will you thank them for me,' she said, 'and wait in the boat? I . . . I won't be long.'

Catalina nodded, her bottom lip starting to wobble, and went back to the boat. Irina wiped her eyes, fumbling in her pockets for the vial.

'I've got something for you,' she said, when she had finally found it. 'It might make things easier.'

'What is it?'

She held out the opalescent water. 'It's from the River Lethe,' she said. 'There's just enough here to let you forget me. If things get too much, I won't mind. I won't mind at all, if it means you don't – if it makes it stop . . .'

Stefan took the vial from her. He gazed at her for a long moment. Then he dropped the vial, and before Irina could react, crushed it under his boot.

'What are you doing?' she gasped. 'That could've—'

He took her hands, scrunching her fingers against the pine needles. 'Irina,' he said, 'I don't want to forget you.' He cupped her cheek, and gave her a smile that broke her heart. 'You're the only thing that's going to get me through Hell.'

Her resolve buckled. It seemed unbearably cruel to leave him when he was looking at her like that. How could she have a life on Earth, when she knew that he was in the underworld, holding onto the memory of her as if it could prevent him from drowning?

'It's going to make it so much harder,' she whispered.

Panic flashed across his face. 'Did you want me to drink it?' He stared down at the ground, looking for glimmers of colour among broken glass. 'I think there's enough to—'

She shook her head. 'Of course not. But I want you to be happy. And if that could've helped . . .'

Halfway through reaching for a shard of broken glass, Stefan stopped. 'I want you to be happy, too. Promise me you won't wait for me, Irina. Don't let me hold you back. I . . . I want you to have all the things you want, even if I can't give them to you.'

The way that he was looking at her was a torture in itself. There was such tenderness in his face, such care. But she could see in his eyes that, in his heart, he had never thought that this would end any other way. He had accepted his fate so fast that, for a moment, she wondered if he had always expected her to leave him. That night in the inn, she realized, he hadn't been lying to the landlady; he'd always thought that she was far too good for him. But, she wondered, after a lonely childhood under the shadow of his father's abuse, did he think that he was unworthy of her, or did he think he did not deserve love from anyone? She recoiled from the thought, filled with revulsion for every single person who had made him think like that. He *was* worthy. How could she leave him, knowing that the second she was out of sight, he would give up on his own happiness completely?

The Blue River glimmered in front of them. Irina remembered what Doctor Emil had called it: the Styx, the river of unbreakable oaths. An idea began to form.

'I'll make the promise,' she said, 'if you'll do the same.'

Taking him by the hand, she led him over to the water's edge, slipping the bridal crown back onto her head. Aqua and ultramarine danced past in a swirling rush, cornflower-blue spray brushing their ankles. Irina knelt down, pulling him down with her, and stuck her right hand into the water.

'What are you doing?'

She smiled. 'Unbreakable oaths,' she said. His eyes widened as she pulled her arm out of the water. Glittering droplets in every shade of blue clung to her fingers. She held out her hand, sparkling blue water dripping across her palm and down her wrist. Stefan did the same. Shimmering blue slid across his purple-black hands, like stars in the sky.

She clasped his hand. His skin was cold. Undulating blue light spilled across his features, sending one half of his face into shadow that rippled like silk.

'If you have a chance to be happy, take it,' she said. 'Swear it.'

'I will, if you will.'

A Steep and Savage Path

'I swear.'

'I swear.'

For a moment, Irina could have sworn that the water clinging to their hands glowed a brighter blue. But she was already leaning forward, her eyes closed, her lips parted. The kiss, when it came, felt like something holy.

They broke apart, got to their feet. Stefan gathered her into his arms, face buried in her hair. Then, the two of them walked hand in hand to the jetty.

Catalina was already sitting in the boat, watching the two of them with wide, worried eyes. The boatman stood behind her, leaning on their pole, hooded face pointed in their direction. A shaft of blue light, thrown by the lapping of the water, shone into the bottom of their hood. For a moment, Irina was sure that she saw them smiling. But then, Stefan handed her into the boat, and shadow passed over the boatman's face once more.

Irina sat down in the prow, next to her sister. Stefan's eyes never left her face. A thousand different blues shimmered across his skin. They said nothing. What was there to say, Irina wondered, in the face of their last vow? Only the things that were truer and more solid than the bones in her body, and sharper than the blade of a scythe. That she loved him. That she did not want to leave. That, even though it was a choice they had made together, and that they had tried to soften the blow, she would always remember him standing on the jetty, watching her sail away into a life that they might have shared.

The boatman pushed off. Irina felt a sudden lurch of panic. She raised a hand, reaching for Stefan, before she could help herself. There was no more river water clinging to her fingers. She turned it into a wave instead, and hoped he did not see the fear in her eyes. He smiled, raised a hand. Then the boat turned, and he was out of sight.

Catalina shuffled over to sit beside her. She lifted Irina's arm and wriggled underneath it, knocking her knees against the seat. She put her arms around her, squeezing Irina tight.

'He's not getting on the next boat, is he?' she asked.

'No,' Irina rasped, her voice suddenly heavy.

Catalina fell silent. The water lapped at the sides of the boat, the boatman's pole slicing through the current in smooth, gentle strokes. Then, there was a small snuffling sound. Catalina squeezed tighter.

'What is it?' Irina asked.

'Nothing,' Catalina said, wiping her eyes. 'I just thought he was nice.'

The dam broke. Irina burst into tears.

PART FIVE

When they reached the other side of the Blue River, it took Irina and Catalina a long time to climb out of the boat. Irina was still sobbing when they docked, and after a journey listening to her sister weep, Catalina was crying too. There was nothing for it but to sit in the boat and wait for the tears to subside. The boatman did not seem to mind. There was no queue of the dead on the other side of the river – evidently, Death was keeping them far away – and they stood and leaned on their pole with a meditative air.

At last, Irina composed herself. She wiped her eyes, sniffling, and drew in a deep, shuddering breath. 'Come on now,' she said to Catalina, who was still crying. 'No more tears. Let's go home.'

'I'm only crying because you're crying,' Catalina wailed. 'It's not my fault!'

'I know.'

Irina lifted Catalina out of the boat and onto the jetty. She was not ready to be on solid ground; her legs folded underneath her when Irina tried to put her down. Irina turned to the boatman, fishing in her pockets for some coins, but they held up a hand and shook their head.

'Thank you,' she said, her voice hoarse. 'Do you know the way to the gate?'

The boatman pointed into the darkness.

'Just keep going that way?'

They nodded.

Irina climbed out of the boat. 'Thank you.' She helped Catalina up, holding her hand. Her sister was still crying; Irina couldn't afford to fall apart again. Not when Catalina needed her. 'Come on,' she said, trying to inject some brightness into her voice. 'Let's go home.'

They set off into the darkness. The blue light darkened to navy shadows, and then faded into black. Stalactites and stalagmites loomed out of the darkness like teeth. Footsteps echoed off the stone, and Irina was not sure how many of them there were, amid all the ringing. With every step, Catalina drew closer to Irina's side. Soon, she was not holding Irina's hand; she was walking with her arms thrown around Irina's middle, peering into the dark.

'I don't like it here,' she whispered.

'Not long now,' Irina replied. 'You'll be home before you know it.'

Catalina made a sceptical noise against Irina's ribs. 'Won't we have to walk all the way back?'

'No,' said Irina, remembering what Death had told her. 'There'll be a big gate up ahead soon. When we go through it, you'll wake up in your bed. Mama and Tata will be there, and this whole thing will seem like a bad dream.'

'It wasn't all bad,' said Catalina, stumbling over a stalagmite. 'I got to fly.'

Irina thought of Stefan, and it sliced her open. 'No,' she said, her voice quiet. 'It wasn't.'

'Will you be there too, when I wake up?' Catalina asked.

'I'll come home as quick as I can,' said Irina. She hesitated; best not for her sister to know the truth. It was far too much to place on her shoulders. 'I'm actually supposed to be working right now,' she lied.

Catalina looked up at her. 'And you ran off to get me?'

Irina nodded.

'You'd better tell them that I was a bird,' Catalina said, her face serious, 'otherwise you'll be in real trouble.'

They kept walking. After a while, her sister started yawning, her feet dragging over the uneven rock. Irina crouched down and let her climb onto her back, then kept going. Soon, Catalina was asleep, slumped over Irina's shoulder. Irina shifted her weight a little and kept walking. Better that Catalina did not see the moment they crossed between worlds. For Irina, it had been painful, but she was living, forcing herself into a place not meant for her. If it was going to hurt for Catalina as she crossed the border into Life, Irina would much rather her sister slept through it.

A distant shimmer in the darkness. Gold and copper and bronze and white, twining around each other. As Irina drew closer to the gate, she could see the points of light swaying and twisting like fronds in the breeze. Swooping up and branching out into the vast archway, the lights filled Irina with relief and hope and sadness. She was still living, after all. Her family would be whole again when she passed through that arch. Her heart would not. There would be no going back.

Catalina let out a murmur in her sleep. The sound bolstered Irina's resolve. She had made her choice. She had made her vow. She was going to honour it – no looking back, not once. Perhaps she would not fall in love again – it seemed unlikely, when love had seemed so alien to her before she'd met Stefan – but she would have her family. There were other ways to be happy. She owed it to Stefan – and to herself – to find out what they were.

The gate drew closer. Soon she was craning her neck to look up at it. This time, there was no pain, no headache buzzing at the back of her skull. But, she thought, why would there be? She was heading back to the land of the living. She was going home. At last, she would be where she was meant to be.

One more deep breath. She planted her feet in front of the sheet of light, staring through the shifting colours. The lights were too bright to see through, but she could just about make out a familiar shape on a distant floor. Her pack? There was only one way to find out.

Irina stepped through.

Light blinded her. Sensation flooded into her – not pain, but thirst, hunger, heat and cold, all prickling across her skin at once. Her sister's weight vanished from her back. She felt a brief flash of panic before she remembered Death's words: her sister's soul was on its way back to her body. She would awake in her own bed, with her loving parents beside her. Catalina was all right. She was home.

Irina staggered forward, the lights dimming as she passed through the gate. She was back in the cave. The light from the gate was just enough to see by, tingeing the enormous rock formations gold. Her pack lay discarded on the ground a few feet away. Mouth dust-dry, stomach cavernous, Irina fell on it, scrabbling for a flask of water. She drained it in seconds, the lights behind her dimming even further. The moment the water hit her tongue felt like striking a match: it was only then that she realized how much she'd been craving it. Next, she scrabbled for a loaf of cornmeal bread and tore into it like an animal. Then water again, then a jar of pickles so tart she nearly wept at the taste, then a chunk of dried sausage that she sliced off with shaking hands. By the time she was finished she was shaking and felt like she would be sick at any moment, the remnants of her feast around her on the floor, but she knew it had worked. Guilt flooded through her. Had this been how Stefan had felt, all this time? The light from the gate behind her had dwindled to a faint glow. The touch of Death was fading. Soon she would not be able to see the gate at all.

Irina hauled herself upright and shouldered her pack. The

weight of it made her think of Catalina, and she felt a pang of triumph and despair. As much as she wished she was not alone, she had to hold onto what was important. Right now, Catalina would be waking up as herself, her parents weeping with joy. By the time Irina came home, she could be her old self again.

She set off, refusing to look at the gate. Shuffling through the darkness, she found her way to the slope that led up to the entrance and climbed it, staring at her feet. The slice of night sky at the top grew larger, stars winking through the gap. Irina was already bracing herself for the pain before she realized that it would not come.

The night air was cold, clean. There was still snow on the ground. A powdery layer clung to everything, sliding down the mountainside. It silvered everything it touched – rocks, shrubs, the needles of pines – and Irina reached out to brush away a fine layer of snow from a young pine. When she saw that one of its branches had one side of its needles stripped off and some were starting to brown, she could have wept. There was no perfection here. She was home.

She set off, trudging back down the mountainside. The path they had taken was clear; there were footsteps in the snow, and branches bent back as she approached the forest. She was glad of it, when she ducked beneath the canopy of the trees and could no longer see the imprint of Stefan's bare feet. Despite how much time had passed in the land of the dead, in the land of the living, it looked as though they had only passed through seconds before. She could not bear to see the reminders of him walking beside her so recently, like the fading echo of a song.

The path wove through the trees, twisting and turning. She could see the leaves they'd trampled, the branches they'd snapped. She wondered if the creatures of the forest could still scent the trace of a vampire hanging in the air. Nothing came close. No distant rustling, no snapping of twigs under a hoof or a paw. She was safe. Stefan's last gift, she thought, and tears welled up in her eyes again.

Eventually, she saw the little house at the edge of the forest. Dropping her pack over the wooden fence, she hauled herself over it, landing in the courtyard with an undignified thump. Irina picked up her pack and went inside. The door was still swinging open, a lingering curl of heat drawing her forward.

She moved as if she were performing the steps of a familiar dance. She put her pack by the door and closed it, lighting a candle so she could see a little better. She stoked up the fire in the oven and held out her hands, marvelling at how sharply the cold could bite. She closed the shutters at the window and shook out the blankets, washed her hands and face. She unpacked her things, placing each carefully wrapped piece of food in the pantry and setting the cooking pot back on its shelf. She straightened the chairs. She took off her bridal crown and laid her necklaces neatly on the table, cleaning her cuts with melted snow. She combed out the tangles in her hair. Throughout it all she did not stop moving. If she stayed on her feet and kept herself busy, she would not have to think about what she had seen and what she had done.

Her bridal crown sat on the table. The pine gleamed rich and dark in the candlelight, the white ribbons shining like moonlight. Some of the needles had been scraped off, the ribbons tattered. A single snowdrop wilted beside it. Irina's hands stilled, halfway through untangling her hair. Her vision blurred. All her momentum bled out of her. She had no more energy to keep moving and stop her thoughts from settling. The weight of what she had been through drew itself over her like a blanket. There was nothing to run from now. She'd done it. She'd brought her sister home and rid the village of a vampire, just like she'd promised she would. Before she'd set out on her journey, she might have celebrated. But she was hollow, exhausted. Now, even the idea that she might have celebrated Stefan being gone seemed like a desecration of the sacrifice he had made for her. She had been a different person then: more innocent, more cruel. It disgusted her. How had she ever been so thoughtless?

For a long moment, Irina stared at her bridal crown, and the flower wilting beside it. Then, she snuffed out the candle, and went to bed.

The next morning, snow was swirling past the little door. Irina was shivering in the courtyard, pack on her shoulder, staring over the heads of the crowd on the other side of the fence. There were far fewer of them than there had been when they'd locked her in. That made sense, she thought, bitterness shrivelling all her thoughts; it was a cold morning, and now they were no longer dying.

Father Simeon came hurrying up to the gate, his black robes brushing through the snow. He was beaming at her, tears gleaming in his eyes. Irina stared straight ahead, keeping a leash on her expression. She couldn't let him know what she thought of him; she was still locked in, after all.

Father Simeon gestured to two men in the crowd, waving them towards the gate. They lifted the bar out of its holds, gloved hands fumbling in the cold, and pulled the door open. The priest spread his arms wide, gratitude etched into every line of his face.

'My child,' he said, tears in his eyes, 'you have delivered us.'

Irina ground her teeth and stepped through the gate. The moment she crossed the threshold, the crowd let out a collective sigh. They clasped each other's hands, closed their eyes in prayer. Some of them rushed forward, reaching for the hem of her skirt as if she were a saint.

'Where are your things?' Father Simeon asked. 'Have you nothing for the snow? You'll catch your death.'

She thought of Stefan, freezing on the mountainside, and anger sliced into her. 'These are all the things you left me with, Father,' she said, before she could stop herself.

The silence curdled. The crowd drew back their hands, looking away.

Father Simeon flushed. 'An oversight, I am sure,' he said. 'You must come in out of the cold. We have many things to discuss.'

He held out an arm, showing the way to the church. Irina hurried past him, pack bumping into her back as she wrestled her temper back under control. She still had to leave the village, and in snow this deep, she would need his help. This was no time to lose her head.

The church was a squat wooden building with narrow windows and a tall, pointed tower, built on a hill and surrounded by a thick wall. It was bitterly cold, and the wind and snow snatched at her hair, but the climb was steep and soon she was sweating. As she passed, Irina saw faces peering through windows. Some of them wept, some of them blessed her as she walked by. Each gesture felt like another piece of silver being pressed into her hand, until she buckled under the weight of it and her fingers were crushed. Keeping her eyes up and a hand on her pack, Irina walked into the church.

Inside, it was dark, cold. The painted faces of saints and angels were shadows in the gloom. Candlesticks glittered on the altar like eyes. For a moment, she hesitated, thinking of Death's monastery and what she had learned in the land of the dead. It felt strange, knowing that there was a part of the afterlife that was not as she had been told. But at least here, she was out of the wind.

Father Simeon bustled in after her. He lit a candle, throwing the painted faces into sharp relief. He waved her over to the altar and said a quick prayer of thanks; Irina watched, feeling nothing.

When he was finished, Father Simeon stood beside her. Joy lit his face from within. He looked twenty years younger.

'I cannot tell you what you have done for us, my child,' he said. 'By the grace of God, you have delivered us from this monster.'

Irina ground her teeth, swallowing her words. *Monster?* Stefan had killed people, she would not deny that. But if he was a monster, then so were the people who had made him one.

'Your duty and sacrifice are an example to us all,' the priest continued, 'and they will not go unrewarded. We give thanks for God's works, in this village, and value his instruments.'

He waited. Irina said nothing, still chewing on the urge to scream in his face.

'Mihai would be glad to have you stay on, if you wish to continue working,' he said. 'If not, he will pay you your wages – just for the time when you worked for him, of course, but he assures me that the sum will be more than fair. Or, if you wish for a husband, Istvan's eldest is looking for another wife. He's a fine young man, a good father to his children – and more than willing to overlook your lack of a dowry, after the great boon you have given us.'

Just the thought of being rewarded by the people who had driven Stefan to his death and back again was making her feel sick. She wanted to grab the priest by the collar and shake him, to scream into his face that Stefan was no monster – just a frightened boy propelled by hunger and neglect. But she couldn't. He'd think she was mad, or in league with some dark power. Irina's hands curled into fists.

Father Simeon saw. His voice softened, smooth as oil. 'But you are troubled, child. Of course you are. Your isolation cannot have been easy. Tell me—' He leaned forward, lowered his voice. 'Did you . . . did you see . . .'

Irina took a deep breath. She closed her eyes, sharpened the edge of her anger. She couldn't hold it back any more; she may as well use it.

'Will you tell me something, Father?' she asked.

'Of course.'

She opened her eyes, skewering him with a look. 'Do you know my name?'

Father Simeon froze. Panic flickered in his eyes. He opened his mouth; nothing came out.

'You did not know that these were the only clothes I was given to keep out the cold,' she said, plucking at her sleeve. 'Or perhaps you did, and you only left me with my wedding clothes because you knew I could not get far in the snow. I am not sure which is true, Father, but I cannot say that either speaks to your character.'

The priest was floundering, a dull flush creeping up his neck. 'It was an oversight, nothing more. But if you are asking about wedding clothes, am I to understand that Istvan's eldest would be acceptable to you?'

It was an effort to wrestle her words into something like civility. 'Tell me, Father: if you don't even know my name, what makes you think you know anything about who I wish to marry?'

'Another man could be found, I'm sure.'

'I'm sure that you could find me another husband, if you set your mind to it,' Irina said, wielding each word like a rapier. 'After all, you found a suitable girl for the wedding of the dead, didn't you? There are plenty of other unmarried girls in the village. You didn't ask them. But I suppose I had no family to object. What would you have done if I'd said no?'

All the colour had drained from Father Simeon's face. 'I did what I thought was best . . .'

'Best for who? Certainly not the village. The attacks had been going on for months before I arrived.'

'I asked. No one wanted to give up their daughters. I tried. I swear, I tried.'

Irina folded her arms. 'There are other ways to kill a vampire. But you didn't want to risk anyone you would miss.'

The priest put his head in his hands.

'I do not want to stay in this village,' Irina said, 'not after the way that I have been treated. What I want for my reward, Father Simeon, is my wages in full, safe passage home, and good warm clothes for the journey. I will not say that I trust you to make these arrangements, because I do not trust you at all, but I am sure that you want to see me gone. I have had a great deal of time to think, and I do not think that you are a man who wants to be reminded of his own failures.' She fixed him with a cold, measured look. 'I can't imagine you want anyone else to be reminded, either. The bishop is very mindful of the reputation of his priests, I hear.'

Father Simeon staggered back a step. All his happiness had fled, leaving him looking gaunt and guilty. Irina tried to pity him. It did not work. When she looked at him, all she saw was a man who could not make hard decisions, whether that was deciding to stop a father beating his son or deciding which of his flock should risk a brush with the dead.

'I will see who can be spared to—'

'No. You will find someone to take me safely home, and you will do it today. I will not stay here a moment longer than I have to. And I want my wages.'

He nodded, unable to meet her eyes.

'I will stay here while you make the arrangements.' Irina tried to summon a little of Death's blank expression, and felt coldness freeze her face. 'I am sure you do not want me to be disturbed while I am at prayer.'

Father Simeon fled. Irina was left alone with the faces of the saints, painted hands blessing her on every side. She stared up at their gentle expressions, jaw clenched, and wondered how she was ever supposed to forgive people who had done nothing but disappoint her. Was it strength, or weakness, to let that anger go? She was not sure. Now, all she could do was cradle it, huddling around it like a flame in the cold. She remembered Stefan's face, dappled with blue light, and something inside her twisted. It would be a long time before she was ready to forgive them.

A sleigh was found, and horses to pull it. The driver – a man from the next village over who Irina did not recognize – seemed just as keen to be gone as she was. He shivered by his horse, sipping at a flask of țuică and muttering about stingy neighbours. Irina's own, warmer clothes were brought to the church, and provisions for the journey. Mihai handed over Irina's wages, in full, with only the slightest sour tinge to his expression. Within an hour, Irina was sitting in the sleigh, nestled among furs, barrels of wine and lumpy sacks of cornmeal.

The driver handed her a flask of țuică, huddling into a sheepskin coat. He was old enough to be her father. 'For the cold,' he said, and went to check his horse's bridle. 'You were in that house on the edge of the woods, weren't you?'

Irina nodded.

'That was a good thing you did,' the man said, not looking up from his work. 'And a hard one, too. They shouldn't have let you do it. It's not right, to ask that of a girl your age.'

She blinked, fast. It *wasn't* right. Nothing about the situation she had found herself in was right – not the things she'd seen or the way she was treated. But here she was all the same, on the other side of it, not quite the girl she had been.

'Don't you worry,' he said, his voice gruff. 'I'll see you safely home.'

They set off. Snow thick as whipped cream blanketed the ground and covered the trees. Irina pummelled the sack of cornmeal she was leaning on into a more comfortable shape – she was sure something inside had frozen – and leaned back, ignoring the snow spraying up in the wake of the sledge. The world rushed by in a haze of white, the odd dark glimpse of a fence post or a tree trunk marring the perfection like a crack in a mirror. Irina caught herself looking for a flash of opalescent colour. Her throat tightened.

The journey was uneventful. Irina spent most of it huddling, either in her nest of packages at the back of the sleigh or directly over the campfire. Most mornings, when the fire had burned low and before the sun had risen, she cursed her own impatience. Would it have been so bad to have stayed in Stefan's village, and waited out the winter? But then she remembered how hard it had been to prise something out of the villagers' shame and goodwill, and how much harder it would have been to pretend that she did not resent scratching at the surface of their charity. Better she was gone. There could be no looking back.

When, at last, she saw the outline of her own village, the last of her doubts vanished. It was hard to recognize it at first. The snow hid its familiar shape like a hand inside a glove. But when she realized that the church at the top of the hill was her own, she scrambled forward in her seat, nearly tipping herself out of the sleigh. There were the fences her father had helped build. There was the tree she'd fallen out of as a child, almost breaking her arm. There was the witch's house, set a little apart from the rest. Someone was brewing spiced wine and roasting pork; an extravagance in winter, and one that made her mouth water. A long line of men were trudging out of the forest, logs strapped to their backs. One of them saw her and waved.

'Irina! Irina, your—'

The sleigh rushed past. Now, they were in the village proper, and Irina's heart was starting to pound. Children's sledges were stacked up against the houses. Smoke plumed from every chimney. Her neighbours nudged each other, and came rushing out of their houses when she passed. Irina saw none of it. She called up to the driver; her own home was up ahead, and it was all she could see. Two storeys, wooden. A large chimney, gently smoking. Red and yellow flowers painted on the shutters. Interlocking designs carved into the eaves – her father had put them there, and the ones where the pattern wobbled were where he'd tried to show her how to do it. Wood stacked up against the byre, to give the animals that extra bit of warmth in the winter. It looked just as it always had, but suddenly, her hands were shaking. Had Death kept her promise?

'Stop,' she said, 'this is it.'

The driver pulled on the reins. Irina stumbled out of the sleigh, nearly losing her footing in the snow. She pushed open the courtyard gate, breath catching in her throat. Why was she so nervous? She'd kept her end of the bargain. Death had to do the same. She was the one certain thing in the world, after all. Irina had to be able to depend on her.

She hesitated inside her own courtyard. Their goat recognized her. It started bleating. Moments later, the front door opened and her mother came out, flushed, shaking cornflour off her apron. 'What's got into—'

She stopped. Gasped. Her eyes widened. Then she burst into tears and rushed forward, arms outstretched. 'Sorin!' she called, 'Sorin! She's home!'

Panic lurched through Irina. 'Mama? Mama, why are you crying? What's—'

A Steep and Savage Path

The door opened. Irina froze.

There, standing on the doorstep, was Catalina.

She was very thin. The months in bed had wasted her away, and she was clutching at the door frame. She was pale, too, and her hair hung limp against her cheek. But her eyes lit up when she saw Irina. She let out a gasp of delight, grinned, and still holding onto the door frame for support, gingerly stepped into the courtyard.

Irina flew forward. Snatching up her sister, she fell to her knees and howled into her shoulder, sobbing. Catalina wriggled loose an elbow – 'You're *squeezing*,' – but Irina wouldn't let go. All the fear and relief and sadness burst out of her in a flood. She felt her mother's arms around her shoulders, her hands smoothing her hair – 'It's all right, my lamb, she's all right . . .' – and cried all the harder. Then, her father wrapping his arms around them all and saying, 'My girls, my girls, all my girls together . . .' before he tearfully extricated himself from the huddle on the doorstep and went to thank the driver.

The novelty of having both their children well and home again did not wear off for Irina's parents. Sometimes Irina would look up from her work to see her father smiling at her for no reason, and every time anyone left the house her mother would insist on them saying goodbye to each member of the family properly, which always seemed to involve a lot of tearful hugs even if they were only going to chop firewood. Catalina was clearly fed up of this, and started scampering off whenever anyone came near her. It was a slow scamper, but they let her do it. It was good to see her on her feet again.

They all knew that something was wrong with Irina.

Her mother had noticed right away. She had clocked the strands of white in Irina's hair from their first embrace, and the shadows under her eyes. When her father had brought out a bottle of good țuică, determined to get happily drunk, Irina's mother had told him sharply that Irina was far too tired from her journey for drink. He'd shared the bottle with the driver instead, set on getting drunk with somebody, and had invited him for dinner. But when he left the next morning, her father watched him go with troubled eyes.

'Irina,' he said, his voice still hoarse, 'is everything all right? Toma said . . .'

'Toma?' she asked, handing him a bowl of cornmeal porridge.

Her father waved vaguely at the door. 'Who gave you the lift home. He had some strange stories . . .'

Irina tried to keep her voice light. 'Oh! I suspect he does. He must be very well travelled.'

The ruse did not work. Her father's hangover faded, his worries did not. She kept the wounds hidden for as long as she could; it was easy to stay wrapped up, in the cold. As the weeks passed, Irina saw him pull her mother aside for whispered conversations, staring at the white in her hair. When Irina heard her neighbours share news from the surrounding villages, and of the great evil that had been laid to rest by a young woman, his face paled every time.

Irina did not mind, much. Not now that Catalina was herself again.

Still weak after her time in bed, Catalina was endlessly frustrated. Her strength had melted away like snow, the muscles on her arms and legs wasted. She got out of breath quickly and hated it, snapping at everyone who came near her when she grew overtired. She was still regaining her balance, too, and Irina could not help but notice that when she fell, she would sometimes flap her arms, as though she had wings that could help right her.

She did not remember what had happened.

A Steep and Savage Path

It was for the best, Irina told herself. Catalina was much too young to understand what she had been through. Irina had asked a series of gentle questions, to work out if anything lingered from the land of the dead. Nothing, except a vague dream of flight. Irina was glad of it. But at the same time, it would have been nice to have had someone to talk to. Only the witch had an inkling of what she had done, and when Irina had sought her out, bursting with knowledge of the other side, the witch would not admit her. She had told Irina that there were some things it was better not to understand, and closed the door of her little hut in Irina's face.

But that was for the best, too. Or at least, Irina was sure it would be, eventually.

The snows began to melt. Catalina grew strong enough to cross the floor of their little house three times without holding onto anything or getting out of breath. Their parents began to talk seriously about spring planting, and whether it was worth taking the goat next door to see if their neighbour's buck could get a kid on her. Irina still dreamed of rivers of colour, of cold hands, of the scrape of teeth on skin. But when the trees began to frill with buds, and the first green shoots speckled the dark earth, the sight was comforting. This was the land of the living. Here, things could change, even heal. She might have broken her own heart, but the flowers would still bloom.

One morning, she awoke to the first blue sky she had seen in a long time. A bright and bitter day, she could feel the sun on her face even as she shivered pulling on her clothes. Today would be spent in the fields with the rest of the villagers, planting what they needed for the harvest. Her mother was already up and making bulz, letting the mămăligă cool before she shaped it into balls filled with creamy cheese.

Irina wandered over, braiding her hair. 'Do you need all of those?'

Her mother shot her a look. 'You'll get one if you're up in the fields.'

'Only one?'

'Yes, only one! These have to go around the whole village, you know.'

'But you aren't the only person making bulz, so couldn't I have two?'

There was a knock at the door. Her mother waved her towards it.

'Go and answer that before you steal anything. Honestly! They're not even filled yet, let alone grilled.'

Irina tied off her braid, snatched up a headscarf and went to answer the door. She picked her way around Catalina's discarded doll – now that she could get out of bed and play on the floor again, she was really enjoying leaving things there. The knock came again, fast, almost nervous. Irina frowned. It was far too early for visitors. They were barely awake; what was anyone doing bothering them at this hour?

She opened the door, and froze. Standing on the doorstep, his hand raised as though he was about to knock for a third time, was Stefan.

The rest of the world fell away.

He was on her doorstep. On her own doorstep, when she'd thought him as good as dead and buried. But he was standing there – on her *actual* doorstep – looking as though he was about to throw up. It couldn't be real. She had to be dreaming. She blinked, hard; he was still there. Her hands began to tremble.

He was staring at her, eyes wide, his hand still raised. His clothes were different: he had well-made boots and a good, warm jacket. His *hands* were different. There was no purple-black colour bleeding up his arms to the elbow; no shadowy veins snaking across his wrist. They were tanned and strong, faintly scarred. His cheeks and nose were red from the cold, and sunlight picked out threads of red in his hair that she had never known were there. She'd never seen him stand in true sunlight, before.

He cleared his throat and tried for a smile. It came out wobbly. 'Hello,' he said. 'How . . . how are you?'

Irina stared. Her heart was pounding. She blinked, again; he still did not fade. He couldn't be real. She'd made her bargain. Her mind was playing cruel tricks on her. It had to be another part of Death's punishment. He couldn't be real . . .

His smile faded. He cleared his throat again. 'I . . . I can go, if you'd like. I don't have to—'

'Don't you dare,' Irina rasped. Every part of her was shaking. She stepped forward, the door slamming shut behind her. Her breath misted in the morning air. Cold pinched at her cheeks. Hanging low in the sky, the sunlight made her eyes water. These things were real. Her feet ground into the dirt, stray bits of gravel crunching underneath her shoes. She'd tied her apron badly; the knot was digging into the small of her back. Her stomach was rumbling. These things were real, too. She reached out a shaking hand. She felt eggshell-thin. The slightest knock would punch a hole right through her. If her hand passed through him, she would crumble into pieces.

She reached for his cheek. Her fingers met warm, living skin.

It was as if a part of her had been kept under ice, and now, it was finally cracking. She smiled, and she was not sure if it felt more like the rising sun or a dam about to break.

'It's you,' she said. 'You're here. How are you here?'

Stefan's hand closed over hers. He was beaming at her, eyes full of tears. 'Oh, Irina. I . . .'

The door opened. There was a flurry of whispers from over Irina's shoulder, a hushed 'For God's sake, Sorin, let *me* handle this,' and then her mother cleared her throat. Panic flashed across Stefan's face as he caught their eyes.

'Irina!' her mother said. 'You didn't tell us we'd be having visitors! Who is this?'

Irina turned around. Both her parents and Catalina were peering through the door, all of them trying to look as though they hadn't been eavesdropping. She took Stefan's hand, and saw her mother's face light up with interest.

'Stefan,' she said, 'this is my family. Mama, Tata, this is Stefan. I thought he was dead, but . . .'

Understanding dawned on her mother's face. 'Why don't we give you two a minute to talk, and then you can come inside?' she said, her voice gentle.

Her father bristled. 'Doina, hadn't we better learn who—'

'A minute to talk, *in private*,' her mother said, shoving her father back into the house. 'But a minute, you understand? And you're not to go beyond the fence.'

'Doina! He could be anyone, we can't just—'

'I swear to God, Sorin, if you don't—'

The front door closed. Moments later, Irina heard one of the shutters creaking open. Irina did not have to turn around to know that at least one member of her family was looking through the window.

She turned to Stefan with a sheepish laugh. 'That's my family,' she said.

Stefan looked worried. 'Do you think they mind me coming here?'

'I don't care.' She threw her arms around him. He was warm, solid, strong. When she laid her head against his chest, she could hear his heart beating. He held her close, his breath tickling her ear. It was so different, holding a living man. Living or dead, she found she did not care. It was still him.

'How did you get away?'

He pulled away, held her at arm's length. His eyes moved over every inch of her, drinking her in, from the silver in her hair to the shoes on her feet. The more he looked, the wider his smile became.

'God, I missed you,' he said, stroking her hair. 'I missed you so much.'

She blushed, and poked him in the stomach. 'Aren't you going to answer my question?'

He gave her a grin. 'Aren't you going to say you missed me too?'

'You know I did,' she said, winding her arms around his waist.

'I know. I just want to hear you say it.'

He was still grinning at her, the kind of grin he knew would make her want to grab him by the lapels of his jacket and kiss him until he was breathless. But her family were watching, so she stood on her tiptoes, kissed him on the cheek, and whispered, 'I missed you.' When she came away, he was blushing. She'd never seen him blush, before.

'Do you remember the vow we made?' he asked. 'I swore that if I saw a chance to be happy, I would take it.' He smiled, smoothing her hair back. 'I saw a chance.'

'But how? I thought you had to stay in the land of the dead. How are you here? How are you *living*?'

'I wasn't sure, at first,' he said. 'But after a few months, things started changing. I started becoming like you – the doors got painful, and when I touched people, they remembered how they'd died. That was when I realized. It was the food.'

Irina stared at him. 'The food?'

He took both her hands, beaming at her. 'Death told us that

if you ate the food of the land of the dead, you were bound to stay there. I didn't. I ate the food of the living—'

The realization dawned on her. 'My blood! So . . . so you're bound to stay here?'

A shadow passed over his face. 'Not forever,' he said. 'I still have to fulfil my end of the bargain. When spring comes, I can return to the land of the living. But when autumn falls, I have to go back to the land of the dead.'

The smile vanished from his face. His hands trembled against hers.

'It'll only ever be half a life,' he said, 'but I knew I had to find you. You deserve to know. Irina, if you don't want a husband that can only stay for summer, I'll—'

She kissed him. For a moment, he was frozen; then his arms wound around her and he kissed her back. The window flew open, and her mother's voice called, 'That has been more than a minute, young lady!' and the two of them broke apart, grinning sheepishly.

Irina took his hands. 'I'll take all the life I can get, if it's with you,' she said.

He glanced back at the house. 'What will we tell your family?'

'We'll think of something. But we'll think of it together.' She tucked his hand into the crook of her elbow and turned towards her front door. 'Are you ready?'

'No. I'm going to make a fool of myself.'

She stroked his forearm, beaming at him. 'And so will I. But that won't matter. I love you.'

Stefan's face split into a smile lovelier than a sunrise, and together, they went back into the house.

Acknowledgements

At the end of writing any book there always seems to be a point where I sit back and say to myself, 'Well that was a Whole Damn Process, wasn't it.' Why stop now? Writing this book *was* a Whole Damn Process and there were many points along the way where I wished all those dead guys would just sort their own problems out. But luckily for me, the Whole Damn Process was made a lot easier with the help of the following delightful people.

A massive thank you to everyone at HarperCollins who has worked so hard on all my books: Rachel Winterbottom, Catherine Perks, Chloe Gough for their insightful editorial feedback and endless patience; Megan Smith and Charlotte Day for another truly stunning cover; Emily Chan, Sian Richefond and Angelica Bowden-Jones for all their tireless work in producing and promoting the book. It really is wonderful to know that I have such a dedicated team behind me. I'd also like to shout out Vicky Leech – even though she didn't get the opportunity to work on this manuscript before she left HarperVoyager, I will always be grateful for her calm and measured response when I threw out my previous project in a panic and pitched her a vampire book instead.

I'd also like to thank my incredible agent, Chloe Seager, who is consistently phenomenal in everything she does. Her support, encouragement, and skill at dealing with me occasionally flapping at her is truly peerless and always appreciated. It's always such a relief to know that I have such an incredibly talented person on my team – people, really, because that applies to every single person at Madeleine Milburn.

Once again I am indebted to the staff at the British Library for helping me with the research for this book. I'd also like to thank Cristina for all her insight and advice when I visited Romania, and for making sure I did not get stranded outside Bran Castle and got on the bus back to Brașov (although I still maintain that being left at Dracula's castle is very on brand for me).

To my friends: I finally published my vampire book, lads, and it wasn't even Dracula fanfic. (Please be proud.) I'd particularly like to thank Nate, Ellie, Moz, Ruaraidh, Sam and Fay for listening to me whine, feeding me, and occasionally scooping me off the sofa and making me go outside and do things. I had a run of pretty bad luck the summer that I was doing one round of edits on this book and was renovating and moving house the round before, and I genuinely don't think I could've got through the Whole Damn Process without the care and support I receive from my friends on a daily basis. Thank you.

And lastly, my family – in particular, Mum, Dad and Lucy. I always have to gear up to writing their part of the acknowledgements because that's the part that will reliably make me cry. Trying to express how much their love and encouragement have made my life better in words is always difficult for me because none of the words I have are enough to encompass how much they mean to me. So I'll leave it at this: thank you, I love you.